Six Minutes Early

Patrick Parker

This book is a work of fiction. With the exception of well-known historical events, the names used herein and the characters and incidents portrayed are fictitious and any resemblance to the names, character, or history of any person, incident, or technology is coincidental and unintentional.

ISBN 10: 1539539792
ISBN 13: 978-1539539797

Library of Congress Control Number: 2016917504

CreateSpace Independent Publishing Platform, North Charleston, SC

Cover by Elizabeth Mackey

Chapter 1

September 18, 2013
Green Iguana Bar
Balboa, Panama

George snuffed out his cigarette and then reached for his Panama beer. The alcohol had already started impairing his judgment, and his dark-brown hand knocked over the bottle. "Dorotea!" he said, his voice dominating the din as he sprang to his feet. "Bring a towel!" Wiping his bare hand quickly across the wooden table, he looked up at the man seated across from him and said, "Felipe, ready for another beer?"

Felipe simply nodded. His attention was elsewhere. Slowly grasping the empty bottle, he threw it at a two-foot-long iguana. Droplets of beer arched across his front, some splattering on George. His aim was good, but the reptile's reflexes were better. Wandering into the old *bohío* bar in search of food, oblivious to the people and blaring music, the lizard wound up being the entertainment. Felipe retrieved a cigarette from the pocket of his tan shirt, lit it, and then offered one to George.

"Make that two beers, Dorotea!" George wiped beer and sweat from his face.

As usual the two men rendezvoused in the bar that evening before going home after their shift. They drank, talked about the day, and shared dreams of a better life. Often their conversations were punctuated with stories of their youth when they'd had even less responsibilities or money. Although their employers were good to them, the two men were envious of the Americans.

"Why did your parents name you George?" Felipe asked, leaning back in his chair and exhaling the smoke.

"When all the Americans were here, my mother worked for one named George and named me after him." Looking around, he saw the voluptuous Dorotea, displaying enormous amounts of cleavage, approach with three bottles of beer.

Setting the bottles on the old table with a clack, she then smoothed her worn but colorful red-and-black skirt and seated herself at the table. Crossing her shapely brown legs and lifting a beer, she said, "*Saludi!*"

The two men did the same and clicked their bottles against hers, and then in unison they took a swig of the local favorite. Each leaned back and watched the sun sink into the green-foliaged horizon. Only four other people, seated several tables across from them, were in the bar.

The Green Iguana bar was located about twelve kilometers west of Balboa, Panama, and about two kilometers from the site where the two men worked. This was a favorite watering hole, and that's about all it was, for the men who worked nearby. It was a no-frills kind of place, open on three sides with a concrete-slab floor. Food, if that's what you chose to call it, was cooked on a grill outside. The beer was always cold, the men always sweat stained, and, of course, there was Dorotea.

Leaning forward and brushing her long, black hair back, Dorotea said, "George, I talked to my cousin, and he'll be here the day after tomorrow." She paused and glanced around the room. Retrieving a slip of paper from her bra and handing it to George, she continued, "Be at this address at ten o'clock Friday night. My cousin wants to look around."

"We can't get him into the site," Felipe said and then took a drag of his cigarette.

"From the outside," she replied.

Felipe looked at George.

"We'll be there," George said, wiping the sweat from his brow with his hand and then drying it on his tan cargo pants.

"Who's your cousin? Why are we looking around the site?" Felipe asked. "We just supply the information."

"Do you want the rest of your money?" she asked, her voice stern and brow furrowed. "Be there the day after tomorrow. No more questions."

She stood, and George grabbed her arm, pulling her close to him. He caught a whiff of her perfume.

"How about you and me—"

"I'm working." She jerked free. "Day after tomorrow, ten at night." She flounced away without waiting for a response.

"I hope you know what you're doing." Felipe took a pull on the beer. "I don't trust her."

"She's got a fine ass." George swigged his beer. "Easy money. We're just giving them information. They're going to do the work. Besides, who'll know?"

"I…I just don't know."

"You didn't have any problems before when we both needed the money. We've worked out there as guards for over a year, and we're still nobodies," George said.

"I know, but it's a job."

"We're making some real money now. Finish up. Let's go."

That Friday night at ten, as ordered, George and Felipe entered the house located at the address Dorotea had provided; it was about one kilometer from where they worked. The airy tropical-style house, located in a small community shielded by dense jungle, was typical for the area and modestly furnished. Handing the two men Panama beers and with her sandals slapping the floor, Dorotea, curvaceous as ever, escorted them into the den. A casually dressed, muscular man with a dark complexion was seated in a side chair. Opposite him was a tanned Caucasian man. A third man, a Panamanian, closed the door and remained standing next to it. A fourth man stood guard outside on the patio. Dorotea steered the new arrivals to the couch.

"This is my cousin, Franco," she said, introducing the forty-two-year-old Latin American man as he and the Caucasian man stood. "He's the commander of the Fifty-Seventh Front, FARC."

FARC, the Revolutionary Armed Forces of Colombia—the military wing of the Colombian Communist Party. The expressions dropped from the faces of George and Felipe as she mentioned FARC. They had not expected to come face-to-face with a FARC member, let alone a commander. The notorious terrorist organization was well known to them and feared throughout Latin America. Knowing that this was bigger than they had anticipated, the two men moved to stand in respect.

"Please…relax, my friends," Franco said, taking George's hand and then Felipe's. "We finally meet. Dorotea has told me quite a bit about you."

Franco was obviously attempting to put them at ease in order to gain their trust and confidence. Intrigued by the information they were providing, Franco wanted to develop them more—a skill he had learned when he had been a Panamanian policeman. "The information you provided us has been very informative."

"Thank you, Comandante," George replied, still wary of the commander and intimidated by the situation.

"This is my advisor, Bart Madison," Franco said as he motioned to the man next to him.

"An American!" Felipe said to himself as he studied the rugged Caucasian man before him. The man's steely gaze made Felipe uncomfortable. "I don't like this. Can we trust this guy? Is he CIA?"

"I wanted to look you in the eye," Franco said, leveling a stern gaze on them. "I am interested in this American site. We'll know tonight if you're trustworthy or if you work for the Americans. If the latter is true, you will not see the sunrise. Do you understand?"

"*Sí*, Comandante! We are loyal to you." George forced the words as Felipe nodded. They both realized that they were in over their heads and that it was too late to back out.

"I want to know more about this place, and then we'll go see it." Franco sat in the chair, and Bart stepped behind to look over Franco's shoulder. "What else have you found out?"

"As I reported last time, the site is guarded around the clock," George said, unfolding a sketch he had made. His hand trembled. Orienting it to the north, he described the small facility, estimating it to be 100 by 150 meters.

"It's located on a knoll, and the jungle is cut back about two hundred meters around the perimeter fence," George continued. "The rear of the compound has a bunker. That's where the activity is. That's where we work."

"The location is strange. Security is very tight in the rear portion of the compound. There is security in the front but not as heavy," Felipe added.

"The sign in front of the building says *NASA Climate Research*." George indicated the building and then said, "That's the only sign, except for a couple of others that say *US Government Property, Keep Out*. We've never been in the main building; we go through an entrance on the side." George pointed to the sketch. "Just inside the entrance is the guardhouse—it controls the entry." He identified the small structure.

"Also in there is a reactionary force—a squad-sized unit. Between the main building and the helipad is the security force's quarters." George pointed to that building. "The rest of the security force—about three squads—stays there for a shift. Only about thirty-eight to forty men provide security at the site at any given time."

"The security force—are they soldiers or contractors like you?" Franco asked, evaluating George's words.

"*Sí*, we all work for an American company, except for a few main people. Those men are all US Special Forces."

"Continue." Franco's face remained expressionless.

"There are automatic weapons in the towers." George handed the sketch to Franco.

As Bart Madison looked over his shoulder, Franco leaned back in his chair and studied the detailed sketch briefly and then handed it to Madison. "Go on," he said, looking at George. "What is stored there?"

"They only tell us that it is highly sensitive equipment. We've seen large, rectangular containers, about the size of a trunk, through the open door of the bunker. Two men usually move them about," George said. "It's always two or more men who go in there together to handle the containers."

"Are these containers dark green?" Madison asked.

"*Sí.*"

"Two guard towers, diagonally across from each other, overlooking the area. Is that correct?"

"*Sí.*"

"Helicopters land here." Felipe pointed to the helipad in an open space between the bunker and the main building.

"How often?" Madison asked.

"Not very often. Maybe three or four times in the last year."

"Do they keep helicopter impediment poles up when the helipad is not in use?"

"Helicopter impediment poles?" George displayed a blank look on his face.

"Poles positioned in the ground about every meter and tied together at the top."

"Yes, all over the open ground."

Madison nodded and then asked, "At night, how is it lit, and is there much activity?"

"Very little activity at night, and the place is locked down. Metal halide lights illuminate the site and perimeter. Felipe and I start on the night shift next month."

"Very good. You have done well," Franco said as he motioned to Madison.

Madison withdrew an envelope stuffed with cash from his briefcase and handed it to Franco.

"For you and Felipe," Franco said, handing George the envelope. "Let's see this place now. I'll want an update after you're on the night shift. Dorotea will let you know what else we want or what we decide to do next. If there are any changes to the routine or anything out of the ordinary, tell Dorotea."

"*Sí,* Comandante, we will."

As George and Felipe led Franco and Bart along the dark jungle path that they had marked earlier, the light from their red flashlights danced about and illuminated the way. The nocturnal rainforest was alive with insects, reptiles, and mammals—many deadly to humans—that thrived here. Any biologist would be fascinated with the variety of life, and many were. Even the US Army maintained a tropical test center in Panama because of the near-perfect tropical conditions there.

Meandering through the foliage, Franco and Bart lagged behind, out of hearing from the other two, and discussed the site and the opportunity it might provide. The vines, branches, and leaves constantly slapped and tugged at their clothes. The bright, full moon was like a beacon in the clear night sky, and the stars shone like diamonds. However, the ambient light was unable to penetrate the dense canopy. Only on occasion did traces of light pierce the darkness as the men followed the markers. The warm night air was heavy with humidity.

"You know about this place, Bart?" Franco wiped the sweat from his face.

"I think so, but I'll verify it with my contact in Washington," Bart replied, guiding a branch out of their way.

"The senator?" Franco looked at him and then flicked off several large insects—beetles, ants, and a foot-long walking stick—from Bart's shoulder.

Bart nodded.

"OK, but what do you think is there?"

"I think it's a nuclear-weapons storage facility."

"No shit?" Franco paused and looked at Bart. "I thought the United States closed all the storage sites down that were outside the borders."

"I thought so, too, but I'll find out for sure. It wouldn't surprise me, though."

"Why's that?"

"When the army closed down the tactical storage facilities, SOCOM took over the sole mission of employing man-portable nuclear devices. Before I left the special forces, I worked on plans for using this type of weapon against a potential adversary. They even considered using them in Iraq." SOCOM, or United States Special Operations Command was a unified combatant command that was legislated into existence to provide command, control, and training for all US special-operations forces.

"Man-portable nuclear devices? Go on." Franco brushed a huge spider from the leg of his pants.

"There was a lot of discussion about scattering a few facilities outside the country in order to conceal the weapons and move them without detection. It was probably as much an effort to conceal them from the politicians as it was from spies. SOCOM didn't want to give up the weapons when DOD was reducing much of the nuclear stockpiles. My guess is that this is one of those locations. The way these knuckleheads sketched out and described the place, it fits in the way I remember them."

"I'm only interested in conventional weapons and ammunition," Franco replied. "If there are nuclear weapons, we can sell them to the highest bidder—ISIS, Hezbollah, Iran, whoever—and they'll pay a good price for them. We just don't want to get caught with them."

"Especially if they belonged to the Americans in the first place!" Bart added with a smirk. "They would all love to get their hands on one; using something like that against the Americans is their wet dream."

"This is what I'm thinking," Franco continued. "We use Los Zetas's mules to deliver the weapons just across the border. We can get a higher price that way."

"Can we trust Los Zetas?" Bart asked, knowing the reputation of the cartel made up of former Mexican Special Forces.

"I think we can, but it will cost us. After we reach an agreement with the top bidder, then I'll contact the Los Zetas commander and work out a deal. You plan it out and figure out the deception and routes. Don't mention this to anyone yet. When we're ready, we'll auction them off and execute quickly. Those Arabs can't keep a secret, so we'll have to move fast."

"What about these two?"

"We'll use them as long as we can and then eliminate them. They don't need to know everything."

***

Monday
September 23, 2013
Darien Gap
Near the Panamanian-Colombian Border

At the jungle compound, Franco Trujillo, commander of the Fifty-Seventh Front, FARC, laid the newspaper on the bamboo coffee table and then refilled his snifter. Two televisions, one tuned to Fox News and the other to the BBC, continuously reported on the chaos in Washington, DC, over the pending government shutdown. Both stations provided commentary on the conflict between the liberal and conservative sides of the government standoff.

The elections were a year away, and politicians were trying to keep their bases happy. Neither side was about to make any move that would jeopardize votes. Votes meant money and, above all, power. Anything outside the domestic issues was given only a cursory attention, mainly for show.

Bart entered the spacious room and started to speak, but Franco held up his hand and indicated for Bart to wait as he listened to one of the pundits.

"This is like watching kids fight over the candy bowl," Franco said, motioning for Bart to sit beside him on the couch. The floral fabric showed its age. "Here, have a brandy." He pointed to a snifter and bottle on the coffee table. "Try one of these cigars too. Montecristo Number Two. I just got them today."

"Thanks, don't mind if I do." Grasping the brandy, Bart filled the snifter to the bowl, swirled it, and then took a sip. Retrieving one of the cigars, he lit it in a cloud of bluish smoke. "Nice!"

"This box of Cohíba Espléndidos is for the senator." Franco lifted the box of cigars off the coffee table and then handed it to Bart.

"Good. The meeting is on for Wednesday evening in Panama City."

"Find out all you can—the real story about the government shutdown," Franco said. "Also I don't want the border closed. Be sure he knows to keep the DOJ and Border Patrol under control."

"Several of my other contacts have told me that the administration is bogged down with domestic issues and isn't concerned with anything else," Bart said. "I'm told that the president isn't even taking the daily intelligence briefings and that the ongoing scandals are eating his lunch. I don't think we have to worry about the US military too much for a while. The president and staffers are micromanaging everyone. He's fired a number of generals, and the others are doing what they can to protect their stars. No one is doing anything without explicit approval. The politicians are jockeying for reelection and fighting with each other. The whole place is screwed."

"Good! All the better for us, amigo." Franco took a sip of brandy and then puffed the Montecristo as he leaned back. "While you're meeting with the senator, I'm meeting with the representatives from the Secretariat and my commander." He sipped his brandy again and then continued. "Bart, this may get me promoted. As you know, the Ivan Rios Bloc commander is an old man and in poor health; they might just retire him. If they make me the bloc commander, that would mean a promotion for you as well, amigo. What do you think?"

Bart simply nodded, lifted his snifter in a salute, and then sipped the brandy.

***

Wednesday
September 25, 2013
Trump Ocean Club International Hotel and Tower
Panama City, Panama

Senator Carlton Bradbourne filled his chair like a pan of bread dough ready for the oven—bulging out of its container. He finished off his Scotch and looked at Bart; the senator's blue eyes signaled another drink. Bart Madison had reserved them a private section in the upscale Tejas restaurant for obvious reasons. Having dealt with the senator on numerous occasions, Bart knew what to expect. Knowing the senator's weaknesses, he exploited them as needed. Bart was no fool, either; he had plenty of photographs, video, and recordings of the senator, should he develop a conscience. Bart motioned to the attentive waiter for another single-malt Scotch for the senator.

As dinner arrived, the waiter filled the wine glasses and set the bottle on the table. Watching the self-absorbed man stuff his face with lobster ravioli, Bart ensured that Bradbourne's wine glass was always full. When the senator mopped up the remnants on his plate with a piece of bread, Bart thought, *What a pig! He's about ready.* Bart signaled for the waiter to bring dessert. He selected a signature cake: apple fusion, a warm-roasted, apple-cinnamon Breton with baked meringue and cinnamon ice cream.

As the waiter cleared the table, Bart placed the box of cigars in front of the senator. "For you, Senator."

"Thank you." A smirk appeared on Bradbourne's pudgy face. "I'm looking forward to having one."

When the waiter left, Bart retrieved an envelope bulging with cash from inside his coat and slid it to the senator. Without speaking, Bradbourne's fat fingers grasped the envelope and tucked it into his inside coat pocket.

"Is there going to be a government shutdown?" Bart asked, observing the senator wipe his face and then pick his teeth behind his napkin.

"I think so. No one is budging. The election is a year out, and several seats are in play. If the government does shut down, it will be for maximum pain in an attempt to get the conservatives to cave in. The White House thinks the people will be up in arms and will demand the government to reopen. They believe the Republicans will take the blame. The White House is in chaos—the scandals, his agenda, the shutdown, the budget—no one is in charge. The president is up to his eyeballs, and the alligators keep biting him in the ass."

"I don't want the southern border closed. Keep the DOJ and Border Patrol under control."

"You don't have to worry. A lot of votes are streaming across the border, if you know what I mean."

"Good. I want it to remain that way."

"Nothing is going to happen until after the election."

"I need some information," Bart continued. "There is a small facility about twelve kilometers west of Balboa. A sign on the main entrance says *NASA Climate Research.* A few other signs say *US Government Property, Keep Out.* I want to know what it really is and what's there."

"I'm sure it's just what the sign says, a climate-research station."

"Senator, don't play games with me. I want to know about it."

"I don't know anything about it. You said climate research; I guess that's what it is."

"Naw, not buying it. You go find out for sure and get back to me fast."

"I dunno. It'll take a while. Besides, I have several meetings and the pending shutdown…I dunno when I can find out."

"Senator, I want the fucking information before any goddamned shutdown! You're on several committees—Appropriations, Defense, and Homeland Security—so you should have no problem getting me the facts."

"Hold on! How dare you make demands on me! Who do you think you are?"

Without displaying any emotion, Bart pulled a folder from his briefcase and slid it in front of the senator.

Senator Carlton Bradbourne opened the folder, and the color drained from his face. His blank expression told Bart that the senator understood.

"Senator, we've had this discussion before," Bart continued. "I'm pretty sure those compromising photos will end your career. You're up for reelection next year. I bet your constituents would be more than a little curious to learn who that is in bed with you. How old is your little plaything? Twelve, thirteen?"

Bradbourne's hand trembled. "I understand. I'll find out what it is right away."

"I thought you'd see it my way. You know how to get in touch with me. I'll be waiting for your call."

Bradbourne nodded. "Yes, Bart."

"Enjoy the rest of your evening, Senator. You have a guest waiting for you in your room."

Bart stood and then walked out of the restaurant.

Chapter 2

Friday
September 27, 2013
Darien Gap
Near the Panamanian-Colombian Border

A map spread out before him, Bart was studying the routes into the southern US border when his special cell phone rang and broke his concentration. "Bart," he said.

"Bradbourne here."

"Senator, I've been expecting your call. Whatcha got?"

"As you suspected, it's not a climate-research station. NASA *is* doing a few things there, but NASA's part is small, just for show, in case anyone checks."

"I'm waiting."

"Bart, please…I've got to back away from this."

"Senator, don't try my patience. I'm very busy today. What did you find out?"

"Bart, no, really, wait—"

"Pictures and election, Senator!"

"It's a nuclear-storage facility that belongs to SOCOM. It's buried in their classified budget. They store special atomic demolition munitions there. I'll send you a complete report."

"Very good, Senator. I'll be in touch." Bart ended the call without waiting for a response.

Bart walked onto the porch where Franco sat in a well-worn, rattan wingback chair, observing the compound guards, and said, "Just as I thought, Franco. The compound east of Balboa is a nuclear-storage facility for SADMs. The senator just confirmed. He's sending a complete report."

"What's a SADM?" Franco asked and then repositioned the cigar in his mouth.

"They're man-portable nuclear weapons from the Cold War days. The design is old—late fifties or early sixties—but they'll do the job. They've been maintained over the years to keep them in a ready state. The Americans and Russians had them; the Israelis are rumored to possess them as well. A soldier parachuting in or a swimmer could implant one at a specific target, such as a dam, bridge, building, or mountain pass, and then set it to detonate at a specific time or on command. They'll bring a good price. Supposedly they were taken out of the inventory about 1989. However, it seems that SOCOM managed to hold on to quite a few and strategically stored them outside the US."

"How many are there?"

"I don't know yet. Hopefully the senator's package will tell us. You know, we talked about taking *one* device. Why not take a few extra?"

"That's what I was thinking." Franco's eyes narrowed as he held Bart's gaze.

"I'm almost finished with the plan, and if you approve, we'll probably have time to take four or five of 'em. But it must be fast and hard. We'll only have a couple of minutes to get into the bunker, load them, and get out. A backup force is supposed to arrive within thirty minutes. That'll probably be the Panamanians." Bart paused and then said, "That's only part of the problem."

"What's the bad news?" Franco puffed his cigar, and the smoke swirled above his head.

"The Americans, especially SOCOM, will be pissed. We'll need to beef up security and move our location a little more frequently."

"What will the American response be?"

"It is just a guess, but with the current chaos in DC and the president's inability to react, the response won't be immediate. Once the president authorizes SOCOM to act, things'll be quite active around here. Drugs are one thing, but nuclear weapons are another. It won't take the Americans long to figure out who took them, but it'll take a little longer to locate them. We just have to get rid of them right away. I've considered all this in my plan."

"The biggest problem will be keeping this quiet. OK, continue."

"It'll require split-second timing and the help of George and Felipe on the inside. After we evacuate the site, we'll rendezvous in a concealed location in the jungle and transfer the SADMs to other vehicles, and then the vehicles will separate and go to different transfer locations for Los Zetas to deliver them."

"I like it. Perhaps we can quadruple our profits."

"That's what I was thinking. I'll finish the time sequence and draft detail instructions for each person."

"Good. I'll call and get the meeting arranged," Franco said, dropping his cigar into the ashtray. "Remember, I want to hand off the nukes quickly."

***

Thursday
October 3, 2013
Zulian Region, Venezuela
Near the Colombian-Venezuelan Border

Franco and Bart walked along with their boss, Luis Marin Guzman, the Ivan Rios Bloc commander, on the grounds of his temporary jungle compound inside the Venezuelan Border. The compound was, as anyone might suspect, heavily guarded, and for the next several days, the security would be very tight. Guzman was hosting an unusual meeting with the Iranian, Hezbollah, and ISIS representatives for the sale of the nuclear weapons. Raúl Cano of the FARC Secretariat was due to arrive later that evening.

The estate, taken over from a Venezuelan rancher and fruit plantation owner for the meeting, occupied high ground overlooking the lush, green valley below. The three acres were well manicured, and various religious and mythological statues adorned the grounds. A swimming pool, decorated with statues of mermaids and cherubs, with outdoor kitchen was in the rear of the house and included in the entertainment.

As the three men turned the corner of the house and walked toward the pool, a strikingly beautiful nude woman—her long, black hair like strands of silk cascading over her tanned shoulders—climbed the ladder out of the pool.

"The guests are enjoying themselves?" Bart asked as he saw another nude woman—her blond hair pulled back into a ponytail—applying lotion to her shapely leg on a lounger by the pool. Her gold bracelet was brilliant in the bright sun.

"Yes, our ISIS friends are very pleased with the entertainment." Guzman smiled and puffed on his cigar. "There are several more ladies inside with the others, and a few more will be here this evening." Guzman motioned to the bartender.

"Nice touch. I'm sure they're thanking Allah for the ladies and booze." Bart smirked from behind his sunglasses. "These girls are really too good for these guys. But this is a big deal, and going all out and getting them boozed and screwed before the meeting tomorrow is good."

"They'll be easier to deal with. I haven't seen the two Iranians for several hours." A smile appeared on Guzman's face.

"How much do our guests know?" Franco asked as he eyed the woman drying herself.

"Very little. We didn't want them talking about this meeting. We've asked them to turn their cell phones off in case the Americans are listening."

"We're ready to go as soon as we have a buyer. Los Zetas are ready as well, but they don't know all the details or their cargo yet. They're scouting the routes now, and Bart has a couple of deceptions planned," Franco said, accepting a cuba libre, a favorite highball made of cola, lime, and white rum, from the bartender. "The delivery into the United States will be to a warehouse in Nogales. Douglas and El Paso are the alternate locations."

"The Chihuahua to Nogales or Douglas routes are in the Sinaloa Cartel's area. Are they going to give Los Zetas a problem?" Guzman asked, his face displaying concern.

"They're working on a deal. As a last resort, if they can't reach an agreement, they'll go through Nuevo Laredo."

"Be careful with the Sinaloa; I don't trust them. Where will the others be transferred?"

"There's an old airstrip about twenty-five kilometers north of here; that's where we'll hand them off."

"As a further inducement for them to work with us," Bart said as he looked at Guzman and then sipped his drink, "tell them we'll pass along intelligence about the US actions on the border and that we have a source inside the US government."

"Good idea," Guzman replied. "But they'll be more than a little cautious."

"Correct," Bart continued. "I recommend that Raúl contact them when he gets here. Ask him to tell his contacts in the cartels to put the word out that the southern US border is open and that their human smugglers will have no trouble crossing. They can keep the profits. All we want is their cooperation. I want maximum chaos at the border when we cross."

"I like it. That just might do it," Guzman said, and then he turned as he sensed someone approaching.

"I need some help with my sunscreen," a redheaded woman said, looking at Bart. She wore only a delicate gold chain around her neck—her firm breasts like ski slopes—as she walked from the house. Her auburn hair glistened in the bright sun, but Bart didn't notice.

"I'll be glad to help." Bart took the tube of lotion. "Gentlemen, please excuse me."

***

11:37 p.m.
Thursday
October 3, 2013
CIA Counterterrorism Center (CTC)
Tysons Corner, Virginia

"OK, what've you got?" Margaret said as she entered the vault. "The boss said it was urgent and that he'd obtained special permission for me to come in."

"Here's the summary," the watch officer said, handing her a folder. "I sent you an electronic file with the info I was given."

"Thanks." She smiled and walked to her cubicle, flicking on the light as she passed.

The vault was actually a sensitive compartmented information facility located in the building, a secure area where the highest classified material was stored and processed. She and the watch officer were the only two people on the floor and two of the few people in the entire building due to the government shutdown. The eerie building, normally filled with people and full of life, was dark and cool as though it were dead. As part of the power-down procedures, the lights and HVAC were turned off.

As she waited for her computer to power up, Margaret poured a cup of tea from her thermos and then removed her coat. She had been called in when the Latin American division of the CIA had sent a query, requesting information after hearing that two ISIS members were attending a meeting in Venezuela. The name *al-Aqrab* was the only one mentioned.

A senior analyst at the center, Margaret, like almost a million other government employees, was off work since the shutdown on October 1. The dedicated and highly respected analyst felt guilty for not being able to finish the cases she had been working on prior to the shutdown; she was so close, and the information she provided was very critical.

Her quad computer monitors blinked to life and waited her input. Opening the case file—Nabi Ulmalhamah al-Aqrab—an active case file spanning many months of work, the attractive brunette wasted no time. Scanning the voluminous amount of information she had amassed on the Arabic man to refresh her memory, Margaret made notes of his associates and contacts.

Al-Aqrab was a senior ISIS member and not known to have previously visited Venezuela. Al-Aqrab was suspected to be on the inner circle of Abu Bakr al-Baghdadi, the leader of ISIS. ISIS or the Islamic State of Iraq and Syria, also known as ISIL, the Islamic State of Iraq and the Levant, is an Islamic extremist terrorist organization. Leading the planning on a number of high-level bombings and attacks, al-Aqrab had extensive authority and worked strategic attacks on the West.

Completing her list, Margaret began the time-consuming task of searching to see if the passports belonging to Ulmalhamah al-Aqrab or his associates had been recently used; she started with his inner circle. Faster than she had anticipated, five potential matches were returned, four of which were false positives. The last one Margaret confirmed as the passport belonging to Abu Bakr al-Muhaymin, a close confidant of al-Aqrab. *It figures,* she thought. *Two dandy young men any mother would invite to Christmas dinner…not!*

The sun was high in the morning sky when Margaret finished her report, which confirmed that al-Aqrab and al-Muhaymin had entered Caracas on Thursday, October 3. Her report was electronically transmitted to the appropriate staff sections, including the Latin American division, all of whom, except for the Latin American division case officer who had submitted the request, would probably not read her report until the government shutdown was over. Immediately starting her next task, Margaret began researching to see if any of her other targets who could be associated with these two had entered Caracas recently. That was enough to keep Margaret busy as she waited for any further communications from the case officer.

By late morning Margaret had discovered that two senior Hezbollah members and two senior Iranians, all on her watch list, entered Caracas at different times on October 2. That in itself would not have piqued her interest or caused her to explore the connection any deeper. However, Iran's recent threats against the United States and their desire for nuclear weapons caused Margaret to take the time for a deeper look. That, and ISIS entering Caracas at the same time, would arouse anyone's interest.

Hezbollah, a proxy of Iran, derived income in Latin America from money laundering, the used-car trade, and drug trafficking, which had strengthened their relationship with the drug cartel, Los Zetas. The cartel, comprised mainly of ex-special-forces soldiers from the Mexican Army, was the most dangerous and second most powerful drug cartel in Mexico. An alliance between Los Zetas and Hezbollah could provide easy access for Iran to enter the mainland of the United States via the southern border along drug-traffic routes, as well as undermine the United States' interests in Latin America.

Hezbollah, Iran, Los Zetas, I understand, she thought. *They've been in bed together for a while now, but ISIS? What's that about, or is it a coincidence? There are no coincidences.*

Margaret prepared a supplemental message identifying the two Iranians, Nasim Shahbazi and Ahura Mazda Namazi, and the two Hezbollah members, Abdalrahman Tabari and Zafir Yasin, and sent the report forward to the same addressees as before. Included in the report was the background on each of the individuals. To Margaret, the representatives converging in Caracas was like an itch she couldn't scratch. She was determined to find out what they were doing.

***

Friday
October 4, 2013
Zulian Region, Venezuela
Near the Colombian-Venezuelan Border

"Franco, you have done very well," Guzman said as he looked out of the window at the sunset. "If this goes as Bart planned, we'll make a lot of money and do away with the nukes quickly. Whatever Bart needs—more men, vehicles, weapons, anything—he gets it."

"Can we trust Tabari or Yasin?" Franco asked and then sipped his brandy.

"Don't trust any of them, but we have something they all want. Shahbazi will keep them under control. It's the two ISIS—al-Aqrab and al-Muhaymin—who concern me. I'm leaving after dinner," Guzman said. "I'm glad to see them leave. You and Bart stay here and enjoy yourselves tonight. The house will be checked and cleaned in the morning."

He watched the redhead stroll to the pool, drop her towel in the chair, and then dive in. "If I were a younger man…"

"Luis, you're never too old to look at the scenery. I don't trust those Arabs to keep their mouths shut. We need to move quickly if we're going to make this happen. The American CIA will find out about this as soon as the Arabs start talking."

"I know. Have Bart ready to go. Oh, and have Bart lean on his senator for information. I want to know if the CIA learns anything about our plan. If anything goes wrong, make it look like the Arabs are responsible."

"Bart is the only one I can trust for this big an operation. He'll lead it, and he knows what to do."

***

Monday
October 7, 2013
Darien Gap
Near the Panamanian-Colombian Border

"Senator," Bart said into the phone, "what's the latest on the government shutdown?"

"No end in sight," replied Senator Bradbourne.

"I want an intelligence update every day. I want to know what the intelligence community knows before the president or whoever is in charge up there."

"Bart…please, I can't—"

"Pictures, Senator. I don't want to hear this fucking shit from you anymore! Got it?"

"I got it."

"I want to know the status of the southern border. What is the Border Patrol doing? Are they detaining people or what?"

"No change on the border. Border Patrol isn't detaining anyone."

"If that should change, I want to know immediately. Also, if the military goes on any kind of alert or deploys any troops, especially to Latin America, call me right away."

"What're you up to?"

"Don't worry about what I'm doing. You just do as you're told. I'll expect your call tomorrow with an update." Bart ended the call before the senator could respond. Sliding his chair back, he stood and paced the floor and rehearsed each step of his plan in his mind.

"How's the plan coming? About finished?" Franco asked as he entered the room.

"I'm finished; just going over the details again."

"You're leaving to go to the Balboa site to get with George and Felipe, correct?"

"In a couple of hours. I want to spend time with 'em and walk 'em through each step. You need me to do something?"

"No, I'll be leaving to coordinate and set up the transfer site in Venezuela. I'll meet you back here in a few days."

***

Wednesday
October 9, 2013
Trump Ocean Club International Hotel and Tower
Panama City, Panama

Seated, his legs outstretched, Bart nursed a Crown Royal Reserve on ice and looked over the Panama Bay. Completing two days of rehearsals with George and Felipe, he had insured they knew exactly what they were to do and when to execute it. The success of Bart's plan relied on those two—not the brightest bulbs on the tree—doing exactly as he instructed. Their duties were simple but key to the operation.

The inexperience of those two individuals concerned him. Neither had actual combat experience of any type, and depending on them to shoot another person without provocation, especially ones they had worked with for over a year, was the weakest part of Bart's plan. A more seasoned mercenary would be better suited for such a task, but Bart didn't have that luxury. If George and Felipe failed in their task, Bart and his force would disappear, and that would save Bart two bullets.

Bart sat the glass on the table and punched in the numbers to the senator's office again, for the third time that afternoon.

"Senator Bradbourne," he answered.

"This is Bart. I haven't received your intel update for yesterday. Why!"

"I…I was in a funding meeting yesterday."

"Bullshit! I want that update and now. Understand?"

"I do. I do. It's—"

"*Unacceptable* is the word, Senator. You're trying my patience."

"I'm sorry, Bart. I'll get right on it."

"Good. I saw a Fox News story that a US antidrug plane crashed in Colombia on Saturday. I didn't see that in your update on Monday. I told you I wanted everything."

"I guess I missed that. I'll find out and call you back."

"I guess you did. No more slipups like this. I'll be waiting on your call." Bart ended the call.

Thoroughly infuriated with the senator, Bart considered a quick trip to DC, but he didn't have the time. Ending the relationship with the senator would require Bart to develop another source; it wouldn't take long, but it would slow him down. Needing to relax, Bart slipped on his bathing suit and went to the pool, where his redheaded companion was lounging in the afternoon sun—a more relaxing and pleasurable experience than sitting around waiting for the senator.

Seated in the recliner next to the woman, Bart examined her nearly perfect curves. She was facedown, taking in the sun on her back. Her red hair was pulled back, allowing the sun to reach her neck and the side of her face. Opening her eyes, she smiled at Bart and then sat upright.

"I'd like a drink," she said.

Bart motioned for the waiter, ordered two cold beers, and then observed the occupants of the sparsely populated pool. *All sizes and shapes,* he thought. *No one is interested in us.* That provided him some relief. Being careful was what kept him alive. His eyes came back around and landed on the woman next to him, her eyes closed beneath her sunglasses. A drop of perspiration gently made its way from her gold necklace down her cleavage and disappeared below her bathing-suit top.

The waiter unobtrusively placed two coasters on the table and then set the drinks on them. Handing one to the woman, Bart drank the other. At that moment, his cell phone rang. Looking at the phone, he saw the senator's number.

"Yes," Bart spoke into the phone.

"Your update is on the way. The news story—"

"Hold on," Bart said. "I'll call you right back, five minutes."

Ending the call, Bart set the drink back on the coaster and then kissed the redhead's cheek. "I'll be back in a few minutes," he said.

She smiled and stroked his cheek.

Five minutes later Bart was seated at the desk in his room. "OK, Senator," Bart said into his phone. "I can talk now. Whatta ya got for me?"

"The plane was a twin-engine turboprop, Bombardier DHC-8, specially outfitted with the latest intelligence, surveillance, and reconnaissance equipment," Bradbourne said. "It was a civilian aircraft operated by JIATF South. It flew out of Panama." The Joint Interagency Task Force South is a multiservice, multiagency task force that conducts interagency and international detection and monitoring operations. It facilitates the interdiction of illicit trafficking and other narco-terrorist threats in support of national and partner nation security.

"Keep going," Bart said. "Why did it crash?"

"Officially it is listed as mechanical failure. But it was shot down by the FARC presumably. What do you know about that?"

"Keep going, Senator."

"The plane routinely flies drug routes; they were supposedly tracking a drug-smuggling vessel. However, the CIA got wind of a meeting between representatives from Iran, Hezbollah, and ISIS, and they suspected the meeting was with the FARC just inside the Venezuelan border. The plane was sent along the Colombian-Venezuela border to see if it could pick up anything. That's when the plane was hit. It managed to fly back to Capurganá, where it crashed in the jungle."

"What'd the plane pick up?"

"I'm trying to find out now. But the damned shutdown is making it difficult. What the hell is going on?"

"Don't worry about it, Senator. Just get me the information on what the plane picked up, and fast!"

"I will, but I've got to be careful on this; CIA, DEA, Homeland Security, JIATF South, and I don't know who all are looking at this."

"All right, stay on top of it, and calm down. I want to know immediately what you find out. No matter what, you ensure that the border stays open. I'll give you the location of a large drug shipment that's going to cross the border; it'll make you look good in the news. You do your part, and I'll have a nice little bonus for you."

"What does all this have to do with the site in Balboa you asked about?"

"Nothing, Senator," Bart lied. "The meeting was just about a drug alliance. Nothing for you to worry about."

"Bart, I—"

"Just start thinking about your next visit to Panama," Bart cut in.

The latest information the senator had provided concerned Bart. *How much do they know?* he thought. *Did the Arabs start talking with all their praise-be-to-Allah bullshit and spill the beans? Hold off on execution, and keep on planning for now. I need to know what the CIA and the military know.*

The next morning, at 7:34 a.m., Bart rolled over to his ringing cell phone and recognized the senator's number.

Throwing the sheet back and sitting up, Bart patted the bare butt of his redheaded companion and said, "Hop in the shower; then we'll have breakfast."

"Good morning, Senator. What've you got?"

"The plane was destroyed, and they aren't going to get much from the crash site. Very little was transmitted that's useful. JIATF South believe that they have the location of the meeting, and the name *Nabi Ulmalhamah al-Aqrab* was used. Most of it is useless babble, but they talked about some big deal and fifteen million dollars. The CIA is checking out the location now. Nothing else has come out of Homeland Security or DEA."

Fucking Arabs! Bart thought. "OK, Senator. What about NSA or Fort Huachuca? Anything from them?"

"I haven't heard of anything, but I'll keep checking. What's this *big deal* and fifteen million dollars?"

"Nothing to worry about; just a drug deal. They're projecting profits. Thank you, Senator. Keep me informed."

The senator's call concerned Bart, but it wasn't a showstopper. The Arabs were talking, which meant that the window for executing Bart's plan was closing. *The meetinghouse was cleaned, so they won't find anything there,* he thought. *Franco will need an update. Franco and Luis can deal with the CIA. They'll need to push to get the money if we are going to move on this.*

Picking up the phone again, Bart entered Franco's number.

"Franco," the voice said.

"We're set on my end. Are you?"

"All set here. The transfer agreement is complete from two, and I have a promise from the third by this evening."

"Good. I just got a call from my contact, and the window is closing for us to move. As we suspected, our friends are starting to talk. I'll fill you in on the details when I get back. Also, they're checking out the meetinghouse."

"I'll take care of it. I'll be ready to go when you are."

Franco ended the call.

Chapter 3

Saturday
October 12, 2013
Headquarters, US Special Operations Command
J3 Directorate of Operations
MacDill Air Force Base, Florida

The general's secretary held the door open for Max Kenworth as he entered.

"Thank you, Helen," he said, smiling, as she closed the door.

Max was every bit what his name signified—with short, jet-black hair, he was built like a freight liner. It wasn't happenstance that the former delta-force officer, now retired from the army, was visiting the J3 on a Saturday afternoon. As a civilian, Max worked for the J3 and headed up the highly classified program at headquarters, having to do with nuclear-weapons planning and counterproliferation of weapons of mass destruction.

"Max," Major General Matherson said as he shook Max's hand. "Thanks for stoppin' by."

The highly decorated Major General Hugh "Chugs" Matherson was the Director of Operations or J3 at SOCOM. The moniker was derived from his college days and had held true throughout his early air-force years as a young lieutenant. Known for his fondness of beer, this lanky officer never seemed to gain a pound and was in excellent physical condition. Even to this day, Chugs never passed up the opportunity for good beer.

"General, when you call me on a Saturday afternoon and ask me to stop in for a visit—if I'm comin' on base—it means only one thing: get your ass in here; I've got a problem." Max broke into a smile as he picked up a knight from the chessboard on the general's desk. "I'm pretty sure it isn't to play chess."

"Max, come in. I'm not that bad." The two-star general grinned. "Have a seat. Wish we *could* play chess."

"Yeah, what's up?" Max eased into a side chair and adjusted the tight-fitting sleeves of his polo shirt.

"Well, I do have a problem."

"I knew it, General. What do you want me to do? Is the DEA stuck some place again and needing help, or is it the State Department this time?"

"Well, worse than that; read this first." Chugs handed him a copy of the CIA summary on a meeting the FARC hosted in Venezuela and the JIATF South report.

Max quickly read the summary. "That's not good. CIA find anything at the meeting site?" He returned the message.

"They've lost all contact with the team they sent in. They're presumed killed. They've asked our help in finding their people. An A-team is already on their way. Max, this meeting didn't happen today." The general paused, looked into Max's brown eyes, and then continued, "We've got a more serious problem. The Balboa site was attacked early this morning."

"Shit! How many casualties?"

"They damned near wiped out the entire place. Three American soldiers are in ICU now. Don't know if they're going to make it or not. Most of the guard force is either dead or wounded. But it's worse than that."

"Don't tell me. The bunker, Empty Quiver?" Max asked, referring to the remote storage bunker containing SOCOM's Mark 54 SADMs. *Empty Quiver* was code; it meant the theft or loss of nuclear weapons.

"They got in. The Panamanians have the site secured, and a team from Fort Bragg'll be on the ground shortly. When they take inventory, I'll know what's missing. The bunker door was open when the Panamanians arrived. Until we've got confirmation, the assumption is that whoever gained access to the bunker made off with one or more SADMs. A Pinnacle OPREP-3 incident report has been submitted." A Pinnacle OPREP-3 is a special report that describes an event of such importance that it needs to be brought to the immediate attention of the National Command Authority, Joint Chiefs of Staff/National Military Command Center and other national-level leadership.

"You're not sending me to Panama, are you?" Max knew that the general had something else in mind, something more than securing the facility in Balboa, something that would probably challenge Max's many years of experience as an operator and as a nuclear-weapons expert. Above all, it wouldn't be at a conference stuffed with supposed intellectuals without any practical experience and with an idealistic view of the world, as they sat in an air-conditioned room and took breaks every hour to shove pastries in their faces and wash them down with bad coffee. More likely it would be dealing with some transnational group that wanted nothing more than to inflict maximum pain on the United States and bring it down.

"I'm not going to send you anywhere. You're a civilian. But if you volunteer…"

"Come on, General. Out with it. What do you want me to do?"

"I need you on this. Find those weapons, wherever they are, and then get 'em back in our custody. The old man has been cooling his heels, trying to brief the president on the attack. He's playing golf. The old man did quickly brief the SecDef but not the details yet. He doesn't trust SecDef either." Chugs was affectionately referring to the SOCOM commander.

"What do the White House staffers know about the weapons?"

"Nothing. The old man is reluctant to tell them anything other than that an attack occurred and that we've got casualties. We're all concerned that if the staff know about the SADMs, it'll be all over the news before you can spit.

That'll cause a lot of panic and compound the difficulty of getting them back. In addition, the international community will absolutely go ballistic and hammer the president. Of course, the Russians'll lambaste the president savagely on reneging on the nuclear arms treaty. Just another scandal or crisis. Shit!"

"This meeting in Venezuela." Max pointed to the reports on the general's desk. "Do we know for sure the FARC is behind the attack or had something to do with it?"

"No direct link has been made as of yet. The chaos in Washington—gridlock, government shutdown, administration's policies, and political infighting—is causing us fits. The old man knows that if he briefs the president and suggests that Iran had a hand in this, he'll be handed his head. The president believes that he can sit down and have a discussion with the Iranians and that everything will be fine then. The president won't do anything he thinks will irritate them. If Iran or Hezbollah is involved, it'll be worse than a disaster. We'll need verification, and if it's the Iranians, we could be in another shooting match. Our big problem is that we can't wait around and get proof."

"General, we should tell the Israelis and Brits—"

"We have been directed by the president to suspend reporting and execution of our contingency plans until we know exactly who has them." Chugs's expression was serious; his brow dipped slightly, and his eyes narrowed. "Low profile for now. I've already put your boys to work on this."

Chugs's guidance left Max almost speechless. He paused and then said, "This is going to cause other problems as well."

"Correct. The president and the Israeli PM aren't on good terms."

"I want to make sure that I understand you correctly—someone stole one or more of our nuclear weapons, and we aren't supposed to make a fuss or aggressively try to find and recover them? Israel is about our only ally in that part of the world now. Iran has vowed to wipe them off the face of the earth, and the Mideast is going up in flames. If we don't bring them in on this immediately, it will definitely end our relationship."

"I have been ordered, Max." The general's eyes bored onto Max's, and his tone was stern.

For the next two hours, the two men discussed the situation and planned a strategy for the recovery of the weapons. The attack on the site had been a complete surprise—there had been no warning, no protests or demonstrations, and no intel. The absence of any reference to the site in intelligence reporting was troubling in itself, let alone puzzling.

"It's highly unlikely the Panamanian Public Forces did it, but a cartel could have. The FARC or Los Zetas, maybe," Max said.

"I agree. So who's got 'em? Where are they? And what're they gonna do with 'em? That's what you've got to find out, and fast. We've gotta get the weapons back before some reporter finds out we had nukes in Panama."

"Understood. Israel needs to know."

"Hold off on telling them for now. I want to see what the old man comes back with after his talk with the president. I've arranged for you to have dedicated support from the CIA." Chugs picked up the message, looked at the name, and continued. "Margaret, the analyst who prepared the report, is your contact there. You'll be out there by yourself and undercover, but check in with me regularly."

"It's not the first time, sir." Max grinned.

"You have carte blanche on this; just let me know what you need." The general paused, looked at Max, and then continued, saying, "As I said when you came in, this meeting never happened. SOCOM will disavow any knowledge about your mission, hasn't authorized it, and you are simply on leave. So don't get caught. However, you'll have whatever you need, and a delta team is on standby to help you as required."

"I understand, sir. Is Margaret furloughed?"

"No, they brought her in. If you need anything, call her. If she is out, the watch officer will get the message to her."

"I'll make contact with her and then head to Panama."

"Good luck, Max. Be careful."

"Thank you, sir, I will."

***

CTC
Tysons Corner, Virginia

On a classified video teleconference between SOCOM and CTC, Max became acquainted with Margaret, an astute Texas woman. Giving him an intelligence update, she said, "The CIA team that went to check out the meetinghouse in Venezuela is confirmed killed. All indications are that the FARC is responsible."

"Shit! I was afraid of that."

"The LA division is trying to get in close to see what's going on. I got permission to tell them you'll be in the area, and they'll provide any support you may need."

"Thanks, I don't want to get caught in the middle if something goes down." Max shifted in his chair.

"The chatter has picked up on ISIS." Margaret scribbled on her notepad. "They are promising something big, but we don't know where or what. I can only guess that it's the missing weapons. Hezbollah has also increased the anti-Israel chatter. I recommend we bring the Israelis in the loop on this."

"Hold off for a bit. I hope we can contain this to Latin America. The Israelis have their hands full right now."

"They'll be pissed off royally if they find out that we haven't told them. As you know, the prime minister and the president aren't on the best of terms right now."

"I know. The makings of another crisis." The corner of Max's mouth wrinkled up, and his head gave a slight nod.

Max and Margaret spent almost forty-five minutes reviewing the latest intelligence. They discussed Max's plan and the specific intelligence he wanted her to research.

"A cartel taking the nuclear weapons doesn't fit with their pattern," Margaret said, placing her pen next to the tablet on the table. "The meeting in Venezuela suggests that the FARC has joined with Hezbollah, Iran, and ISIS—"

"I agree. The cartel sells the nuclear weapons to one or more of the members at the meeting, and they, in turn, take them out of the country."

"That's right." Margaret's expression was serious. "The cartels don't have their own capabilities to deliver the weapons to the Middle East. So they'll distribute them somewhere in Latin America for transportation elsewhere. We won't have much time to locate them."

"I know. The drug routes are the key, so really look close at that traffic."

"Hezbollah likes the used-car trade for smuggling their drugs, so that'll mean a shipping port. Iran could be using ship or plane. ISIS, that's the tricky one. If they want them in Afghanistan, it could be by plane or ship; if it's not Afghanistan, it could be the United States."

Margaret, expressionless, held her gaze on the monitor.

"Let's hope we can find them before they leave Latin America."

"I have a couple of cell-phone numbers I'm trying to run down," Margaret continued. "The calls are between a US citizen and someone in Panama. NSA is compounding my problems in getting information. Everyone is under the microscope right now when it comes to getting phone records. Approval is a bitch!"

"OK, let me know if you turn up anything. Are you seeing anything new or any pattern changes in the FARC or Los Zetas?"

"Not too much. Just the usual drug-related stuff."

"Watch for anything that changes in their routines, no matter how slight. I'll check in with you regularly, and if you find something I need to know about immediately, call my cell. If I don't answer, leave me a message. I'll get back to you when I can." A smile emerged on Max's face.

"Will do. Good luck, and be careful."

***

Sunday Afternoon
October 13, 2013
NASA Climate Research Facility
Balboa, Panama

A sergeant of the Panamanian Public Forces, armed with an M4 carbine, challenged Max outside the exclusion area as he eased the rental car to a stop in the parking lot at the site. After providing sufficient identification, Max was escorted inside the compound to meet Captain Greg Garnett, officer in charge of the special-forces team from Fort Bragg. Observing the exterior of the compound, Max saw Americans in full combat gear manning the towers, while armed Panamanians, also in combat gear, were posted outside the fence. A Panamanian helicopter patrolled overhead. A large truck—obviously used as a ram for entry—was overturned just inside and beyond a gaping hole in the security fence. Pockmarks covered the doors and walls of the guardhouse and security force's quarters. Several armed American soldiers, in combat gear and carrying M4 carbines, were scattered about the compound.

"I was told to expect you, sir," Captain Garnett said, shaking Max's hand. "This way, sir. I'm set up to brief you inside."

"Thank you, Captain. It's quite a mess out here. What's the status?"

"Confirmed Empty Quiver. The bunker has been secured, but four mark-fifty-four SADMs are missing. Power and phones have been restored."

Leading Max into a small conference room, Garnett motioned for him to sit at the table and then began his briefing. A diagram of the site, with numerous markings, was propped on an easel next to the captain. A laptop, connected to a projection system, displayed the PowerPoint presentation on a screen behind him. Piecing together the details of the attack from his observations when he had first arrived, Garnett presented the time line of the attack.

"At approximately zero five forty-five," Garnet started, "two of the contract guards initiated the assault. One entered the guardhouse and killed the sergeant on duty, opened the bunker doors, and kept the reaction force pinned down in the building, killing all but one. The second guard kept the rest of the security force bottled up inside their building. A force outside the fence took out the two tower personnel. A roadblock was set up here," he said, pointing to a red-circled area on the sketch, "and made to look like an accident. That was just after the last turnoff from the main road and delayed the backup force. Electricity, phone lines, and the generator were knocked out."

"The two guards who started the inside attack, what did you learn from them?"

"Very little. Both were killed in the fight. Their company representative is on his way here."

"Let me know immediately what you find out from him."

The briefing lasted another twenty minutes and covered each detail as pieced together by Garnett. "The attack was a well-coordinated military operation, hitting hard and fast. The force took all the mark-four rifles, four mark-forty-six lightweight machine guns, two mark-two fifty-caliber machine guns, four mark-nineteen grenade launchers—"

"Thanks, Captain," Max said. "In other words, all the weapons were taken. I guess ammunition as well. The complete inventory is in your report, correct?"

"Yes, sir, it is."

"Did you find much evidence?"

"We swept the area very well. They did take a few casualties. We found a couple of blood trails and one Kalashnikov. The overturned truck by the fence was stolen."

"That's not much to go on, but it's a start. I'm going to have a look around for a bit."

Standing, Max shook the captain's hand and then left the room. Max strolled around the compound and reconstructed the attack as told to him by Captain Garnett. Though confident that the diligent captain hadn't missed anything, Max wanted to see with his own eyes if there were any telltale clues that his experienced eye might pick up.

It's obvious the attack was to gain entry into the bunker and the SADMs, Max thought. *Someone had inside information. The two guards were part of it, but who turned them? Who paid them? And one Kalashnikov. Very few people know about this place. Even the guards don't know exactly what they're guarding.*

The sun was dipping low in the western sky by the time Max completed his inspection. Looking for weak or unprotected areas, he had examined every angle of the compound—view from the towers, guardhouse, entrance, and approach to the facility. Nothing escaped his inquisitive eyes.

Satisfied that Captain Garnett had things under control and that his further inspection of the site wouldn't reveal much more than he already knew, Max returned to his car. He looked over the compound again as he walked out.

Heading back toward Balboa, Max mulled over each detail. *It appears they left very few clues to the untrained eye,* he thought. However, what Max had seen told him a lot. *Military style, fast and hard. Truck stolen, all guards taken out, and all weapons and ammunition taken along with four SADMs, and then they vanished into the jungle. It's not a military; probably a cartel, but which one?*

Realizing that he was driving ten miles per hour under the speed limit, Max sped up as a car behind him honked and flashed its lights. Max waved, signaling his apology. *Military-style operation,* he thought. *Los Zetas is mostly ex–Mexican Special Forces, the logical ones. But this is way outside their operating region. This is closer to FARC territory; they run drugs through Panama. Margaret thinks it's the FARC. A military advisor. She didn't mention if they had one; that's something to check out.*

Instinctively Max turned into the drive of the Green Iguana bar. *A beer on the way home. That's what bored, lowly paid guards would do.*

Max slid onto an old wooden stool at the bar and then ordered a Panama beer. Two bewhiskered older men in sweat-stained clothes sat in the back and nursed their preferred drink. Seeing the two men confirmed what Max had suspected—this was the local watering hole for the men at the site. *The incident at the site is taking its toll on this place as well,* he thought. *Unfortunately business will be off for a while.*

Setting the bottle on a coaster in front of Max, the bartender picked up a smoldering cigarette from the ashtray and stuck it in the middle of his badly shaped, shaggy, vandyke beard.

"Kinda quiet around here this evening," Max said, hoping to get a conversation going.

"It's dead, amigo. There was a little excitement up the road at the NASA facility early yesterday morning. I heard it was some terrorist attack or something like that."

"I heard about it."

The bartender, wiping his hands on a soiled white towel, paused, inquisitively looked at Max, and then said, "I haven't seen you around here before."

Watching the bartender dry his hands, Max thought, *How long has it been since he last washed that towel and his hands?* "I'm a reporter for NewsMax," he lied. "I heard something was going on and thought I'd just check it out. They wouldn't let me get anywhere near the place."

"The soldiers won't let anyone get near it."

"What do they do out there?"

"Something to do with climate research. Most of the workers come in here after their shifts. I hope this doesn't last long. No customers—no business."

"I know whatcha mean; kinda tough to make a living without any customers."

"I have a girl who helps me, but she hasn't been in for two days. No big deal, since there isn't any business. I'd just have to send her home."

"That's an idea," Max continued, retrieving a notepad and pen from his pocket. "That would make an interesting story to go along with the attack on the facility. If I could, I'd like to mention you and the way the incident has affected the local business. I'll be sure to mention the Green Iguana. Free publicity, you know."

"OK, man, but I don't know anything. Dorotea, the gal who helps me, knows the customers and things going on better than I do. She's, well, pretty good window dressing, if you know what I mean. A couple of the regulars chase her around, but I think she just leads them along."

"Gotcha!" Max grinned. "Her name is Dorotea, and her last name?" Max entered her name in his notepad.

"Trujillo, Dorotea Trujillo."

"How can I get in touch with her? She might be able to give me some information about the men and the site for my story." Max laid a twenty-dollar bill on the bar.

"I think it'd be OK." The bartender slid the twenty toward himself. "When you talk to her, tell her that I don't appreciate her not letting me know she wouldn't be working. Have her call me if she wants to keep her job. This shit at the NASA facility won't last long, and I'm going to need some help." The man scribbled her address on a scrap of paper as cigarette ashes rained onto it and then flipped the paper to Max.

"Thanks for the info," Max said as he stood, laid another twenty-dollar bill on the counter, and retrieved the address. *That's a start,* he thought as he walked to the car.

Driving back into town, Max checked the time, and then entered the number for Margaret in his cell phone.

"This is John," the voice said, indicating that he was the CTC watch officer.

"Max," he replied, "pass to Margaret the name *Dorotea Trujillo.* She's a waitress at the Green Iguana bar about two kilometers from the facility. It's the favorite watering hole for the workers. Have her check it out, and I'll be back in touch."

"Got it. Anything else?"

"Tell her that I agree with her that it's probably the FARC, and see if she can find out if they have a military advisor, an ex-combat-arms type."

"Anything else?"

"No, thanks." Max ended the call and then punched in the number for General Matherson to give him the latest information, which wasn't much.

"General," Max said, "confirmed Empty Quiver. I did get a briefing on the situation at the site and also picked up a name at the local watering hole. Looks like a FARC operation. I don't have much more than a hunch at this point, but it looks that way. I got the name of a barmaid, who might provide more info. I passed it along to Margaret."

"Great, Max. I'm to get an update from the Panamanians in the morning. I'll let you know what they've got. The old man did brief the president, and it didn't go well. The president has instructed us to keep it quiet for now. He's worried about another scandal. I don't know how long he'll be able to keep this quiet. The old man did try to get the president to authorize us to go into Panama and Colombia to search for the weapons. He said he'd consider it. He wants to talk with the Panamanian president first. He thinks he should have an active role in this."

"Goddamn it! When will the administration learn? They can't keep this kind of stuff quiet. That means not long. I'm going to stay here for a day or two to see if I can pick up anything. I'll be in touch."

***

Tuesday
October 15, 2013
Darien Gap
Near the Panamanian-Colombian Border

"Senator, you've been doing well with your reports," Bart said. "What about the shutdown? The news says they're close to an agreement."

"We are close, but there are still a couple of sticking points. I got wind of something happening in Panama. Bart, that facility in Balboa—"

"You didn't mention anything about it in yesterday's intel update. I told you I wanted to know what's going on before the president. What did you hear, and whom did you hear it from?"

"It came from one of the White House staff."

"OK. I'm waiting."

"There was an attack on the facility, and several people were killed. It's hush-hush, and SOCOM is leading the effort. What do you know about this?"

"Find out all you can about SOCOM's efforts, and keep me posted!"

"I will. There is an A-team at the place now, and there was one sent to look for a missing CIA team on the Venezuelan border. What's going on?"

"Senator, I promised you something big to get your name in the paper. There's going to be a big drug shipment through a Sinaloa Cartel drug tunnel the day after tomorrow. The tunnel is from Tijuana and connects to a warehouse in an industrial district in Otay Mesa, on the south side of San Diego. I'll get you the address. I want you to make it public. You figure out a way to tell everyone how you found out. Make it a big splash, and get all the major networks there. Push all the relevant agencies—Border Patrol, DEA, Homeland Security, and whomever else you can think of—to be there. I want them all looking at this. I want to see on the news where everyone is slapping each other on the back and congratulating each other on a great bust. You got it?"

"I do, but—"

"Don't worry about it, Senator. Just get everyone focused on the drug tunnel."

***

CTC
Tysons Corner, Virginia

"Glad you called, Max," Margaret said. "I've got some info for you."

"Whatcha got?" asked Max.

"Two men were taken to Hospital Santo Tomás in Panama City with gunshot wounds. They're under guard and are members of the FARC. They're talking. I'll have a summary for you shortly, and I'll send it. Hezbollah has ramped up their rhetoric against Israel. They're planning something big. There's talk of Iran sending another shipment of arms to Syria. ISIS has ramped up its chatter. Sounds like they're planning an attack on the United States."

"Anything on Dorotea Trujillo?"

"We haven't located her yet, but we did find out that she is the cousin of Franco Trujillo, commander of Fifty-Seventh Front, FARC."

"Well, you're just full of good news," replied Max. "That explains how the FARC got all the information about the site. Let your guys know I'll be going to the hospital."

"Will do."

"Start looking for any information on senior bomb makers for our three watch groups. I'm interested in senior guys who are actually scientists. In order to use the SADMs, they'll have to bypass the permissive action link. The PAL is an electronic interface requiring a special code to activate the weapon, and if they screw it up, they won't detonate. They'll know that and will have their best guys working on it. My guess is that it will take a scientist one to two weeks to complete the task."

"That doesn't give us much time. I'll highlight that part in my summary for everyone to see," Margaret said.

"Good. Bypassing the PAL and ensuring the trigger is functioning properly is going to be their biggest challenge. To work on the device, they'll need a stable work environment. It could be a hideout somewhere or on board a ship. This isn't a job that some run-of-the-mill turban head can do."

"I understand. We've got a pretty good list of their scientists. One other thing."

"I'm afraid to ask," said Max, "but go ahead."

"The White house is very nervous. They've brought in Homeland Security and assembled their crisis team. They are quietly working in the background and have been instructed to keep this quiet."

"Shit! That's like printing it on the front page. Everyone I've come in contact with from Homeland Security is short on experience and long on ego. I don't think any of them have progressed farther than the comic-book level."

Margaret continued, "The Brits and Israelis have been briefed as well. They're not happy campers; the Israelis are furious and will contact you for a meeting."

"OK. I know those guys; they're good. I'll be in touch."

"Be careful."

Chapter 4

October 15, 2013
Mossad Safe House
Balboa, Panama

"Max!" Danya Mayer said after a brief pause; her face had lit up as he had entered the room.

"Danya," he replied with outstretched arms. The two embraced and kissed each other on the cheek. "It's good to see you again."

"You, too. It's been too long," she whispered in his ear. Danya was an Israeli intelligence officer for Mossad in Panama.

"I guess introductions aren't necessary," said Thaddeus Nussbaum, senior Israeli intelligence officer for Mossad, Panama. He stood motionless and looked at the couple with curiosity.

"We go back a while." Danya smiled and then grasped Max's muscular arm and escorted him into the living room.

Max sat on the couch as Danya and Thaddeus sat in chairs across the coffee table from him. With the cordialities complete, the meeting quickly got down to business.

"Max, what the hell is going on in Washington?" Danya asked as she leaned forward in her chair.

Max was meeting with the two agents assigned to find the missing SADMs and prevent them from reaching Hezbollah or Iran. Israel, taking the threats against their country or people very seriously, had, for years, kept their defenses up—many times taking preemptive strikes to protect themselves. This threat was no exception. Max knew the meeting would be contentious.

The safe house was located in Balboa near the international airport and Ancón Hill. The well-appointed house, of traditional French and American design common to Panama, had formerly been an American senior officer's quarters. Danya, a very experienced agent in her late thirties, was in her sixth year working in Panama.

Brushing her short, wavy brown hair from her face, she continued, "The prime minister is furious and thinks your president is going to get us into a war—"

"Danya," Thaddeus said, his tone commanding. "Max, we have received intelligence summaries from the CIA." Thaddeus, a former naval officer and member of Shayetet Thirteen, carried his six-foot frame with confidence, and his demeanor was serious. "This is very frustrating to us. We're supposed to be on the same team. Level with us, and keep us informed. Danya is already working her sources. Activity has picked up with Hezbollah, and it coincides with the attack at your Balboa site. We understand that four weapons were taken."

"Our estimation is that the FARC took them and has sold them to Iran, Hezbollah, or ISIS—or all three." Max's eyes shifted from Thaddeus to Danya.

"That's great." Thaddeus's sarcasm was thick. "Your president is being lied to by the Iranians; they think he's weak. He's fallen victim to the charm offensive of the new Iranian president. They're just stringing him along. We believe if they do have one of the weapons, they'll use it as a bargaining chip or really *use* it if the negotiations fail."

"I know, and that's the problem," Max replied. "He won't do anything that he thinks will upset the Iranians. The president believes they'll discuss things like gentlemen."

"Shit!" Danya's voice exploded in anger. "They've vowed to wipe Israel off the map. You can't have a gentlemen's discussion with those fanatics! We've been on the verge of war with them for thirty-five years. Can't the Americans see that Iran continues to build strength in the region? They want more prestige on the world stage, and a nuke is prestige. Iran has avowed not to be caught shorthanded, like they were when Iraqi troops attacked them with chemical weapons during the Iran-Iraq War in 1980 to 1988. Iran couldn't retaliate in kind, as they didn't have any WMDs. What does that tell ya?"

"I know." Max shifted in his seat and wiped his forehead. "They're justifying their desire for WMDs on Shi'ite tradition—use any means to attack those who don't believe in their version of Islam."

"Iran is convinced the United States will not attack a nuclear-weapons state for fear of retaliation. If Iran becomes a nuclear power, it will be war in the Middle East." Thaddeus's tone was serious.

"I know," Max said as he shot a glance to Thaddeus and then back to Danya. "We've got to solve this problem now, here, in Panama. I seem to recall your motto—*Where there is no guidance, a nation falls, but in an abundance of counselors, there is safety.*" Max looked at the fiery Danya. "They're going to be a bitch to find in the jungle."

"We're watching the used-car-collection points, airports, and ports, but, frankly, it is going to be a challenge." Thaddeus's face was void of expression. "I talked to the British this morning, and they are beefing up their team down here."

"I agree. The CIA and JIATF South are covering the drug routes and along the coast," Max said.

"Your devices, the SADMs, the core is plutonium?"

Max nodded. "Pu-239. Yes, almost impossible to detect as long as the plutonium isn't exposed. Even if it is exposed, it's difficult. And the shipping containers provide additional shielding."

"That's what I thought." Thaddeus paused and looked down and then back to Max. "It'll be a challenge to find the weapons, since Pu-239 only emits alpha particles. Sensors won't detect them."

"A sheet of paper or heavy dust covering can shield the particles." Max looked into his eyes. "They were designed to prevent an adversary from easily detecting them and for maximum protection for the individual employing the weapons. It was never envisioned that we'd someday need to find one."

"This is just fucking great, Max!" Danya uncrossed her shapely legs and then stood. "Your president is treating this with no more enthusiasm than if he were going after a cartel smuggling marijuana. The heroin traffic is about seventy billion dollars a year, and on a good day, only about twenty percent is confiscated in transit. So our odds are twenty percent or less of finding the weapons." She paced and ran her hand through her brown hair.

"That's about the size of it." Max watched her pace. "And they have over a three-day head start into the jungle."

"I'm going back to talk with the two casualties at Hospital Santo Tomás," Thaddeus said. He slipped a map of Panama from his desk, glanced at it, and then glanced back at Max. "We checked out the two transfer points they told us about, but they were clean. The two in the hospital were either purposely not told any more than the transfer locations, or they are very good at concealing it." He handed the map to Max.

"I'm betting on the latter," Danya said. "Our people are working the Caracas area to see if anyone can find out any more about the meeting in Venezuela. The CIA has Bogotá covered. It'll just take time, which we are short of."

"We'll help you all we can, but Israel comes first." Thaddeus's eyes locked onto Max's.

"I understand. That's all I ask." Max was humbled, understanding what Thaddeus actually meant—Israel wouldn't go out of their way to help the United States because of their strained relationship.

"Your president's policies toward Israel are making this very difficult. A team from Shayetet Thirteen will arrive here this evening and prepare to strike as soon as we locate the weapons. They will not leave the region," Danya said, referring to Israel's highly secretive unit, equivalent to the US

Army's First Special Forces Operational Detachment-Delta or Delta Force.

"We would like the weapons back when you locate them." Max's expression was serious as he made eye contact with Danya and then Thaddeus.

"We can't guarantee it, but we'll try." Thaddeus shot a look at Danya. "Is the United States prepositioning a team here as well? I'd like to link our unit up with them as soon as possible."

"No, just me for now, Max said, then his eyes dropped and focused on the coffee table. "The president has not authorized the prepositioning of combat troops outside the United States. He wants to keep a low profile on this."

"Let me get this straight!" Danya's voice exploded. "Because of his weak and nearsighted policies, the president of the United States has allowed four of the country's nuclear weapons to be stolen, and he isn't actively trying to get them back? The Iranians are rattling sabers and proceeding with a nuclear-bomb program. Russia is fanning the flames in Syria and Ukraine. What the hell is going on? You're good, and you are special to me. But you are just one person. What are you going to do? Threaten them with spitballs?"

"The CIA is actively working it, along with the ISR assets from JIATF South. We've got to locate them first. Then we can move on them." The acronym ISR stands for intelligence, surveillance, and reconnaissance assets. Max knew that he was losing the diplomatic war and that help from the Israelis wouldn't be as robust as he had hoped. He didn't want to bring up the subject about how the sequestration was impacting the coast guard's drug-interdiction mission. "I can have a team here on short order, but we must locate them first."

"The CIA. What's going on there?" Thaddeus looked deep into Max's eyes.

"What do you mean?"

"They're very reserved and risk averse now. It's as if they are reluctant to do anything."

"They have taken some bad hits lately, and they're not in favor with the administration." Max shifted his position and shot a look at Danya. "Several of their people were hung out to dry, and the administration didn't back them up when needed. A couple of politicians are embellishing those incidents and using them for their own political gain. They're a bit demoralized right now."

"You're saying the CIA doesn't trust the US administration?" Danya's brow furrowed and eyes narrowed. "Great! So we're leading this effort?"

Max wrinkled up the corner of his mouth and gave a slight nod. "They'll come through. They're professionals."

"Make no mistake." Thaddeus was straight-faced, his eyes piercing. "We'll take action wherever and whenever we deem appropriate."

Max simply nodded. Unable to reassure the Israelis, Max was able to extract an agreement for them to notify him if they received any new information on the weapons or discovered their location. However, Max's request to meet with the Shayetet Thirteen team commander received a tepid reception.

The cold meeting with Mossad seemed to do little in calming their frustrations with the United States.

***

Panama Marriott Hotel
Panama City, Panama

In his hotel room, Max, frustrated with the frigid Mossad meeting, connected his laptop and made the secure connection with SOCOM Headquarters to retrieve his e-mail. It was time to update Chugs, and with a bit of luck, Chugs might provide additional information. As it connected, Max dialed the number to Major General Matherson.

"General," he said, recognizing Matherson's voice.

"Max, how's the beer down there?"

"Not cold enough." Max's tone was serious. "The Israelis are pissed, and my meeting with them was a bit chilly. Can you get the president to call their prime minister? That would help the situation. They're sending a team down here. They want them prepositioned to strike quickly when the weapons are located. I asked to meet with them when they get here. Can you get authorization to get a delta team down here as well? It would sure make the Israelis feel better."

"I'll see what I can do, but don't hold your breath. You know the situation. We haven't turned up anything on our end yet that you need to worry about. Margaret has an update for you, and I have a copy. Things are not improving. JIATF South has picked up activity along the drug route through Panama, Mexico, to San Diego. Homeland Security is watching it. They think that's the route into the United States that'll be used for the delivery."

"Possible, but that seems too easy," Max said. "The attack on the site was too well planned, more of a military strike. I bet it's a deception."

"That's the way we see it, too. But Homeland disagrees."

"Figures. Just a bunch of grandstanders! Very little experience and a lot of ego. Do you want me to go back to the United States and meet with them?"

"No, stay on it down there. The CIA has picked up the girl, Dorotea Trujillo. They're talking to her now."

"That's something. Let me know what you find out."

The phone conversation lasted another five minutes, but very little information was exchanged that could lead them to the weapons.

The next call made was to Margaret at CTC. Living up to her reputation, she was ferreting out pertinent information from the seemingly superfluous bits that flowed into the center.

"Margaret, I had a dismal meeting with the Israelis. They're not very happy right now."

"I didn't figure they would be. Did you learn anything?"

"Not really. The best I got from them was that they would call me if they turned up any information on the weapons."

"LA division has picked up Dorotea Trujillo, but I don't have anything back yet."

"OK. Chugs said that JIATF South has picked up activity on one of the drug routes into the United States."

"Yeah, Homeland is working on it. They're convinced that's where the weapons will enter the United States, and they've got all the monitors tuned up and focused over there. I don't think so." Margaret paused, anticipating Max's response. "I think it's a ruse."

"You and I agree. Keep me posted. I don't have much faith in Homeland."

"Know what you mean. The chatter has really picked up from ISIS. Al-Aqrab used his passport again in Caracas, along with the Iranian Shahbazi and Hezbollah Yasin. The three entered at different times."

"Another big meeting. This could be it." Max's tone was serious. "If you get a location, I'll get a strike on it."

"The agency people down there are on it and working their sources. They have a bounty out for the devices, and they're passing out money right and left for information. The same goes for Panama and Mexico. The State Department is posting a million-dollar reward as well. And there's more. The top ISIS bomb guy, Dhul Fiqar, has dropped out of sight."

"What do you mean dropped out of sight?" Max's tone was full of astonishment.

"Disappeared. I can't find him anywhere."

"Great. Surely he won't be at the meeting. But he may be sending or instructing someone who is there. My guess is that he has gone to some secret lab he has or is setting one up. Keep looking for him. He could turn up anywhere."

"Agree. Best guess is that he's setting up a lab. Someone in Venezuela will probably act on his instructions and provide him with pictures, diagrams, and things like that. When he gets the devices, he'll be ready to start working to bypass the PAL. As soon as I find him, I'll let you know," Margaret said.

"Stay on the drug-route lead as well. That concerns me."

"Maybe just another big drug shipment, or they're going to ship one to the United States and work on it later."

"Yeah, it could be a drug shipment, but I doubt it. The others could be put on board a freighter, and the bomb guy could figure out how to bypass the PAL en route to their destination. He could easily have a week or two aboard a ship. Figure out how the system works, and then it would only take a short amount of time to use the same procedures on the other three."

"ISIS brags a lot, and the chatter goes up just before something happens. I'm on it. You asked about a military advisor with the FARC; they have an ex-special-forces officer by the name of Bart Madison. Know him?"

"Bart Madison…I know him," said Max. "He worked for me for a little while. A smart officer but got a little carried away in Afghanistan. I reprimanded him, and then I rotated out. Never knew what happened to him. I'll check at SOCOM to see if they still have anything on him."

"He was court-martialed and forced to resign his commission six years ago," Margaret continued. "Dropped out of sight for a while and then hooked up with the FARC. He's now the advisor to the commander, Fifty-Seventh Front, FARC."

They discussed Bart Madison for several more minutes. The fact that an ex-special-forces officer was advising the FARC was another problem for Max. Madison would know how the special-operations community operated—tactics, operations—and, of course, he would know the terrain. Learning of Madison told Max a lot, and that explained how the FARC had been so successful over the past several years. It also meant that a number of good operators could die. Max also knew not to believe what was on the surface or what seemed obvious. Madison could be a formidable foe.

"Margaret, see if Madison has any family, wife, or girlfriend. They could provide us some valuable information on him. Do the Israelis know that the bomb scientist, Dhul Fiqar, has disappeared and that the other two have returned to Caracas?"

"They should have that info by now. Anything else?"

"Not for now. Keep the information coming, and let me know what you find out right away."

Max ended the call and turned to review the intelligence update Margaret had sent him. Most of the points Margaret had covered in the conversation. However, one entry she hadn't talked about was the phone numbers she had previously mentioned to him. One phone number, highlighted with an asterisk, indicated a US citizen. Since it was a US citizen, she had requested special permission to research the number. Upon approval, NSA would release it for research. The current NSA scandal of eavesdropping on US citizens without authorization made Margaret's request extremely painful and time consuming. She listed the entry as *in for request.*

Finished with the intelligence update from Margaret and an e-mail to Chugs about Bart Madison, Max leaned back to contemplate his next move. Waiting for intelligence was the hardest part, but as he knew very well, the better the intelligence preparation, the better the outcome. Just as he leaned back and stretched, the phone rang.

"Yes," Max said.

"This is Danya. Meet me in the lounge of your hotel at five thirty." Her voice was much more charming than previously.

"I'll be there." Max replaced the receiver and checked his watch and then switched on Fox News. *Danya,* he thought. *Is there a development, or is this an apology meeting? In any event, it's time for a drink.*

***

Seated alone in a back area of the lounge, nursing a glass of red wine, Danya smiled as Max entered. A second glass of wine across the table from her waited his arrival. A simple but elegant gold necklace lay exposed against her tanned skin beneath her beige blouse. The hint of makeup and her charming demeanor revealed a very attractive woman.

"Max, I apologize for our meeting earlier," Danya said as Max eased into the chair in front of her. "We're frustrated with your president, and we take threats to Israel very seriously."

"Thank you for the wine." Max smiled and took a sip. She was good, and Max knew it. He raised his guard even more; a charming and attractive woman making up to him signaled caution. There is no such thing as a friendly foreign intelligence. It did cross his mind that she could be trying to rekindle their previous relationship. His first priority was to stay on equal footing with the Israelis and not provide information without something in return. Falling into the trap of an attractive woman wasn't in his plans.

Danya gave a nod of her head. "Pinot Noir, right?"

"You remember." Max looked into her sparkling eyes. "Don't worry about the meeting; I understand. We're frustrated with him, as well."

Still maintaining his guard, Max studied Danya. *She's good looking,* he thought. *Is this change really an apology meeting, or is she appealing to me for something else? I do like this person much better.*

"Did you remarry?" Danya fingered her glass and then looked up at him, her head slightly cocked.

"No, the job is not conducive to marriage."

"The same in my world."

"Sharing with someone special would be nice. Someday maybe." A slight smile emerged on his face.

"Yes, someday. In any case, I'd like you and me to have a cordial working relationship." She gently touched his hand and allowed her hand to linger.

"I'd like that as well. We'll get more accomplished that way."

"Thaddeus had a productive meeting at Hospital Santo Tomás," she said, her tone soft. "The two casualties there are talking. They said an American was leading the operation."

Max remained stone faced. *Wonder what else she knows.*

Danya took a sip of wine. *Hmm. That didn't work,* she thought. *Obviously he already knows that. He's not giving anything up without something in return.*

"Two of the SADMs were transferred to the Los Zetas cartel, and they headed north. The American went with them. The other two were transferred to another FARC team, and they headed south."

"Los Zetas, they're pretty good." Max massaged the stem of the glass and then sipped his wine. "It looks like two are headed to the United States and two are headed out of the country. Splitting them up is going to make it more difficult on us, and they know it."

"The girl, Dorotea Trujillo, is a bit feisty." Danya brushed her wavy hair back from her face. "I was with the CIA when they questioned her. She's coming around but claims she doesn't know where the headquarters of her cousin, Franco Trujillo, is located. She says all she knows is that it is somewhere in the Darien Gap, near the border. They're going to have another round with her later tonight."

"Wherever his headquarters was, he must have relocated it by now."

"Probably. What do you say we take a walk down to the bay?" Danya finished her glass of wine and touched his hand.

Without speaking, Max stood, signifying agreement, and the two of them walked out of the lounge together.

***

7:16 a.m.
Wednesday
October 16, 2013
Panama Marriott Hotel
Panama City, Panama

Max was greeted by the ringing telephone as he entered his hotel room.

"Max," he said as he placed the receiver to his ear.

"Danya," came the voice. "Did I wake you?"

"No, just went for breakfast. What's up?"

"I'll be there in half an hour. I think we've located a FARC base. It could be the Fifty-Seventh Front, FARC headquarters. Our team has already departed to secure it. I thought you'd want to go. I've got a helicopter meeting us at the airport."

"I'll be ready. See you then."

Max changed into tropical-weight cargo pants and a shirt and then slipped on his jungle boots. As Max picked up his camera, the phone rang again. *Busy day already,* he thought.

"Good morning!" Margaret's voice was chipper. "How's your day going?"

"Good morning! Already busy. Just got a call from Danya, and they think they've found a FARC location. I'm flying down there to have a look. What's up?"

"The phone number that belonged to a US citizen, I've checked it out, and it's a good one."

"Whom does it belong to?"

"Senator Carlton Bradbourne."

"Bradbourne! Shit! Did you run the other number?"

"Bart Madison."

"Well, well, well," said Max. "That's quite a connection. A presidential hopeful and an ex-special-forces officer who is now advising the FARC."

"The FBI has the info. I know the agent who has the case, and she's very good. She's as tough as woodpecker lips and doesn't take shit off anyone. More to follow on this."

"That's good news. When is the FBI going to have a talk with him?"

"They've gone for a wiretap and are full speed ahead. They want to see what else they can pick up on him. So it could be a while. They want an airtight case. He'll pitch a fit and cause a lot of grief otherwise. That's why they put this particular agent in charge of it."

"Thanks. Anything on Madison's family, girlfriend, or wife?"

"Nothing yet. One more thing on Bradbourne. He's got all the news media—DEA, ICE, FBI, Homeland Security, and God knows who else—heading for California. He's got them convinced a major drug shipment is going to be smuggled into the United States tomorrow. He's turning it into a media circus to use for his campaign."

"Figures. He's focusing everyone on the drug routes into San Diego, and the SADMs will be smuggled in someplace else."

"It's beginning to look that way. The chick who's heading up the Homeland team to intercept the SADMs believes they're with this drug shipment. I attended a VTC briefing she held. I'm not sure she's old enough to be out of school yet. She sounds like a little girl. God, how can anyone take her seriously?" The acronym VTC is commonly used for video teleconference in the government.

"I know the one you're talking about," said Max. "Well, better put on your flak jacket, and don't fall for their shit. If Madison and the senator are connected, which looks as if they are, that's not the entry point. The SADMs aren't with the drug shipment. Did you see the e-mail I sent to you last night?"

"Yes, Los Zetas are transporting two of them north."

"The show tomorrow is a deception."

"Yeah, but no one is listening to us."

Margaret's comments echoed the agency's sentiments. The CIA was out of favor with the administration. Politicians up for reelection took the opportunity to grab headlines to beat down the agency at every opportunity. Demonizing the entire intelligence community for political gain was the norm. The director of national intelligence seemed to be out of touch with what was actually happening in the world.

The president's handpicked replacement for the director of CIA, although a career-agency officer, didn't have the respect of the agency's career staff and only echoed the president's view of the world. The current director had assumed the position when the previous one had resigned in disgrace.

The administration desperately sought positive victories and continuously tried to shift focus from controversies plaguing the administration. Capturing a major drug-smuggling operation and especially intercepting nuclear weapons about to be smuggled into the United States would definitely shift the focus from real-world events for a while and raise approval ratings. It was all about politics and getting reelected.

***

Darien Gap
Near the Panamanian-Colombian Border

The Bell helicopter transporting Max and Danya to the suspected FARC site landed in a clearing in the dense jungle about a kilometer from the Panamanian side of the border. Just as the helicopter touched down, Danya was out of the door and greeted by one of the Shayetet Thirteen team members wearing full combat gear, his M4 in his arms across his chest. Max secured the door and watched as the aircraft lifted off en route to a safe location.

The Panama side of the gap was mountainous rain forest, while the Colombian side was river delta and swampland. The entire Darien Gap, controlled by the FARC, was considered a no man's land. No improved roads were in the gap, only primitive dirt roads or jungle trails. Most of that area was under dense canopy, making detection from overhead very difficult.

"Max, this is Aaron." Danya turned toward Max and then looked up at the ascending helicopter.

"Good to meet you." Max shook the man's firm hand. "Have you found anything?"

Rav-Seren Aaron Friedman, having the rank equivalent of lieutenant commander in the US Navy, was the team's commander.

"We'd better move out of the clearing." Aaron motioned for them to follow him. "Be extremely careful. They left quite a few booby traps. We've also taken a few shots but haven't got the shooter yet."

Aaron led them along; they meandered to the edge of the base camp. The dense canopy held in the humidity, making the humidity almost 100 percent, and the thick foliage blocked any breeze from entering. Their clothes were soon wet with perspiration. As they entered the perimeter of the former camp, gunfire erupted, spraying bullets into the area and ripping through the vegetation around them. The three hit the ground and rolled behind a fallen mango tree for cover. A hail of machine-gun fire from the Shayetet team answered the incoming gunfire. Then silence, as bits of vegetation rained down around them.

"Probably a couple of their fighters left behind to see who shows up looking for them. The FARC commander is smart; he knows we're onto them now, and he knows who we are." Max cautiously raised as the gunfire ended and looked over the fallen tree before standing.

"They're just harassing us," Aaron said as he lowered his carbine. "We do need to move quickly and get out of here."

"You've got my vote." Danya rose, ran her hand through her hair, straightened her shirt, and then brushed off her pants. "Someone could get hurt."

The location was eerily silent; there was no noise of any kind—no animal sounds, no wind rustling the leaves, nothing. They cautiously continued into the center of the suspected headquarters. The Israeli team had established a perimeter guard, and three of the commandos were methodically searching the entire location. For over an hour, they searched each building—*shacks* was a more accurate term—only to find a couple of cigar butts in what they figured was the commander's quarters.

Just as Danya and Max entered one of the dimly lit rooms adjoining what they considered the main living room, they saw a box on top of an old wooden table with papers strewn about. Several old, broken chairs were scattered about the musty space. It appeared as though the box and papers had been overlooked in the FARC's haste to evacuate the area. Max shone his small flashlight on the box and then quickly around the room. Danya stepped forward to investigate the box; Max reached out, grabbed her shirt collar, and jerked her back.

"Stop!" His voice was cold and commanding.

Startled by Max's outburst, she fell back into him. "What is it?"

"That's an old trick." His attention remained on the box. "You should know better than that. That box is bait, and you were going for it." Max shone the light low and around the table. "There it is."

The focused light beam illuminated a trip wire. Following the wire with the light, Max found the primer and then disarmed the device. "I don't want to lose you."

"Thanks. That was close."

"I'm sure all those papers are worthless."

"I'll take them back with us and go through them. They may've let something slip through."

Max nodded.

The retrieved booby traps were from a variety of countries—Russia, the United States, and Iran. The FARC had cleaned the site very well. Obviously they had done this before when vacating other locations.

Frustrated at the lack of any useable intelligence, Danya called for the helicopter to return to pick them up. Aaron and two other commandos escorted them to the landing zone and provided security until the helicopter was safely out of the area and on the way back to Panama City.

Chapter 5

Los Zetas Staging Area
Sonoran Desert
South of Nogales, Sonora, Mexico

A safe distance from the US border, Los Zetas picked a remote location in the desert for the staging area in preparation for crossing the border and delivering the devices. The location was far enough away to avoid the prying eyes of the ISR assets employed by Border Security, yet close enough to the cell towers supporting the city of Nogales, Sonora, Mexico, for communications. Large rock formations provided seclusion from linear observation from almost any direction, especially from the north-south Mexico Highway 15.

Planning the border crossing at the noon rush hour, Bart needed to coordinate with Senator Bradbourne to ensure he was doing as instructed. It was imperative that attention be on the tunnel into Otay Mesa, on the south side of San Diego, with all the ratings-generating hoopla the news media was famous for.

For added insurance, Bart planned two other deceptions, just in case the senator fell short. One was an anonymous tip through one of the FARC contacts in the United States about a shipment of red mercury being smuggled into the United States at the Andrade Port of Entry in southeastern California. The elaborate story told of how terrorists planned to use the red mercury to make a ballotechnic-triggered fusion bomb. Red mercury could also be used to line the container of a plutonium bomb to enhance the yield ten times.

The third ruse was for Los Zetas to send an unsuspecting person seeking to enter the United States with a container of iridium-192 in the person's belongings. Bart previously had directed Los Zetas to steal a container of iridium-192 from a medical-supply warehouse in southern Mexico. Iridium-192, a radioactive isotope of iridium that emitted beta particles and gamma radiation, would be detected as it passed through a radiation detector at any of the border crossings.

These two deceptions were to cause confusion and panic at the border. Assuming the senator did as he was instructed in getting the relevant agencies focused on Otay Mesa, these two incidents would put the media into hysteria in reporting the story. However, if the senator failed, these two were Bart's backup deceptions. He felt confident that Homeland Security would take the bait on either of, or all, the stories, since they knew that four SADMs had been stolen from a secret site in Panama and that at least one was headed for the United States.

Bart calculated that the red-mercury story and the detection of the radioactive material—iridium-192—crossing the border would get the media's full attention and would explode in the news at about the same time as the Otay Mesa tunnel discovery. Watching the news, like most other people in the world, Bart knew pundits and news reporters would rush the story out in an attempt to be first and gain ratings without first checking the facts of the story. Also, he believed that the inexperienced and naïve people at Homeland Security would fall for the ruses, at least for a few hours, and by then it would be too late.

The FARC associate in the United States whom Bart had contacted was ready to pump information into the TV pundits, along with the tip, as soon as Bart gave the word; it was full of stories of the potential uses of red mercury as well as information on the American physicist, Samuel Cohen, father of the neutron bomb. Pointing out that red mercury contained no radioactive materials and emitted no detectable radiation ensured that the pundits would devour the story.

The politicians would declare, "We can't afford to take a chance," and, of course, they would throw in a reference to children. In election years, politicians used every opportunity to get their names and faces in the news. This was no exception. It didn't matter whether the topic was true or not. If the news ran with the stories, as Bart figured, it could also cause a bit of a panic at the border crossings and major populated areas. In any event, the focus would be more on the news and would distract the border guards just enough to ensure a successful crossing.

If Bradbourne didn't do as instructed, Bart would deal with him later. He would have to make a decision to cross the border as planned, choose a different location, or cancel altogether. This was the position that Bart didn't want to be in—relying on a self-absorbed senator with a number of flaws, reliability being the main one. Bart knew that the senator would grab a headline, but he didn't know if the senator could create the fanfare Bart wanted for the crossing.

Retrieving his phone, Bart entered the number for Senator Bradbourne and listened to it ring.

"Senator Bradbourne," came the deep, raspy voice.

"Is everything set for tomorrow?"

"Yes, all the major networks have been alerted, as well as the cable networks."

"You said alerted. I want them there, not just alerted. Do what you have to ensure they are there. I want to see coverage like we had when we invaded Iraq. Got that?"

"Not to worry, Bart. It's all arranged," the senator said.

"I'll be watching. Maximum coverage, no screw-ups."

Bart ended the call and then paused to reflect on the conversation with the senator. Next he entered the number for the FARC contact in the United States.

"Yes," came the man's voice.

"This is Bart. Release the story."

"Watch the news," the man replied, and then the phone went dead.

***

Stretched out atop a large boulder, overlooking their inconspicuous staging area in the Sonoran Desert, Bart admired the bright stars against the black night sky. The desert had given up its heat to the cool, dry evening air, which had made a jacket mandatory. Pleased with the light and noise discipline of the mules, Bart scanned his temporary position and then booted up his laptop. The term *mules* was used to describe the people actually smuggling the contraband across the border. These mules had been handpicked by Los Zetas and had been paid extra for this special mission.

Bart was escorting these mules with the SADMs to ensure delivery and to coordinate the border crossing. They weren't told what they were carrying, only that it was very valuable. The mules took it as an honor that Los Zetas entrusted them for this special trip. They were veterans, having smuggled drugs and people into the United States several times before. But this was their first trip into Nogales, Arizona.

Chapter 6

Zulian Region, Venezuela
Near the Colombian-Venezuelan Border

In his utility vehicle, secluded in the tree line near the abandoned airstrip, Franco wiped the sweat from his face and burr-cut head and then looked over the airfield again as he waited. He led the transportation of the two SADMs to Venezuela, supported by the Fifty-Seventh Front, FARC, for transfer to al-Aqrab, Shahbazi, and Yasin.

As soon as he had arrived in his field position, Franco had directed his force to establish a perimeter defense under the concealment of the trees, which provided some relief from the sun. However, the trees held in the humidity, and the absence of wind made for a very warm position.

Franco's experience dictated that his temporary location be as secure as possible for this meeting. All vehicles were hidden from overhead ISR assets or from the probing eyes of any ground reconnaissance team that might be working in the area. Knowing that the Americans and Panamanians were actively looking for senior FARC members and his cargo, Franco wasn't about to be surprised—especially now with the nuclear devices in his possession.

On the far end of the old runway, two Toyota Land Cruisers emerged and raised a billowing dust cloud as they raced up the runway toward Franco's position. He alerted his men to the approaching vehicles. Instantly they took up their fighting positions and were ready to defend themselves if needed.

As the two approaching SUVs slid to a stop in front of Franco's vehicle, the dust cloud enveloped all three of them. Doors opened. Shahbazi, a lanky man with a large black mustache and sunglasses, swung out of the first SUV and paused to observe the situation; he provided theatrics more than anything else. Shahbazi and the others exchanged greetings with Franco.

"The nukes. Over here," Franco said as he motioned to the two containers with open lids under a nearby tree.

"We will take pictures and make drawings," the stone-faced al-Aqrab said as he set a small bag on the ground next to the devices. The three-inch scar across his cheek and dark eyes gave him an evil look.

Yasin, stockier and shorter than the other two, smoked constantly. His eyes darted right and then left; he was uneasy with Franco's men, whose weapons were trained on the three. As he reached the first weapon, Yasin removed his sunglasses.

The three men hovered over the box, snapped pictures, made notes, and discussed each piece, before they removed the cylindrical canister housing the nuclear material. Pictures were taken at every angle, and diagrams were made with annotations of each component. After about forty-five minutes of photographing, sketching, and making notations, al-Aqrab said, "I must make a phone call." Without waiting for a response, he walked several meters away, retrieved his cell phone, and then punched in a series of numbers.

Completing the call, al-Aqrab wheeled around and stepped back to where the others stood. "Praise be to Allah! We accept. The money, fifteen million dollars for each device, is being transferred to your account." For an instant, the fanatic looked like a pleasant human being—his death eyes sparkled, as his face seemed to light up with a toothy grin.

"As soon as I have confirmation of the deposit, you can take them." Franco turned on his laptop. Within a few minutes, he received a message from Guzman that thirty million dollars had been deposited in their account.

Receiving the confirmation, Franco motioned to his fighters. His mission was almost complete. Evacuating the area and returning to his camp was the final task. Two of his men returned the components to the containers and then loaded them into the two SUVs. At the same time, the other FARC members loaded their gear and the crew-served weapons onto their trucks.

Al-Aqrab watched as the men carried the containers. He withdrew his cell phone and placed a quick call. Within five minutes, a helicopter emerged on the northern skyline.

Franco maintained a wary eye on the lone aircraft as it landed. As soon as it touched down, its rotors continuing to spin, the SUVs sped to the waiting bird. Once the two containers were on board, al-Aqrab got in, and the helicopter took off. The two Land Cruisers raced back the way they had come. A dust cloud followed them. Franco signaled his men as the aircraft headed back north, led his convoy back onto the dirt trail, and disappeared.

Al-Aqrab took the two nukes to Maracaibo in northwest Venezuela. Upon arrival in the port city, the devices would then be loaded onto a freighter, *Amira Fatima*, for transport to a secret laboratory location for the ISIS scientist Hamdan Talib Dhul Fiqar to bypass the PAL.

***

Thursday
October 17, 2013
Los Zetas Staging Area
Sonoran Desert
South of Nogales, Sonora, Mexico

Bart gathered the three drivers to ensure that they were up and ready to go. He rehearsed with them once again the roles they were playing and then orchestrated the details of the crossing, using the ground to diagram the events. Once finished, he directed the men to check their vehicles. His scheme was that a lead SUV would depart ahead of the two vehicles carrying the SADMs, make a reconnaissance of the border checkpoint, and look for anything unusual as well as the number of guards at the crossing—heavy manning could be a sign of trouble. The scout would also pay particular attention to how diligently the guards were checking the cars and trucks. Once the lookout reported back, the two vehicles carrying the weapons would depart at intervals, with Bart following.

A young Mexican man and woman, posing as a middle-income, married couple traveling to the United States to shop and visit relatives, drove the first SUV. Their hair was neatly trimmed, and they were conservatively dressed in jeans and pullover shirts. In the second, a starry-eyed couple posed as newlyweds going to the United States on a honeymoon. These two appeared to be in their midtwenties and wore shorts and polo shirts.

The SUVs were appropriately packed and decorated to resemble what the occupants were supposed to be. Luggage, clothes, and various foods and canned goods were stacked in the rear around the box. Both containers were decoratively painted and placed in cardboard boxes and then wrapped with brown paper. In the first vehicle, the box was wrapped and tied with a bow and resembled a large gift. In the second, luggage, clothes, food items, and various other items you would expect to see in the car of a couple traveling on an extended trip concealed the boxes. Wedding ornaments were strewn about inside the second SUV, and *el lazo*—a large loop of rosary beads that symbolized unity—hung from the rearview mirror.

Bart was confident that the camouflage of the boxes would suffice to satisfy the inquisitive eyes of the border guards who might happen to see them. As an added precaution, Bart had affixed a piece of a dental x-ray apron to the portion of the containers, about where the nuclear device and electrical components were located. He had acquired the apron, used to protect patients from exposure to the x-rays, by draping it over the patient and then cutting pieces from it that were just large enough to shield the components inside the container. He figured that the pieces of apron and various items around the container were sufficient to block or diffuse x-rays and obscure, or make unrecognizable, the contents in case a diligent guard did x-ray the vehicle.

Counting on the administration's push to keep the borders open and instructions not to arrest immigrants crossing borders, Bart was confident his simple plan would work. A demoralized border force and entering the country at peak traffic time added a few more points in Bart's favor for a successful crossing. The dramatic increase of illegal immigrants infiltrating the US border was an added benefit. This influx of immigrants further strained the resources of the Border Patrol. Bart was sure that the guards would only go through the motions and make a cursory inspection at best.

Satisfied that his preparations were complete and his people were ready to go, Bart started up his laptop to check the latest news and wait times at the port of entry. As he waited for the machine to fully boot up, Bart called the senator once again.

"Yes, Bart," Bradbourne said. "All the major networks are here, as well as cable news. Homeland Security, Border Patrol, ICE, state police, and almost everyone else you can think of are here."

"Good. The other crossings, anything on them? Is everyone focused just on that area?"

"Yes. I haven't heard anything about the other border crossings, other than comments on the heavy traffic and increased number of illegals crossing. The woman in charge of the operation here is flitting around and keeping everyone focused."

"OK, keep me informed. Are you sure that no alerts or notices have been posted to the Ports of Entry?"

"Nothing."

"Hold on for a minute, Senator."

Bart accessed the Internet and opened Fox News. A banner streamed at the top of Fox News home page, alerting viewers to a major drug-tunnel discovery in California. Bart went to the live coverage, and as anticipated, it was nonstop, with pundits babbling incessantly.

Politicians grasped at every opportunity to get into the spotlight. Senator Bradbourne was in the middle of the circus, making the biggest splash. He boisterously orated about the need to secure the borders. Bradbourne hammered relentlessly on about the irresponsibility and negligence of not doing more to stop the drug flow into the United States—as well as the illegal immigrants. He called for senate investigations on border security and the illicit drug flow into the United States.

"Bart, Bart, what's this about red mercury?" Bradbourne's voice was full of excitement. "There's a breaking story about it being smuggled across the border."

"Don't worry about it. Take advantage of that story as well."

"But, Bart—"

"Don't worry about it. Go make a speech on the need for tighter border security."

What a fucking, slimy hypocrite, Bart thought, shaking his head.

"You're doing great, Senator. Keep it up. I'll call you later."

Bart ended the call and motioned for the first vehicle to depart. He looked back to the breaking news on the laptop; the story was on all the networks. Excited reporters, each trying to give an accurate report but failing miserably, were bouncing between the tunnel discovery and the story of red mercury.

Pandemonium, Bart thought, a slight smile emerging on his face. *Now where's the Homeland chick with the horn-rimmed glasses?* The news went back to the Homeland Security briefing; standing at the podium and struggling to maintain her composure was Dawn Blakey, the Homeland Security woman in charge of the operation. Bart smiled at the woman's obvious stress and then shut down his laptop.

***

CTC
Tysons Corner, Virginia

Meeting in the conference room with Margaret was Gail Summers, the FBI agent assigned to investigate Senator Bradbourne. Margaret turned on the large TV that hung on the wall. "Senator Carlton Bradbourne has been on TV all morning, grabbing face time and talking up border security," Margaret said as she switched the TV to Fox News.

"I know him." Gail ran her hand through her short, blond hair. "It's going to be dicey with this slime bag." She slid a folder marked *Senator Carlton Bradbourne* across the table to Margaret. "Here's some information that could be of use to you. Can you tell me why you're interested in him and how he ties into what you're working on? I know the CIA doesn't look at US citizens."

"Not much right now," Margaret replied. "Still gathering information, but it ties in. I'll let you know when I can. Make sure you've got a tight case on him, or he'll make our lives miserable."

The two glanced up as the news switched back to the Homeland Security update. Dawn Blakey elaborated again about the discovery of the drug tunnel, the capture of eight illegal immigrants coming out of the tunnel, and the packages of cocaine with a street value of about $500,000. Dawn said they believed more people and cocaine were still in the tunnel.

The news then switched to a consultant wearing a dark suit and tie who expounded on red mercury. "It's a very explosive chemical substance. Originally developed in Russia, it has been around for quite a while." The man was straight-faced, his tone serious with an air of authority.

He continued, "Red mercury was responsible for the crash of SAA Flight 295 off the coast of Mauritius in 1987. A small amount ignited in the cargo compartment and destroyed the plane. Because of its explosive power, red mercury is the solution to the briefcase-sized neutron bomb. Terrorists could make an undetectable bomb the size of a baseball capable of wiping out several square blocks or more. When this type of ballotechnic bomb explodes, it produces tremendous heat and pressure. It is many times more powerful than a nuclear bomb of the same size—"

Gail grasped the remote and then muted the broadcast. "I can't take any more of that shit! Where do they find these guys? There's the Homeland chick again!" She pointed to the TV. "Is she even old enough to drive? Goddamn it, where do they get these chippies?"

"That's Homeland for ya."

"Makes me feel real safe." Gail's voice was full of sarcasm as she retrieved a pen from her jacket. "Something's not right about this news coverage." She scribbled a note in the file.

"Yep! And not just the selection of the Homeland bimbo to lead this event." Margaret laid her glasses on the table and then looked at Gail. "Everyone knows Homeland's story—but the entire setup and the senator and now this breaking story of red mercury…it just doesn't seem right. I've gotta check this out." She glanced up at the TV. "Wait, what's that headline?" Margaret picked up the remote and then canceled the mute.

An agitated reporter started explaining that a nuclear device had been intercepted at the Columbus New Mexico Port of Entry. The station headquarters broke into the news as soon as the word leaked. The highly excited reporter, his head and eyes shifting right and then left, began talking away, stalling mostly, until his crew could provide the details.

"One person is in custody," the reporter said, his voice full of emotion. "No details of the size of the bomb or his target." The reporter continued to babble and made very little sense. "The border is closed, and there's a large traffic jam at this small port of entry. A hazmat response team has been contacted, as well as technicians from Department of Energy, the military—"

The news switched to the Otay Mesa tunnel, where Dawn Blakey tried to give an update on the current situation at the border. Her presentation was disjointed and, at times, confusing. She lost control of the briefing and contributed to more confusion at each border location. Cell phones continuously rang, and agency radios blared, as everyone sought information.

The news switched to Andrade Port of Entry, where another overly animated reporter jabbered away about the red mercury crossing the border there and the implications for the United States. Short video clips from experts were interjected to support the story. Then broadcast headquarters abruptly switched to the Columbus New Mexico Port of Entry for the latest breaking news on the nuclear-bomb story. The news station switched back to Otay Mesa.

Margaret muted the TV again.

"Something isn't right. This smells. Red mercury, Otay Mesa, and now a nuclear bomb." Margaret shook her head. "There's been no intel on any of this. That's unusual. I've got some work to do. I need to sort this shit out."

"Let me know what you find out, and I'll see who the senator's been talking to about Otay Mesa. It should be interesting. I'll let ya know what we get on this character," said Gail.

"Ya know, the senator was really promoting this event in California." One of Margaret's eyebrows rose. Her tone was full of curiosity. "He's been hounding all the networks, Homeland, Border, ICE, and everyone else you can think of to be there."

"Hmm. I've got a bit of snooping to do." Gail stood and then straightened her jacket. "I'll be in touch."

Margaret stood up with Gail and then picked up her glasses and notepad. "Talk to you soon."

***

Mossad Safe House
Balboa, Panama

At Danya's invitation, Max met with her to discuss the latest developments and possible next steps. Information was sparse, but it was still coming in from the British, Americans, and Panamanians.

"Thaddeus is at the hospital, talking with the casualties again." Danya sipped her *limonana* (mint lemonade). "Dorotea Trujillo has decided to cooperate, but she's not a very big player. She doesn't have much. The two in the hospital are providing a lot more info."

"The weapons are probably out of the country," Max said. "Turn the TV to Fox News."

Danya stood, grasped the remote, and pushed the buttons.

"This is why I think they're out of the country." Max pointed to the broadcast. "There's a lot of hype on this drug tunnel, too much actually. Now these stories on red mercury and a nuclear bomb at the Columbus New Mexico Port of Entry. It's all a deception to draw attention away from the real crossing."

"The two in the hospital confirmed that two devices were going to the United States and two were going to Venezuela," Danya said. "From there, they didn't know."

"Splitting them up means we're going to have to split up, too. Have you got anything back from Caracas?"

"I'm expecting to hear from them pretty soon."

"Danya, I'm going back to the United States. Homeland Security is over their head on this and will screw things up. They won't know what they are looking at if it's standing in front of them."

"I understand and agree. I'd do the same thing. Let me know what you find out." Danya smiled and then kissed Max. "Stay in touch. *Shalom aleikhem.*"

"I will. *Aleikhem shalom.*"

Seated in his car, Max paused and looked back at the building and then punched in the numbers to Chugs at SOCOM.

"General Matherson," the voice said.

"This is Max."

"Hold on, I need to close the door. OK, whatta ya got?"

"I'm heading back to the United States on the first available flight. Have you seen the news?"

"It's on now. You saved me a call."

"I am sure two of the devices are in the United States now. The other two, according to the Israelis, went to Venezuela."

"Figures," replied the general. "On their ISR run, JIATF South picked up a helicopter landing about twenty-five kilometers from the location, just inside the Venezuelan border, where the CIA team was killed. The helicopter was on the ground only a few minutes. We normally wouldn't pay any attention to it; aircraft land and take off all over the place. But one of our diligent analysts got a little curious and connected the dots. That landing could be to pick up the other two devices. We've asked the agency for more info."

"That's probable." Max mulled over Chug's statement. "The weapons could be anywhere by now—on a ship, on a plane, or even in Caracas somewhere. The Israelis are focused on those two and will keep us informed. I'm going to DC to see if I can pick up the trail from there."

"Got it." Chug paused. Then, his voice full of caution, he said, "Remember, you're on leave and not officially involved in this."

"Understood. Margaret's going to introduce me to the bureau agent, Gail Summers, who is investigating Senator Bradbourne. She may be helpful. If the weapons are in the United States, the bureau will be in charge of the investigation to find them. Pretty sure Bradbourne is connected to the SADMs. Can you arrange to have Gail Summers head up that investigation?"

"I'll see what I can do. Keep a low profile with her for now. We dug up an old photo of Madison and a few notes. I've asked if anyone in the command has anything else on him. You'll have the photo and notes shortly."

"Thanks, that might help."

"Have a good flight back."

"Talk to you soon."

***

12:18 p.m.
October 17, 2013
Nogales-Mariposa Port of Entry

Bart received the signal back from the recon vehicle; it indicated normal operations at the port of entry. Then he sent the two loaded SUVs at five-minute intervals to make the border crossing. Scanning the skyline ahead for aircraft or anything that would signal trouble, Bart eased onto the highway toward the border and blended into the traffic.

As he approached the port of entry, the traffic slowed. Finally it came to a stop and then inched along, with a long line of cars building behind. Ubiquitous signs directed traffic that snaked to the checkpoint; trucks went in one direction as cars went in another. The occupants of the cars seemed to take the delay in stride.

The couples in the two SUVs played their parts well, all the time discreetly observing the guards. No one was in a hurry. Finally Bart inched to the head of the line and knew that the others made successful crossings as planned. He watched the guards perform cursory inspections and give quick glances at the occupants. He saw the large monitor inside the guardhouse and several guards talking, obviously not interested in him, and paying more attention to the monitor.

Once clear of the checkpoint, Bart breathed a sigh of relief. *Now to the warehouse and make the transfer,* he thought. *Just a couple more miles—and hopefully no random stops or Border Patrols getting curious this close to the finish line.* He accelerated with the traffic, and the GPS indicated he would arrive at the destination in about six minutes.

Bart pulled into the building located in the warehouse district north of Nogales, Arizona. The metal doors rattled closed behind his vehicle. In the rearview mirror, he saw the armed guards behind him closing the doors. The scout vehicle and the two SUVs with the nukes were in front of him, the occupants standing silently beside the vehicles. Florescent light strips illuminated the sparsely filled space. No noise, no movement, just daunting silence filled the hot interior of the building.

"The man. Your contact," Marco, riding with Bart, said as he leaned slightly toward Bart and nodded when the vehicle came to a stop. Marco was Los Zetas representative in charge of the team transporting the devices. "He goes by the name of Bari."

Bart watched Marco ease out of the seat, look around, and then step toward the man he had identified as Bari, whose beard was heavy and complexion dark. Bari, the ISIS representative, was to take possession of the nukes and then deliver them to the makeshift laboratory once it was established. The two men quietly talked, and then Bari motioned to the two SUVs. Bart cautiously opened the car door and got out.

The two couples unloaded the boxes, unwrapped them, and then opened the containers for Bari's inspection. The eerie silence continued as Bart and Marco stood aside while Bari inspected the cargo. He made sketches and notes and then took pictures of all the components. Finally he looked up and said, "I must make a call."

He stepped several meters away and punched in numbers on his cell phone. During his conversation, Bari referred to his notes and photographs several times. Ending his call, he stepped back to Bart and Marco.

"We accept," he said with a toothy grin. "You may go now."

"Hold on there, bubba." Bart wiped the sweat from his brow and then rubbed his hand on his trousers. He felt the pistol in his cargo pocket. "You forgot one little detail—thirty million dollars. When I get verification that the money has been deposited in our account, we'll go."

"Oh yes, my mistake." Bari displayed a toothy grin. "Your money is being transferred now."

Bart entered a series of numbers into his cell phone. "They accept." He ended the call and then looked at the two men. "Now we wait."

No one spoke. The warehouse fell silent, once again.

Could be a setup, Bart thought. *They renege on the deal, overpower us, and take the weapons. Don't like hanging around. Not many options if they decide to start shootin'.*

Sensing the tension, Marco passed out Cuban cigars. "This calls for a celebration." He retrieved a bottle of bourbon from the first vehicle. "Dig out some glasses." He nodded to the driver.

Pouring the drink into the glasses, Marco purposely filled Bari's glass. "*Saludi!*" He raised his glass and then took a sip. "We're a little short of ice. I hope that's OK."

"Very good," Bari said. "It has been a pleasure doing business with you."

Bart nodded and tipped his glass toward Bari as a sign of acceptance and then sipped it. He maintained his eyes firmly fixed on Bari and looked for any sign of trouble.

Bart's cell phone rang; he set his glass on the hood of the SUV, his gaze on Bari all the while. "Bart," he said, paused, and then ended the call.

He pointed to the containers. "These are yours."

"May Allah be with you."

Bari held up his hand.

***

10:05 a.m.
Saturday
October 19, 2013
CTC
Tysons Corner, Virginia

Margaret introduced Gail Summers, FBI; Dawn Blakey, Homeland Security; and Max Kenworth, DOD, to each other before the meeting began. "Thank you for coming over this morning." Margaret opened the folder in front of her. "Since we're all working together on this, we needed to meet each other and coordinate our efforts."

"Hold on a minute." Gail stood and leaned over to enter numbers into the phone that sat in the middle of the conference table. She spoke into the phone. "Sweet pea, get your ass in here; we're waiting for you."

Within a few moments, David entered the conference room in a flurry and sat next to Gail. It wasn't his dramatic entrance that captured everyone's attention; it was his choice of a flamboyantly colored shirt—neon magenta. He crossed his legs and folded his perfectly manicured hands in his lap. "I'm so sorry for being tardy; I was on the phone to that fellow in Panama."

"This is David Elsworth." Gail rolled her eyes. "He's an analyst assigned to help on this. Margaret has him pretty much up to speed with what information we have."

In a dripping-sweet voice, David said, "Thank you, Gail *dahling*." He took the opportunity to start a short speech. "I'm so happy to be working on this with you. I'll be the FBI focal point. I'll—"

"Cut the crap, David," Gail said as she glared at him with a furrowed brow.

"I'm leading the Homeland Security operation to find the nuclear devices or prevent their entry into the United States." Dawn Blakey's tone was condescending.

"I am leading the investigation into the theft and recovery of the devices." Gail's tone was assertive, and she looked at each of them. "As David said, he is the bureau's counterpart to Margaret."

"I'm from DOD and will provide any technical advice or assistance as required." Max gave as little information as possible and kept his true mission secret.

"Here is some background information on the theft of the devices to date." Margaret slid a folder across the table to the others. "I'll also coordinate with David on information. We don't have much to go on so far. The thought is that whoever has them will be making a move very soon. It could be anything. We've picked up quite a bit of chatter and believe that two are headed for Israel and two are already in the United States. Look for anything. Any clue could lead us to the weapons."

"Margaret," Dawn said as she laid her black horn-rimmed glasses on the table, "we believe that we stopped them at the border in California. However, the report of red mercury being smuggled into the United States bothers me. Nothing was found at the Andrade Port of Entry. Also, the guy with the iridium-192 didn't know what he had. He was just a stooge. We think this was just a test run."

Already irritated with Dawn, Gail said sharply, "What makes you think you stopped the fuckers at the border?"

"Because we nabbed about eight illegals and a load of cocaine. That was it. We searched everyone and thoroughly inspected the tunnel. None of the radiation sensors picked up anything unusual, either."

"And you didn't find any red mercury," Gail said. "This is just fucking great! This is the biggest bunch of bullshit I've heard in a long time. I guess the illegals were released?"

"Dawn," Max said, "did it occur to you that the news story was a ruse to get you to focus on California, while they were crossing someplace else?"

"Uh, no. Why would they do that?" Dawn's eyes opened wide as bewilderment washed across her face. "But the red mercury could be—"

"Dawn," Max said, "there is no such thing as red mercury. That's an old scam. The purpose behind that story was to cause a little chaos and distraction for a couple of hours. The same goes for the iridium-192. That was from a medical-supply warehouse in southern Mexico. You may want to get up-to-date on the intel."

Dawn struggled to process the information and then said, "But the news reported it…all the consultants. What about the crash of SAA Flight 295 the consultant talked about?"

"All a bunch of crap, sweet pea." Gail's tone was stern, and her eyes glared at the woman as she fought the urge to smack Dawn.

"Well, we have sensors on the border to pick up any radiation—"

Max paused before replying; he was astonished that the naïve young woman had been so easily taken in by the story and obviously had not done her homework. Moreover, she was the person in charge of protecting the homeland from immediate threat. "The material in the weapons is plutonium, Pu-239, which is an alpha emitter. In other words, it doesn't take much to shield it. These are military-grade nuclear devices and have adequate shielding around the plutonium. Your sensors detect radiation from nonenhanced materials. Detecting Pu-239 is very difficult and time consuming, especially when it is shielded."

"We think that the weapons are already in the country," Margaret said. "The stories of red mercury are false—a distractor."

The florid-faced Dawn sat back; she was obviously embarrassed that she had fallen for the ruse and the false assumption of the sensors. "Now what?" Her voice was barely a squeak.

"That's what we're doing this morning," Gail said. "We'll tell you what to do."

"I…I'm—"

"In over your head, chickie," Gail said. "We're in trouble, and every minute counts. This is real shit! I don't want to hear any crap; just facts that you've verified."

The meeting continued for a little over an hour. Margaret provided clear and pertinent information for background and about who had stolen the weapons.

"This must be kept quiet," Dawn said as she tried to reassert her position. "I'm instructed to keep this quiet and out of the news. This can't be another scandal for the president. We've got to keep this away from the public."

"We need the public's help on this, and they do need to be warned," Gail said, her voice stern.

"No, the president doesn't want to scare anyone; besides, there's an election next year. There's no proof that the weapons are actually in the United States."

"We're talking lives here," Gail replied, her tone sharp.

"No, I'm in charge, and until I am told otherwise, we keep it quiet," Dawn said.

"Well, you may be in charge, but I'm leading the investigation." Gail looked over her glasses. "You'll do as I tell you, when I tell you, or I'll shove one of those devices up your ass! Have you got that?"

Dawn folded her arms as she sat back in her chair and sulked. "OK," she said.

"We'll keep it quiet—for now." Gail understood the politics, but she didn't like it. "Dawn, I want you to contact all the ports of entry along the southern border and interview them. See if they've noticed anything—anything at all—that was unusual. David is working with Panama and Caracas to develop leads. Coordinate with David on what you find out."

Chapter 7

October 19, 2013
CTC
Tysons Corner, Virginia

Max retrieved his cell phone, turned it on, and then slid behind the wheel of his rental car. Seeing the blinking light notifying him of a voice mail, he accessed the message and heard Danya's voice. "Max, call me." He tapped the screen to return her call.

"Hi, Max." Her voice was chipper.

"What's up?" Max's thoughts went back to their evening walk to the bay in Panama. He smiled.

"We picked up Madison's girlfriend a couple of days ago and been having a nice little chat with her."

"I bet she was real eager to talk with you. What does she know?"

"Not much. She's supposed to meet Madison in Vegas tomorrow evening. We got a couple of names from her. We're checking them out. The agency will have the summary shortly."

"Good. Can we use her to trap Madison?"

"Thaddeus has been stalling the agency; they've asked the same question. They're eager to have a talk with her, as well. Let me check and get back with you. Her name is Maurine Rowen, red hair, quite attractive. She was a high-priced escort working out of Caracas. Since she hooked up with Madison, she hasn't been seen around much."

"Gotcha. Anything else from Dorotea Trujillo?"

"She's provided a couple more leads. I'll let you know what turns up. Call you back later."

Ending the call, Max immediately entered the number for Agent Summers. "Gail, this is Max."

"I know you're not calling to ask me out tonight, so what's the news?"

"The Israelis picked up Madison's girlfriend. She's to meet him in Vegas tomorrow evening. I've asked the Israelis to allow the meeting so that we can get Madison. Margaret'll have their summary shortly. I hope to get their approval pretty soon, since this is short notice."

"Ah, Sin City! Well, well, a nice place to rendezvous. I'll get the Vegas field office spun up on this. Let me know as soon as you can. I'm not doing anything this weekend, so Vegas would be fun. Want me to notify Dawn Blakey?"

"No, let's just keep it between us for now." Max thought back to their meeting earlier where Dawn demonstrated her incompetence.

"Fine by me. She'd just be in the way. What're the details on the girlfriend?"

Max provided the description of Maurine Rowen and her background as told to him by Danya.

"Can we get a photo of her?" Gail's tone was serious. "Have you been to Vegas? Hell, you've just described about one-third of the high-end call girls. Red hair seems to be *in* these days."

"Margaret is working on a photo. Get David to start looking at Vegas and the surrounding area. Madison is in the country for a reason, and it's not to party in Vegas. I doubt he has the devices with him, but he knows where they are."

"I'll start things rolling on my end. Talk to you soon."

***

October 19, 2013
InterContinental Hotel
Caracas, Venezuela

Remaining in Caracas before returning to Lebanon, Hezbollah representative Yasin was enjoying his last few days of what the Western world had to offer before returning home: good whisky, women, and a fancy car. He had already received praise by phone of the job he had done and was assured of being welcomed a hero upon his return. Clad in only a bathrobe, Yasin switched on the TV and then emptied his glass of whisky. A black-haired woman of Spanish descent lay nude in the bed, covered with a sheet. At ten forty-five, a knock came from the door.

"It's about time," Yasin said as he stomped to the door; he was expecting the arrival of another bottle of whisky.

"Room service," came a man's voice from beyond the door.

Yasin opened the door, saw a man carrying the whisky on a tray, and began a belligerent outburst. "It's about time! What am I paying you for—"

At that instant the door burst open fully; three Mossad men, accompanied by three Shayetet commandos in civilian clothes, rushed in with their pistols drawn. Yasin was immediately taken to the floor. One man grabbed the woman and held his Glock 21SF under her chin. With his left hand, he motioned for her to remain silent. Two men raised Yasin, removed his robe, sat the nude man in a chair, and bound his hands behind him with double zip-tie handcuffs.

"We're going to have a little discussion," said Ethan, the Mossad team's lead; his expression was serious and his voice firm. "We want the right answers without any shit!"

"Who are you?" Yasin's voice was loud and full of fury. "What do you want? You can't do this to me. I—"

Ethan popped Yasin, and his head shot back.

"I said no shit!" Ethan said as he motioned to one of the other men, who grabbed the ice bucket and then left the room. "Where are the nuclear weapons? Before you answer, I want you to think very hard for just a minute. You know what I am talking about, and you will eventually give me the answers to my questions. Make it as painful as you like or not, but I will get the answers."

Yasin's eyes, wide with fear, darted about the room. Outnumbered and outgunned, he knew what to expect. His years of training—brainwashing actually—would save him, or so he thought. He was defiant and struggled with every bit of his strength. He spat at Ethan.

"Fuck you, you son of a Zionist pig!" Yasin replied.

Ethan wiped the man's spit from his cheek. "That's good. So you think you're a badass. Better have a talk with Allah. You'll need it. We'll cool you off a little and then perhaps castrate you, or who knows what else we'll think of. But you'll tell me what I want to know before we are finished with you."

The man returned with a full ice bucket, dumped it into the bathtub, and then continuously repeated the process. Another man turned on the cold water and filled the tub. Two other men lifted Yasin, placed him in the tub, and held him down. Ethan placed a cold, wet towel over Yasin.

Ice Man returned and poured the ice on top of Yasin. The tub filled slightly and covered Yasin. Within a few minutes, the goose pimples formed on Yasin as his body temperature began dropping. Ice Man continued until ice filled the water. Ethan signaled the two men, and they stretched out the squirming man's legs. Ice Man dumped a bucket of ice in his crotch.

Yasin struggled against the two men, trying to wiggle free, but the men holding him down were too powerful. Ethan draped a wet hand towel across Yasin's face and slowly poured water on it. When the container emptied, he removed the towel and then looked into the wide, fear-filled eyes of Yasin as he gasped for air.

"Are you ready to answer my questions?" asked Ethan. "I haven't even begun yet."

"Fuck you!" Yasin pushed the words through blue, shivering lips.

"Are your balls cold enough? I wouldn't want you to be in too much pain when we remove them." Without waiting for a reply, he returned the towel to the Arab's face and then poured water across the towel again. Ethan left the towel in place a little longer and then removed it once again. Yasin gasped for air and struggled once more. Ethan retrieved a stiletto and pressed the button, and the razor-sharp blade appeared with a click. Making sure that Yasin saw the blade and had time to contemplate his options, Ethan wiped the blade and waved it about as he got close to Yasin. Then Ethan whispered into Yasin's ear.

Anticipating what they were about to do, the Spanish woman in the bed started to scream. Seeing their brutality, she could only imagine what they had in mind for her. The Israeli guarding her shoved his pistol harder into her throat. He motioned again for her to remain silent. Her eyes, wide and filled with fear, darted about. She then turned her head and vomited.

"Hold his legs," Ethan said. As the two men spread Yasin's legs, he taunted Yasin with his knife once again and then laid the towel back across Yasin's face and poured more water. Gasping for air, Yasin struggled. Ethan slightly pricked the skin of Yasin's lower abdomen, just enough for him to feel the pain, and then looked at the man. As Yasin started to yell out, Ethan stuffed a wet washcloth in his mouth. He grabbed Yasin's scrotum, stretched it outward, and then cut slightly into the skin—more for the pain and effect. Then Ethan stopped.

Ethan leaned close to Yasin and then, with a harsh voice, said, "Where's the device?"

Ethan pulled the washcloth from Yasin's mouth. "Your choice—tell me or never have the pleasure of a woman again."

Yasin's tear-filled eyes signaled that he was contemplating the alternative. Then Yasin said, "Two are on board the *Amira Fatima* out of Maracaibo, Venezuela." His voice was full of fear as he forced the words.

"The other two, where are they?"

"The United States. Nogales, Arizona."

Ethan motioned to the two holding Yasin. They released Yasin's legs, stood him up, and quickly dried the shivering man. The other Israeli guarding the woman pulled her out of bed.

"Dress," he said and motioned to her clothes.

Ethan pitched Yasin's pants to him and said, "Get dressed." When Yasin finished, one of the commandos produced a syringe and injected Yasin with a sedative to ensure he would be quiet and unable to resist. Ethan pulled the woman's head back by the hair.

"Do as you are told and be quiet, or you will get the needle, too."

Two commandos steadied Yasin as he and the woman were then ushered out of the hotel.

***

October 20, 2013
Bellagio Hotel
Las Vegas, Nevada

The aroma of freshly brewed coffee wafted through the air of the sparsely populated dining room. The tantalizing smell was wasted on most of the occupants. Their bloodshot eyes told of their activities the night before. They just wanted coffee—lots of it. Unlike the others' eyes, Bart's cold blue eyes were clear and his mind fully alert. Seated several tables away from anyone else and away from the main flow of traffic, Bart refilled his cup from the carafe on the table. The coffee was every bit as good as he expected.

He wasn't in Vegas for fun; he was there for business, and his first appointment arrived as expected. Senator Carlton Bradbourne shuffled his large frame into the room, paused to look around—more out of habit than of one looking for a familiar face—and then produced a wavering smile as he approached Bart's table.

"Good morning, Senator." Bart studied the man and then glanced about the room to see if anyone recognized the senator. "You look like you enjoyed yourself last night."

"I worked late last night. I need some of that coffee." Bradbourne filled his cup, added cream and sugar, and then went to town on the drink.

"Cut the bullshit, Senator! I paid for your prostitute. Remember? I know she was just a little older than you prefer; obviously you didn't mind."

Bradbourne cleared his throat and then quickly finished off his coffee. Without hesitation, he reached for the carafe and refilled the cup. Leaning forward, he said, "What's going on? That story of red mercury scared a lot of people."

"Nothing to it." Bart withdrew a bulging envelope and slid it to Bradbourne. "You did very well. There is a little extra in there this time."

"Bart, thank you, but all this…I don't like it." The senator tucked the envelope into his coat pocket.

"You like the money, don't you?"

Bradbourne lowered his head just slightly. There was no question; he belonged to Bart.

"When you get back to DC, I want you to keep your ear to the ground and me informed about what's going on. I expect you to keep the intelligence reports coming."

"Bart, I—"

"I don't want any shit from you, and no whining," Bart said through clenched teeth. "I'll be in touch."

He stood and walked out of the room.

Later that same afternoon, Bart met with the ISIS member, al-Muhaymin, as arranged by al-Aqrab. When ISIS had agreed to purchase the weapons at the meeting in Venezuela, al-Aqrab had arranged for another meeting in Las Vegas after they had taken possession. Although ISIS had dormant cells in the United States, al-Aqrab wanted someone with native knowledge of the United States to assist them in choosing the best place to detonate the devices for maximum impact and shock to the nation.

Many disgruntled citizens would strike out at the US government, including—possibly—ex–service members offering their services to take out their frustrations on the government. Numerous others had become radicalized, for whatever reason, and had joined the Islamists in the fighting in Iraq, Afghanistan, and Syria as well as other countries around the world. However, all the aforementioned lacked the experience, discipline, and proven skills that the ex-special-forces officer possessed. He was a professional for hire. As a mercenary, Bart had agreed, for a price, to advise them on the planning and deployment of the devices.

Al-Muhaymin had slipped into the country through the southern border the day before and had been escorted to the desert metropolis by one of the ISIS contacts inside the United States. Bart had arranged for his room, a prostitute, and plenty of booze—all awaiting his arrival.

Meeting in the Arab's suite, they sat across the coffee table from each other. Bart turned on the TV for background noise as a precaution to thwart any eavesdropping. Not only did he not trust his employer but also didn't trust the government. Believing that al-Muhaymin was probably on the government watch lists, Bart wanted to conduct his business with the ISIS representative as soon as possible. That wouldn't be very difficult, as the Arab was like a child in the candy store, his eyes popping at every temptation. Bart had made it clear that business came first, but he anticipated that al-Muhaymin would be consuming his fill of liquor and women until his departure.

Careful not to be seen publically with the ISIS representative, Bart planned to avoid him after their meeting ended. Being seen with the Arab would cause Bart problems, not only because of his association with a known ISIS member but also because Bart himself wasn't on the most favored list with the government, either. However, since he was in Vegas, Bart planned to spend a couple of days relaxing and enjoying a little entertainment with his girlfriend, Maurine; he anticipated her arrival early that evening.

As a city where almost anything goes, Las Vegas was easy to hide in. People of all walks of life roamed the streets and casinos at all hours of the day and night. Alcohol, sex, drugs, and anything else that suited your desires could be found there. It was easy enough to go unnoticed in Vegas, as the streets and casinos were always buzzing with activity.

"A cigar?" Bart offered the Arab a Cuban Montecristo No. 2. He watched the man clumsily reciprocate the hospitality by sloshing Glenlivet XXV into two glasses and then adding a couple of ice cubes. *That's a waste of good single-malt Scotch,* Bart thought. *He'd be just as happy if it was Old Crow.*

"Allah is pleased. We will defeat the infidels," Al-Muhaymin said, took a drink, and then puffed the cigar. His arrogance was as thick as the smoke. "We will blow up New York and Washington, DC."

"Cut the crap," Bart replied. "I'm not here to listen to your bullshit. I'm paid to do a job, so let's get to it." Bart placed his cigar in the ashtray and then unfolded a map of the United States. "If you want major impact and damage to the United States, one should be at Hoover Dam and the other at the Port of Los Angeles. Then have a car bomb or suicide bomber in DC."

"Hoover Dam. Why there?" With raised shoulders, the foreigner displayed a questioning look.

"Blow up that structure, and you will knock out power to almost one-third of the country or more. The shortage will overload the rest of the grid with demand. The rushing water flowing downstream will cause thousands of casualties and a tremendous financial loss. The military will be sent in to help, which will affect the country's ability to deploy forces and tie up the National Guard. The entire focus will be on that part of the country."

"That is good. But New York City—"

"They expect and are more prepared for a strike in New York City."

Bart pointed to Los Angeles on the map. He said, "The Port of Los Angeles is the main import-export center for the West Coast. Millions of people live in Los Angeles; it is the high-profile financial center of the West Coast, and that'll put the entire country into shock. The electromagnetic pulse will fry all electrical components and knock out the western electrical grid. Hell, you may even get lucky and set off a major earthquake along the San Andreas Fault."

Bart traced the fault line with his finger. "That'll hamper recovery efforts. A strike at the center of the homeland will also set the United States into panic mode, and chaos will ensue. Either one is a high-value target and will cause great financial loss and panic."

"I see. What about the stock market in New York?"

"Not to worry," replied Bart. "The attack and news will set the market into a tailspin. Eventually the demand on the electric grid will affect the rest of the country and cause power outages. The government shutdown is just now over, and people are getting back to work. Explode a car bomb in the DC area, and it will disrupt the government and cause even greater anarchy in DC."

Bart picked up his Scotch and leaned back in his chair. He took a sip and then puffed on the cigar.

"A very brilliant and aggressive plan," said al-Muhaymin, and he gulped his drink.

The two spent the next two hours planning each detail of the attack. Step by step Bart guided al-Muhaymin through what needed to occur and when and how to emplace the nukes. They planned for each contingency. Bart continuously emphasized the need for secrecy.

"No one must talk or boast of what is going to happen," Bart insisted. This concerned Bart the most, as these fanatics could never keep anything secret. "We must work quickly. The longer we take, the more our chances of discovery. The FBI'll, no doubt, be investigating the theft of the devices. They probably know by now that the devices are in the country."

Bart's brow dipped. *If I'm caught or associated with these rag heads, I'm as good as dead*, he thought.

"I understand. The CIA?" Al-Muhaymin nodded.

"I'm sure, but they don't investigate inside this country."

"I will discuss your plan with Nabi Ulmalhamah al-Aqrab," al-Muhaymin said. "We will contact you. May Allah be with you."

"You keep him with you," said Bart. "When I hear from you again, bring money." Bart stood and stepped to the door. "A lot more money!"

***

6:26 p.m.
October 20, 2013
McCarran International Airport
Las Vegas, Nevada

In the throng of people near the gate, Max Kenworth and Gail Summers stood awaiting the arrival of the flight carrying Bart Madison's girlfriend, escorted by Danya Mayer. The Israelis had agreed to allow Danya to escort Maurine Rowen to Las Vegas to bait the trap in order to capture Bart; Israel deemed it in their best interest. The FBI special agent in charge of the Las Vegas division was en route to the Bellagio to scout out the hotel and position her team. Anticipating that the hotel would be a beehive of activity at seven thirty in the evening, the FBI planned to apprehend Madison with the least disruption to the hotel routine and avoid harm to the guests or staff.

Passengers, many wrestling with their carry-on bags, began to emerge from the gate and quickly made their way to their connecting flights or baggage-claim areas. Overhead speakers blared out the arrival and departures of flights in rapid succession. Finally Danya emerged, followed by the redheaded Maurine.

"Danya." Max's loud voice competed with the flight announcements. He waved his hand.

Max and Danya embraced and exchanged kisses on each other's cheek, and then he made the introductions. Gail took charge and said, "Maurine, you've been told what this is about, correct?"

Maurine nodded.

"Good. We're going to walk out of here and take a taxi to the hotel. An agent outside is holding a cab. There'll also be an FBI car following to the Bellagio Hotel. At the hotel, you'll walk in by yourself and meet with Bart as planned."

Maurine nodded again.

"Don't fuck this up. Don't try to run or warn Bart. You'll meet with him as you planned. You got it?"

Maurine glared at Gail for an instant and then nodded. "I am supposed to call him when I arrive at the airport," Maurine added.

Her eyes studying the woman, Gail paused and considered the alternatives. Everything was supposed to look normal. Anything out of the ordinary could spook Madison. A call to him could be a subtle warning to him; however, up to that point, Maurine had been cooperative. On the other hand, it was commonplace for couples or travel companions to call and let the others know of their arrival or changes in schedule. Gail was sure that Madison knew the time Maurine would arrive. The absence of a call could also be a warning.

Evaluating the options, Gail agreed. "OK, call him."

Gail nodded at Danya, as a signal to return Maurine's cell phone. "Play it straight, and no tricks. You'll be watched every step of the way. Just do as you were instructed. Remember, screw this up or try to run, and I'll fuck up that pretty face of yours."

Maurine nodded again, and then Danya handed the cell phone to her. Maurine punched in the numbers as Gail and Danya looked over her shoulder and watched each of her moves.

"Hi, love," Maurine said into the phone as soon as she heard Bart's voice. "I'm at the airport. I'll grab a taxi and be there in a few minutes."

"Did you have a good flight?"

"It was long and bumpy at times. I'm exhausted. Would you mind if we don't go to the performance this evening? I'd just like to shower, eat, and then go to bed early."

"Not a problem. I'll change our reservations. I'll meet you in the lobby."

"Thanks. See you in a few minutes." Maurine hung up the phone.

"That was good," said Gail in an authoritative voice. "Keep it up. Let's go."

Danya held out her hand and indicated for Maurine to return the cell phone. The four then proceeded to the exit. On the way, Gail rehearsed the sequence of events again. They needed Maurine to identify Madison early on so that the agents could get into position. The only photograph they had of Madison was a US Army photo more than eight years old, and he probably had changed quite a bit since the photo had been taken.

Madison could have deliberately altered his appearance for his trip into the country anticipating the authorities might be looking for him, Max thought. *Or simply a hard life as a mercenary living in the jungle could have taken a toll on his former youthful appearance.* This worried Max, and he was cautious about whether he could recognize Madison without him speaking or seeing a familiar gesture.

***

Seated in the Petrossian Bar inside the Bellagio Hotel and nursing a glass of wine, Bart waited Maurine's arrival. The pianist played the grand piano and competed with the noise of the slots, the tables, the overhead speakers, and the growing din of the evening crowd. The bar, located off to the side near the check-in desk, was a popular stopover for people waiting to go to dinner or for friends to arrive or to just have a drink. Nestled in the crowd, Bart sat at a table where he could observe the entrance and reception desk.

He ended the call from Maurine and sat back in his chair. *She called me on this phone,* he thought. *She knows to call me on the other one. Reservations for this evening? We didn't have any. Something's up. What've I missed? Better grab my bag. If I've gotta bug out, I'll have my stuff.*

Having been around the block several times before, Maurine was smart, and even though Mossad and now the FBI were calling the shots, she wasn't about to be rattled and fall apart. Bart had given her his special cell-phone number and had instructed her to use it only in an emergency. It was a part of the unspoken rule of the underworld not to help the police, and, of course, he was her lover. Maurine was confident that if Bart avoided the authorities, he would help her as soon as he could.

Returning to the bar and dropping his bag at his feet, Bart sat back and ordered another glass of wine. Looking over the activity of people entering and leaving the lobby, Bart's eye caught a man and woman as they emerged from the main entrance and then disappeared into the depths of the hotel. His eyes roamed over the crowd and spotted a man enter from the north end of the hotel and walk to the front desk. Bart's eyes continued, landing on a third man who stepped from the elevator and then sat in a chair near the entrance. All four people were dressed in black.

Typical FBI attire, he thought. *Dude, I'm not stupid enough to register under my own name. Are they looking for me or al-Muhaymin? You'll find al-Muhaymin in his room, banging his prostitute. But I'm not taking any chances on who you're after. Time to go.*

The man who had gone to the desk returned and sat across from the previously seated man. Overhearing the couple sitting at the adjoining table, Bart engaged them in a conversation, all the while keeping an eye on the FBI men. The man and woman were on holiday from Oklahoma. The woman—a bit on the large size—favored the slot machines, and her husband—a short, potbellied man—played blackjack and craps. He boasted about playing craps and taking money from other soldiers during his days in the military. They were waiting on the shuttle to take them to the airport to catch their flight back home.

"Well, Jim," the woman said with a high-pitched, nasal drawl. "I'll, for sure, be glad to get back to my bed. I'm looking forward to some good fried chicken, mashed potatoes, and gravy with hot rolls. That stuff they call fried chicken here *ain't* chicken. They don't know how to cook."

The woman talked incessantly, but no one was listening to her. She looked around to the young woman—displaying lots of cleavage and wearing tight, short shorts—serving drinks at an adjacent table. "*Hun,*" the woman said without taking a pause, "would you bring me another one of these?" She held out her hand with the glass. "Well, where's that shuttle? I'm ready to go."

Bart continued his careful watch on the two men by the door and tried to locate the other two. He was sure that the man and woman who had come in the front entrance were FBI as well and were probably checking out any possible escape routes. Then the announcement came for the guests to load the shuttle for the airport. As Jim and his wife stood,

Bart did the same and acted as if he were headed to the airport as well.

The talkative woman set her glass on the table with a click. She then grasped the sides of her shirt and bra and gave them a couple of twists to adjust the large undergarment. She then grabbed her bags and said, "Well, Jim, let's go home."

A crowd of tourists heading for the strip merged with the Oklahoma couple's group bound for the airport and enveloped Bart and his newfound friends. As they walked, Bart was careful to keep several people between him and the suspected FBI men and obscure their view of him. Bart maintained the conversation with Jim as they made their way to the doors and the waiting shuttle outside. Out of sight of the scrutinizing eyes of the two agents, Bart broke free of the Oklahoma couple and continued with the group venturing back onto the strip.

Within minutes, the taxi pulled to a stop at the front doors of the hotel; Maurine got out and walked in. Gail, with Danya and Max in the car, timed her arrival at the hotel entrance as Maurine entered the doors. The agents inside scanned the lobby and bar, looking for Madison as she stepped in. Maurine stopped near the center of the lobby and looked around the interior, obviously looking for Madison. After an awkward few minutes, Gail followed by Max and Danya approached her. "Well, goddamn it!" Gail Summers said, frustrated at missing Bart. Then she turned to Maurine. "You warned him."

"How did I warn him?" replied Maurine. "I've been stuck to your ass ever since I've been here. I haven't even been able to go to the bathroom by myself."

"Madison is pretty smart," Max said, looking around the lobby again. "If she didn't warn him, he spotted the stakeout. In any event, he's not here and probably out of the city by now."

"Danya, I need that number off the cell phone to compare it to the list of numbers going to Madison's phone," Gail said.

"I thought you'd want it. Here's the number." Danya handed Gail a piece of paper with the number on it.

"Thanks. I'm going to talk to the division chief here; they're going to hold her overnight for us." Gail pointed to Maurine. "They'll bring her to the airport in the morning and hand her over to us there."

"Do you want to meet later for a drink?" Max asked.

"Meet you in the bar in about an hour. I need several drinks," Gail said as she tugged on Maurine's arm and led her away.

Chapter 8

2:12 a.m.
October 22, 2013
West-Southwest of Western Sahara
Atlantic Ocean

In the black of night, the British ship HMS *Bulwark*, of the United Kingdom's Response Force Task Group, launched the Shayetet Thirteen team from Panama in their rigid-hull, inflatable boats. The coxswains shoved the throttles forward and propelled their light craft across the low swells of the central Atlantic. Once the two boats cleared the ship and were en route to the freighter *Amira Fatima*, two Lynx helicopters departed HMS *Bulwark* with a team from the Forty-Second Commando Royal Marines to support the Shayetet commandos in boarding and controlling the *Amira Fatima*.

The captain of HMS *Bulwark* hailed the *Amira Fatima* and ordered it to stop. With no response, he repeated the order for the freighter to stop once again. No response from the freighter. Ordering a third time without any effect on the *Amira Fatima*, the captain of HMS *Bulwark* directed the gun crew to fire a short burst from the forward-mounted twenty-millimeter GAM-BO1 cannon.

High-explosive rounds impacted into the water across the bow of the freighter, which brought an almost-immediate response. As the freighter slowed, the frantic Pakistani captain's voice came over the speaker.

"No more shoot! We are stopping. No more shoot! We comply. This is international waters. Why you stop us? This is international waters. This is violation of maritime law." The captain's protests had no effect on the captain of the *Bulwark*.

Hovering above the freighter, forward of the bridge and approximately the center of the ship, the marine commandos began fast-roping onto the ship. In fewer than twenty seconds, the commandos were on board and moving to the bridge. The Shayetet team boarded the ship from both sides and immediately began assembling the crew.

"I want to see your manifest," said the marine captain, his voice stern.

The Pakistani shook his head and pretended not to speak English.

Shoving his assault rifle into the man's chest, the marine said again, "The manifest!"

The manifest appeared and was handed to the commando captain. Scanning the list of crew and passengers, he circled the name *Abdalrahman Tabari.* As he continued down the cargo list, it revealed nothing other than general cargo, cars, machinery, parts, stores, and so on. Seeing the Shayetet team assemble the crew, the marine captain descended the ladder to deliver the manifest to Rav-Seren Aaron Friedman.

"The manifest lists one name that'll interest you." The captain handed the list to Friedman. "Nothing out of the ordinary on the cargo list."

Friedman took a quick look and then returned the paper. He said, "Start searching the automobile shipping containers." His voice was crisp. "Find Tabari." Friedman motioned to one of his men to accompany the captain.

After numerous protest and denials of Tabari's existence on board and, of course, a little persuasion from the Israelis, the Pakistani captain led the commando to Tabari's cabin. Bursting in, the commandos were surprised to find Tabari still in bed. A half-empty bottle of Scotch sat on the small desk and provided the explanation. In the cluttered room, cigarette butts filled the ashtrays, several used glasses sat on the desk, and clothes were scattered about. They rousted Tabari up, bound his hands behind him, and then sat him in a chair. The marine captain reported the capture of the man and told Friedman where they were located.

After about an hour and fifteen minutes of intense interrogation, Tabari agreed to show them where the SADMs were concealed. The battered and disheveled man, still wearing only his underwear, led them to a shipping container and nodded toward it. "Inside."

Opening the steel doors, Friedman saw the trunk of a late-model Lexus. "The keys," he demanded.

"In the ignition," replied Tabari, his voice trembling more from fear than the cool air.

Another commando squeezed into the container and retrieved the keys, while another methodically checked the car for booby traps. He nodded as the other commando brought out the key. As they slowly raised the trunk lid, the olive-green container was revealed. Two commandos retrieved the box, set it on the deck, and then opened the lid. Friedman inspected the contents and verified that the components were undisturbed.

Friedman faced Tabari and said, "Where's the other one?"

Tabari turned and, without speaking, led them to another stack of shipping containers. Then Tabari nodded. The commandos repeated the process. As they opened the steel door, a Cadillac was exposed. After verifying the contents, Friedman reported to HMS *Bulwark* that they had seized both devices. A Lynx helicopter was dispatched to transport the two nukes and Tabari back to HMS *Bulwark*. Rav-Seren Friedman and his men departed the freighter in their boats and returned to HMS *Bulwark*. The marine commandos stayed aboard the *Amira Fatima* as it was directed to a controlled harbor.

Chapter 9

9:15 a.m.
Tuesday
October 22, 2013
CTC
Tysons Corner, Virginia

"ISIS chatter has been very quiet the last couple of days," Margaret said as she looked around at the others with her hazel eyes. "That concerns me."

Dawn Blakey's tone was incredulous as she replied, "Are you still thinking the SADMs are in the country? We haven't seen anything to indicate that they are, and the White House doesn't think so, either."

David leaned forward, rested his arms on the table, and said, "Dawn, love, didn't you read the summary I sent over to you? Madison was in Las Vegas, and we're looking for leads there."

Margaret said, "This report from Mossad was waiting for me when I got in this morning." She passed out copies to the others and then continued. "Two SADMs were loaded aboard the freighter *Amira Fatima* out of Maracaibo, Venezuela, and two were to enter the United States at Nogales, Arizona. The Israelis are working on the freighter."

Dawn's mouth gaped open, and her eyes filled with fear as she said in a panic-filled voice, "Oh my God!" She stood and ran her hand through her hair. "That means New York and DC are the most likely places. There're some big gatherings coming up that are potential targets—football games, conventions, and the like. I've gotta send out an alert and notify the president."

"Dawn *dahling*," David said, his tone soft. He fingered the pencil on his tablet. "Max has it under control. The FBI is posting a reward for information on the devices and Madison."

"Settle down." Max's tone was commanding as he looked at the panicky woman. "Yes, those places should be considered, but they're the obvious targets. We need to look very closely at other potential objectives. Think of other infrastructure, large congregations of people, or places of significance whose destruction would terrify the country."

"We routinely send out alerts," Dawn replied as she sat back in her chair.

"That's the problem," Max said as he tapped the eraser end of his pencil on his tablet. "You send out ambiguous warnings to everyone, but nothing specific. It's become commonplace—like the boy who yelled wolf too often. No one pays any attention to what you send out. Frankly it's all crap."

Gail entered the conference room and sat at the table. "Sorry I'm late," she said. "Just got approval to arrest the senator." She beamed.

"Oh Gail, that's wonderful," David said, his eyebrows raised and eyes open wide. His grin went from ear to ear.

"I hope you've got your shit together," said Margaret. Her hazel eyes narrowed slightly as she handed Gail a copy of the Mossad message.

"Me too," agreed Gail. "I've checked everything over several times and have a really good team. And, yes, David, you have done a great job on this." Gail looked around at him and warned, "But Bradbourne will be out on bail before the ink dries. Then he'll be in front of every camera he can find."

"This'll be another 'right-wing conspiracy' with all the drama," Margaret said and rolled her eyes.

"That's not fair," Dawn said. Her brow dipped, and her eyes narrowed. "Don't talk about Senator Bradbourne that way." She held her scornful look on Margaret.

"He's a fucking crook." Gail's voice filled the room. She was in no mood to put up with the young woman and her naïve liberal leanings.

Recognizing that the meeting was rapidly deteriorating into a political scuffle, Max said, "Ladies, let's get back to the topic at hand. Anything of importance come from the interviews with Maurine Rowen?"

"Not much really," Gail said, wrinkling up the corner of her mouth and shaking her head. "The agency and FBI interrogators have been at it for a while. Madison didn't talk about his activities around her. Even when he got phone calls, he ushered her out of earshot. The call she made from the airport was to the same cell phone that placed and received numerous calls to and from the senator."

"Any leads on Madison?" Max scribbled on his notepad and then looked at Gail.

"I'm afraid he has gone *poof!*" David said as he lifted his hands to indicate exasperation.

"David, no one goes poof!" Gail said. She took a deep breath and looked at David and then Max. "No, we don't have a goddamned thing on him."

"Margaret," Max said as he looked at her, "have you located the ISIS bomb guy, Dhul Fiqar, yet?"

"Nothing on him either," replied Margaret. "The agency and FBI are stirring the dregs of the underground and passing out money all over the place."

As he looked around the table at each of them, Max questioned sharply, "Why would Madison be in Las Vegas if he was involved in the theft of the SADMs? He's too smart for that. My guess is that he's working with ISIS. Think about it for a minute."

Max paused and tapped his pencil. He continued, "Madison plans the strike on the Balboa facility and coordinates transportation of the devices into the United States; it makes sense for him to meet with ISIS representatives and plan where to place them. If he is helping them plan a strike, I bet it won't be on the obvious places.

Since he was in Las Vegas, I suspect it'll be out west. If it's the East Coast, I'd think he'd be closer. He'll want to recon the area and walk the terrain. Keep looking for anything unusual, no matter how slight or benign it might appear."

When their meeting broke up, Dawn scooped up her things and marched out of the room in a hurry. As soon as the door closed, Max raised his hand.

"Hold up just a minute," Max said. "The Pentagon is frustrated, and their hands are being tied by the president. It's going to be up to us all the way now. SOCOM is still in the loop and will back us. They'll continue to provide us support and provide a delta team when we're ready. This is all *need to know*. Don't say anything to Dawn until it is absolutely necessary."

Max unyieldingly looked at each of them in the eyes. Margaret, Gail, and David all nodded in agreement.

That evening's lead news story on the networks and cable-news providers was about the arrest of Senator Carlton Bradbourne, a presidential hopeful for the 2016 elections. News anchors played the videos of the arrest and added their commentary on how this surprise would shape the elections. Political strategists for both parties put their spin on the senator's arrest. Without any inside information, all expounded and gave their views.

Depending on the channel, the slant was different, from a right-wing conspiracy to a corrupt politician getting his deserved reward. Each clip ended with Senator Bradbourne just out on bail, standing at a lectern, denying all charges, and vowing to vindicate his good name.

He boasted defiantly and shook his finger. "I am innocent of these slanderous and fabricated charges. I have done nothing wrong. This is purely a conspiracy to tarnish my good name. I am appalled at such dirty tricks. I have never done, nor would I commit, such offenses against my country and the constituencies of our great state." He continued his rant and played to the camera as long as anyone would listen.

The news editors showed just enough of the video to capture the audience's interest.

When he heard the news story on the TV about the arrest of the senator, Bart wheeled the desk chair around and turned up the volume. *Well, they arrested the good senator,* he thought. *Time for a little tidying up of the loose ends. It won't be too difficult to get a replacement. The leeches will grab at anyone with money during election season. The more money you have, the better friend you are. Hmm, slimy bastards!*

After slipping out of Las Vegas, Bart had checked into a family-owned hotel on the outskirts of Boulder City, Nevada, about ten minutes from Hoover Dam. The quaint inn was quiet and clean, and it provided what he needed. He had started reconnoitering the area, gathering maps and information about Hoover Dam, as well as locating a suitable house close to Lake Mead.

Madison anticipated word back on his plan from al-Muhaymin anytime. He also gathered data on the lake's water level, temperature, visibility, popular sites, and anything else he could find out about the lake. Unfortunately Senator Bradbourne's arrest would cost Bart a couple of days' time, but the senator was a pressing matter needing Bart's urgent attention. He checked his watch and then entered the phone number for Senator Bradbourne.

As soon as he heard the senator's voice, Bart said, "I saw the news."

"We shouldn't be talking—"

"We aren't." Bart's voice was stern. "Just listen. We've got to deal with your problem, and I can take care of it. I know what to do. Tomorrow night at nine, meet me at the park. You know where."

"Yes, but, Bart, I don't know. I may be—"

"You do want me to get you out of this, don't you?"

"Yes, but—"

"Tomorrow night, nine o'clock. Be there."

Bart ended the call and sat back to think through the next forty-eight hours. He took a sip of Crown Royal Reserve and then booked a flight to DC using an alias and phony Canadian passport.

***

Old Ebbitt Grill
Washington, DC

Seated in a cozy booth, Max poured another glass of Pinot Noir for Danya and then refilled his own. Rich in history, the famous establishment with Victorian decor made for a perfect spot to have dinner. The unobtrusive staff was attentive to every detail. Max started to speak when his cell phone rang. He paused and looked at the number and then said, "It's the boss. Please excuse me."

Danya nodded. "Of course."

"Max, Chugs," came the voice from the cell phone.

"Yes, sir. You're working late tonight."

"The old man had a very one-way and brutal meeting with the president. Did you see the evening news?"

"The senator's arrest? I saw it."

"That's just part of it. The Israelis and Brits stopped the freighter *Amira Fatima* off the coast of Africa and recovered two of the SADMs. They're returning them to us tomorrow."

"That's good news."

"The bad news is that some reporter found out about it," said Chugs, "and they've been breaking into the broadcast regularly over the last couple of hours with updates on the weapons. The same reporter also is trying to confirm that the attack on the Balboa site and these devices are tied together. The press is hounding the president, and the administration is denying the news reports. Everyone in the administration is asking about the devices—if they're really ours. The president is trying to kill the stories, but they are getting lots of attention. A bigger problem is that the Russians know about it. They're outraged and accusing the United States of reneging on the nuclear-weapons treaties. This is another scandal for the president. He's squeezing the SOCOM commander."

"Shit!" Max said. "It's his policies that are causing the problems in the first place. He won't give us the resources we need, and he's not actively engaged. His entire staff and appointees are very inexperienced. Is he going to let the military do its job, or are we still going to run around with our hands tied behind our backs and be his whipping boys?"

"The Israelis are definitely taking this seriously. They have one person in custody, Abdalrahman Tabari, who was on the freighter. I don't know if he'll be of value, but see what they have on him. If you need to, have a talk with him. Push and see what you can find out. The president is about to hand the boss his head. He's already looking for a fall guy."

"Will do. General, you know intel takes time and lots of resources."

"I do, the old man does, and you do. The president doesn't. Do what you need to do, but make it quick. Oh, and so far, no one knows about the other two weapons. Find them before anyone hears about them."

Max ended the call and then looked at Danya. His mood had obviously changed. "We need to go. I'll tell you in the car."

The smile dropped from Danya's face. The call wasn't good news. Without hesitation, she grasped her handbag and stood. Her hand clutched his as they walked out.

Max pulled the car out of the parking space, and as he eased onto the street, he told her of the phone call from Chugs. "Danya, I need to know what your team has learned from the guy they took from the freighter. They recovered two SADMs."

"I don't know anything. Honest."

"Let's find out. Will your people here in DC help us? I need to know tonight."

"Take me to the embassy, and I'll start working on it."

Max headed the rental car north to Connecticut Avenue Northwest, toward the Israeli embassy.

After dropping off Danya at the embassy, Max returned to the Sheraton Pentagon City Hotel. *Not how I wanted to spend my evening,* he thought as he entered the lobby. Once in his room, he turned the TV to the news. He glanced at the screen as the commentator was recapping the program and showing the arrest of Senator Bradbourne. He poured a glass of wine and sipped it and then sat to watch the remainder of the newscast.

Switching channels, Max saw that another reporter was reporting on the attack on the Balboa facility in Panama. Quizzing the press secretary, the reporter asked, "Why would terrorists attack a NASA climate-research facility in Panama? What was there? How many Americans were killed?"

The arrogant spokesman became agitated at the reporter's questions.

"I have no idea," the representative said. "You'll have to ask them. The president has met with the staff, and they're looking into it. It appears that it was not terrorists but simply disgruntled workers. They were striking for higher wages. There were a couple of people hurt after a scuffle when the Panamanian police tried to open the street they were blocking."

"Why were nuclear weapons stored at a NASA facility?" the reporter asked pointedly, hoping the secretary would slip and divulge more. "How many were taken?"

"That's nonsense. I have no knowledge that any weapons were stored in Panama. It's a NASA climate-research facility."

"This is turning into a disaster," Max mumbled to himself. "The entire world knows what happened and is looking for answers, while the president is playing golf and fundraising." Max shook his head and then sipped his wine.

"The nuclear weapons the Israelis recovered from the freighter *Amira Fatima* belong to the United States. How did they come to be on a Venezuelan freighter headed for Western Sahara?" the reporter continued, probing the secretary.

"I don't have that information, but I know the president is checking with his commanders."

"How stupid do you think the American people are, Baghdad Bob?" Max muttered. "Yep, another scandal." Baghdad Bob was the nickname for Iraqi Information Minister Mohammed Saeed al-Sahhaf—known for grand and grossly unrealistic broadcasts—during the 2003 invasion of Iraq in which he denied that there were any American tanks in Baghdad, when, in fact, they were seen in the background during a press conference he was giving.

***

Bart struggled and fought his way out of the deep sleep as he woke to the noise and then realized that his cell phone on the nightstand was ringing. Looking at the clock, his eyes focused on the digital numbers: 1:05 a.m.

"Shit!" In a sleep-filled mumble, he moaned, "I was sleeping hard. Who the hell is calling me at this hour?" Bart looked at the display of the cell phone, only to see *Unavailable* where the number should be displayed. Rubbing his hand over his face, he picked up the phone and said, "Bart."

"This is Abu Bakr al-Muhaymin." The accented voice was crisp. "Your plan is approved. We are to proceed at once to make all preparations."

"Good. I have a task to complete and will be back day after tomorrow. I'll send you a list of things I want you to acquire and complete instructions. Get the exact items outside of the country. Start working on the list. I'll call you when I get back. There are three houses I want you to go look at to rent. Make sure that the one you pick is secluded. Whichever one best fits our needs, rent it for a month. Tell the real-estate agent we are going fishing. Don't say anything else; be polite. All the information will be in the e-mail."

Bart ended the call after al-Muhaymin acknowledged his instructions and confirmed Bart's price.

***

9:10 a.m.
Wednesday
October 23, 2013
CTC
Tysons Corner, Virginia

Margaret passed out the latest intelligence summary to Gail, Max, David, and Dawn, who were already in the conference room, waiting on her.

"The Israeli summary is the first item," said Margaret. "The Hezbollah representative they picked up in Caracas, Zafir Yasin, is talking, but he hasn't added much new information. Hezbollah Tabari, the one they apprehended on the *Amira Fatima,* is being defiant but talking. He's corroborated Yasin's story. These two *fine young men* were to deliver the two nukes to ISIS scientist Dhul Fiqar at a remote location in Western Sahara. They only know that two devices went to the United States but not where. The Brits and Israelis have been very proactive on this."

"They're definitely taking this a lot more serious than the United States is," said Max as he flipped his pen onto the tablet and leaned back. "Even though the Israelis have taken the lead in this, our president and the PM still have a cold relationship. Unbelievable!"

Margaret's tone was serious as she read from her notes. "When they learned that ISIS scientist Dhul Fiqar was in Western Sahara, the Shayetet Thirteen, supported by the British Response Force Task Group, raided the location." She laid her glasses on the table and then brushed her hair back with her hand.

"Let me guess," Max said, leaning back and placing his hands behind his head. "The location was clean, no bomb maker."

"That's correct." Margaret nodded and then looked at the others. "Two down and two to go but no bomb scientist. We do know that two weapons are inside the United States somewhere. Dawn, anything from Nogales yet?"

"No, they're still reviewing the recordings at the port of entry. I've talked to all but two guards, and nothing seems to have been out of the ordinary."

"The Russians are outraged at the president," Margaret continued. "We're going back into a cold war."

"This could lead to a shooting war," Max said. "They're rattling sabers and putting pressure on NATO. The deteriorating situation in Ukraine could just be it."

"Oh Max! Don't say such things," David said, wringing his manicured hands.

"Have the money or rewards produced anything?" Max asked.

"Mostly the usual sleazeballs trying to tap Uncle Sam's ATM. Panama thought they had something, but before they could make the deal with the contact, he was found floating in the canal."

"Well, crap!" Max said, his tone full of frustration. He ran his hand across his mouth.

"Not to worry, Max," replied Margaret. She leaned forward, and her hazel eyes sparkled. "The ATM is fully stocked and spitting out money. Another source will come forward."

"I know," Max said and scribbled on his notepad. "The question is *when.* At least Dhul Fiqar is on the move again.

He'll set up some place else and contact whoever has the devices. Gail, be ready to move fast. I'm sure they'll be using throwaway phones. Internet traffic could give us a good lead if they happen to divulge something."

"David is already working on the Internet and phones sources," Gail said as she wrote on her notepad.

"These guys will probably want to shoot it out if we find them. I have a delta team ready to go as soon as you locate 'em," Max said.

"That won't be necessary." Dawn laid her glasses on the table and then sat upright. "The local police and FBI will handle it. We won't need the military."

Gail made eye contact and winked at Max, signaling she understood the situation and accepted his offer.

"Anything more on Madison?" Max asked, tapping the end of his pencil as he looked at David.

"We've alerted the major cities and field offices. Nothing new yet. The agents are working their informants."

"Figures," Max said. "At least we upset their plan a little by keeping the bomb scientist on the run. Undoubtedly Madison is waiting to be contacted by the bomb maker. That means they have the SADMs at some secluded location. The scientist needs time to bypass the PAL. He may already know how to do it but needs the devices to do so. That probably gives us a few extra days. Watch for anything—something subtle, slightly odd, or out of the ordinary. That could be the clue we need."

"I've started with Las Vegas and am working out at one-hundred-mile radius," David said, turning his head slightly upward.

"What about DC and New York?" Dawn asked, trying to sound important.

"I am working with them as well, *dahling,*" David reassured her.

"Madison was in Las Vegas for a reason. At that time we were just looking for him. Did you check all the names registered at the Bellagio Hotel?" Max's eyes slightly narrowed as he looked at David.

David, his mouth gaped open and eyes widened in astonishment, replied, "Oh my, no! We just looked for him."

"Go back and check all the hotels in the vicinity. Get a list of occupants the day before and the day after Madison's girlfriend was supposed to meet him," Max said. "If Madison met his contact there, the contact may have been registered at one of the hotels. It's worth a look."

"That'll take some doing," David said as he wrote on his notepad. "It'll take time."

"Well, sweet pea," Gail said, her tone direct and harsh, "you'd better get on it. Look for any Middle Eastern names first."

"Yes, *ma'am*." David's eyebrows rose, and then a slight smile emerged.

"Margaret," Max said, "any change in the electronic traffic?"

"It's about normal now. We did have a little spike. NSA is looking for anything related."

"How big are these devices? Wouldn't they need a truck to move them around?" Dawn asked, her expression clouded but her tone serious.

With an astonished look on his face, Max controlled his frustration with Dawn. "In the shipping container, it's about the size of a trunk. It'll fit in the back of your car. Outside the container, it's about twelve inches by eighteen inches with an aluminum and fiberglass frame. Does that give you an idea of how difficult they are to find?"

Dawn sheepishly acknowledged his reply and sat back in her chair.

At the conclusion of the meeting, Max hung back and waited for Dawn to leave the room. Once the door closed, he said, "Hold up a minute. Gail, I know you have the FBI working on Las Vegas, but I've got a hunch. Send David to Las Vegas and have him just snoop around and see what he can find out."

"I don't know, Max." Gail bit the side of her mouth. "Let me think about it."

"I don't mean police work. Just keep his ears open; watch for anything unusual."

"Unusual?" Gail's eyes opened wide; one eyebrow rose. "Sweetheart, everything about Las Vegas is unusual."

"That's what I mean. He'll fit in; all he needs to do is observe and listen."

"That's not a bad idea," Margaret said as she stood and scooped up her folder. "ISIS is trying to recruit Americans, and we know they have cells in the United States."

David's gaze shot to Max, Gail, and Margaret; he was not sure what he was about to get into. "Excuse me," he said. "Do I have anything to say about this?"

"Yes, sweet pea." Gail looked at him over her glasses. "What do you want to say?"

"That sounds exciting!" he replied. "I'll go."

"Do you feel better now?" Gail asked. "No James Bond stuff. Just observe and listen. Got that?"

"Yes, *dahling*."

Chapter 10

October 23, 2013
Courtyard Hotel
Alexandria, Virginia

The rain turned to drizzle as the clouds hung low in the evening sky. Streetlights struggled to provide basic illumination; what they did provide seemed to be mostly swallowed by the darkness. Bart looked at his watch as he walked into the hotel. The stops he had made along the way from the airport had taken him longer than he had anticipated. Traffic was slowed by the rainy night, and lines were long. Sojourns were necessary, and with a little over two hours before his meeting with the senator, Bart was almost ready. *Not a lot of time, but it will do,* he thought.

Once in his room, he completed his final preparations.

Unfolding a map, Bart examined the park area and closest neighborhood where he was to meet the senator. "The rain will keep all but the most die-hard bikers and joggers in tonight," he said to himself. "By nine o'clock even they won't be a problem." His preparations complete, Bart stretched out on the bed and waited until it was time for him to depart for the rendezvous with Bradbourne.

Rock Creek National Park in Northwest DC was a nature area with numerous jogging and bike trails crisscrossing the park. Light fog settled in the wooded area, with intermittent drizzle. Bart pulled up the hood on his dark rain slicker and stood in a tree line not far from where he anticipated the senator would park his car and then make his way to meet with him. Motionless, Bart blended in with the surrounding vegetation; the soaked leaves on the ground would muffle his footsteps when he moved. Bart watched and waited.

Headlights appeared and then slowed to a stop at the northern end of the park. The driver's door opened; the interior light revealed that the senator was alone. Bradbourne wrestled his frame from behind the wheel, grasped an umbrella as he slid out, and popped it open, and then the senator closed the car door. The burly figure paused and looked over the quiet, rain-soaked area. Satisfied that he was alone, Bradbourne flicked on a flashlight and began negotiating the terrain. He made very little noise as he walked along the path to where he was to meet Bart, a safe distance from the road, inside the park.

Bart watched as the flashlight led the way for the hefty figure. He searched for anyone following the senator to ensure that there would be no surprises. Water dripped off the hood of his slicker as he slowly turned his head, looking over the area once again. Bart saw the senator stop and glance around—obviously looking for him. Bart remained motionless momentarily as he studied the senator and then silently stepped out, his eyes fixed on the large frame of the man.

The senator's back was now in front of Bart. Bart saw Bradbourne move his arm and then look down. Bradbourne turned his head to look around, evidently looking for Bart, as he placed a cigar in his mouth and lit it. The flame illuminated the silhouette of his head and ears; the smoke swirled above his head as he puffed. The umbrella captured the rising smoke from the Cuban cigar, and the aroma was thick in the moist air.

Continuing to approach without the senator realizing, Bart stopped behind him. "Good evening, Senator," Bart said in a low voice.

Bradbourne jerked around. "Oh…Bart! You startled me."

"What did you tell the FBI?"

"Nothing! Absolutely nothing. They were asking about you."

"About me? What about me? What'd you say?"

"Hell, they asked me all kinds of questions. My attorney kept telling me not to say anything."

"Good. What else?"

"They're accusing you of leading the attack on the NASA facility in Panama, smuggling, working with the FARC, and all kinds of things. The FBI is saying I furnished you the information."

"They're just trying to scare you. They don't know anything."

"They're looking for you. I went to the Pentagon this morning for a meeting, and while I was there, I saw the deputy assistant secretary of defense for nuclear matters. I found out, by accident, that SOCOM is calling the shots on this and that they've got their top guy working it. It's very hush-hush. Homeland Security is just a front."

"Who's the SOCOM guy? What does he know?"

"I don't know what he knows, but he's teamed up with the FBI, Homeland Security, and CIA. His name is Kenworth, Max Kenworth."

"Kenworth! I know him. I've got a score to settle with him."

"Bart, you've got to get out of here."

"What about the administration? What's the president doing? You're behind on your daily intel updates."

"The entire administration is running around without their heads. There's no action, and no one is in charge. But all the people at the White House say they're in charge. It is completely dysfunctional. The president is swamped with scandals. Frankly I don't think he wants to deal with this. He's not engaged; he ducks out constantly to play golf. So nothing gets done, and everyone is running amok."

"What about the military—any deployments, large domestic exercises, the border, and things like that?"

"Nothing. The White House won't hear of it. When the SecDef and generals bring the subject up, he throws them out. All the generals are playing it very cool and keeping their heads down to protect their positions. They won't do anything without explicit approval from the White House. The border is wide open; no one is interested in closing it."

"Have you told me everything?"

"Yes, Bart. Everything."

Bart pulled his hand out of the slicker pocket and quickly jammed the short barrel of a Smith and Wesson revolver, model 43C, under Bradbourne's chin and shoved his head back. Reflexively the senator's arms reached for Bart's, but his actions were too slow. Madison squeezed the trigger; the twenty-two-caliber round popped.

Bradbourne's cheeks puffed out with the shot and partially muffled the sound. His body jerked and then slumped backward. Bart removed his glove, stooped over the body, and checked the lifeless eyes of the senator and then his pulse. Satisfied that he had taken care of a loose end, Bart returned the revolver to his pocket and looked for any evidence that he may have inadvertently left near the corpse. One of the stops Bart had made prior to the meeting was a gun store along the way, where he had purchased the pistol using forged documents.

He made his way back to the rental car, removed the slicker and gloves, and then wadded them in a ball. He drove out of the park area into a nearby residential neighborhood, found a curbside trash bin, and deposited the rolled-up slicker and gloves. Driving a little farther, he deposited the revolver, wrapped in a McDonald's bag, in a suburban strip mall's dumpster and then drove off. Trash collection would occur the next morning and would take care of the garments and revolver, which would never be found. Early morning joggers would find Bradbourne's corpse, another notch in the legacy of the park as a dumping ground for bodies.

Once back in his hotel room, Bart stripped off his clothes and then took a hot shower. After getting dressed, he took the clothes, devoid of any identifying marks, to a vacant laundromat. As a conscientious but somewhat inept bachelor doing laundry—should anyone see him—he deposited the coins for extra wash, added the soap and bleach, and then walked out. The clothes would be considered abandoned.

***

Thursday
October 24, 2013
Tysons Corner, Virginia

As she eased to a stop on the drive of CTC, Gail entered a telephone number into her cell. She quickly checked traffic and pulled out.

"Hello," David Elsworth said, his voice slow and sleep filled.

"Sweet pea! It's Gail. Wake up!"

"Gail *dahling*. What is it?"

"I'll pick you up in thirty minutes."

"It's five forty-six in the morning! Come by at eight?"

"Wake up! We've got work to do."

"Work at this hour? I haven't even had breakfast yet."

"Bradbourne is dead. Now get a move on. You can get a coffee on the way."

"Dead? What happened? Where're we going?"

"I'll tell you in the car. Max is meeting us. We're going to the crime scene. You might need your raincoat."

"Can I just meet you at the office later? I'd rather not see any corpses this early in the morning. In fact, I prefer not to see them at any time."

"Thirty minutes, sweet pea! Be out front of your building, or I will come in and haul your ass out!" Gail ended the call.

Gail, Max, and David were standing near the senator's body and discussing what the Rock Creek Park police had found at the scene when Captain Hadley, DC Metropolitan Police, walked up to them. Hadley said, "Well, good morning, Summers. It's a bit early for you, isn't it?"

"Mornin', Hadley," Gail said. She preferred to eat dead bugs than see Hadley, especially at this hour in the morning. "Don't start with your shit; it's too early."

"Who're your running buddies? This one looks like his scrambled eggs didn't agree with him." Hadley motioned toward David.

"His first homicide," Gail said and then made the introductions.

"That's all right, kid. I puked for two days with my first one. Best thing to do is go straight from here and get a big breakfast—eggs, bacon, biscuits, and gravy. The works."

"Back off, Hadley," Gail said, her tone harsh; she was irritated at his sarcasm.

"I saw the news yesterday where you arrested him." Hadley pointed to the corpse. "You saved the taxpayers a lot of money."

"Just tell me what you have, Hadley."

"Are you finally accepting my invitation to go out with me?"

"Hadley, please. The situation here?"

"The senator was shot once at point-blank range under the chin. Small caliber—probably twenty-two or twenty-five. We'll know later today. Nothing on him except wallet, watch, and the things you would expect to see. He met someone he knew and smoked a cigar, and then whomever he met shot him. The place is clean. The rain didn't help us. So far no witnesses."

"I guess you haven't found the murder weapon?"

"Not yet."

Max withdrew a copy of Madison's photograph from the folder he carried and handed it to Hadley. "It's possible this is the shooter. Looks like a professional job; it fits with his style."

"I guess he's part of the case you had against the senator?" Hadley briefly held his gaze on Max and then shifted to Gail, expecting answers. "What can you tell me about him?"

"Ex-special-forces officer, now a mercenary." Gail brushed her blond hair back.

"Mercenary…nice. Can I keep this?" Hadley tapped the photograph. "Anything I need to know about, Summers?"

"It's yours," replied Gail. "Let me know if you turn up anything on him. I'll let you know if there's anything you need to know about."

"Now about that date, Summers—"

Gail turned and stepped away. She was ready for a coffee. Max and David followed.

"This is Madison's work," Max said after they had walked about five meters away. "He took care of Bradbourne; now he's gone back to ground someplace. I doubt he stayed in the city. David, we know for sure that Madison was in Las Vegas on Sunday evening."

"That's correct," David said, his voice weak.

"If he came here after Bradbourne's arrest and silenced him, Madison probably flew in yesterday. I guess, but he may have gone back to the vicinity of the devices—either last night or this morning."

"That's a good start, more than we had." Gail turned her head to Max and then to David. "You all right, David?"

He nodded.

"I'll get on it as soon as I get to the office," Gail said. She knew David was down for the count.

"When are you going to Las Vegas?" Max asked David. One look at David, and Max knew the sight of the corpse would plague David for a while.

"Tomorrow."

It took Max about forty-five minutes to drive back to CTC. He hadn't been at his desk for more than ten minutes when Margaret slid a chair up next to Max and sat. She said, "I thought you'd want to see this."

"What've you got?" he replied, taking the paper from her.

"I saw this report that listed items being found near the border. The list contains several noteworthy articles," Margaret said as she pointed to several entries. "Prayer mats, Urdu-to-English dictionary and phrase book, Korans, backpacks, underwear, and a book titled *In Memory of Our Martyrs*. This is the most curious." She pointed to the Urdu-to-English dictionary and phrase book.

"A dictionary and phrase book," said Max. "This signifies a more educated person—possibly more of a senior type. This raises a big *why* question. Of course, the owner of this book could be anywhere, but it is worth looking into further. See if you can get the book and have your folks go over it. They might find something of value."

"That's what I thought, too. I've already got the wheels rolling on this."

The phone on Max's desk rang. He looked at Margaret, and she said, "I'll get with you later."

Max nodded to her and then answered the phone, "This is Max."

"This is Danya."

"Hello! What's up? Are we still on for dinner?"

"Sure. I'm looking forward to it. We've received word that one of Dhul Fiqar's lieutenants is on his way to Panama. We lost track of him when we raided their temporary lab in Western Sahara. There's just one problem."

"OK, that's the good news. What's the bad news?"

"We don't know where he is now or when he's going to Panama. Thaddeus is working on it now. If we can find him, we'll follow him to see where he leads us. We've sent the information to the agency. I wanted to give you a heads-up on this."

"Good, thanks. What's his name?"

"Habib Abd al Jabbar."

"I'll pass his name on to the folks here to start working on him. They may have something. Whatever I turn up, I'll pass along to you. Are you getting anything of importance from Maurine Rowen?"

"I think we've got everything she knows. She was Madison's piece and wasn't included in anything. Thaddeus and the agency are discussing the next steps with her. More to follow up on, but I don't think it's of much value."

"Thanks, I'll call you later."

Max lifted the receiver again and then punched the numbers to Margaret's desk.

He gave her the information from Danya and the ISIS bomb-scientist lieutenant's name. "That's right, Habib Abd al Jabbar; supposedly he's heading to Panama."

"I'll see if we have anything on him. Back to you in a few minutes."

While he was waiting for Margaret, Max took the opportunity to update Chugs. Specifically Max gave Chugs the name of the bomb maker's lieutenant and the fact that Abd al Jabbar was headed to Panama. This was a significant piece of information. Also Max believed that Abd al Jabbar might lead them to the SADMs. He was well aware that senior bomb makers normally did very little traveling and would avoid any high-risk areas for fear of being captured. However, Max believed that ISIS might be emboldened by the news and the state of the border and might take the unusual step to send a bomb maker to the United States.

Since the Israelis upset their operation in Western Sahara and captured the two SADMs destined for the remote lab, the terrorists had two inside the United States, waiting for their scientist to take action on them. They had the nuclear devices, and the temptation to move forward to activate the bombs would be too much for ISIS to resist. Logically a skilled scientist would need to be with the devices to bypass the PAL, even after the senior scientist had studied it. Max felt that Abd al Jabbar could be on an errand for Dhul Fiqar to set up a lab in the United States or to investigate the devices in more detail—possibly even test out his theories.

"That's correct, General. Habib Abd al Jabbar. I just have a hunch that he is on his way to the devices. I think that was their plan all along—activate all the devices at the same time."

"All right. I'll get all our assets looking for him," replied the general. "JIATF South is searching all the drug routes; I'll add this to their tasker. The rangers are doing intelligence training in Panama; I'll put them on to Abd al Jabbar. Maybe they can pick up something if the coyotes are going to escort him across the border. It's a long shot, but we've got to cover all bases. What about the FBI? Have they come up with anything yet?"

"They thought the senator was going to be a big help to them, but that ended with his death. Homeland is almost worthless on this."

"I was afraid you were going to say that," Chug said, his tone full of exasperation.

"I am working with some very good people—Margaret; Gail Summers, her analyst; and, of course, Mossad. They all get it! It sure would help if the administration took more interest in this," replied Max.

"Well, they *are* interested but in the wrong way," said the general. "The old man is catching hell; they've got his hands tied."

Max and Chugs continued their conversation for another five minutes, discussing possibilities and options. The more they discussed the situation, the more they came to believe that Abd al Jabbar was already in the United States. As Max ended his call, Margaret entered and sat in the chair next to him.

"Abd al Jabbar," said Margaret as she flopped a folder on the desk in front of him.

Max looked at her and then the folder. Without speaking, he opened it and began scanning the two-page summary. "Pakistani, mother tongue Urdu, Muslim, radicalized. That could be *his* dictionary and phrase book that was found," Max said as he looked up at Margaret.

"I thought the same thing."

"It looks more like he is in the country, but where? Does David have a copy of this?"

"I just sent him one. The ISIS chatter is picking up. Indications are that they are getting ready for something. They've been trying to recruit Americans for a while, but they're really putting emphasis on it now—specifically targeting ex–service members."

"I'll get with David and have him focus on areas around the military installations."

"He's working on it now. Remember, he's heading to Las Vegas tomorrow." Margaret slid her chair back and then stood.

"Right, keep me posted. I've got a phone call to make," said Max. He looked up at her and signaled that he was focused elsewhere. Margaret smiled and walked out of the room.

Max checked his watch and then punched in a series of numbers for Ludwig Steiner in Lucerne, Switzerland. Steiner was a German soldier of fortune, one of the best mercenaries Max had ever known. The two men had worked together on numerous occasions in Iraq, Afghanistan, and a host of other hot spots around the world. Well connected, Steiner could raise a sizeable, well-equipped force in about twenty-four hours. He had reached a level where he could pick and choose jobs.

After a quick round of pleasantries, Max got down to business.

Sensing the shift, Ludwig said, "Hold on for just a minute." To thwart any possible eavesdropping, he turned up the volume on his sound system that was playing Johannes Brahms and then slipped on a set of earphones. Steiner took a sip of Brandy and then said, "What have you got for me?"

"Right now I am looking for information and hoping you can help."

"*Ja*, probably. I heard about the trouble at Balboa. Is that what you are calling me about?"

"Yes, have you heard anything about the devices they took?"

"Well, the Israelis cost Hezbollah and Iran thirty million dollars. The rag heads were more than a little pissed off, as you can imagine."

"Have you heard anything about two in the United States?"

"I did hear that ISIS was looking for a few American ex–service members to join their fight," said Steiner. "You need to get a hold of those things pretty quick. They're planning something big in the United States. That's all I know."

"Are you available for a job?"

"*Ja*, I am available. What do you want me to do?"

"For now, snoop around; see if you can get any information on the devices. We'll go from there."

"*Ja*, sounds easy enough. Information costs a hundred grand. People are more. If we agree, I will send the contract for signature."

"OK, I'll get approval from Chugs."

"Chugs? He's still there? He's got deep pockets. Tell him he still owes me a beer—German. One more thing, I heard that the agency and State Department have put out a reward. I want that, too, if my information leads to their recovery."

"You're getting expensive, Ludwig."

"I have expenses, and dealing with the rag heads can get dangerous in a hurry. *Auf Wiedersehen!*"

"*Auf Wiedersehen!*"

The line went dead, and Max returned the handset to the cradle.

Chapter 11

8:05 a.m.
October 25, 2013
Boulder City, Nevada

Bart had arrived back at the same hotel in Boulder City the previous afternoon. Finished with breakfast, he set his coffee cup down and then looked at his watch. *Where is he?* Bart thought. *He was supposed to meet me over thirty minutes ago. You can't depend on these rag heads for shit.* His coffee emptied, Bart walked out of the dining room, smiled and nodded to the waitress as he passed, and then headed to al-Muhaymin's room.

Bart surveyed the hall to make sure no one would see him enter the room and then gently tapped on the door. No response. He tapped again. The door opened, and al-Muhaymin stood with a towel around his waist, his hair dripping wet. Bart walked past him and saw a woman drying herself in the bathroom. The bleached-blond woman made eye contact with Bart as she dried her bare breasts. She was the same prostitute he had seen al-Muhaymin with several times at the Bellagio Hotel in Las Vegas.

"Hurry up, and clear out of here," Bart said to her, his voice harsh. He then looked at al-Muhaymin. "Get dressed; we've got work to do. You were supposed to meet me over a half hour ago."

"What's your hurry? I've done everything on your list."

Bart turned to the woman and said, "Get a move on! Clear out." He picked up her dress and pitched it to her. She grasped the garment, slipped it over her head, and wiggled it in place. Her eyes signaled her disdain for him. She stumbled, trying to slip into her shoes, and then grasped her purse and stomped to the door. Bart gave her a little shove and closed the door behind her.

"When I agreed to this job," said Bart, "I told you and al-Aqrab there must be secrecy. No bragging, and no one is to say anything until all this is finished. I made it very clear to both of you."

"I didn't tell her a thing."

"Bullshit! You rag heads can't keep a secret for anything. The FBI, military, and no telling who else is looking for us. No more women; keep your mouth shut, or I'm out."

"But, Bart, she—"

"No buts. There'll be plenty of women for you afterward. Besides, you're going to wear out your pecker before you meet Allah. Then what're you going to do with all those virgins?"

"I didn't tell her anything. She's just a piece of meat."

Bart picked up the empty bottle of Glenlivet XXV. Holding it in front of him, Bart said, "You fuckers like to brag. A little booze, and you spill your guts. There's no telling what you bragged to her about. *That piece of meat*, as you called her, could say something and land us in jail or the morgue. Let's go; we've got a lot to do."

Bart's apprehension about working for the ISIS operatives was quickly growing. He believed that al-Muhaymin had probably said something to his prostitute that would compromise what they had planned to do. Bart hadn't noticed any bruises on the woman that would indicate that he liked rough sex and would definitely prompt a call to the police. Something less than rough sex might not cause her to mention it, but if she were questioned about him, his actions might introduce a comment.

Bart wasn't taking any chances. He would free himself as soon as possible and set up al-Muhaymin to be the fall guy.

Two and a half hours later, he and al-Muhaymin pulled out of the slip on Lake Mead in a twenty-one-foot Bayliner powerboat to conduct reconnaissance of Hoover Dam and several nearby coves. The two were dressed much like the other tourists out for a day of sightseeing on the lake—blue jeans, light jacket, and hat. The sun was already high in the sky, but the morning temperature was still cool enough to warrant a jacket. Bart had given al-Muhaymin explicit instructions to remain silent until the boat was well clear of the marina; he didn't want anyone to hear al-Muhaymin's accent.

Bart slightly nudged the throttle forward, and the pitch of the engine changed to a huskier rumbling, signaling the engine was ready for any challenge as the boat slid away from the dock. A number of other boats—ranging from smaller powerboats, pontoon boats, and popular houseboats, as well as the occasional personal watercraft—were already on the lake, making it easy for them to blend in.

Bart headed the boat into Black Canyon, where Hoover Dam sprawled across the Colorado River, to get a firsthand look of the dam and the surrounding terrain. He identified vulnerabilities in the dam security as the boat eased across the water. Retrieving a pad and pencil from his bag, Bart made a terrain sketch of the area and dam and took pictures with his smartphone to supplement his sketch. In the margin, he estimated the distance relative to the dam and canyon walls.

The boat slowly bobbed across the water from one side of the canyon to the other as Bart and al-Muhaymin discussed the dam, approach, and metal halide lights. They stayed outside the marker buoys but close enough to get a good look at the steel-wire net draped across the lake three hundred meters in front of the dam, which prevented anything from getting any closer. Enough pictures were taken and the sketch completed by the time the boat reached the other side. Bart shoved the throttle forward; the bow raised on the water as the engine raced and propelled the craft faster.

For the next several hours, they explored numerous coves in Boulder Basin on the west side of the lake. They started with the closest coves to the dam and then worked farther out, looking for a secluded spot out of sight of the watchful eyes of the Hoover Dam police. Bart sought the cove that provided the most cover for an approach to the dam. It had to have a suitable place to land a small boat without damaging it and road access of some type.

The dam police, a federal police force actually belonging to the Bureau of Reclamation, was a highly trained organization and employed surveillance capabilities to protect the dam. Bart anticipated that the authorities would be on an elevated alert, since the dam was a national landmark. However, no facility was completely secure; Bart would exploit those vulnerabilities in their defense to make his plan work. Finally a suitable cove was identified a little farther from the dam than Bart preferred but still close enough. Buying supplies and making a trial run were the last tasks to accomplish; those would happen in the next few days.

Bart and al-Muhaymin were back at the hotel by late afternoon.

"Meet me in my room in about an hour and a half," Bart said as he paused and looked at al-Muhaymin. "I have several things for you to do."

"I will be there," al-Muhaymin said, and then he inserted the key card into the lock and stepped into his room.

Bart entered his suite, latched the door, and then switched on the television to get the latest news. Seated at the desk, he looked over his sketch and then to the pictures on his smartphone and then back to the sketch. He repeated the process several times and made additional notes. Satisfied, Bart laid the drawing aside and then began making a list of items al-Muhaymin was to buy.

After his meeting with al-Muhaymin, Bart planned to drive to Los Angeles to make contact with two operatives who were to handle the Port of Los Angeles operation. While there, Bart would make reconnaissance of the port to decide on the best course of action. Leaving al-Muhaymin in Boulder City and unchaperoned made Bart uneasy, but he didn't have any alternative. Al-Muhaymin had several tasks to complete before Bart returned from Los Angeles, and one of those tasks was to meet with four ISIS operatives the next day.

As instructed, al-Muhaymin arrived in Bart's room and sat on the couch. Bart turned the volume up on the television before he spoke.

"Here are the items you are to buy," Bart told the man. He handed him the list. "Look it over, and let me know if you have any questions." Bart eased into the chair across the coffee table from al-Muhaymin.

"What is all this shit?" al-Muhaymin asked, looking up from the list.

"It's fishing tackle and camping gear. Get everything on the list."

"I thought—"

"I do the thinking on this. Just buy all that stuff. When will the diving gear I told you to buy from outside the United States arrive?"

"Tomorrow."

"Good. Check it over to ensure that everything arrived and nothing is damaged. The four operatives you are meeting with tomorrow, tell me about them." Bart's eyes remained fixed on al-Muhaymin as he listened intently.

"All four are from our cells in the United States. Two are Americans, one is Arab, and the other is Syrian. The Americans and the Syrian are qualified divers, as you requested. The Americans are ex-military."

"Good." Bart scribbled on his notepad. "Get those items on the list. You and the two Americans need to get a fishing license. Contact al-Aqrab and have him send us two sniper teams. We'll get the arms locally but will need money to make the purchase. When I return, we'll buy the weapons, so get the money right away. Also, collect all the cell phones, thumb drives, iPods, and any other recording devices from these guys. Take the batteries out of everything."

His voice stern, Bart continued, "Yours too. We'll get new phones. I'll be back from Los Angeles Monday afternoon. Keep a low profile; stay away from women and booze. Understand?" His brow furrowed, Bart glared into al-Muhaymin's eyes.

Al-Muhaymin nodded. "I know, Bart." He shifted his weight and grinned.

Bart didn't believe al-Muhaymin for a minute. He just hoped that there would be no trouble and prayed that al-Muhaymin wouldn't start bragging.

***

Saturday
October 26, 2013
CTC
Tysons Corner, Virginia

"Max," Margaret said as she slid her chair closer to the conference table. "I just got word that Abd al Jabbar's fingerprints were confirmed to be on the dictionary and phrase book."

"Damn! Our bomb-maker lieutenant is in the United States already." Max shifted in his chair and then rubbed his forehead. "Anything else?"

"Lots of Internet chatter about the United States drowning in the blood of its infidel citizens. We've had several cases of people claiming to know about ISIS attacking the United States. Nothing solid yet."

"I haven't seen Gail. Where is she?" Max's eyes darted around the room.

"She's checking out a couple of leads," replied Margaret. "David discovered something about a car-bomb plot for New York, and the FBI has picked up several young women who are supposedly recruiting Americans for ISIS. David and Gail have updated the FBI field offices and police departments in the major cities across the country. The bigger problem is that the president doesn't believe there's a threat to the United States and thinks such talk is overblown. Of course, Homeland Security is following his line. And the State Department, well, they're out to lunch as usual. That's about it so far."

"Great! The southern border is wide open, and foreigners are pouring across. It's business as usual." Max closed his eyes and shook his head. "I got a call from Ludwig Steiner just before you came over here. He heard through his contacts that a Pakistani is on his way to the United States to take part in an attack on the mainland. Ludwig is going to try to pick up his trail; it's a long shot. ISIS has stepped up its recruiting efforts. That's all Ludwig knows so far. He's still snooping around. Did anything turn up on the person who provided the tip of red mercury crossing the border last week?"

"In a word, no." Margaret shook her head and twirled her glasses in her hand. "They did identify him, but he's nowhere to be found."

"Damn it! We're sitting ducks," said Max. "Something has to turn up on these guys. Has Dawn discovered anything out of the ordinary from her contacts at the major police departments?"

Margaret rolled her eyes and wrinkled up the corner of her mouth. "Nothing yet. She just flits around mostly. I don't think she'd recognize anything unusual even if it hit her in the face." Margaret gave a slight shake of her head.

"Danya is following up on a lead. The Israelis are very serious about this; they're leaving her in the United States for now." Max scrunched his face. "ISIS will tip their hand pretty soon. I just hope we have enough time to react when they do."

"You and me both," Margaret said as she stood and then walked out of the room.

***

October 26, 2013
Port of Los Angeles, California

For over an hour, Bart cruised along the streets within the complex of the Port of Los Angeles, getting a feel for security, traffic flows, and potential places for the SADM. As he paralleled the main channel, Bart meandered along the streets and gazed at the ships, massive cranes, and landmarks as any tourist might do.

Along South Harbor Boulevard, Bart checked his rearview mirror and saw a Los Angeles Port Police vehicle behind him. *Don't want to get a ticket*, Bart thought as he focused back on the street. *Am I in your way or of interest to you?* He turned the car into the parking lot for the USS *Iowa* battleship as though he were going to visit the massive vessel. The patrol car sped on past as he turned in.

Bart sighed and relaxed. When the car stopped, he got out and started looking over the ship to ensure that the police were not interested in him. Admiring the battleship and watching visitors enter the museum, Bart felt a tinge of patriotism and remorse for what he was about to do. But the money was too good to deny.

Bart continued his reconnaissance of the port for a few more hours. He had developed a good sense of the sprawling port facility and had found countless suitable places where the bomb could achieve its desired effect; he would repeat the recon process again that night. However, Sunday and Monday wouldn't be as leisurely. Those two days Bart would use to orient the two operatives with the port and instruct them on what they were to do and where to place the nuke. Satisfied with his daylight progress, Bart headed the car back to the Crown Plaza Los Angeles Harbor Hotel, where he would meet the two Pakistani operatives activated by al-Aqrab to emplace the SADM at the port.

***

Saturday Afternoon
October 26, 2013
Bellagio Hotel
Las Vegas, Nevada

Al-Muhaymin had rendezvoused with the four ISIS operatives—two Americans, one Arab, and one Syrian—and got them checked into the Bellagio Hotel. Their rooms were well stocked with liquor and cigars. He said to the others, "I will need to collect your cell phones and recording devices, iPods, thumb drives, or any other recording device."

"What *da* fuck for?" said the muscular black American as he stepped close to al-Muhaymin. The others looked on.

"One of our rules. If you don't like it, you may leave now."

His face puffed out, the black man glared at al-Muhaymin. Then he relaxed.

"Other questions? If you want anything, let me know," al-Muhaymin said, eager to start their weekend party. "Monday morning we start to work. But until then, enjoy yourselves. Come to my room at seven, and we will eat. Bring your cell phones and recording devices. I will have other treats for you."

"Women?" The Syrian asked what the others were thinking.

"I have taken care of everything," said al-Muhaymin as he displayed a broad smile and then walked away.

He treated his newly acquired Muslim brothers as long-lost relatives and catered to their every desire. The food arrived in al-Muhaymin's suite, where his guests were already enjoying the liquor. The women would arrive later. Smoke from Cuban cigars filled the air and challenged the ventilation system. They attacked the smorgasbord as though they were at a desert campfire, piling their plates with food, slopping it everywhere.

At eight thirty, their dessert arrived—four very attractive and very expensive women led by al-Muhaymin's bleached-blond love interest, Candy. As they entered, each of the women surveyed the situation and men. The women's expressions revealed that their tricks were not the class they expected. However, they were professionals and knew how to handle them. After all, they were paid well and anticipated a nice tip for a job well done.

None of the men saw the women's expressions—partly because of the Glenlivet and partly because of their hourglass figures. Each of the women quickly paired up with her target, and in no time, the crowd in al-Muhaymin's room dwindled to just al-Muhaymin and Candy.

The couples settled in their respective rooms for a weekend of passion—at least that's what was supposed to happen. At eleven thirty, al-Muhaymin heard loud voices, a woman's scream, and then a crash. He threw the sheet back, covered his nude body with a robe, and then stepped into the hall. Several doors down from his room came loud voices again.

"The Syrian's room," he said to himself. He hadn't taken more than three steps when the door opened, and the prostitute staggered out. The woman's lip was bleeding, and her eye was red. Al-Muhaymin moved to help her up and was joined by his love muffin.

The prostitute yelled at the closed door, "You're too kinky for me!" Her voice filled the hallway as she straightened her clothes. "He's a freak." Tears streamed down her red face.

Candy took the shaken woman back into al-Muhaymin's room, while he went to talk to the Syrian.

Al-Muhaymin grabbed the Syrian and pushed him back into the room. "What's the matter with you?" he said as soon as the door latched shut. "There is to be no trouble. You were told that."

"She is nothing," said the Syrian, his jaw tight and fists clenched. "She was to fulfill my desires. She is a bitch. A dog." He spat to the side.

At that moment a knock came from the door.

"Be quiet. I'll handle this," al-Muhaymin said in a low voice, glaring into the man's eyes. He turned back to the door and opened it, revealing a uniformed policeman and a man wearing a polo shirt and slacks.

"Mr. Jones?" the man in the polo shirt said. "I'm Tom Buckner, hotel security. This is Officer Ortiz."

"I am Haris Jamil," al-Muhaymin said, his tone cordial and his brow slightly dipped in apparent confusion. "This is my cousin, Sol Jones. What can we do for you?"

"We have several complaints of loud noise and a woman screaming. We'd like to come in and look around," Officer Ortiz said as he walked past the two men.

"Oh, that was just a lover's spat. Everything is OK." Al-Muhaymin shifted his stance; he knew that his response hadn't worked.

"Where's the woman?" Buckner's tone was stern.

"She's just fine. Everything is all right—"

"I want to talk with the woman. Where is she?" Buckner's eyes shifted between al-Muhaymin and the Syrian.

"She is in my room, talking with my fiancée. I'll get her. You will see that everything is fine." With Officer Ortiz, Buckner, and the Syrian in tow, al-Muhaymin marched out of the room and down the hall. *Mr. Jamil* slipped his key card into the lock and opened the door. The three men paraded in behind him.

"Well, hello, Ruby," Buckner said as he saw the woman applying makeup in the bathroom."

"Buckner," she replied.

"Are you with Mr. Jones?" Buckner motioned to the Syrian.

Ruby nodded.

Buckner then looked into the rest of the room. "Evening, Candy," he said as he saw her seated in a chair, smoking a cigarette. "You all right?"

Candy nodded.

"Did he do that to you?" Officer Ortiz asked, pointing to Ruby's cut lip and red, swollen eye.

"There's no problem, and no, I don't want to press charges," said Ruby, her tone harsh, as she glared at the Syrian.

"OK, Ruby, get your stuff and clear out," Buckner said.

Officer Ortiz glowered at both men. "Mr. Jones, if there is any more trouble, we'll be back, and you'll be out," he said. "That goes for you too, Mr. Jamil. Got it?"

"Yes, sir," Mr. Jamil said, displaying a toothy grin, and nodded.

Officer Ortiz and Tom Buckner waited in the hall outside the Syrian's room, while Ruby collected her things. They followed her as she tramped toward the elevator.

Chapter 12

9:05 p.m.
October 28, 2013
Boulder City, Nevada

Bart entered the hotel they had been staying in the last several days and looked forward to a drink and a good night's rest. The trip to the Port of Los Angeles had been long and tiring. As he turned and stepped down the hall, a faint but distinct heavy, sweet odor captured his attention. As Bart approached al-Muhaymin's door, the odor became stronger, and he could hear the TV blaring from inside the room. He knocked on the door.

"Son of a bitch," Bart said under his breath and then knocked again. The door opened, and the stench of marijuana and then al-Muhaymin greeted him. A look of surprise covered his face, and then his usual toothy grin appeared.

"What the fuck are you doing?" Bart's voice was harsh, his eyes squinted, and his red face contorted. Bart closed the door as he stepped inside the room.

Displaying a toothy grin, al-Muhaymin, said, "Bart! Glad you are back." His words were slurred.

Bart looked around the room. An empty bottle of Glenlivet XXV lay on the floor by the coffee table, and a half-empty bottle sat on the dresser next to a nearly empty bottle of Crown Royal Reserve. Two roaches smoldered in the full ashtray on the table. Fast-food wrappers, soda cans, and pieces of food were strewn about. Empty pizza cartons were on the counter. Two men, one white and one black, sat slumped in the wingback chairs opposite the couch. Two other men with dark complexions, whom Bart presumed were the Arab and the Syrian, sat on either end of the couch.

Their eyes drooped. Both men, in their early twenties, had dark, curly beards. Their faded, dark-cotton pants were past due for the laundry.

The white man's disheveled clothes matched his brown hair and scraggly beard. He drooled from the corner of his mouth and farted. His well-worn blue jeans were split open at the knees. As he lay against the side of the chair, the left sleeve of his polo shirt was bunched up, revealing a skull and crossbones tattoo on his shoulder.

The black man wasn't any better. His long, bleached-out dreadlocks spread across his face and disappeared into his curly black beard. A dingy T-shirt stretched around his burly chest. Various tattoos spread across his arms and exposed shoulder. Both men appeared to be in their midtwenties.

Bart motioned with his hand and commanded, "This is a dump; air it out. Wake those guys up, and get this place cleaned up. I told you no booze and a low profile. It's a wonder the police haven't been called."

"We were just having a little welcoming party for our brothers," al-Muhaymin said, ill at ease, as he stepped to the end chair and rousted up the black man and then nudged the white man. He shook him awake.

"Huh, what? The drowsy man looked around and then sat forward and rubbed his face. "Yeah." His mouth slurred the word. He sat upright, yawned, and reached for the glass of booze that sat on the coffee table in front of him. He farted again.

Al-Muhaymin shook both the Arab and the Syrian and then kicked their feet.

"Move your asses! Clean up this pigsty," Bart commanded. His face was florid, and his words were crisp.

"Who *da* fuck are you, *maaan*?" The black man's words were slurred. He stood, and a knife appeared in his hand.

"I'm the man you work for and probably your worst nightmare. Either use that knife or get rid of it. What'll it be?" Bart stared into the man's glassy eyes.

The black man hesitated and then dropped the knife on the coffee table.

Bart nodded.

"Fuck you!" the white man said and then leaned back in the chair.

Bart knocked the drink from his hand, and the booze flew across the room. "I said move."

Grumbling, the five men stood and began to comply with Bart's orders. Attempting to get back in Bart's good graces, al-Muhaymin coached the others and turned on the exhaust fans.

"Y'all get this place squared away and then get to bed," Bart said, his words sharp. "Take a shower, and shave the beards. Meet me for breakfast at seven in the morning."

Then, looking at the black man, Bart said, "Cut the dreadlocks."

The black man started to speak but didn't.

"Everyone is to get a haircut and new clothes," Bart continued. "We must look like mainstream Americans so as not to call attention to ourselves. We are going to look and act like everyday Middle Americans." Bart scanned the men. "You got that? Leave now if you don't."

The men nodded.

"Don't be late in the morning," Bart said in a stern tone and then left the room, closing the door behind him.

The next morning all five men arrived before the designated time. Bart, already seated, watched the men straggle in and take their seats. Al-Muhaymin motioned for each one of them to sit around the table as they entered. Although no other guests had arrived for breakfast, Bart had arranged for a table in a secluded portion of the restaurant for the meeting and meal. As each man emerged in the doorway, Bart noted his appearance. They were bathed and cleanly shaven, except for the black man, who was the last to enter and had not shaved or cut his dreadlocks. He wore the same T-shirt and ragged jeans from the night before. It was his obvious challenge to Bart's authority, which Bart took note of but did not mention.

"First thing this morning, get haircuts and then buy new clothes—jeans, sport shirts, and running shoes," Bart said in a low voice. He looked each of them in the eye. "We must blend in with the rest of the people. From now on, we're just on a fishing trip. Speak only English. We have a lot to do. Get back here as soon as you can. Have breakfast and then get going. Each of you will be given an alias. No Muslim names.

"From now on, you are Americans. Your names will be simple names, something like Gary or George, on your identification. Al-Muhaymin will take your pictures for the identification and provide you with a few basic documents with your alias. Get rid of everything that identifies your real name and address. Burn it. Have you all turned in your cell phone and recording devices to al-Muhaymin?" Bart asked, holding his gaze on each man briefly. He already knew the answer.

All but the black man nodded. He sat defiantly, challenging Bart.

Bart held his steely eyes firmly on the black man. Finally the man produced his cell phone and flipped it onto the table.

No one spoke for the remainder of the meal. Bart sipped his coffee and watched as they left the table, one by one. Al-Muhaymin slid his chair back to get up, and Bart placed his hand on his arm, signaling for him to wait. As soon as the black man, the last to leave the table, left the room, Bart said in a low voice, "Get rid of him. See if you can get a replacement."

Al-Muhaymin simply nodded. "A key to the house I rented," he said and handed Bart the key. "It is secluded like you wanted."

"Good. I'm going over there to scout out the area and access to the lake. As soon as y'all get back here, check out and then meet me at the house. I'll expect you by noon."

Al-Muhaymin leaned into Bart and said in a low voice, “Al-Aqrab called me this morning,”

“I’m listening.”

“We are to expect a couple more guests and equipment this evening.”

Bart nodded. “OK. Keep a fire under those guys’ asses, and don’t get sidetracked—haircuts and new clothes. Get moving; we have a lot to do.”

Bart stood and was followed by al-Muhaymin. Bart started to leave and then stopped, turned to him, and said in a low voice, “I want to make a walk-through rehearsal this afternoon.”

“We will be ready,” al-Muhaymin said, with an ice-cold expression.

***

9:17 a.m.
October 29, 2013
CTC
Tysons Corner, Virginia

Margaret slid a paper across the conference table to Max. “David sent me this report on Las Vegas.”

He read the summary and then looked up at Gail from across the conference table. “Have you seen this?”

“I saw it. Usual Vegas stuff. Lots of drunks, loud parties, and prostitutes. Sin City—remember?”

Max scanned the notes and then looked back to Gail and then Margaret. His expression displayed his curiosity. Max asked, “What about this item, the disturbance at the Bellagio Hotel? A prostitute was escorted out of the hotel. Anything on the two men, Haris Jamil and Sol Jones? He didn’t provide a very good description.”

"David hasn't found anything on the two names," Margaret replied. "He thinks they're bogus. That happens regularly in Vegas. Men and women sometimes go to Vegas without their significant other to party, and they run a bit wild, especially the younger ones. Know what I mean?"

Margaret's left eyebrow rose as she looked over her glasses. A slight smirk appeared on her face. "I wouldn't get too excited about it, but I told David to dig deeper with the hotel security guy. And to send us a better description."

Max tapped his notepad with the pencil. "That's too coincidental. I think there could be more to the story of just kicking out a prostitute; it could be who we are looking for. Muslims tend to go wild when they get out of the Mideast. They always want to drive around in fancy cars and booze it up. I'd like to talk with that prostitute."

Gail wrote on her notepad and then said, "I'll send David a note and let him know."

"Anything from the Israelis?" Margaret asked, fingering her delicate gold necklace.

"I haven't heard from my contact," Max said. "I've got a call into them. I should've heard something by now."

"Let me know as soon as you do," Margaret replied, lowering her hand.

"Ludwig Steiner confirmed that the Pakistani he had heard was traveling to the United States is Abd al Jabbar," Max said, marking on his pad and then shooting a glance at the two women. "ISIS is keeping guards around him. Ludwig tracked the Pakistani to the US border in Nogales, where he lost him. He's trying to pick up the trail again."

Max paused and then looked at Gail. "Pass Ludwig's information to David. Tell him to pay attention to any Middle Eastern men. Just keep on the lookout and then let us know. Don't follow them. Margaret, have you heard from Dawn? Where is she?" Max's brow dipped as he looked up.

Margaret rolled her eyes and then said, "She's in New York. Remember the report last week, where David learned of a car-bomb plot in New York City and several women were supposedly recruiting Americans for ISIS? Dawn went up there to coordinate the efforts. She's convinced that's where the terrorists are going to strike."

With a red face and harsh tone, Gail said, "I told that blond-headed bimbo that the car-bomb story was one of many that New York receives all the time. David and I checked it out. The FBI and police are watching, but no other evidence has turned up. However, one of the women who are supposedly recruiting Americans for ISIS did say that she recruited two ex–service members, one white and the other black. She didn't know where they were sent. The New York office is still working on her."

With a serious expression, Max said, "Did they get names on the ex–service members?"

Gail shook her head, wrinkled up the corner of her mouth, and said, "Not yet."

"As soon as you get names on those guys, get their service records. I want to review them. What else you got?"

Gail scribbled on her notepad and then continued, "Dawn is checking in regularly. A friend of mine there told me that she is being a pain in the ass. I asked him to keep her, but his price was too steep."

"Let her stay up there, but if she turns up any hard facts or more on the Americans, let me know."

Back at his desk, Max had barely settled into his chair when the phone rang. "This is Max," he said into the receiver.

"Thaddeus," the voice said. "I got your message."

"Have you turned up anything?"

"Danya has a lead. She's on her way to Los Angeles. She's on to a couple of Pakistani men who might be involved with the SADMs. I sent a report over to the CIA."

"Did she say where in Los Angeles she was going?" Max asked.

"Everything she had is in the report, but it isn't much. The two men were to meet their contact at the port. She's checking it out."

"It's logical the port would be a target," said Max. "It is big, open, and high value. Did she have much confidence in her information?"

"She was fairly confident."

"I may go out there. I want to have a talk with a woman in Las Vegas who may know something. Then I'll head on over to Los Angeles. I'll keep you posted. Let Danya know that I'll be heading her way and want to link up with her."

"OK, I'll get the word to her. Talk to you soon."

Max pressed the button to end the call and then dialed Gail.

"Summers," the voice said.

"Max. I may have a lead in Los Angeles. And I wanna talk with that prostitute in Vegas and then go to LA. Wanna go?"

"Hell, I thought you were going to ask me out tonight. Sin City is even better. Do I need to bring anything besides my handcuffs?"

"Your badge and Glock."

"Oh, work. When do we leave?"

"Alert David and tell him we're heading that way. Have him set up an interview with the prostitute. I'd like to be on the morning flight to Vegas."

"I'll give him a heads-up."

"One more thing. The cell-phone number Maurine Rowen used to call Madison at the airport last week—any luck with the collect on that number?"

"Nothing. It looks like he may have trashed it."

"He's more than likely got another one. Tell your folks to keep an eye open for his name to pop up again."

***

October 29, 2013
Rental House
Boulder City, Nevada

The rental house—a large, five-bedroom, southwestern-style house with privacy fence surrounding the perimeter—was located on the edge of the city in a middle-income neighborhood. The property had easy access to the main roads leading to the national recreation area. The spacious residence fit Bart's requirements very well.

Bart pinned large maps of the lake and dam on the wall of the great room over the garage, which he turned into his operations and briefing room. Data on the lake level was posted next to one map and an article from the paper describing the fourteen-year drought that had made the water levels drop historic lows—more than 130 feet low.

Bart leaned back in the chair and stretched and then checked his watch. The numbers displayed 12:07 p.m. Hearing the sound of a car door outside, Bart stood and stepped to the window overlooking the driveway below. Al-Muhaymin and only three men emerged from the Lexus and headed to the front door. From his vantage point, Bart could see that the men had complied with his instructions: each had neat, short-cropped hair and wore sport shirts, light jackets, and jeans. They carried bulging plastic bags from several clothing retailers in the area, obviously changes of clothing.

They looked like average Middle Americans, Bart thought. *They'll blend in very well.*

Al-Muhaymin led them into the house and gave them a quick tour and then ushered them upstairs where Bart was waiting.

"Pull up a chair, and sit where you can see the map," Bart said, motioning to the map on the wall. Bart leaned close to al-Muhaymin, as the last man was far enough away so as not to hear him, and said, "Any trouble with the other one?"

"No trouble," al-Muhaymin said, his tone apathetic. "It will be a long time before his body is found."

Bart's brow furrowed and, in a harsh tone, said, "I didn't mean for you to kill him."

Bart stepped back in front of the seated men and methodically began to explain their specific duties but not the exact details of the mission. For the time being, as he didn't trust them to keep quiet about what they were doing, all he told them was that they were to look as if they were going night fishing.

"I'll rent a boat, and then four of us will motor to a secluded beach al-Muhaymin and I have selected. We will rendezvous with a SUV and transfer some equipment to the boat, and then al-Muhaymin, the Syrian, you," he said, pointing to the American, "and I will depart in the boat and return to the beach several hours later. When we return to the beach, the SUV will pick us up and bring us back here."

Bart paused. "We're one American short to drive the SUV. Do we have a replacement for the man who left us?" Bart asked, looking at al-Muhaymin.

"Not yet," he replied.

"Push them. We need a replacement right away."

"We could get someone local just to drive the SUV, pay well, and say nothing."

"Not an option. Keep trying to get a replacement through your channels."

Al-Muhaymin nodded. "I will need to set up a meeting with our contact in Las Vegas."

Bart studied al-Muhaymin for a moment and then nodded. "There and back. Make it quick."

Bart gave them a time sequence for each event and their assigned locations for each minute. He repeated the series several times until all the men responded correctly with what they were to do and where they were supposed to be. As an added security step, Bart wouldn't tell them the exact plan until the last minute.

When all the men responded correctly, their next step was an actual walk-through of Bart's scenario during that afternoon while there was still daylight. They made a recon of the route and made notes of the speed limits, turns, landmarks, and time to reach each designated point. The loss of the black American hampered Bart's planning rehearsal. He would make a decision about how to proceed after he found out how long it would take for al-Aqrab to provide a replacement.

***

2:36 p.m.
October 30, 2013
FBI Las Vegas Field Division
Las Vegas, NV

For over an hour, Ruby, the prostitute involved in the incident at the Bellagio, had been questioned in the interview room. Up to that point, she had been tight-lipped and had refused to answer any of the various questions put to her by Gail or Max. Tom Buckner, hotel security manager at the Bellagio, had also been unable to coerce her into providing information. Officer Ortiz stood silently by the door.

"Tom, would you and Officer Ortiz please step outside for a few minutes?" Gail asked, her voice calm.

As soon as the door latched clicked, Gail leaned close to Ruby's face; Gail's demeanor changed. Her eyes narrowed, and her voice was harsh. "OK, bitch, I'm tired of fucking around with you. Out with it. Who was the trick you were with? I want to know everything he said. Everything."

"Listen," Ruby replied, "I told you he said his name was Sol Jones. He got too kinky for me, and I left. That was about it. What the fuck is going on here? I've been rousted before but not like this."

"You left out a few minor details," Gail said as she glared at Ruby. "Your black eye and split lip, for instance. You'd better start providing me some detail, or I'll fuck up that pretty face some more. Got that?"

Ruby's mouth wrinkled up, and her face was florid when she said, "Bitch! What's this all about?"

Gail slammed her hand on the table and said in a stern tone, "Damn it! Who was he? What did he say?"

"Why should I help you? What's in it for me?"

"We need your help, Ruby," Max said, looking deep into her eyes. "It's very important. We'll keep you out of this if you help us. If you don't help us, you'll be in the middle, and your name will be all over the place. We'll spread the word around that you are providing us a list of all your tricks, along with anything else we can come up with. There'll be a few new charges as well."

"You asshole! What gives?" Ruby asked. Having played this game before, Ruby wanted something in return. She was not willing to tell all just yet.

Max's eyes narrowed as he stared into her eyes.

"He said his name was Sol Jones, a Syrian," Ruby said. "Lived in the United States for the last year or so. He mostly bragged a lot, trying to impress me. I didn't particularly like him, but his money was very good. Didn't pay any attention to what he said."

"Why was he in Las Vegas?" Gail asked, steely eyed.

"He said he was working for his cousin and starting a new job, making a lot of money."

"His cousin. Would that be Haris Jamil?"

"Yeah."

Stone faced, Max asked, "What was the job?"

"Hell, I don't know. I wasn't paying any attention to him. Then he started doing that Muslim thing—washing and Islamic prayer ritual—and I got scared. I just wanted out of there."

"Where was the job?" Gail asked, her brow furrowed.

"He didn't get that far."

"Was there anyone else there besides Jones and Jamil?" Gail asked.

"Yeah, when we arrived, four other men were in the room. They were drinking Glenlivet, as if it was punch. We all had a few drinks and a joint. I needed it."

"Who were the other men?" Max asked.

"I don't know who they were, no names. Two were Americans, one white, and the other black. The other two had dark complexions. Middle Eastern, I think. Frankly they all needed a bath and clean clothes."

Max shot a look at Gail when Ruby mentioned the two Americans.

Ruby, her guard up, anticipated that the time for a deal was close; she went on to provide descriptions of the two Americans as Max wrote down the details on his notepad. He placed a star by the information on two Americans. Ruby was reluctant at first, but after another round of Gail's encouragement, Ruby provided the names of the other women. They would be interviewed as well. The bits and pieces were finally starting to materialize.

Max withdrew a copy of the eight-year-old army photograph of Bart Madison from his briefcase and then slid it in front of Ruby. "Was he one of the men, or have you seen him?" Max tapped the photograph.

She looked down at the photograph and then back at Max. "No, he wasn't the white man," she said. "I don't think I've seen him."

"Are you sure?" Max pressed. "Take another look. His hair could be longer; he could be a little older, and he would be dressed differently."

"Not a bad-looking guy, though. I know he wasn't the white guy in the room." Ruby paused and slumped slightly.

Max looked up at Gail and then back at Ruby. "We need to find this guy."

"If word gets out I helped you," said Ruby, "I'm finished in this town."

"OK, what do you want?" Max asked.

"Money and out of this town."

"You little bitch. I—" said Gail.

Max held up his hand. "We might be able to work out a deal if you level with us. I need more to go on. Agent Summers and I'll see what we can come up with."

Ruby gave a slight nod.

"Back to the photo. Would you have seen him at the Bellagio?" asked Max.

"No, I don't think so. Let me think about him for a while; I might remember. I don't usually pay much attention, unless they have lots of money," Ruby said, and then she glanced at Gail and then back at Max. Ruby knew they understood that she wouldn't provide any more information without an agreement.

At 7:15 p.m. Officer Ortiz escorted the last prostitute Ruby had named into the interview room. Like the others, she protested the entire time. As anticipated, none of the girls agreed to answer any questions.

"OK, Candy, we'll let you go." Max's tone was calm and gentle. "Think about what we've said. Ruby had a rough night at the hotel. All we want is a little more information about who these men were and what they talked about. We'll keep you and the other ladies' names confidential if you will help us."

"I'll think about it."

"Take another look at the photograph," Max said as he tapped Madison's picture. Max knew that Candy was holding back on him. "Are you sure you haven't seen him?"

"Can I go now?" Candy held her gaze on Max.

"You can go." Max's tone had a hint of weariness. "I can help you if you will help us. Think about it."

Candy stood and gazed steadily for a moment and then nodded.

Chapter 13

11:18 a.m.
October 31, 2013
CTC
Tysons Corner, Virginia

"This is Margaret," she said as she placed the receiver to her ear.

"Margaret *dahling*," came the voice.

"Morning, David. Whatcha got?"

"I sent you my latest report. Just wanted to give you a heads-up. Some progress on my end. I got word of a possible weapons buy; I'm meeting with them later."

"That's not procedure, David. You are not supposed to get close. Remember what Max told you."

"Not to worry, *dahling*. I have everything in the report. This is a low-threat meeting. It's probably a dead end, but I need to check it out."

"David! Have you talked to Gail about this?"

"Gotta go. Check you later."

The line went dead.

Margaret paused and then dialed Gail's number.

"That little shit!" Gail said, her tone harsh. "I just talked to him last night, and he didn't say anything about a meeting. Let me know as soon as you hear any more from him. We drove over to LA last night."

"I thought you'd want to know," said Margaret. "Do you need me to do anything?"

"Not for now. I'll get you an update soon."

The call ended, and Margaret made a note in her file to expect another update from David by the time she returned in the morning.

***

October 31, 2013
Long Beach Museum of Art
Long Beach, California

Danya nibbled on banana bread pudding as she sat at a table with an umbrella and looked over the bay. The sun was bright in the blue morning sky, and a pleasant breeze danced about. As she glanced around, she saw Max, followed by Gail, entering the patio. Danya scanned the area once again. Satisfied that no one was near, she gave a nod for the two arrivals to join her. Max and Gail took seats at the table as though they were old friends. The patio behind the museum provided a relaxing atmosphere; it was a popular place.

After placing drinks on the table, the waiter stepped away, and Danya got down to business. As she sipped her cappuccino, she began to say, "This place is a mess. Drugs and aliens crossing the border are making things difficult. It's damned hard to keep up. But I've got a lead on a guy who wants to buy weapons. It could be gangs, drugs, or our target. The Sinaloa Cartel is operating freely across the border and even recruiting inside the United States. They're increasing their meth shipments. I also hear that ISIS is crossing into the United States. The lax security is their golden opportunity. It's taking a lot of time and resources to sift through this crap. Just don't know."

Danya wrinkled up the corner of her mouth and gave a slight shake of her head. "It doesn't look good."

Gail leaned into Danya. "Want me to bring in the FBI and DEA on this?"

"Not yet," said Danya. "If it's one of our targets, I want him. If the United States picks him up, he'll clam up and be right back on the streets. I'm not interested in the drugs or aliens, just the nuclear weapons. We gotta get them back before they figure out how to bypass the PAL. Once they solve that problem, our stockpiles—yours and ours—will become even bigger targets."

"This could get dangerous real quick. I'll go with you to the meeting," Max said as he shot a look at Gail and then at Danya.

"I was hoping you'd say that," Danya said and nodded. "I want to know about these guys, and if they're our targets, we need to be able to talk to 'em."

"Backup?" Gail asked, looking at Max and then Danya.

"They'll spot reinforcements before you can spit. Just the two of us," Danya said. She took another sip of her drink and looked over the area again.

"Where's the meeting?" Gail asked. Her brow dipped, and her face was serious. "I think you should have some backup."

"No. Too many people. A vacant warehouse not far from here. Ten thirty."

"Who'll be at the meeting?" Gail asked.

"Aside from my contact, two Pakistani guys. We'll qualify them tonight. If they aren't our targets, you can have 'em," Danya said, looked at Gail, and then lifted the cup to her lips. Gail did the same.

"What's the layout of the warehouse?" Max asked, holding his cup, his expression serious.

Danya withdrew a pen from her purse and slid a napkin close to her. Within a short time, a sketch emerged of the warehouse and its immediate area. Danya identified key features: the streets, blind spots, and potential choke points. Once the sketch was completed, Danya explained the concept for the meeting. Max interjected a couple of times and then made suggestions.

Danya continued, "We'll set the deal and then arrange for a meeting to make the exchange." Danya paused and looked at Gail. "Then we pick 'em up. I don't want them in police or FBI custody."

Gail started to speak.

Danya read her intentions. "My way or no way."

Gail nodded.

I'm not staying out of this one, Gail thought. *Just hang back a little.*

***

10:20 p.m.
Vacant Warehouse
Port of Los Angeles, California

Scanning for any threat, Max and Danya cautiously entered the empty building through the personnel door. The expanse was a shell—dark and musty. A conical industrial light near the entrance interrupted the blackness. Anyone standing beyond the meager cone of light could not be seen. Max and Danya's footsteps intruded on the eerie quiet, and every little sound echoed into the nothingness. Several wooden pallets were scattered across the floor, and a row of empty steel shelving units lined the wall. It was a good setup if someone wanted to catch them off guard or observe them prior to making their presence known.

Max motioned Danya to wait at the edge of the light as he disappeared. If someone was lurking, he wanted to find that person. His gait was slow and deliberate; he felt the floor as he placed each foot. Every inch of Max's body became a sensor, attuned to the slightest possible hazard. His eyes searched, and his ears strained for any sound or movement indicating a threat. From the corner of his eye, Max could see Danya standing, watching, and waiting.

Danya pressed her hand against the pocket of her pants—feeling the Beretta Model 70. It was her reassurance if the situation went south; she wanted to be ready. She stood motionless and strained her senses to detect anything, even the slightest movement of air, that would signal someone close. The bitter taste of adrenaline filled Danya's mouth as her heart pounded. She was ready to react to any danger.

Danya could not hear Max. Her instinct was to call out, but her training controlled her. Then a slight sound of something being dragged along the floor permeated the silence. Danya crouched and scanned the darkness as she tried to determine what caused the noise—silence—then it started again and abruptly stopped. *What the hell is that? Max?* she thought.

Max finally emerged and then nodded to indicate that no one else was present. "The other doors are locked," Max said, his voice low and full of concern. "I've stacked a couple of those pallets up for a little protection. Straight behind me. Just know where they are. We can expect them at any minute. You ready?"

Danya nodded.

"OK, step out of the light," Max said as he returned to his vantage point behind the stacked pallets.

At 10:31 p.m., the small door squeaked open. One by one, five men filed in and paused in the cone of light. The single fixture overhead was sufficient to affect their night vision—they could not see beyond the cone. As the first man entered, Danya thought, *Bob.* He was her contact. *The next two must be the Pakistani buyers, and these last two thugs must be hired guns. They won't be much of a problem. It was just supposed to be the four of us, Bob.*

Danya slipped the Beretta from her pocket and tucked it in her waistband behind her back and then stepped into the light.

"You ready to deal?" Bob asked. His eyes darted about as he continuously shifted his stance. His agitation was annoying.

"I didn't expect a crowd," Danya said, her voice cold. *He's on cocaine,* she thought. *Great! His paranoia could lead to shooting.*

"You like it in private?" Bob asked, his voice daring. "Why don't we step over there in the dark? A little pleasure before work. You're a good-looking bitch." Bob stepped closer and caressed her breast.

"Asshole, I didn't come here to give you a cheap thrill," Danya replied. In a quick thrust, Danya shoved the nose of the Beretta under Bob's chin and grasped his lapel. The two Pakistani men on her side were between Danya and the two thugs.

"Do you want to buy weapons or just act stupid in front of your friends? Tell them not to move," Danya said. Her reflexes were faster than his.

His head back and eyes glaring down, the startled man didn't move. As the pistol pressed into his neck, Bob forced the words, "Don't move. Do what she says." His voice was deeper and partially garbled.

The four others stood rigid. Pistols were already in the hands of the two thugs, but a clear shot at Danya was nonexistent. For a brief moment, there was silence. Eyes shifted about, looking for a signal.

"What'll it be, fight or buy weapons?" Danya said through clenched teeth.

"Weapons." The word struggled over Bob's raised chin. Tears emerged from his eyes, and his nose started to run. He sniffed.

"I'm going to relax," said Danya, "but if you so much as fart, I'll start firing. Got that, asshole?"

Bob nodded. His nose began to bleed. He started to raise his arm.

Danya shoved the pistol back into his throat. "Easy!"

"My nose," Bob said. He sniffed again as the blood continued to ooze from his nose.

"Slowly," Danya replied. She released her grip on Bob and motioned with the pistol.

Bob dragged his arm across his nose, smearing his sleeve and face with the bloody snot.

Shifting her glance, Danya could see the gunmen, their eyes darting about. She didn't like their demeanor and held her pistol ready. "Tell them to holster their guns."

Bob looked at them and nodded. He slid his sleeve under his nose again.

"Gotta list of what you want?" she asked.

"In my pocket," he said in a nasally voice. He rubbed his neck.

"Gently…give it to me."

Bob shifted his stance. His hand trembled as it disappeared into his jacket pocket and then emerged with a folded piece of paper.

Danya snatched the paper from his hand and glanced at the others as the two Pakistani men started to move. "Just stand still," she commanded. Danya shot a look at the two goons.

She read over the list of weapons and looked up at the man before her and then to the two Pakistani men. "This is quite a list," she said. "Sniper rifles. Hmm, you guys are serious. Whatcha gonna do? You need anything else? I can get most anything."

"Not for you to worry about," one of the Pakistani men said. "Can you deliver all the weapons?"

"It'll take a couple of days. The sniper rifles will take a little extra time. Day after tomorrow, here, same time?"

"We'll tell you where. What's your price?" the other Pakistani said.

"They'd better be quality, bitch," Bob said as his eyes glared at her.

"Do you want the fucking guns or not? This isn't my first rodeo. My terms or no deal. Where, when, and just the four of us."

In a crouched position behind the pallets, deep inside the darkness, Max watched as Danya played out her part—his Glock 21SF pistol was in his hand, ready to fire. *She's good*, he thought. He felt the urge to start shooting when he saw the man fondle Danya's breasts. Then as Danya shoved the pistol into the man's throat, Max thought, *She's got it under control.* Her actions were quick, and she controlled the situation before the thugs could react. *Make the deal, and let's get the hell outta here.*

Although the meeting only lasted a few minutes, time seemed to creep along. Max could almost feel the thick tension. Anything could go wrong at any second, and bullets could start flying. Danya would be in the center of it. She was well aware of the risks and running the show. Max felt a sense of relief as he watched Danya look over the paper the man handed her. The meeting was finally about to end. He couldn't hear what Bob and Danya were saying, but he watched their mouths move in several exchanges. Bob began to fidget and shift his weight. He became more animated—obviously at something Danya had said.

Suddenly a gun appeared in Bob's hand; it looked like a forty-five-caliber automatic. The man fired at Danya twice in quick succession, the shots thundering in the confines of the warehouse. Danya fired at almost the same time as his first shot and twice more. She quickly shifted her aim and fired at the two gunmen.

Max's rate of fire matched Danya's. He fired at Bob and then at the man next to her. Shifting his aim, Max fired at one of the thugs. Bob and one of the Pakistani men went down. The two thugs fired several rounds wildly and then pulled the other Pakistani out the door. Max believed that his last shot struck one of the retreating thugs as he exited the door. The odor of burnt propellant from the gunshots was thick as silence slammed into the humid air of the warehouse.

Max paused to analyze the situation and ensure that the two men on the concrete were not getting up. He cautiously rose before stepping into the light. He checked the first man.

Dead.

Then the Pakistani.

Dead…shit!

"Danya," Max said as he saw Danya go down on one knee and then sit on the floor. Blood stained her upper left abdomen. Max quickly checked her for other wounds.

Danya looked into Max's eyes. "Max…" Her voice was filled with pain. "He got me in the left side."

Max retrieved his handkerchief from his pocket and gently pressed it against the seeping wound. At that moment the door squeaked open again. Max swung his pistol around and was ready to fire. Gail stepped through the door and crouched with a pistol in her hand. Recognizing her, Max relaxed and stood.

"We've got a little mess," he said to Gail. "Can you get an ambulance for Danya?"

"Is it bad?" Gail asked as she dialed 911, ready to make the report. Unfortunately that would bring the police and lots of questions that the two of them were not ready to answer.

"Not sure. She was hit in the left side."

"Are these our guys?" Gail stood over the Pakistani.

"That one is. The other one was the go-between."

"We do have a fucking mess," said Gail. "I'll run as much interference as I can, but the local cops will be a little pissed off because they weren't notified."

"I figured as much," Max replied. "Ya know, I'm not supposed to be here. By the way, thanks for following."

She nodded. "Like I said, it's a mess."

As soon as the local police released Max and Gail, the two sped to Harbor-UCLA Medical Center, where the ambulance took Danya. Max and Gail sat in the waiting room and fidgeted as they waited to talk with the doctor about Danya's condition. The room was well lit with florescent light bouncing off the shiny floors, but it wouldn't have been restful even if the situation had been different. Every time someone entered the room, Max and Gail's anxiety peaked. The vicissitudes were exhausting.

"I'll see if there's an update on Danya," Gail said, and then she stood and walked down the hall.

Max nodded and watched Gail step away. He glanced at his watch again and compared the time to the clock on the wall—the same time. Looking back to the coffee table, Max picked up a worn magazine he had flipped through earlier. Nothing interested him; all he could do was wait. Looking back to where he anticipated Gail would be, Max saw her walking toward him with two men in tow. The developing situation didn't look good. As Gail approached, Max saw her clenched jaw. He stood as the trio stopped before him.

Detectives, he thought, briefly studying the two men in suits.

"Max, this is Captain Baker." Gail motioned to the taller and heavier-set man. Her tone was curt. It was apparent they'd already had words.

The stone-faced Baker didn't speak, but he scrutinized Max.

Gail motioned to the other one. "This is Sergeant Tolan."

Max noticed the nicotine stains on the man's fingers as he shook his hand. His suit wasn't tailored as well as Baker's.

"Gentlemen," Max said as he shook hands and then paused to let them speak first.

"We want to talk with you about the shooting earlier this evening," Baker said, his expression serious. "We've read the initial report. Let's have a seat over here, out of the way."

Gail touched Max's arm. "I'll wait here for the doctor."

Max nodded and stepped away with the detectives.

Gail looked over to the three seated alone in an out-of-the-way area and noted Max's composure under the detectives' grilling. *He's doing well,* she thought. *Baker looks a little frustrated. Not looking good.* She looked back the other way and saw a doctor, in his surgical scrubs and white smock, walking toward her.

"I'm Dr. Pierce." He extended his hand to Gail. "You're asking about Danya Mayer?"

"Yes, I am." Gail stood, produced her identification, and introduced herself. *This should cut through the red tape,* she thought. "How is she? What's the extent of her injuries?" She raised an eyebrow.

Dr. Pierce got the message that Gail didn't want to bother with the bureaucracy. "Danya is in recovery right now. They'll have her in a room after she wakes up. She did well. The written report will be ready later this morning."

"How bad is it?" Gail asked, her tone commanding. "The details, please."

"The bullet entered her left upper abdomen and then traversed along a superficial path, exiting the lateral midchest wall with fractures of ribs nine and ten." He motioned, tracing the path of the bullet on his abdomen. "The abdominal and chest cavities were not penetrated. No bullet fragments were recovered. The wounds were irrigated and then closed. We'll keep her in the hospital two to three days for observation for infection and pain management."

"When will she be able to go back to work?"

"She's pretty lucky," Pierce said with a nod of his head and raise of his brows. "She'll have subsequent moderate-to-severe pain for a couple of weeks to a month, with movement and respirations. Pain tolerance is the major limitation for mobility and returning to normal activities. She needs to take it easy and not exert herself."

"Thank you, Dr. Pierce," Gail said as she smiled and extended her hand.

Captain Baker and Sergeant Tolan, escorting Max, stopped in front of Gail as she stood in the main waiting room. Max's eyes signaled to her the situation was not good.

"How is she?" asked Max.

"She's in pretty good shape—two broken ribs and no internal damage. The bullet just traveled under the skin and then exited. They're keeping her in here for a couple of days for observation. She'll have quite a bit of pain for about a month."

"Thanks. Let the others know right away."

Gail gave a slight nod of her head.

"Agent Summers," Baker said, his voice sharp, "the district attorney is pissed off. You're supposed to notify us beforehand—this is my turf. We're taking him downtown. What the hell's going on?"

"Nothing now, Baker," Gail said. She couldn't tell him what they were working on, as it was classified, and Baker had not been cleared. *Not telling you shit until I'm ordered to*, she thought. *Asshole.*

"Summers, I want to know what's happening on my beat—in advance," Baker insisted. "We're holding Kenworth until we get all this crap you caused sorted out. I'll be back to talk to the woman when she wakes up."

"Baker, you can't do that. He's working with me," Gail said, her face florid. Her fists were clenched as she struggled not to smack the detective. *That would cause me problems I don't need right now,* she thought.

"Call the DA," Baker said as he tugged on Max's arm.

Gail stood rigid for a moment, and her jaw tightened as she watched Baker and Tolan escort Max out. A nurse approached Gail as the three men disappeared around a corner.

With a smile and compassionate tone, the nurse said, "Danya is in a room. You may see her now." The nurse directed Gail to the ward.

Back in her hotel room after spending most of the night at the hospital, Gail was working on her third cup of coffee. The TV was just noise until the news switched to a black-haired female reporter standing in front of the courthouse. Gail sat upright as the woman told about an army veteran with several tours in Afghanistan and Iraq who had been in a shootout the night before. Her slant was obvious.

"It's unclear if it was a drug deal gone bad or a veteran with posttraumatic stress disorder who went on a shooting spree," the reporter said. "Two men are dead, and the police are searching for a third man wounded in the shooting. A woman is in the hospital, recovering from a gunshot wound to the abdomen. The woman was with the man, who is currently in jail, when the shooting started."

Gail switched off the television and said to herself, "Well, shit. I see where this is going. They're going to use Max as a political football." She checked her watch and then dialed the number for Margaret at CTC.

"The TV has been on all morning," Margaret said. "It's getting nauseated. I've talked to General Matherson twice already today."

"You saw my notes about what really went down?" Gail asked.

"Yes, and I forwarded your e-mail onto General Matherson. He's livid. He said the president called the old man earlier this morning. The one-way conversation was quite heated. The president reamed the old man out about Max investigating this with the Israelis and ignoring Homeland. He had to tell the president that Max was working it undercover. After melting the phone lines to SOCOM, the president went to play golf."

"That's just great," Gail said, her sarcasm thick.

"Several politicians have already started twisting this for their gun-control efforts and face time in the news. More gun control. Max is the current poster child."

"I'm going to try to talk to the DA here," Gail continued. "We've gotta get Max out of jail. He and Danya were getting close to locating the devices. Max is the only one of us who could recognize Madison."

"SOCOM is trying to get Max out," said Margaret, "but the feeling is that everyone is stalling."

"What's the latest from David?" Gail asked.

"Nothing. He's past due reporting in."

"What the hell is going on?" Gail's voice was full of frustration. "I've got to get a move on. I'm heading on over to the DA's office. After that, back to the hospital to talk with Danya. I want to be there before Baker shows up."

"Good luck."

Chapter 14

Friday
November 1, 2013
Rental House
Boulder City, Nevada

"Bart! Bart." Al-Muhaymin's voice was crisp as he walked into the operations room, where Bart stood looking out of the window. "One of our men in California was killed."

Bart turned to look at al-Muhaymin and nodded.

Bart said, "I saw it on the TV. Kenworth. It's time to execute. They're getting close. We're two men short. We'll set up the forward position at the campground and make a complete practice run tonight. I want at least two men there around the clock. Start with the American and one of the others. This is to look like a bunch of guys on a fishing trip. The American will know what to do."

Bart paused, held his gaze on the Arab, and then continued, "Get in touch with al-Aqrab. Tell him we need two men *now*. If we don't move soon, we'll miss the opportunity. Remember to limit your call to two minutes or less."

Kenworth is a threat, Bart thought. *In jail. Hmm. He's good for a couple of days, if he really is in jail. I can go with just one man in LA. I'm too thin here; I need another native speaker on this end. Too risky otherwise. Kenworth is smart and will find us. Make the escape plan ready.*

Moving his timetable up, Bart believed, would have little impact on his mission and leave less time for his men to get bored. He had considered that he might only have the opportunity for one rehearsal, but Bart had planned for several to perfect his operation. Additional practice runs would also keep the men occupied until they actually placed the nuke.

Establishing the lakeside position was necessary for the dry run as well as the actual strike. The fishing camp would allow the surrounding campers to get used to the men and was necessary for the practice. After a couple of days, no one would pay any attention to Bart's men, as long as there was no trouble. The two men Bart directed to be at the lake would observe and note the routines as well as emulate the others already there.

Al-Muhaymin shifted his stance; his voice was full of concern when he said, "Abd al Jabbar doesn't have the bomb working yet."

"I'll talk to him. He's gotta speed it up. You tell him the same so he understands." Bart paused and then continued, saying, "Remember I told you about Kenworth? I'll find out when he'll be released and send you a note. Check with your contacts; get a couple of guys who can take him out. Set it up for me to meet them in Los Angeles. I've got to make a quick trip back there to coordinate with our guy who's handling the port."

"Why not just use one of our sniper teams?" al-Muhaymin asked, staring blankly at Bart.

"They'll be busy here." Bart's answer was curt.

"I will need to go to Las Vegas to check with my contacts."

"Remember what I told you," Bart said, his voice stern as he pointed his finger at the Arab.

"I know. No booze, no drugs, no bragging. You want me to set up another meeting with that guy on the weapons?"

Bart locked eyes with al-Muhaymin. "Don't stay anywhere you have stayed before, and don't use your real name. Set up the meeting—I may meet you there. Everyone else stays here. Make damn sure they keep the twenty-four-hour guard."

A slight grin appeared on al-Muhaymin's face. He was already thinking about Las Vegas and his bleached-blond love muffin, Candy.

***

2:42 p.m.
November 1, 2013
CTC
Tysons Corner, Virginia

"Have you heard from David?" Gail's voice was blunt over the line. "He's not in his room, and he doesn't answer his cell phone."

"No, not a word," Margaret said as she tapped the file on her desk with her pen. "Hold on for a minute, and I'll check again. Might have missed it." She opened her received e-mail folder and scanned the list. "No, nothing from him."

"I have no idea where he can be," Gail said, her voice full of anxiety. "I don't have a very good feeling about this."

"LA division picked up a senior FARC member," Margaret said. "At first they thought they had the Ivan Rios Bloc commander. As it turns out, he is only the Caribbean Bloc's number-two guy. They operate in the northern areas of Colombia and the Caribbean coast. He provided support and security to the Fifty-Seventh Front when they transferred the nukes at the abandoned airstrip in Venezuela. He doesn't know much."

"They're not making it easy for us, are they? They keep secrets better than ISIS."

"How did your meeting go with the DA?" Margaret asked. "When are they going to release Max?"

"The DA is an ass!" Gail's tone was sharp. "I couldn't get a straight answer on when Max'll be released. You might want to give SOCOM a heads-up. They may need to authorize the DA to be briefed on all this. However, the DA's office is very much pro–gun control. For now, the DA is using Max. My guess is that they'll hold him as long as they can."

"I don't think SOCOM will authorize it. The president has told us to keep all this close hold. When are you heading back here?"

"Don't know yet. I need to check on David. I just hope he isn't in any trouble. I also need to keep working on the DA to get Max out."

***

9:11 p.m.
November 1, 2013
Lake Mead, Nevada

The camp on Lake Mead was set up by nightfall. The American did an excellent job of making it look as Bart expected, right down to two men nursing beers and a low fire in the fire pit. A radio playing urban contemporary music from a Las Vegas radio station matched the volume from others in the vicinity. The music, a part of their charade, masked their communications.

Inside his tent, Bart laid out the diving equipment and made the final preparations for the dry run. He refilled the rebreather with the carbon-dioxide-scrubbing chemical used to prevent hypercapnia, while the American sorted out the fishing tackle and made it ready. Bart rechecked all the gear again.

Satisfied that everything was prepared, Bart gathered the others close around him. Using the sketch he'd made of the dam with updated information, Bart stepped through the sequence once more with the others. Everyone answered correctly. The final step before they departed was the synchronization of their watches to his. Bart shoved his ball cap up and looked at each of them.

He asked, "Any questions?"

They shook their heads.

Bart motioned to the fishing tackle and diving gear. "Load the equipment," he ordered.

As the men packed the twenty-one-foot Bayliner that gently rocked in the water nearby, Bart pulled the Syrian aside. He went over their course to the target with him again. Bart handed the Syrian an underwater writing slate, a duplicate of his. Their course with way points and times to the steel-wire net three hundred meters in front of the dam was drawn on the slates. Although the two were supposed to stay together, Bart ensured that the Syrian knew the course and plan.

"Once at the net," Bart said as he touched the sketch, "we'll determine the best place to breach it and then mark it." He flipped over the slate and touched where he had plotted tick marks on a more detailed sketch of the dam area beyond the net. "These are the possible places to anchor the device."

"I understand." The Syrian nodded, his expression serious. "If we get separated…" He looked up at Bart.

"Stay on your course to the net. Watch for me there. If I don't make it, follow the plan and then return to the boat. Local dive reports estimated water visibility at forty feet and the current negligible."

The Syrian dipped his head and tucked the slate in his open wet-suit top.

The diving equipment Bart had selected was state-of-the-art, closed-circuit rebreathers. They emitted no bubbles and were nonmagnetic and acoustically safe, which meant that they were undetectable by any sensors the police might have employed.

Bart motioned to the others to start the practice run. They all checked their watches and started the timed sequence.

After the simulated rendezvous to pick up the nuke under the moonless night sky, the American steered the Bayliner to a small cove, near the entrance to Black Canyon but still out of sight of the dam, and stopped. The only sound was the low rumble of the MerCruiser engine and the occasional hum of another craft on the lake. The only light emitted from them was from the three required running lights.

With the aid of night-vision binoculars, Bart examined the rugged terrain down to the water in all directions to ensure that no one was in the vicinity. Satisfied that they were alone and unobserved, Bart nodded, and then he and the Syrian donned their diving equipment. When ready, they quietly slid over the side. They grasped the tow harnesses Bart had rigged for them to hold on to as they dangled just under the surface on the side of the boat.

As soon as the two in the water signaled they were ready, the American eased the throttle forward and slowly guided the small vessel to the specific point on the water Bart had identified. Towing the men into position at a slow speed prevented their silhouettes from being seen entering the water after arriving at the prescribed location, which could have otherwise raised the interest of Hoover Dam police. A diver at night in an unusual spot and the absence of a diver-down flag would definitely elevate the curiosity of the authorities and prompt an investigation. The two men in the slow-moving Bayliner looked like many others on the lake for a night of fishing.

Reaching the designated position, the American slipped the throttle lever back and into neutral. When the two divers were ready, Bart signaled, and they slipped beneath the surface, descending to forty feet. Using their diver-propulsion vehicles at a speed of three kilometers per hour, they headed for the target. The American and al-Muhaymin pretended to fish while they watched for any threats, alarms, or problems with the divers.

The two sniper teams had taken up their positions earlier. Their mission was to protect the divers through their escape and evasion, should the police detect them. They had picked spots that provided good visibility overlooking Bart's course to the dam. However, their vantage point did not allow them to see the cove position where the boat made the stop to pick up the nuke. Bart accepted that risk, as the two in the boat would be armed on the night when the device would actually be emplaced. The snipers studied the activity at the dam and the routine of the dam police and gathered other pertinent intelligence.

***

10:21 a.m.
November 2, 2013
CTC
Tysons Corner, Virginia

"Gail, a friend of mine at the cyberunit sent me a block of numbers," Margaret said into the phone receiver. "I'm sending it to you and Max."

"He's got several e-mails waiting on him," Gail replied. "Did you find something?"

"You tell me." Margaret's tone had a hint of excitement. "The phone number we've been collecting on, the one that belongs to al-Aqrab, was called by a US phone number, area code seven zero two—Las Vegas."

"What was the duration of the call?"

"Twenty-six seconds."

"Don't get excited about it. It's most likely called by mistake."

"I think it's more than a wrong number," Margaret said, her tone full of agitation. "I think you should check it out."

"It's a pain in the ass to get authorization for a collect and identification on a US number. It's nothing. That short of a call is just a wrong number."

"Gail, I think it's worth it."

"All right. I'll do it. It'll take a few days. I'll let you know if we get anything."

Margaret could almost hear Gail's eyes roll but felt certain the call was a good lead.

"I'll let Max know," Gail said, her tone dismissive.

"When are they going to release him? How's he doing?"

"He's pretty anxious to get out of there. They're gonna release him Sunday. The DA's got about all the mileage she can out of him."

"I'll pass that along to the general."

"I think Danya will be released Sunday or Monday. I'll keep checking on her."

"I got a sketchy e-mail from David," Margaret said. "He thinks he's on to something. He didn't say what it was. I think he might be taking some chances."

With a tone of concern, Gail said, "I'll have a talk with him. We'll head back to Las Vegas when they release Max. I've got nothing but dead ends here."

***

Monday
November 4, 2013
Interstate 5, California

The DA had quietly ordered Max to be released late in the afternoon the previous day. Danya was released from the hospital Monday morning, with instructions to rest. However, she didn't have time for that. Gail headed back to Las Vegas with Danya and Max. Although proud of David and his initiative, Gail was concerned that he might be taking unnecessary chances. She encouraged Max to return to Vegas, mostly because she felt an obligation to watch over David. They would set up there until they could get a substantial lead on Madison. The incidents in Los Angeles—Danya getting shot and Max jailed—had set their investigation back and turned their leads cold.

Max looked over to Gail and then to the speedometer, which registered eighty-five miles per hour. He watched her glance into the rearview mirror. A moment later, he sensed the car slowing. He checked the speed again and then asked, "Trouble?"

"I think we're being followed," Gail said as she shot a look back into the mirror. "They're pacing us. I can't really be sure. They're just hanging back."

"Keep an eye on 'em, and let me know if they make any changes." Max turned around to look at Danya in the back seat. "How you doin'?"

"It hurts like hell, but I'll make it."

Max watched Danya retrieve her Beretta and then check it. She placed it on the seat next to her.

"I want to be ready if need be," Danya said. "I can't move very fast."

Max nodded and then turned back around. He slid his Glock into the open compartment on the console.

Gail continued to monitor the car that she suspected was following them. It maintained a steady distance from them and lingered back far enough to make any identification impossible. Outside of Barstow, California, on a desolate stretch of the interstate, traffic lightened. Gail began to relax, thinking that she had imagined the car was following them. Then suddenly she stiffened and sat upright.

"He's making a move," she said, glancing between the rearview mirror and the road ahead.

Max turned around to look out the back, saw Danya asleep, and shot a glance out the rear window. Danya was slumped in the seat; the pain medications were working. Max released her seat belt and eased her over. Danya moaned but cooperated.

"She's out," he said as he turned back around.

"They're coming up quick on the left," Gail said as she shot a look at Max and then looked back at the rearview mirror.

"I'll watch 'em."

Max scanned the road ahead, looking for any other possible hazards and the next exit. He turned to keep watch on the car and sank further in the seat. The car gained on them quickly. He glanced down at the sleeping Danya. No change. The trailing car's speed continued to increase, and it started to overtake them.

When the front end of the approaching vehicle was about even with Gail, Max saw the passenger shove a double-barreled shotgun out of the window. The engine of their car roared as Gail stomped the gas pedal. In no time, the chasing car was gaining again. Looking at the business end of a shotgun just a few feet from your face is an extremely harrowing experience. It is like looking into the bore of the cannon sticking out of a Spectre gunship. Howitzer or shotgun, it doesn't make any difference if you're that close when it goes off. Dead is dead.

"Get down!" Max shouted.

Gail jammed the brakes and turned the wheel just in time. The shotgun unleashed its payload, spitting out fire and death. The blast was deafening. They were lucky. The buckshot missed them.

Gail cut the wheel and leaned over as she hit the brakes. The car jolted to the right, and the tires screeched. The left rear of her car bumped the right front of the other car, causing it to veer to the left. The driver overcorrected, and the car jerked back to the right and then rolled over twice, sliding to a stop.

Gail sat upright as their car left the interstate and entered the ditch. Dirt and chunks of desert vegetation filled the air. The occupants bounced around the car's interior as Gail worked the steering wheel, guiding the car onto the service road before stopping. She and Max didn't move. Danya moaned from the back and captured Max's attention. He turned around and saw Danya on the floor. He then opened the door and helped her back onto the seat. Blood from Danya's wound seeped into her blouse.

"How is she?" Gail asked while she surveyed the area.

"Her wound is bleeding. We'll need to get her checked out."

"The other car first. I'll deal with the police. You see what you can get from the two in the car."

As soon as Max closed the door, Gail stomped the gas pedal, and the back end shot around. She headed back to the wrecked car. Danya moaned again. Gail parked behind the mangled vehicle that sat askew on the interstate. Pieces of chrome, plastic, and glass littered the asphalt. Max sprinted to check the occupants. Arriving at the passenger's side, he reached in to check for a pulse of the motionless man lying over in the seat.

Dead, Max thought. His eyes roamed quickly over the interior of the car. *No shotgun in here.* He stepped around to the driver's side and checked the bleeding man. *He's alive.* Turning to Gail, Max shouted, "The driver is still alive but unconscious! The other one is dead."

As she talked into her phone, Gail held up her hand and motioned to signal that she understood.

Both men appeared to be Middle Eastern—dark complexions; black wavy hair; and thick, black facial hair. Both had mustaches. Max copied down the identification he found on each man, which was very basic—driver's license and credit card. The rental-car information he retrieved from the glove box matched that of the driver. In the passenger's pockets, he found four twelve-gauge shells. A dozen more were in the console. Each man had a forty-five-caliber automatic. Max needed them alive for information. The driver, whom Max feared was in critical condition, was a possibility—if he lived.

Looking for the shotgun, Max backtracked along the path to where the car had first flipped over. He searched along the roadway and then off to the side. He found it several feet from the road. Max believed that the fingerprints on the weapon would be of little value to him, but locating where they'd got it could provide a clue.

Gail looked up at Max as he approached. "I just got a call about that US phone number, area code seven zero two; it's the same number that called al-Aqrab. It made a call to one of our ladies in Vegas. Candy."

A smile slowly emerged on Max's face. He winked and said, "Have them stay on that number and geolocate it. We're close to Madison. Tell David to arrange another interview with her."

Gail nodded. "I'll ask the Las Vegas office to find out where the phone was purchased and see who bought it. I'm sure it will be bogus. It always is."

"I know. But you've gotta check."

***

10:43 a.m.
November 4, 2013
Luxor Hotel
Las Vegas, Nevada

With Ludwig Steiner, David walked onto the pool deck, glanced over the area, and looked for his contact. Ludwig had close-cropped blond hair and was ruggedly handsome, with deep creases in his weathered cheeks. He carried his well-built frame with an air of confidence.

Across the deck from the two men, a man at one of the umbrella tables raised his hand in the air. David smiled as he recognized his contact, Jerome, and gave an acknowledging wave.

David turned his head slightly toward Ludwig. "That's my contact," he said in a low voice and nodded toward the uplifted hand.

Ludwig gave a slight nod.

David led the way to the table. The man looked to be in his early thirties. His hair was bleached blond, and he wore a gold chain around his neck. Matching earrings were in each ear. Although the blush on his cheeks was a little too heavy, the rest of his makeup was well done. Clear nail polish coated his nails. Another man, seated next to him, had dark hair combed back and appeared to be slightly older. He smoked a cigar and wore two diamond-studded rings on each hand. A pair of opera glasses lay on the table in front of him.

"Hello, David," Jerome said, his sultry voice seeming to float in the air. He held his gaze on David.

"Hello, Jerome. This is Ludwig." David looked to his right.

"A pleasure," Jerome replied through a wide smile. "Have a seat."

"This is Al," Jerome said as he motioned to the man on his left.

"David, Ludwig," Al said and then lifted the opera glasses to his eyes as a voluptuous, tanned woman in a white bikini floated across the surface of the pool on an air mattress.

Jerome motioned to a nearby waiter. As soon as the attentive man stepped to the table, Jerome looked at David and asked, "A drink?"

"Piña colada." David smiled.

"Strawberry daiquiri for me," Jerome said.

"Crown Royal Reserve on ice," Al said, never dropping the glasses from his eyes.

"Water for me," Ludwig said.

Ludwig studied the two men. *Jerome is no problem,* he thought. *The other one could be dangerous.*

Al placed the glasses back on the table and looked over Ludwig and then David. "Jerome said you can supply us?" He cut to the chase.

"Weapons. You have a list, *ja*?"

The table fell silent as the waiter set their drinks on the table. He smiled as he put the last glass down. "Will there be anything else?"

Al shook his head. "No, nothin' else." After slipping the guy a tip, he paused until the man was several steps away. Then Al dipped his fingers into his shirt pocket, withdrew a folded paper, and handed it to Ludwig.

Ludwig took a sip of his water and then unfolded the paper and read over the list. "No problem. When do you want delivery? What about ammunition?"

"Day after tomorrow. Yeah, about five hundred rounds each, and add a couple of Uzis with a couple thousand rounds each. Call Jerome with the price. Your boy knows how to get in touch with him."

Ludwig nodded his head. "I can get most anything. Just let me know."

Al gave a slight nod and then puffed on his cigar. He lifted the glasses to his eyes again. It was a definite signal the meeting was over.

Without speaking, Ludwig led David out of the hotel. Once they were clear of the pool, David asked, "Well, whatta you think? Is it them?"

Ludwig shook his head. "*Nein*, druggies."

***

11:28 a.m.
Monday
November 4, 2013
Rental House
Boulder City, Nevada

"Abd al Jabbar thinks he is almost finished bypassing the PAL. Most likely it will be ready tonight or tomorrow." Al-Muhaymin's voice carried a hint of excitement.

"Tell 'em to keep going," Bart replied, his own voice serious. "Collect all the phones. We need to replace 'em. Send the Syrian to a different convenience store for new ones." Bart checked the time on his watch.

Bewildered, al-Muhaymin asked, "Why?"

"The FBI is probably on to us, and I'm not taking any chances. They could have captured any of these cell-phone numbers. Contact al-Aqrab, and tell 'em Abd al Jabbar will have his work done by tomorrow. I need approval to execute. Tell him it is now or never. I believe the Americans are closing in. Also, where are the additional men I requested?"

Al-Muhaymin nodded. "Praise be—"

"Knock that shit off!" Bart's message was punitive. "You're to talk and act like an American. Remember?"

"Yes, Bart."

"Find out if your guys have taken out Kenworth. Lean on 'em. If they haven't, why not? Keep me updated. Get someone else if you need to, but get him."

Chapter 15

8:28 a.m.
November 5, 2013
Bellagio Hotel
Las Vegas, Nevada

"The coffee, it is terrible, *ja*." Ludwig's face wrinkled as he set the cup on the coffee table. "You were very lucky yesterday."

Max nodded.

Max had gathered Gail, Ludwig, David, and Danya together. Although Max wanted Danya to rest in bed, she refused to be sidelined. They met in his suite to review all the fragmented information they had each discovered and to plan their next steps. Margaret was on the phone with them.

"Yesterday's attempt on us could be Madison's first mistake," Max said, lifting his coffee cup to his lips. "He verified that we're close to him. Everyone be careful and ever vigilant. He'll try again."

"David," Gail said, her expression serious, "I think you should go back to DC. It's getting too dangerous here for you."

"It's not any more dangerous for me than you. I want to stay, love."

"David, I—"

"Let him stay," Max said as he looked at Gail. "He can be useful working out of his room and coordinating with Margaret."

"I'm gonna get my ass fired," Gail said, her eyebrows rising as her eyes opened wide. "All right, you can stay."

A slight smile emerged on David's face.

Max looked at David. "Anything yet on the two men who tried to take us out?"

"Nothing yet. IDs were bogus. It could be a while before we get any good information on them."

"What else ya got?"

David glanced at his notes and then back to Max. "Since I've been here, I've picked up on five meetings: three drug and two arms buys. None of 'em were close to our targets." David scooted his chair closer to the table and rested his hands in his lap.

"We thought yesterday's meeting at the Luxor was promising," Ludwig said. "It turned out to be just druggies. David did a good job in that meeting." Ludwig paused as he looked into his cup, hoping it had been transformed into a delicious drink. He took a sip, and his face revealed it hadn't been. "Why am I drinking this?"

The others looked at David. He smiled.

"Are we still on to talk with Candy?" Max shifted his attention to Gail.

"Yes, Buckner will call me when they get here. He has us in one of the meeting rooms about ten thirty."

David had arranged the meeting with Candy after they learned that it was her number that had been called by the phone the FBI was collecting information on. They intentionally set the conference in a neutral place in the hopes that she would be more cooperative. If they were successful with Candy, they believed that Ruby would then be more receptive to an agreement. Her interview would be after Candy's. The two were separated; they were friends and had probably collaborated on their stories beforehand. In the last encounter, both women had made it clear that they wanted to make a deal before they told all they knew. Gail was prepared, should the meeting go in that direction.

Their morning meeting continued for an hour. Margaret provided an update on the increased Internet chatter and rhetoric of ISIS with their nonstop threats to America. She provided the latest information from Homeland Security that Dawn had given her.

"She's still in New York, coordinating defensive activities there," Margaret said. The smile on her face was easy to detect.

"They've had enough time to bypass the PAL," Max said and looked at each of them. "We don't know where or when they may try to use it. We may even be too late. Dig deep. Find out what's going on, and turn over every dirty rock."

"I'll work with David and my sources, since I can't move around very fast," Danya said as she shot a determined look at Max.

Max nodded. "Ludwig?"

"*Ja*, I still have a couple of things to check out as a result of our meeting yesterday with the druggies. I got word—actually David did—of another potential weapons buy. I'm going to check it out. I'll be digging around."

"Tom Buckner, the hotel security, might be a good source for you to talk with," Max continued. "He should know what's going on around here. I'll introduce you to him at our meeting at ten thirty."

Ludwig nodded.

***

9:17 a.m.
November 5, 2013
Rental House
Boulder City, Nevada

"Are you about finished?" Bart said as he approached Abd al Jabbar.

Al Jabbar stood in the kitchen smoking a cigarette and sipping chai. The Pakistani man's thick, heavy beard had not been shaved in several days, and bags under his eyes revealed his long hours laboring over the PAL device.

"It is very difficult," al Jabbar replied. His native tongue of Urdu heavily influenced his English syntax. "The circuitry, it is very complex. This is an implosion device, and to produce the nuclear explosion, the circuits must fire precisely at the right time with the correct current. The electrical charge ignites the high explosives surrounding the core that, in turn, compress the mass of plutonium to produce the nuclear explosion. There is still a small problem. It will happen at most any time."

"Spare me the lecture. We don't have *most any time.*" Bart's tone was stern. "The Americans are getting close. If we don't execute very soon, we won't have another opportunity. You've gotta get it workin'. You should've finished by now."

"Go away, and let me think. I will finish." Al Jabbar knocked the ashes of his smoldering cigarette into the sink.

"When will you finish?"

"It is very difficult to say. Maybe today…maybe tomorrow."

It was the frustration in Abd al Jabbar's voice that bothered Bart the most. The PAL was a challenge for him, as it was supposed to be. Although the circuitry was thwarting his attempts to bypass it, eventually he would succeed. But when?

The longer they stayed static and his men waited to go forward with their mission, the more likely they were to be discovered. Staying on the edge and being ever vigilant was exhausting. Bart knew that they couldn't maintain that posture much longer. Soon they would become bored and let their guard down. The women and booze a short distance away would eventually be too tempting and would threaten Bart's control of them. That would expose them to an unacceptable risk.

Bart walked back to his operations room and began his final preparations for his escape. He packed his necessary identification, credit cards, cash, and, of course, his forty-five-caliber automatic with extra ammunition. Also, a change of clothes and a few other items he deemed necessary were placed into his backpack. It would go with him everywhere he went. Bart was prepared to leave at a moment's notice and disappear.

"Your new cell phone," al-Muhaymin said, holding the phone in his outstretched hand, as he and the Syrian entered the room.

Bart looked up at the two men and said, "Thanks. For the next several days, be careful, and don't use them unless it is important." Bart knew it was a waste of his breath to tell them this.

"Yes, Bart," al-Muhaymin replied with a toothy smile.

"I want you to execute the diversion in New York. Make sure your guy there knows how to set off the bomb. I wanna see it on TV."

"It will be a good one. Not to worry. He knows how to set it off."

"He screwed up the last one. Tell him to spread the word through his circles that he's gonna destroy the city. I want the word to get out. We only need a couple of days more. I want Kenworth to think it is New York City. Make it good, or Kenworth won't take the bait. Oh, and push Abd al Jabbar. He's taking too long."

Al-Muhaymin nodded.

***

10:37 a.m.
Meeting Room
Bellagio Hotel
Las Vegas, Nevada

Gail and Max sat across the table from Candy. Officer Ortiz stood guard just outside the room like an ancient warrior, and Ludwig talked with Tom Buckner in the hall near the room where Ruby waited. Candy lit a cigarette and then crossed her shapely legs and sat back in the chair. She shot a look at both of them and then dropped her eyes. She gently picked at a piece of lint on her dress.

Max noticed Gail's glare, her obvious displeasure at Candy's smoking. He touched Gail's arm and gave a slight nod, indicating for her to allow Candy to smoke. He wanted Candy relaxed and hopefully nonconfrontational.

Without speaking, Max and Gail sat back in their chairs and casually observed Candy. They wanted her to speak first. Candy began swinging her foot, as her leg draped over the other. She fiddled with the hem of her dress and avoided eye contact. The cigarette finally consumed, she uncrossed her legs and leaned forward and then snuffed out the butt in the ashtray on the table.

"Got anything to drink?" Candy asked. "I'm thirsty." Her eyes landed on Max.

"What'd you like?"

"Perrier."

Max looked at Gail and nodded. A scowl covered Gail's face as she stood, briefly held her eyes on the woman, and stepped into the kitchen. Gail retrieved a small bottle from the fridge and glass from the cabinet and then set both on the table with a *clack*. Candy looked up at her with a piercing stare.

As Gail returned to her chair, Candy opened the bottle, filled her glass, and took a sip. She withdrew her lipstick from her purse and refreshed her lips. After Candy dropped the tube into her handbag, her eyes returned to Max. "Look, I've got things to do. Are we going to talk or just sit here and listen to each other breathe?"

"You received a phone call on Saturday," Gail said as she slid a paper with a phone number highlighted, in front of Candy.

"Since when is it a crime to get a phone call? I get lots of calls." Candy held her guard and wanted to see their hand before she committed to anything. She didn't trust them.

"We want to find the person with that number." Max motioned to the paper.

"I don't know whose it is. Why do ya want to find him?" She shifted her eyes between Max and Gail.

"You do know whose number it is," Max said as he locked his eyes on hers.

"I didn't say that. I said I don't know."

"You said, 'Why do we want to find *him*?'"

"So?"

"I said *person*."

"I just assumed a man. Everyone knows I don't do women."

"We'll keep you out of it if you cooperate and help us find him."

"Like I told you before, if I help you, I'm finished," Candy said. She looked deep into Max's eyes. She lit another cigarette.

"We think that number belongs to a pretty bad dude. You could be in trouble, too."

Their banter continued for another thirty minutes without Candy providing any useful information. Max took note of her increased smoking with each round.

"Another Perrier," Candy said, her attitude contemptuous. She held up the bottle as she looked at Gail.

Without speaking, Gail stood and stepped to the fridge. *You little bitch,* Gail thought. *You're enjoying this. I oughta just beat it out of you.* Gail set the bottle on the table and then, with a shove, slid it to her. Candy poured the glass full and took a drink. Her eyes returned to Max's.

Candy was scared. She sensed that this was serious but didn't know what to do. The two people in front of her were the authorities. At least Candy knew that Gail was FBI, but Max had never provided any information on his background or identification. He was mysterious but in command. He was firm and well built, not like the other cops his age. He didn't act like the police. He did show compassion toward her. All this intimidated Candy.

Max held his gaze into Candy's eyes momentarily. He sensed her fear and reservations about cooperating. He also knew that she wanted to reach out to him. She just needed a little help. He looked to Gail and gave her a slight nod.

Gail opened a folder that was on the table in front of her. She slid the paper across the table to Candy.

"We want you to help us, Candy," Max said. He watched her read the document. The letter was an agreement between her and the US government. "This letter says that in exchange for your full cooperation, you are being recommended for the Federal Witness Security Program. You will receive two hundred fifty thousand dollars and be relocated with a new identity."

Candy's eyes welled up. "What about Ruby? Help her out, too." She wiped her eyes with a lace-trimmed handkerchief.

Max nodded. "We have a letter for her if she'll help us."

Candy nodded.

"Sign at the bottom, above your name," Gail said as she slid a pen to Candy.

Candy told them all she knew about Haris Jamil and confirmed that he had called her on Saturday. She answered their questions covering what he talked about and what he liked and disliked.

"He thinks he's in love with me," she said with a tinge of arrogance in her voice. "We were together this past weekend.

Like I said, I don't know what he does, but he always has lots of money. Pays well too. He treated me OK."

"When're you gonna see him again?" Gail asked. "Do you know how to contact him, or where he's living?"

"No." She gave a slight shrug of her shoulders and shake of her head. "He just said that he would call me in a few days. I don't know how to get a hold of him or where he lives. He did ask me not to call him on that number." Candy nodded to the paper on the table.

"Did that strike you as a little odd?" Max realized how illogical that question was before she answered.

Gail grinned.

"Honey, that happens all the time. Men use their cell phones, business phones, and even their home phones. They don't want to take the chance of me calling them and their wife answering. So I don't. It's not good for business. Know what I mean?"

Max nodded as a smile emerged on his face. He withdrew a photograph from the folder beneath the notepad in front of him and slid it in front of her. "I showed you this picture the last time we talked. Have you ever seen this man?"

Without hesitation, she said, "Yes, a couple of weeks ago. Haris and I were together. It was about eight in the morning, and I had just stepped out of the shower when he came barging in. He's an ass. I barely got dressed, before he booted me out of the room."

"Which hotel?" Max asked.

"It was in Boulder City. The small family-owned one on the main drag. I can never remember the name."

Max looked over to Gail and saw her nod. He made note of the new location in his pad.

Candy continued answering their questions but was unable to provide any more details. She would help them and agreed to call Gail when she heard from Haris again. Finally Max looked at Gail and nodded toward the door. Without speaking, Gail walked out of the room. Max leaned back and engaged Candy in lighter, casual conversation. She lit another cigarette.

Gail returned within a few minutes and held the door as Ruby entered. Her eyes scanned the room, and her gait slowed. Ruby's face was void of expression as she looked to Candy for reassurance. She hesitated, not knowing whether to sit at the table or bolt out the door. Candy nodded and slid back the chair next to her, indicating her support and for Ruby to sit.

Max gave a synopsis of what they had discussed with Candy. He cut to the chase and laid out what he was offering Ruby as Gail slid the letter of agreement in front of her. Ruby looked at Candy for approval. Her trusted ally gently nodded her head. With that, Ruby signed the letter where Gail indicated.

Max led off with the questions to Ruby. He followed the same style and format with her as he had done with Candy. Ruby was apprehensive at first, but with Candy's support, she became forthright in her answers. Ruby told them of the evening with Sol Jones until she stumbled out of the room.

"He was kinda freaky, ya know. And rough."

Ruby's information was not as extensive as Candy's, obviously, since she had only been with Jones that one evening. However, she did corroborate several details in Candy's statement and was able to give a detailed description of Jones.

Both women's cooperation was a positive step forward in locating the weapons, but Max still had a long way to go. Confirmation that Madison was in the area reassured Max that he was right and that New York City was probably not the target. However, there were still countless possibilities of potential targets in the heartland. Any one of them would strike fear into the American people and cause more chaos in the Beltway, if that were even possible.

Max could employ any number of assets, but the amount and type depended on where the bomb was located. If Max miscalculated the location or located just one, disaster would occur if he didn't locate Madison or interrupt his plan. Prematurely deploying the assets would alert the press and cause mass hysteria and would impede Max's ability to locate and recover the nukes before they exploded.

***

1:37 p.m.
November 5, 2013
Bellagio Hotel
Las Vegas, Nevada

"*Dahling*, that's what the fellow said. They haven't collected anything on that US phone number that called Candy since yesterday." David sat, with his hands clasped, in the side chair across from Gail as they met in Max's suite to coordinate their activities.

"Crap! That isn't good news." Gail checked her watch and then picked up a cookie from the plate on the coffee table and bit off a piece. With the cookie pinched between her fingers, she waved it as she spoke. "I bet he's already pitched the phone. I was hoping we'd have his location by now. They're pretty good."

Once they had the location, the FBI could follow the phone and do a temporal analysis to see where the user was spending his time. With that information, they could predict where the user would be at any given time.

"That's Madison," Max said. "He's smart." Max looked toward David. "Tell Margaret to stay on her cyberpeople and that the seven-zero-two-area-code number has probably been trashed. The next collect they get on al-Aqrab's number with the same area code, stay on it; that'll be our guy." He looked at Gail.

"I know. Candy's number," said Gail. "That's going to be a bitch. That woman gets a lot of calls."

"Just look at the new seven-zero-two area codes that call her."

"I just got off the phone with the local office," Gail said and then shoved the rest of the cookie into her mouth. "They've located the convenience store where the cell phone was purchased. They're heading over there, but don't hold your breath on 'em finding anything."

David had made contact with each of the security officers at the Vegas hotels and was routinely checking with them all. However, none of them was able to provide any information. David had also made inroads into the underworld that thrived around the city. So far all he had been able to discover, aside from the numerous people wanting to buy drugs of all kinds and quantities, was one possibility in addition to the meeting to buy weapons he and Ludwig had attended at the Luxor Hotel.

Gail grudgingly agreed to allow David to continue exploiting the contacts he had made so far, as long as Ludwig was with him. Gail insisted that David cease his involvement as soon as Ludwig gained traction. David, however, never actually agreed to Gail's demands. Danya's activities were limited to the phones. Her restricted mobility made her irritable.

Max focused his attention on Danya. "Do you still have Madison's girlfriend, Maurine, locked up?"

"Yes." Danya moaned. "What do you have in mind?"

"Release her."

"What?" Danya winced again.

"Yeah, release her. Coordinate with Margaret, Gail, and your people to track her. She may just lead us to Madison. Monitor all her calls, and keep surveillance on her, but let her think she's free. My guess is that she'll contact Madison right away."

"Sounds reasonable. I'll talk with Thaddeus."

Max's cell phone rang, interrupting him. He paused to look at the number and then said, "It's Chugs." He stood and walked into the kitchen.

"No, sir, we're just putting our heads together," Max said into the phone.

"Are you making any headway?" Chugs asked; the frustration was noticeable in his voice.

"We've got a thin lead on Madison—well, on one person linked to him. He's been around the area. One of the prostitutes we talked with this morning identified Madison."

"That's something. Is she going to cooperate?"

"Yes, we have an agreement signed. Danya is going to coordinate to have Madison's girlfriend, Maurine, released. She may lead us to Madison."

"Good." Chugs paused. "The president is putting pressure on the old man. Homeland has convinced him the attack is going to be in New York City. He's suggesting that you move everyone there. We're stalling, but I don't know for how long. You've got to locate Madison."

"Yes, sir. We're turning over every rock, but there're a lot of 'em. Madison isn't tipping his hand, aside from the attempted assassination on us."

"What do you need, Max?"

"For now, can you get SOUTHCOM to include us in their Global Hawk ISR runs along the border? They may pick up something." SOUTHCOM, or United States Southern Command, a unified Combatant Command, is responsible for Central and South America, as well as the Caribbean. The Global Hawk is a high-altitude, long-endurance unmanned aerial reconnaissance system.

"Send me the coverage area, and I'll see what I can do. Las Vegas is quite a way from their normal route. That could be a little tricky."

"I'll get you the area I want covered," said Max. "It's probably a long shot, but we've gotta try. I'm out of options, and they could have the PAL bypassed by now."

"Got it. I'll buy you as much time as I can. Just find Madison."

Chapter 16

9:14 a.m.
November 6, 2013
Bellagio Hotel
Las Vegas, Nevada

"I just received this," David said as he slid a folder across the table to Max. Straight-faced, David paused in anticipation of Max's reaction. "The service records of the two Americans that ISIS recruited."

"St. Louis sure took their damned time getting this to us." Max's sarcasm was thick. "Have you looked at 'em?" His eyes returned to David, and then he opened the first file. "Wyman, Drew." Max mumbled the man's name as he scanned the information. Then he looked at the other one. "Bron, Edsel."

A grin spread across David's face as he nodded. "I've already sent out a request for a national agency check. Nothing so far on the two. I also updated the FBI database with these guys."

Max took several minutes to study the files of the two men. Scanning their assignments, service schools, and type of discharge, Max was forming his mental evaluation of the men and their character. In addition to being enlisted army veterans, both were also qualified army divers.

Reading *divers*, Max looked up with a blank expression. He didn't speak for a moment. *I should've known,* he thought. *Hoover Dam. Is Madison going to use them both on the structure or one somewhere else? The Port of Los Angeles? Is that one of his deceptions?*

Max looked at Gail and Ludwig, who also sat at the table.

Max said, "Gail, set up a meeting with the Hoover Dam chief of police. Ludwig, I want you to have a good look around the dam and vicinity. Gail, better contact Dawn in New York and tell her there's a high probability that Madison'll use divers. There are a number of dams and reservoirs in New York State that would make good targets. Oh, and notify the manager of the hotel in Boulder City that Candy told us about yesterday; we want to meet with him."

Gail shot a look at David and then gave a nod of her head—finding out about the hotel and arranging for them to meet with the manager would be a task for David.

"*Ja*, dams would be good targets." Ludwig nodded. "I am not familiar with the ones in New York State, but the one here, Hoover Dam, would be excellent."

"What makes you think the dam is his target?" Gail's brow dipped, and her eyes narrowed. "They've got pretty good security—all vehicles are subject to search, they've got control of who enters and leaves, and only small backpacks are permitted. It is high profile, but I'd think it would be too difficult to put a bomb in there."

"Madison and these two Americans," Max said, holding the files of the Americans, "are trained military divers, and this is the type of challenge Madison would go for. In the information Chugs provided from SOCOM, Madison worked on plans for using nukes against a potential adversary. He would know how to employ them, and he'd know suitable targets. The dam fits in with his expertise."

"Do you know how many dams are on the Colorado River?" Gail's eyes were wide and her face pale. "Fifteen. We don't have the assets to cover all dams on the Colorado River, let alone those in New York."

Max nodded. "I know. I'll talk with Chugs and see if we can get more people. Be careful what you say to Dawn. She'll probably freak out. Crap!"

"*Ja*, we must call it right, Max." Ludwig leaned forward with his arms on the table, his expression serious. "I can have a hundred and twenty men here within seventy-two hours, configured however you want them. I can double that number in ninety-six hours."

Max paused, briefly returned Ludwig's gaze, and then nodded. "I'll pass that on to Chugs," Max said and then looked at David. "Start collecting information on Lake Mead and the dam. Get everything you can."

David nodded and scribbled on his notepad.

Looking at Danya, Max said, "Help David out."

"I'm OK, Max. I'm not gonna be sidelined and miss this." Danya grimaced in pain from the force of her words and placed her hand to her side.

"This is just a first meeting with the chief," Max replied. "I need you to help David. You'll be in on the takedown."

Danya leaned back in her chair. She knew Max was right to hold her back because of her wound, but it was hard for her to accept that she was benched, at least for now.

***

10:38 a.m.
November 6, 2013
Rental House
Boulder City, Nevada

"Bart," al-Muhaymin said as he entered the operations room where Bart sat at his desk. "The weapons, they will be delivered tomorrow night to a warehouse in Barstow, California. It is all set."

Bart dropped his pencil and looked up at him. "All right. Send a note to al-Aqrab, and tell him to be ready to transfer the money to their account. I don't want to spend any more time at the transfer than necessary. Got an address?"

"Yes, here it is." Al-Muhaymin placed a piece of paper on the desk in front of Bart.

"I'll take the two snipers with me to inspect the rifles. Keep everyone on alert." Bart's tone was stern. "No partying while I'm gone. That means no women and no drugs, and stay off the cell phones. Got that?" Bart's words were as piercing as his look.

Al-Muhaymin shifted his stance. A slight grin emerged, displaying his stained teeth. "Yes, Bart."

Bart's steely eyes remained fixed on al-Muhaymin for an instant before he spoke. "Get on to Abd al Jabbar. Tell him he's out of time. He needs to finish up on the devices."

"Yes, Bart. But—"

"I don't want any excuses." Bart's eyes narrowed, and his brow furrowed. "Get it working. We must go by this weekend. If not, we'll need to move from here."

Al-Muhaymin nodded and walked out of the room.

***

3:10 p.m.
November 6, 2013
Bureau of Reclamation Police Headquarters
Boulder City, Nevada

Meeting in the conference room with Gail, Max, and Ludwig was Scarlet Taite, Hoover Dam chief of police. Scarlet, as her name implied, was an attractive, auburn-haired woman in her midforties. Like many female government employees, she didn't bother with makeup at work.

The introductions complete, Gail was quick to get to the point of the meeting. "Scarlet, we have credible intelligence that a terrorist attack will occur against the dam soon."

"I've read the Homeland Security alerts. We receive them regularly, and my people are vigilant and well informed. What do you have that's not in the alerts?"

"I've been authorized to brief you," Max said, withdrawing a folder from his briefcase and placing it on the table in front of him. "Before we proceed, this is a classified meeting, and you must sign this standard form three one two, Classified Information Nondisclosure Agreement. Basically you must safeguard this information and not discuss it with anyone. Do you understand?" Max removed the form from the folder and placed a pen on top of it. "Tell your staff only what they need to know."

"I understand and agree," said Scarlet. "I've got top-secret clearance."

"I know. I've checked." His expression serious, Max locked eyes with her.

The smile dropped from Scarlet's face, and her demeanor became serious. She pulled the paper toward her, glanced over it, signed it, slid the paper back to Max, and said, "What've ya got?"

Max began to speak. "In the early morning hours of October twelfth, a classified nuclear-storage facility belonging to SOCOM was attacked, and four weapons were taken. Their core is plutonium, Pu-239. Two weapons were subsequently recovered. Two were smuggled into the United States, and we believe that at least one of the devices will be used against the dam."

"Well, you're a bearer of good news. How big?" Scarlet's eyes flashed wide open.

"One kiloton."

"We have pretty good security," said Scarlet, "and our nuclear sensors are regularly checked."

"Scarlet," replied Max, "the core is plutonium and very difficult to detect. Your sensors are for dirty bombs and won't detect a military-grade nuclear device. In this case, *pretty good* isn't good enough."

"Well, shit!" Her excitement increased. "Do you know how they plan to attack us? What intel do you have? We can tighten up our inspections and searches. I'll need to bring on more contractors to beef up security. What help can you give me? I can increase our patrols and things like that. But we can't guard against an aerial attack. We have a security net three hundred meters in front of the dam. Why haven't I seen anything about this on the Homeland Security alerts?"

"Slow down, Scarlet. We believe there are at least three Americans involved and several Middle Eastern men." Max paused, returned the signed form back to the folder, and withdrew a copy of Madison's photograph. "This man is leading the operation against the dam."

"An American?"

"Yes. Make no mistake. He's very dangerous."

"He's not familiar to me," said Scarlet, looking at the photograph, "but I don't have much contact with the visitors to the dam. Can I have this? I'll pass it around to my officers and post it in the briefing room."

"It's yours. I have a high level of confidence that they'll make a water approach to emplace the nuke. His name is Bart Madison. He and the other two Americans are qualified divers, and Madison is trained in this type of operation. I want you to understand that if anyone can breach your security, he can. Remember, no installation is one hundred percent secure."

"We've got sensors, lights, and cameras watching the dam around the clock," Scarlet continued.

"When we finish, can you have someone take Ludwig around to have a look at your security and look for possible weak areas?" Max asked.

"Of course." She glanced over to Ludwig. "I've been told the dam can withstand a nuclear blast unless it's really big. What's your estimate of this bomb?"

Max replied, "This weapon was designed to target bridges and dams and to collapse a mountain pass. It's difficult to say the amount of damage that will occur. It'll depend on where and how deeply it's placed. For your planning, even *if* the dam survives, there will be *significant* damage. The initial blast could knock a hole in the dam, or at the very least, it could seriously weaken the structure. The intake towers will be destroyed, and the canyon walls could collapse, choking off flow to the dam. There could be an earthquake, fires, an electromagnetic pulse, and possibly damage to the turbines that could shift them out of alignment."

Max paused and looked at the others and then back at Scarlet. "After the initial explosion, there is another problem. The energy released from the detonation will force the water away from the center of the blast, and then the water will refill that void, causing a water-hammer effect on the dam. In other words, it could shove against the structure with tremendous force—several times. Any slight flaws or weak areas in the construction will be exacerbated by the initial explosion. It's probable that the first shock wave will create additional fissures, thus weakening the structure. The kinetic force of the returning water may push the dam into the canyon."

"What do you want me to do?" Scarlet asked. The color had drained from her face, and her hand trembled slightly as she picked up her pen to write on her notepad.

Gail replied, "Increase your patrols, and look more closely at the campers and boaters." She took off her glasses and held them in her hand. "Look for anything out of the ordinary or anything that seems odd—no matter how slight or insignificant. I'll send you complete descriptions of those we suspect to be involved as well as a list of everyone on our team."

"If your people should spot them, don't confront them," Max said, his voice emphasizing his words. "Call Gail immediately. We'll take it from there. I'll need some of your men to assist us. These guys no doubt have people watching your routine. Try to keep all your activities as normal as possible. If they detect any change in your routine, that may spook them. I want to catch them and not just run them to ground and have them turn up someplace else."

"Understood," Scarlet said.

"I'll get back with you soon." Max took the folder and his notepad and returned them to his briefcase. "Do you have any other questions?"

"Not for now," the pallid-faced Scarlet replied.

"Don't hesitate to call me," Gail said, handing Scarlet a business card.

"Have someone show Ludwig around now, please. We have a few other things to discuss," Max said.

Scarlet nodded, stood, and stepped out of the room.

***

3:47 p.m.
November 6, 2013
Rental House
Boulder City, Nevada

"Bart, Kenworth is still alive," al-Muhaymin said as he ended the call on his cell phone.

"Damn! OK, get someone else on him. Tell them not to miss this time. No, have them call me. Tell Abd al Jabbar to finish up on the nuke. If it isn't working when I get back, we'll need to change locations. We've been here too long. I'll look for a couple of houses for you to check out while I'm gone."

"I told Abd al Jabbar this morning. He told me not to bother him." With his arm extended and his palm down, al-Muhaymin flicked his hand a couple of times, motioning *go away*.

"I don't give a damn; tell him again! Where are the two men I asked for? What's the problem?"

"It is very difficult. These things take time—" Al-Muhaymin's voice was whiny as he emphasized his reply with a gesture to be patient, bunching up the fingertips of his right hand and moving his hand up and down in front of him.

"I don't want to hear that shit. We don't have time."

"Yes, Bart."

Abd al Jabbar stepped through the door; his clothes looked as though he had slept in them for days, and the bags under his eyes seemed to be larger than before. A cigarette with a long ash drooped from his lips.

"It is working," he said; the ash dropped on his dingy, wrinkled shirt.

"Good," Bart replied. "Is it ready to go?"

"I must, how you say, weld a few connections?"

"The word is *solder*," Bart said. "When'll it be ready? I'll take it with me tomorrow when I pick up the small arms."

"Yes, it will be ready. The other one will be ready when you return. Come with me, and I will show you how to set the timer."

"As soon as the other one is ready, clear out."

Al Jabbar nodded. "Come with me now."

"Hold on just a minute," Bart said and then looked at al-Muhaymin. "Send al-Aqrab a note, and ask him again for approval. Tell him we're ready and must execute Friday or Saturday. After that it'll probably be too late; the Americans are very close to us."

"Yes, Bart," al-Muhaymin replied.

"Let's go." Bart nodded his head as he looked back to Abd al Jabbar.

Bart didn't like the sudden flurry of messages going to al-Aqrab, as he knew that the Internet traffic would spike and possibly alert the CIA something was about to happen or allow them to locate their base of operations. He was uneasy about leaving al-Muhaymin unchaperoned, but the options were limited. Also, keeping al-Muhaymin and the others off their cell phones was a struggle.

Bart suspected that al-Muhaymin, knowing they were ready to execute the plan, would use the opportunity to have a last fling with his prostitute and brag to her. He did consider sending al-Muhaymin to deliver the nuke and pick up the small arms, but that could be even more risky—al-Muhaymin could stop off in Vegas on the way, with the bomb right in the trunk.

Even if he didn't stop over for a romp in the rack with his love muffin—which was unlikely—al-Muhaymin still needed to drive to Barstow and back without getting stopped for a traffic violation or involved in an accident. About the best Bart could do was give him enough things to keep busy until Bart returned.

***

6:23 p.m.
November 6, 2013
Bellagio Hotel
Las Vegas, Nevada

Max, seated at the table, was reviewing the information David had collected on the dam as well as what Scarlet had provided. His focus was on trying to determine where Madison would place the device and at what depth. Max's list of things to discuss with Chugs was growing, as well as the list of resources he needed. Two items to discuss with Chugs were the Nuclear Accident or Incident Response Assistance and an updated Pinnacle report. Nuclear Accident or Incident Response Assistance (NAIRA) refers to the policies and procedures prescribed in regulations for nuclear accident or incident response and assistance operations.

Max confined his true thoughts—about what he felt Madison may already have accomplished and how probable his nemesis's success was—to himself and Chugs. *He may already have bypassed the PAL and employed the device,* Max thought. *We could be too late to the ball game. Only one chance, and it is getting slimmer. Is he using both weapons here or just one?*

Gail slid a chair back and sat next to Max, breaking his concentration. "The Clark County coroner's office has Edsel Bron, or his remains."

"He's dead? What happened?"

"Bullet to the back of the head."

"Why would they kill him?"

"Good question. Do you want to go see the corpse?"

Max looked toward David and saw David looking at him and Gail, obviously listening to their conversation. David's eyes opened wide, and the pale, expressionless gaze told Max that he didn't want to see the corpse.

"No, no need to," Max replied. "They're in the vicinity of Lake Mead, and I'm certain Hoover Dam is the target. If Glen Canyon Dam were the target, I'd think the body would have been found in Coconino County. Look at the map."

Max pulled over a map with the fifteen dams plotted on the Colorado River from his stack of papers on the table. "Glen Canyon Dam is upstream about three hundred miles, near the Utah border. That's a pretty good haul from here. I don't think Madison would risk bringing a body all the way down here to throw us off; neither would he bring someone down here to kill them. Although I wouldn't put it past him. He's cold-blooded enough to do just about anything."

"OK, that makes sense, I think," Gail said, her expression inquisitive. "But why not the next dam downstream?" She leaned over the map for a closer look. "Davis Dam."

"It is almost seventy miles downstream." Max paused briefly before continuing. "If I picked the target, it'd be Hoover. Higher profile, and if Hoover is destroyed, the tsunami of water rushing downstream would overpower Davis, knocking it out, and Parker Dam even further downstream would probably go as well. Madison would know that, and I think he would look at it the same way."

Gail looked reassured. "OK. Hoover. It's a big place. Where'll he put the nukes?"

"That's what I'm trying to figure out. I don't know if he'll use both of them here or one somewhere else. The incident at the Port of Los Angeles concerns me."

"Why not load it in a speedboat and head straight for the dam?"

"A suicide bomber is possible but unlikely. It's a straight-in shot down the canyon to the dam. A speeding boat heading for the dam would catch the attention of the police. The boat would need to breach the steel net and continue to a suitable place to do damage to the dam, if that was their goal. One other thing, the actual timer is mechanical and may function as much as eight minutes early or thirteen minutes late—not very reliable for a suicide mission. I don't think Madison would risk that kind of attack. If their goal is just to terrorize, sure. Then just set it off in Las Vegas, New York, Los Angeles, or some other major city. That'll terrorize and kill a lot of people."

"Gail!" David said in a loud voice. "Your cell is ringing." He held it up for her as she stepped to where he sat.

"This is Gail," she said as she placed the phone to her ear.

"Candy," came the voice. "I'm scared."

"Why, what's wrong?"

"I got a call from Haris Jamil. I…I don't know what to do."

"You did fine. Tell me what he said." Listening intently, Gail stepped back to the table and sat next to Max.

"Haris wants to have a party tomorrow night and be with me." Candy sniffed and then continued. "He wants me to get two other girls. What do I do?"

"First thing is calm down. I want you to agree to be with him. Can you and Ruby meet me tomorrow morning at nine?"

"I think so."

"Good. Come to the Bellagio Hotel, and we'll go over with you what we want you to do. I want you and Ruby to go. I'll arrange for the other girl."

"That's sounding a little dangerous. Ruby won't have anything to do with that freak, Sol Jones."

"She doesn't have to. Just pair her up with the third man, whoever he is. Who'll be there besides Haris?"

"I don't know; he didn't say. It was a very brief phone call."

"Don't say anything to anyone else."

"OK."

"Did he say where?"

"No, he just said he was very busy and would call me back later."

"If he calls before we talk again, make him think you are in love with him and that you'll arrange for a hotel room. You want to throw him a party. You've missed him. Got it?"

Gail detected a smile in Candy's voice as she listened to Candy say, "I think I can do that, if I don't gag."

"Tell him you'll make all the arrangements since he is so busy. Everything'll be fine, Candy." Gail's voice was reassuring. She ended the call and dropped her phone onto the table. Gail looked at Max with a smile.

"Candy got a call from our boy?" Max asked, knowing the answer.

Gail nodded. "She's scared, but she'll be fine. You heard my end of the conversation. She and Ruby will meet us in the morning at nine."

"Let's get it set up here at the Bellagio. I'll talk to Buckner. Have you got someone for the third—"

"I'll be the third woman," Danya said, inserting herself into the conversation.

"No!" Max replied sharply.

"Max!" Danya was not going to be sidelined.

"No. You can't get around very well, and you're wounded. That'll give you away."

Danya frowned and sighed. "I *will* be in on this."

Max nodded and then looked back at Gail. He said, "Don't skimp on the sensors. I want to hear every breath they take, wherever they are. I need information before we take them down. Otherwise, they'll clam up, be out of custody in a couple of days, and disappear. Let me know if you need any assets. I'll have Chugs send them if you do."

"I'll let you know. I'll have them put enough stuff in there that we'll know when his pecker gets up. Do you think one of 'em will be Madison?" Gail asked as she folded her arms across her chest.

"I doubt it. I can't figure out why Madison is allowing these guys out to party—another mistake." Max dipped his head as the corner of his mouth wrinkled up. He ran his hand across his forehead.

"Maybe he doesn't know about it," Danya said as she slid her chair closer to Max.

"It's possible he has already placed the nukes and is gone," Gail said. She made eye contact with each of them. "This might be their victory party."

"I'll send a note to Margaret with an update and have her dig deeper. Her cyberguys may have picked up something," Max said and looked at David. "Contact your sources again."

"I'm on it," David said with a nod.

On the phone in the next room, Ludwig ended his call and joined the others. "Word on the street has it that ISIS is looking for two more people for a mission in the United States—one of them must be a diver. The rest is the usual death-to-America crap. I could have someone infiltrate them, *ja*?"

"That's an idea," said Max. "I'll pass that along to Chugs. I've got a list of things to talk to him about. I'm expecting his call anytime. We've got a lot to do before our morning meeting. First let's get our questions down so that we can get the information we need without getting anyone hurt."

Chapter 17

9:38 p.m.
November 6, 2013
Luxor Hotel
Las Vegas, Nevada

"Your price for the weapons is too high," Jerome said, sipping his strawberry daiquiri.

Ludwig shrugged. "The rifles, they are getting expensive these days, *ja*."

David, Ludwig, and Jerome were meeting in the Aurora Bar across from the front desk. This meeting was to lend credibility to David's cover and enhance Jerome's belief that David really does work for Ludwig—an arms dealer. Ludwig believed that networking with Jerome could lead to the terrorists. They sat around a small, round table away from the main flow of people, and after about half an hour, the conversation became lighter and more social. It became obvious that Ludwig wouldn't lower his price on the quote he provided Jerome for the arms and ammunition.

Jerome admired the ambience brought on by the distinctive lighting. "This is my favorite place," he said, waving his hand upward. "The lighting, it's marvelous, don't you think?" He held his gaze on David. "The lights are supposed to look like the Aurora Borealis."

"Very nice." David returned his smile and then tasted his piña colada.

Ludwig nodded as he scanned the room. "I see a client. I'll be back in a little while." He rose and walked out of the bar.

"Hello, Jerome," a physically fit, well-built man with a golden tan said as he walked by their table. His tone was soft and silky.

"Hello, Tommy," Jerome said with a wink as the smile spread across his face. He returned his attention to David. "He's so cute," Jerome said, lightly touching David's forearm with his soft fingertips. "He's the lifeguard here."

"He's nice," David said as he watched Tommy take a chair across the room from them.

"Are you and Ludwig a couple?" Jerome's manicured fingers with their polished nails slid over David's arm.

"No, just work."

"Perhaps we can do more business together." Jerome stroked David's arm. "I have lots of contacts."

"I would like that. Ludwig can get all kinds of weapons. Vehicles and people too," replied David.

"Would you like another drink?" Jerome asked and signaled with his hand for another round before David could answer. "Where do you work? I don't remember seeing you here before."

"Where the money is. All over."

Ludwig, seated by himself in the centrally located Centra Bar and Lounge, sipped a club soda with a lime twist. He adjusted the volume in his earpiece so as not to miss any of the conversation between David and Jerome. No one paid any attention to him, as his behavior was the same as others taking a break from the action in the casino. Ludwig occasionally glanced up at the monitors. Sipping the drink rounded out his performance.

Ludwig had schooled David beforehand to get friendly with Jerome and get him talking. He had also provided David with a simple cover story. This was David's first foray into the seedy underbelly of intelligence gathering. Gail had reluctantly gone along with Ludwig's potentially dangerous deception. David was an analyst, and the closest he had ever been to this kind of danger was walking into the CTC building at night—not at all.

Ludwig wanted an experienced person. But David had already established himself with Jerome, and there wasn't anyone else. Danya would have been his preferred choice, but her wound was the problem. Ludwig was close by, in the event that something went wrong with the meeting. Not knowing what information Jerome could provide, Ludwig had outlined to David, prior to the meeting, that he wanted to know Jerome's contacts and the extent of Jerome's connections.

Obviously the German was looking for information on weapons buys, Middle Eastern men in the area, and any big operation Jerome might know about. It was an exploratory meeting to see if Jerome could provide any relevant information or if he was simply trying to impress David. Ludwig had advised David not to ask direct questions but just to engage in subtle conversation. He hoped that Jerome might get talkative after a few drinks. David's eagerness bothered Ludwig, but this meeting should be simple and of very little threat.

Ludwig, a professional, couldn't help but smile as he listened to Jerome's comments. "Doing good, David, *ja*," he said under his breath. David followed Jerome's lead, and it wasn't long before Jerome became more talkative. Although Jerome was mostly interested in David, David was doing very well at extracting information from him. Ludwig, impressed with David's performance, was a little concerned after David ordered the second drink but not enough to bail him out. Jerome was beginning to provide some valuable information.

David picked at the mixed nuts on the table as Jerome finished off his drink. David had two drinks waiting as Jerome ordered another round.

"There was this Arab fellow looking to buy some weapons," Jerome said as he stroked David's thigh. "I think he was looking for a couple of people as well. I don't know if he found a supplier. I could find out for you, if you like."

"Is he local? Does he have money?"

"He's been hanging around town and flashing a lot of greenbacks."

"What's he looking for?"

"I don't know exactly. All I know is guns and a couple of people."

"Set something up," David said, dropping his hand to Jerome's hand, stroking his thigh. "I'd like to meet him."

Ludwig disconnected the earphone, removed it from his ear, and then slid it into his pocket. "Time to rescue the boy," he said to himself. Taking another sip of his drink, he scanned the surroundings again and then stood and nonchalantly walked out of the Centra Bar and Lounge and back to the Aurora Bar. David had done well, and Ludwig didn't want to risk the young man's cover any longer than necessary. Ludwig believed that Jerome's attraction to David would be to his advantage in setting up the meeting with the Arab, whom he suspected was one of the men he was looking for.

Ludwig stepped toward the table where Jerome and David were sitting. Jerome was about as close to David as he could get. David looked as if he welcomed the rescue. "We must go. There is work to be done," Ludwig said as he neared the table.

David turned to Jerome. "The boss. I gotta go. I'll see you later."

***

10:06 p.m.
November 6, 2013
Rental House
Boulder City, Nevada

Bart was seated at his desk, watching the news on his laptop. The lead story was about a video released by ISIS threatening to destroy New York City. In another video recorded earlier, the mayor, flanked by the police commissioner and Dawn Blakey of Homeland Security, was holding a press conference to reassure the citizens that everything was being done to protect them.

"There is no credible threat," the mayor continued. "All New Yorkers should go about their business as usual. Their objective is to terrorize the citizens and shut the city down because of fear. We will not be intimidated by their rhetoric."

The reporter talked about the ISIS video showing images of the city and key areas. He reiterated the video translation about ISIS threats to destroy the city and the usual death-to-America chant. The police commissioner took his turn at trying to convince the people that New York City was the city most prepared for meeting any terrorist attack. He repeated the mayor's remarks and spoke about preparedness of the police force.

Dawn took the podium next. She also spoke of readiness and confidently stated, "The full resources of Homeland Security, the FBI, and local law enforcement are working closely to prevent any attack." Her remarks were for reassurance, but like the other two's, they did little to inspire confidence in the citizens. Dawn added, "There is no credible threat to the city, but we do take these threats seriously."

Bart switched to the other networks to see the coverage they were giving to the situation. Each of the news broadcasters devoted about equal coverage, some more dramatic than others. Their pages contained videos, headlines, and articles. Bart leaned back in his chair.

Now if they can make it impressive enough and keep the rhetoric up, Kenworth may bite, he thought. His cell phone rang, interrupting his thinking. Bart assumed that it was al-Muhaymin calling him, as he was due back from the lake.

"Bart," he said into the phone.

"Al-Aqrab," the voice said. "You have approval to execute."

"What about the two men I've asked for?"

"The police arrested our recruiters. It is taking a little time to get reestablished. It will be a few more days." The call terminated.

Bart flipped the phone onto the desk and leaned back. *I don't have a few more days! Friday night*, he thought. *That's when we go. Busy day tomorrow.*

***

7:21 a.m.
November 7, 2013
Bellagio Hotel
Las Vegas, Nevada

"Max," he said as he placed the phone to his ear.

"This is Margaret," came the reply. A hint of excitement was in her cheerful voice.

"Whatcha got?"

"The Internet is very active. Lots of the usual garbage. We did pick up on increased emphasis on recruiting English-speaking fighters for the United States. They've referenced New York City several times, and there was one reference to Los Angeles. I talked to Dawn, and she is convinced more than ever the attack will be in New York. It doesn't seem right to me. It's almost overdone."

"I saw the news about the threat to New York City. I don't buy it as the primary target."

"You need to get some hard intel pretty quick; Dawn has everyone thinking New York." Margaret's words were filled with caution. "The president keeps pressuring SOCOM to focus there. An attack in New York is possible, but our best guess is that it is elsewhere. We think you're going in the right direction."

"Have you been able to come up with a photo of al-Muhaymin or Abd al Jabbar?"

"Not yet. I'm still working on it."

"Did you see my note that Edsel Bron is dead?"

"I did. Why was he killed?"

"I don't know. Can't figure it out."

"OK, Max, I've got a meeting. Let me know what you need."

No sooner had Max ended the call than his phone rang again. It was Chugs.

"The Global Hawk image didn't show anything out of the ordinary," Chugs said, his tone serious. "SOUTHCOM will keep flying the mission for us."

"Good. We're set here for the meeting tonight. Our ladies are nervous but willing to cooperate. We'll start bugging the room this morning."

"Get them to push it. The president is putting lots of pressure on the old man. We're still trying to buy you some time. Fort Sam Houston has sent their representatives from the Joint Task Force Civil Support to New York. They've had discussions with Dawn Blakey at Homeland. That's helped. She believes the army is committed to her efforts."

"Thanks, General. I'll let you know what we find out tonight."

"I'm sending a delta team to your location. They'll arrive about midmorning. The commander will contact you when he gets there. Good luck, Max."

"Thanks, General."

Max checked his watch and then picked up his coffee cup to take a sip but realized it was empty. Just as he started to reach for the pot on the table, he heard a knock. He stepped to the door. Opening it, he admitted Gail, Danya, and David.

"Ludwig will be up in a minute," Danya said with a smile and kiss on the cheek. "He said he is getting a good cup of coffee."

"Let's go ahead and get started," Max said. "Our ladies will be here before you know it."

Within a few minutes, Ludwig arrived carrying two cups. Handing one to Max as Ludwig entered, he said, "A *kaffee* for you."

Max took the cup and sipped it. A smile spread across his face.

Ludwig returned his smile and nodded. He knew Max would like it.

Candy and Ruby arrived as scheduled at Max's suite, where the others waited. The undercover FBI agent, posing as the third prostitute, wouldn't arrive until that evening. Max gave Candy and Ruby another opportunity to back out, which they declined.

"Anything you hear or see in the course of this operation cannot be divulged," Max said in a commanding tone. "Should you reveal anything, your agreement for the Federal Witness Security Program will be revoked, and any money paid to you must be repaid. Do you understand?"

Both women nodded as Max looked at them. He continued, "Gail has a form for you to sign, attesting to what I just told you."

By 10:15 a.m., Max and Gail were well into the rehearsal of the ladies for the evening. The electronics team was busy emplacing the sensors and ensuring that there were no dead spots in the entire room. The women were instructed to keep the men talking and to supply them with drinks.

"At the first sign of trouble or if you feel threatened, just sing out. We'll be listening constantly," Gail said as she looked at each of the women. "Keep the conversation casual and questions light. If the men start bragging, which they probably will, encourage them."

"Appeal to them," Max said, his tone reassuring. "I want to find out how long they're going to be here, where they're going from here, and what're they doing—things of that nature. Make it part of general conversation. As a precaution, this is a sedative." He handed them a small envelope. "Just add it to their drink, and they'll be out in about ten minutes. It's colorless, odorless, and tasteless. Put it where you can get to it quickly and discreetly. Got it?"

Each of the women nodded.

"Max!" Gail's harsh words flew at him. "We can't drug these guys."

"There're a lot of things we're not supposed to do, but I'm taking every precaution with these girls. If one of the ladies slips it in a drink, tomorrow morning the guy won't remember a thing. Blame it on the booze. I'll do what I need to get those items back."

Gail nodded. Her eyebrows rose, and the corner of her mouth wrinkled up.

***

10:30 a.m.
November 7, 2013
Rental House
Boulder City, Nevada

Since waking at dawn, Bart had worried about his plan and, most importantly, his survival. He was not happy with al-Aqrab taking so long to give him approval—and neither with the time it had taken Abd al Jabbar to bypass the PAL. Their position at the rental house had been static for too long. As a professional, Bart followed his employer's instructions and understood that his operation was part of a bigger plan. He wasn't concerned about anything other than the execution of his mission and, of course, his preservation.

Shorthanded, Bart thought al-Muhaymin to be unreliable, needing close supervision, which caused him another problem. There were still a number of tasks to complete—deliver the nuke to Barstow, get the other one to the lake, clear the house, and modify his scheme to get the bomb to the fishing boat. If he didn't need to deliver the one device, he would forgo the rifles and not drive to Barstow. Bart was faced with a Hobson's choice.

"There's a change of plan," Bart said as he stood before al-Muhaymin. His expression was serious, his tone foreboding. "I want you to deliver the nuke and pick up the small arms. Take one of the snipers with you to check them out."

"Bart, I—"

"I don't want to hear any shit from you. Pick up the weapons, and go to the lake location when you get back. I've got to get everyone out of here and check this place thoroughly to ensure nothing was left behind that the authorities can use."

"I can do that, Bart," al-Muhaymin said as his enthusiasm evaporated. He had counted on his night with Candy, and with this sudden change, his mood turned sour.

"No. You're going. Obey all the traffic signs, and be a model citizen. Think you can do that?"

"Yes." Al-Muhaymin sighed.

"Allow at least three hours' travel time. Plan accordingly. After you make the pickup, get a room, and spend the night. It'll be too late to drive back. Be at the lake by eight thirty in the morning."

Al-Muhaymin nodded and walked out of the room.

***

10:46 a.m.
November 7, 2013
Bellagio Hotel
Las Vegas, Nevada

"Hi, love," Candy said into her cell phone. Her words were soft and seductive. She motioned to Max and Gail as she stood and walked to the table where they sat. She pointed to her phone and mimed that it was al-Muhaymin. Max and Gail stood close to her in order to hear him. Max grabbed a pencil and tablet from the table.

"I must reschedule our party tonight. I am required to go out of town for business."

Max scribbled on the tablet: *Keep him talking. Tell him you love him. Turn on the charm.*

"I'm so disappointed, honey. I miss you. I was really looking forward to being in your arms tonight." Candy was more delicious than a hot fudge sundae.

"I am most sorry. I want you, too. These things happen." Max scribbled again: *When will you be back?*

"Haris, I need you. When will you be back? It is so difficult to be away from you."

"I will be back tomorrow. But I must work late."

Max held the pad where Candy could see what he had written: *When will I see you again?*

"When will I see you again? I miss you so much. I need you." Candy was good and convincing.

"Perhaps Saturday night."

Max scribbled again: *Can I go with you?*

Gail's wide eyes shot to Max.

"Haris, I can't stand it," Candy said. "That's too long. Can I go with you? We could be together tonight."

There was a pause on the line.

Max shot a look at Gail and then at Candy. Then he scribbled again: *Please, Haris. I love you. Just you and me tonight.*

"Please, Haris. I've been miserable these last few days without you. I love you so much. Just you and me tonight—all night. Don't you miss me?" Candy looked at Max and smiled.

"I…I don't know."

"I'll wait for you in the hotel while you conduct your business. I'll have everything ready and waiting for you—including me."

Gail's eyes darted to Max and then back to Candy. The tension was visible on Gail's face. She struggled not to speak.

Al-Muhaymin was silent once again.

"I need you, my love." Candy was as sultry as a summer night in Venice.

"I will pick you up about six thirty," al-Muhaymin finally said.

"I can't wait to be with you. Pick me up at the Bellagio. I'll be waiting."

When the call ended, Gail looked at Max and said, "You're quite the romantic."

Max began to blush and then said, "Change of plan. Let me think just a minute."

Candy and Gail sat at the table as Max paced the floor. "Very good, Candy," Gail said with a smile.

"I was so nervous, I thought I was going to pee in my pants. Now what?"

"Let's see what Max has to say. Just relax for a moment."

Within a few minutes, Max stepped back to the table. "Gather around. Here's what we're going to do."

As soon as the others took their places at the table, Max began to speak. "Al-Muhaymin is going somewhere this evening. We don't know where or why, but he'll be back tomorrow. He's working late tomorrow when he returns. Possible party Saturday night."

"It sounds to me as though they have not executed, but maybe tomorrow night, *ja*," Ludwig said as he doodled on his notepad.

"That's what I was thinking," Max said. "Danya?"

"I agree," Danya said as her eyes darted from Max to Ludwig and then Gail. "He may be thinking Saturday night for their victory party. I don't know about going out of town—"

"For weapons," Gail said. "Or, possibly, to transfer the other item to someone."

"Candy, you don't have to go with him tonight. It might get a little dangerous." Max's tone was calm and supportive.

"I don't know. Let me think. I don't know what to do. Can Ruby stay here?" Candy looked up at her friend. "These are pretty bad guys, aren't they?"

Gail squeezed Candy's arm to reassure her.

Max nodded. "Al-Muhaymin could be going anywhere. Gail, you're going to need a few more sensors and a GPS emitter with equipment to track Candy."

"Got it," she said.

"Al-Muhaymin is the key. He's staying overnight somewhere. Unfortunately we don't know where. We'll follow him, and he'll lead us to the items. Then we can take them."

Max looked at Danya; her eyes were fixed on him. "Danya, you and Gail are with me. We'll follow al-Muhaymin." Max glanced at Gail and then at Danya. He saw the slight smile emerge on Danya's face. "Ludwig, you and David stay on Jerome and see where he leads you. Candy, will you help us?"

Candy looked at Ruby, Gail, and back to Max, and then she nodded.

"Good. Gail will put sensors on you so that we can monitor you." Max touched Candy's arm to soothe her. Then Max continued, saying, "We'll start following al-Muhaymin as soon as he picks up Candy. Wherever he goes, we go. At the hotel he stays at tonight, Candy will be waiting for him as you suggested."

Max turned to Candy. "I want you to be very sexy right away. Mix him a drink, and tease him. When he has his third drink, mix him another, and put the sedative in it. He'll be out in about ten minutes. When he's out, we'll come in and help you get him in bed. I want to get his photograph, fingerprints, and DNA. Tomorrow he'll feel hung over. We'll stage the room to look as though he drank so much that he passed out. He won't remember anything, so just convince him you had sex with him. Do you think you can do that?"

A grin spread across Candy's face. "I can do it."

"The aftereffect of the sedative is similar to alcohol, so it will be fairly easy for him to believe he is hungover. You'll need to drive back."

Candy nodded.

"The time frame from when he takes the sedative and it kicks in can seem like a long time. Tease him, toy with him, and just keep him entertained. Can you do this?"

Candy nodded again. "How long will he be out?"

"About six to eight hours."

"You'll be listening?"

"Yes, so if you get into trouble, we'll be there," Max reassured her.

"Are we taking al-Muhaymin when he returns?" Gail asked.

"We'll take him with the others when we have the items located," Max said. "We'll take 'em all. Got it?"

Max looked at each of them.

Each person nodded.

Chapter 18

9:48 p.m.
November 7, 2013
Barstow, California

Max pulled into the parking lot of the outlet mall just up from the Hampton Inn and Suites on the southwest side of Barstow. The hotel faced out toward the desert, and the line of sight from the outlet mall was unobstructed. When al-Muhaymin had turned off the interstate and passed a couple of fast-food places, it had been easy to deduce that the Hampton was his choice for the evening. The road circled back to the interstate, and nothing else, except desert, was along the road. Max and Gail kept a constant vigil on al-Muhaymin's Lexus. Danya was asleep in the back seat—her pain medication working.

They watched the three occupants get out of the Lexus and enter the hotel. Within fifteen minutes, the two men—without Candy—emerged, got into the Lexus, and turned back toward the interstate on Lenwood Road. Max turned around and hesitated for a minute and then reached over the seat and gently shook Danya. "Wake up. Looks like it's about time to go to work."

Danya moaned.

"Danya, wake up."

She eased up and ran her hand through her hair. "Where are we?"

"They just dropped off Candy at the hotel. We'll find out in a few minutes what this trip is all about."

Max's cell phone vibrated, indicating a text message. He looked at it and then held the phone so that Gail could see it. "Candy's room number."

Gail nodded.

When the Lexus passed the mall, Max eased back onto Lenwood Road in anticipation that the car was getting back on the interstate. Instead it crossed under the highway and cruised into an industrial area.

Following their route on a map, Gail said, "There's not much down here. A couple of truck stops, and off to the right about a quarter mile is a complex of three warehouses. Just desert beyond."

Max watched the Lexus slowly drive past the truck stops and then the warehouses.

"They're looking for an address and checking out the area," Max said as he pulled into the first truck stop. He continued to watch the taillights. A quarter mile beyond the warehouses, the Lexus turned around at an intersection and drove back to the warehouses.

"That's it," Max said as he placed the binoculars to his eyes. Gail and Danya watched intently. The car eased to a stop at the entrance of one of the buildings, and then the driver got out and knocked on the door. Within a moment, a man's head emerged. The trio watched as the two men spoke briefly, and then the driver returned to the car and drove around to the large doors, which opened as the car arrived. The doors closed once it was inside.

"Let's find out what's going on," Max said, and he drove to the warehouse complex and parked just inside the entrance, in a secluded spot.

"Danya," Max said as he looked back at her. "Get behind the wheel. We may need to get outta here quick."

Danya's eyes narrowed as she started to speak, but she didn't. She nodded.

"Gail, go to the big door. I'll check around back."

"OK," Gail said, signaling with a thumbs-up.

Scanning the area with each step, Gail cautiously approached the door. She reached the side of the door and looked across to see Max making his way to the personnel door where the head had emerged. She found a crack in the door and tried to peer in. Unable to see clearly, Gail moved to the center, where the doors still gapped enough to allow her a good vantage point.

The Lexus had pulled in to the right, an SUV was to the left, and a Mercedes had backed straight in. Six talking men stood under one of the industrial lights in the center space between the cars. Gail watched and tried to figure out who the players were; Bart Madison was not one of them. She shifted her position to gain a different perspective of the interior in order to ensure that no one else was lurking in the room's shadowed corners.

One of the men turned and opened the SUV hatch. At that moment Max eased up beside Gail, and she held up six fingers to indicate the number inside.

"We're a little outgunned," Max whispered softly. He moved to where he could see inside as well.

Gail's head nodded. "Looks like this is a weapons buy."

They watched as the man accompanying al-Muhaymin inspected the weapons. Finally after examining the rifles and handguns, something was said, and al-Muhaymin nodded. Another man handed him a canvas bag.

"That's probably the ammo to go along with the guns," Max whispered as he glanced to Gail.

Al-Muhaymin retrieved his cell phone and placed a call. The movement of his lips indicated that very little was said. Then he nodded.

"He must be verifying the guns were satisfactory," Max whispered to Gail. "They're probably transferring money now."

"So we drove over two and a half hours to just watch a weapons buy," Gail replied. Her whisper was sarcastic.

"Don't get in a hurry," Max whispered. "Quick, get back! They're leaving. This way."

Max gave a gentle tug on Gail's arm and led her around to the back of the building where they hid behind a Dumpster. The warehouse doors opened, and the light from inside spilled out. The SUV slowly emerged from the building and headed for the exit. As soon as the SUV cleared the building, the old doors rattled closed but still left a small opening. Max and Gail looked at each other.

"Well, what's next?" Max said in a low voice. "Is it social hour or something else? Let's see." Max touched Gail's shoulder, and they crept back to their former positions at the door.

The trunks of the Lexus and Mercedes were open by the time they reached their observation point. "They're splitting up the weapons," Gail whispered.

"No, wait," Max replied.

Al-Muhaymin and the man with him, the one who had inspected the weapons, pulled out a green container from the Lexus.

"Bingo!" Max whispered. "That's what we've been looking for. But only one."

"One of the nukes?" Gail's whisper was full of surprise. "Shit! What now?"

Gail held her focus on Max. She shivered. *It's so small. I never thought about it before. It was always so far away,* she thought. *I am now only a few feet from it. Damn, it's intimidating; we're helpless here.* "If it goes off, it'll level everything around here, right?"

Max nodded. "Just about everything for a quarter of a mile will be leveled, and about ninety percent'll die from radiation out about half a mile. Don't worry; if it goes off, you'll be vaporized before ya know it."

To Gail, Max's whispered words seemed cold and nonchalant. "Thank you for the reassurance," she replied.

Max glanced at Gail. There was nothing else to say. He turned his attention back to what was playing out inside the building.

"We're still outgunned four to two," Gail whispered.

Extending his hand, Max replied in a soft tone, "Wait, let's see what's going on."

After placing the container in the Mercedes, the four men inside talked briefly.

"They're about to leave," Max warned. "We want the Mercedes; we know where the Lexus is going."

Max and Gail retreated to their hiding place behind the Dumpster. The doors opened again, and then the Lexus emerged and drove toward the exit of the complex. The doors closed.

"We may've just got lucky," Max said, a smile spreading across his face, his tone barely over a whisper. He shot a glance back across the parking lot and saw the Lexus driving down Lenwood Road. "Candy is up next. As long as she does as she was instructed, al-Muhaymin isn't going anywhere for a while."

"She'll be fine. I'm just worried about the other guy with them. We didn't count on him, and he could be a problem."

Max nodded. "What's in the back of that Mercedes is our problem right now. Cross over to the other side, and we'll nab them when they come out. That's the only big door in the building. That personnel door is locked."

Gail nodded and cautiously made her way to the other side of the building. She waved, indicating she was ready.

Max tiptoed to the split in the door and peered in. The two remaining men were smoking a cigarette and casually talking. *They are leaving at planned intervals,* Max thought. He looked back at Gail. His eye caught the flashing light of a police car speeding toward them on Lenwood Road.

"Shit!" Max grimaced and waved to Gail and then pointed to the flashing lights.

Gail nodded and sprinted to the front of the complex to meet the oncoming lights. She retrieved her identification and held it high as she met the police officer, a stocky man, just opening the door. A small, dark-haired policewoman got out of the vehicle on the passenger's side.

"Stop right there," the policeman said, his voice loud.

"I'm Special Agent Gail Summers," she replied, holding both arms high.

He shone his flashlight onto her identification. "We had a report of suspicious activity. What've you got?"

"I need you to block the entrance with your vehicle. I have two others with me. We're after the dark Mercedes in the warehouse. Two armed and dangerous men are in the vehicle. I need them alive."

He nodded, and the two climbed back into the vehicle, shot to the entrance, and parked sideways to block the exit.

Gail had turned to sprint back to her former position to support Max when a shot rang out. *Bam! Bam!* More shots cracked in the night and then another. The engine of the Mercedes raced and sounded like an angry beast. Gail stopped as the lights of the car were barreling down on her.

Danya got out of the car and made her way to where she thought Max was positioned.

"Max!" Danya said, holding her side as she ambled to the corner of the building. She arrived just as Max lowered his pistol. He waved, indicating he was unharmed. Danya turned and hustled back to the car.

Max ran after the accelerating car, but it was too fast. He slowed and veered to the right and saw Gail holding her identification as she stood in the path of the beast.

Back in their car, Danya tore out after the Mercedes. She rounded the corner, sped up, and came up alongside Max.

Gail leveled her Glock and fired twice, before she sprang to the side. The Mercedes swerved to the left and continued. The two police officers fired at the approaching vehicle. The right rear wheel blew out when one of the bullets found its mark. The weaving car continued toward the fence and struck one of the palm trees at the entrance.

The two officers reached the car with their pistols ready. The policewoman opened the passenger's door, and a man fell out. The stocky officer opened the other door and checked the driver.

"He's alive, but he'll need an ambulance," he said as Gail, followed by Max, reached the car.

Danya pulled up behind them and got out of the car. She walked to Max, and after verifying that he was all right, Danya stepped to the dead man on the asphalt and began examining him.

Gail quickly identified that Max and Danya were with her.

Max reached into the car and retrieved the keys from the ignition and then went to the rear of the car. After raising the trunk lid, he opened the container and started inspecting the nuke inside. Out of the corner of his eye, Max saw the flashlight beam bounce off the rear fender and into the trunk. Looking toward the source of the light, he saw the inquisitive female officer approaching.

"Officer, please," Max said, his tone cold and commanding. "Stay in front of the vehicle."

She stopped. Her defenses went up. "What's in the trunk?"

Max closed the lid to the container and saw the officer's hand resting on her side arm.

"Sir, step away from the trunk." She focused her flashlight on his face.

"Gail, I've got a problem. Step back here." Max didn't move but held his eyes on the policewoman's hand.

The officer drew her pistol. "I said, step away from the car."

Seeing the woman's actions, Max didn't budge but planned his next move. If he reacted too soon, someone would get injured, and it probably wouldn't be him. He hoped that Gail could defuse the situation. Max didn't want to escalate the situation unnecessarily. However, he would do whatever was necessary to protect the weapon—even take action to deny the officer access to the contents of the container.

Gail recognized the situation as soon as she saw the woman. "Lower your weapon," Gail commanded.

"What's in the trunk, and what's going on?" the officer asked, maintaining her posture. "I need to see your identification."

"He's with me."

"I want some identification. I'll need to check both of you out. We haven't received any word on an FBI operation here."

"I'm with the Department of Defense. I'm going to get my ID out of my pocket."

"Slowly," the officer said, still holding her pistol ready.

"Ma'am, step to the rear of the vehicle," the stocky officer said, looking at Danya as she approached the driver's door.

"I'll call this in," he said, looking at his partner, and then headed for his vehicle.

Max handed his ID card to the woman. "I'm going to close the trunk, and we can talk."

She glanced over his ID card and then said, "What's in the trunk?"

"Classified government equipment. I need to make a phone call. If authorized, I'll give you the details." Max knew the answer before he asked and was stalling. He was well aware that if he told the officer or showed her the contents, it would cost him more time in answering bureaucratic questions—not to mention tons of paperwork.

In addition, the media would descend on them before he could spit and turn the situation into a circus. That would produce disastrous consequences for the entire situation and probably cost the careers of the SOCOM commander and Chugs.

Max's concern—after taking care of the nuke—was to get back to the hotel, as Candy was in the clutches of two very dangerous men. He had promised her protection if she felt threatened. If anything went wrong on her end, it could very well jeopardize his entire recovery operation—probably her life too.

The policewoman nodded.

Max withdrew his cell and entered the number for Chugs.

"Sorry for the late call, sir."

"What've you got?" replied the general.

"We recovered one," Max told him. "Unfortunately the police are here and want to know what's in the container. We're at a bit of a standoff. One of the bad guys is dead; the other one's been shot. The paramedics aren't here yet."

"Max, you know the answer. Don't tell them anything. Stall as long as you can. I've got a delta team on standby, but it'll take about thirty minutes to get to ya. They're prepared to take the device off your hands."

"Thanks, General. I'll call you back when they leave."

The connection went dead, and Max returned the cell to his pocket. Looking at Gail and then the policewoman, he said, "I'm sorry, ma'am, but I'm not allowed to show you or tell you any more than that this is a piece of classified government equipment. The army'll be here in about thirty minutes to take possession of it."

The stocky police officer walked up and said, "There's no information about any FBI or government operation in our area. The ambulance'll be here in a few minutes. I'm afraid the three of you'll have to go to the station with us."

"I'm sorry, sir, but we can't do that." Max locked his eyes on to the other man's and didn't budge.

The policeman withdrew his pistol and said, "Turn around and put your hands behind you. You too, ma'am."

"Hold on. I can clear this up," Gail said as she placed her phone to her ear. "We have a situation here. We've recovered one, but the police on the scene want to take us to the station. They want to know what's in the container."

Gail paused as she listened; her eyes went to the man and then the woman. Her head nodded as she said, "Thanks." Gail dropped her hand. "You'll be receiving a call in just a few minutes that'll clear things up. In the meantime, I suggest we relax before someone gets hurt."

"Let's all step back to the front of the car," the policeman said. "We'll get started with some paperwork while we're waiting." He looked at the woman and said, "Watch 'em. I'll get the forms and let the station know what's goin' on. This all sounds a bit fishy to me. I'll request the supervisor to meet us."

"I'm worried about Candy," Max said as he looked at Gail and then Danya.

Gail nodded. "She's been on her own for too long."

Within a few minutes, another police vehicle, with its lights flashing, appeared on Lenwood Road and approached the warehouse complex. The stocky policeman returned and said as he looked at his partner, "Relax. Holster your weapon. The supervisor is on his way." He looked at Max and continued, saying, "We're to follow your instructions."

"Good," Max said. "I've a few things to do. Please, everyone stay in the front of the vehicle."

Max returned to the rear of the car, opened the trunk, and continued with his inspection of the nuke. The ambulance arrived at the same time as the supervisor. The senior police officer immediately took charge and introduced himself to Gail. She, in turn, identified Max and Danya by name only and then briefed him as the other two officers looked on. Gail kept all classified information to herself. The paramedics evacuated both men and had departed by the time Max finished his inspection. As he rejoined the others in front of the car, the sound of helicopters could be heard in the distant night sky.

It didn't take long until one helicopter, an MH-60 Blackhawk, circled overhead, and the other, an MH-6 Little Bird, circled lower and then made two low passes above the six standing in front of the car. Max signaled, and the Little Bird landed in the parking lot. It was very intimidating to see the black, smaller armed helicopter—with its machine guns pointing directly at them—land.

Four commandos, seated on the outboard benches, departed the aircraft with their weapons ready. They formed a security perimeter around the disabled Mercedes and the six people. The Blackhawk landed next; its 7.62 miniguns on either side of the aircraft pointing at the six people were unmistakable. There was no doubt as to who controlled the situation. Three more armed commandos exited the Blackhawk.

Max walked toward the approaching soldiers and talked briefly to them. He led them immediately to the trunk of the Mercedes, raised the lid, and then opened the container. One commando verified the contents and then signed a receipt and handed it to Max. Without a word, the other two commandos took the container from the trunk and carried it to the Blackhawk. The other one saluted Max and then returned to the waiting helicopter.

The rotors of both helicopters sped up. The Blackhawk lifted off first, and then the four commandos on the perimeter returned to the Little Bird, and it took off. Both disappeared into the night sky.

***

Hampton Inn and Suites
1:17 a.m.
November 8, 2013
Barstow, California

After arriving back at the hotel, the three checked into the hotel and then converged in Max's room to listen to the situation in the suite with Candy. They were later than anticipated, and Candy was probably frightened. The only thing they were able to hear was the TV. That indicated that the sensors placed on Candy and in her handbag were working.

"Max, I'm worried," Gail said as she stood. "Let's check it out."

"I don't like it, either," Danya said. "She could be—"

"All right. Gail, you lead; Danya and I'll back ya up," Max said and then sighed.

The hallway leading to Candy's room was well lit and vacant. As the three walked to her suite, no sounds came from any of the other rooms. In front of her door, they listened. Sounds of a movie playing on the TV emitted into the hall. Gail, flanked by Max and Danya, stood in front of the door. She looked at Max and then at Danya. Both nodded; they were ready, their pistols drawn. Gail took a deep breath, exhaled, and knocked. She listened and then knocked again. The door opened.

"Oh, thank God you're here," Candy said, her voice filled with excitement. She stepped to the side and allowed them to enter. "I was so scared. I didn't know what to do."

Gail, Max, and Danya filed into the room. Two pizza cartons sat on the coffee table with two partially filled glasses in-between the boxes. Al-Muhaymin was slumped in one of the wingback chairs, and the other man lay on the couch asleep. A half-full bottle and an unopened bottle of Glenlivet XXV were next to the ice bucket on the dresser.

"Tell me what happened," Gail said.

"Just as Max said, on their third drink, I added the sedative. They did start to get a little aggressive, but I kept them entertained. Next thing I knew, they passed out. I was getting really worried when you didn't come back." Candy's eyes welled up, and she began to cry.

Max put his arms around her and hugged her. "You did fine. We just got a little delayed."

"I was so afraid they were going to wake up and hurt me," she sobbed.

"You gave them both a sedative?" Max asked as he looked down at her.

"Yes. When the plan switched, Ruby gave me hers as a precaution."

Max smiled and wiped her tears away.

Danya and Gail started setting the room up to look as though they partied most of the night. Danya took the two bottles of Glenlivet and poured them in the sink.

"This makes me want to cry," Danya said as she shot a look at Gail.

"I think that's probably a crime to pour out such good whisky. At least it should be," Gail said and then emptied the remaining pizza, except for two pieces, into the trash can. "I'm going to get my camera and bag. Can you finish up here?"

"I got it. I'll get the bed turned back. Do you want to get their pictures in here or in the bedroom?"

"In here first. Be right back," Gail said as she left the room.

Max guided Candy to the vacant chair next to al-Muhaymin. "Just relax here. We've got a few things to do."

Candy nodded.

Max sat al-Muhaymin upright and then removed his trousers and pitched them into the bedroom. "Where's his room?" Max asked as he looked at Candy and pointed to the man on the couch.

"Straight across the hall."

Max slipped the key card from the man's pocket and then sat him upright, with his head against the back of the couch. Satisfied, Max went to the room across the hall. In a few moments, he returned, followed by Gail. "OK, we're set across the hall," he said.

Gail started taking pictures of both men and then took DNA samples. As soon as she finished, Max carried al-Muhaymin into the bedroom and removed the rest of his clothing. Gail took several more photos. Next Max carried the other man across the hall and repeated the process with him. Danya took one of the partially filled glasses from the coffee table in al-Muhaymin's room and set it on the dresser in the other room. Content that this room was staged well, Max, Gail, and Danya went back to the other room. They made one last check and were pleased that the room looked like they partied late.

"You can sleep in my room if you like," Danya said, looking at Candy.

"Thanks. I don't think I could sleep here."

"Did he say anything about what time he planned to be back in Vegas?"

"Yeah, I think he said about eight thirty."

"OK. We'll get a few hours' sleep," Max said and then looked at Danya. "Get her up and ready to go. She can make it look like she showered in here, and then she can wake him. I'll be monitoring this room as soon as Candy leaves your room."

Danya nodded, picked up the trash bag full of pizza, and tied the top. It would be deposited elsewhere. She replaced the bag and then dropped a crumpled tissue into it as an extra touch.

Max led the others out of the room and switched off the light. "One more to go," he said. "Hopefully these two guys will lead us to it, if we don't have any slipups, and we'll find it before anyone discovers we recovered the other one."

"And before it explodes," Danya added.

Chapter 19

9:14 a.m.
November 8, 2013
Bellagio Hotel
Las Vegas, Nevada

"OK, what's the address?" Gail said into the phone and then scribbled on her notepad. "Yeah, got it. Thanks." She looked at Max and said, "That was the cyberguy. We've got a good location on where al-Muhaymin has made and received most of his calls. It's a residence, and here's the address." She held her notepad where Max could read it.

In case Candy had needed help, the trio had followed al-Muhaymin's Lexus back from Barstow. At a short distance from the entrance and several cars back, so as not to be seen by the occupants of the Lexus, they watched as Candy emerged from the car and then walked into the hotel alone.

"Gail, you and Danya go in and debrief her," said Max. "I'll tail al-Muhaymin." He began entering the address of the residence into the GPS of the rental car. "Send David to relieve me. I need to coordinate with the delta commander." He looked at Gail, anticipating her response.

"Max, he's not field—"

"He's just observing. He'll be fine." Max touched Gail's shoulder. "Make sure his cell phone is charged."

"It's going to take a little while for me to get a search warrant. I don't want this scumbag to walk on a technicality," said Gail.

Max nodded and then said, "Bring Ludwig back with you. I'll call Chugs. We'll go as soon as we can." Max pushed the buttons to activate the GPS.

The Lexus they were watching pulled away from the hotel.

"Keep me posted," Max said as Gail and Danya got out of the car.

He picked up the Lexus as it headed south on Las Vegas Boulevard. He stayed well behind the car but adjusted his distance as the traffic density changed. The sun was high in the clear morning sky, and keeping track of al-Muhaymin was not difficult. Max began to relax somewhat as they entered Interstate 515 or US Highway 93 to Boulder City. Finally, on the east side of Boulder City, the car exited the highway and began the meandering route displayed on the GPS to the address.

The moderate city traffic was as expected for that time of the morning, and the number of vehicles thinned out as they reached suburbia. Max started paying closer attention to the neighborhood as he drove deeper into the residential district. The drive through the well-kept neighborhood of southwestern-style houses with colorful desert-type shrubs and trees was quite pleasant.

The kids are thinking about Thanksgiving, he thought. *Probably already planning their activities for when school is out.*

The Lexus, a couple of blocks ahead of Max, slowed and then stopped for a traffic light. Max reduced his speed and stopped at an intersection, taking time not to get any closer. He glanced in the rearview mirror to see an SUV approaching. *Going too fast,* he thought. Then the sound of screeching tires filled the tranquility, and *bang*! Max's car jolted as the SUV bumped hard into the rear of him.

"Well…shit!" Max said to himself. "This is going to be a delay. At least I've got the address." Max opened the door, got out, and walked to the rear of the car. A young woman with purple hair, matching fingernails, vast amounts of cleavage, and shapely legs extending from beneath a short dress met him.

"I'm so sorry," she said, smacking her gum as she poked at her cell phone.

"You were going a bit fast." Max struggled to suppress his frustration with the young woman.

"Ha-ha! I guess I was. I dropped my phone."

Max motioned to the church parking lot across the street. "Let's pull over there so that we're out of the street. Let me get a couple of pictures first." He took several photos of the damage as well as the woman's license tag. "OK, follow me across the street."

"OK." She worked the gum; her glossy lips never seemed to meet.

Max determined that the damage hadn't disabled his car and was minor. *Minor,* he thought. *Ya can't get out of a body shop these days less than fifteen hundred dollars.*

He got back into the car, glanced into the rearview mirror, and saw the woman climb into the SUV. He drove slowly across the street, leading the vehicle. When he parked, the purple-haired woman stopped behind him. Expecting to meet the woman, Max got out of the car and walked to the rear again.

At that instant a tan sedan slid to a stop in front of his car, and a dark Mercedes came to an abrupt stop beside him. Before Max could react, two men with pistols drawn were on either side of him. The one to Max's left—a block of a man with a wrinkly, short-muzzled face—looked like a pug dog, and the other man, a little shorter, was the spitting image of a bulldog—a pushed-in nose and protruding jaw. Both had close-cropped hair, and their stature was muscular.

I should have known, Max thought.

"Put your hands behind you, Kenworth," Bulldog said as he held his forty-five automatic level with Max's abdomen.

Max analyzed his situation. Outgunned and outnumbered, he was in no position to refuse. He complied without a word.

Pug bound his wrists with double zip-tie handcuffs. "Your phone?"

"In my pocket."

Pug slid the phone out of Max's pocket and then passed his hands over Max to check for a weapon. He nodded to the woman. She turned, got into the SUV, and drove off.

"Get in," Bulldog said as the rear door of the Mercedes opened.

Max ducked his head, sat on the seat, and then worked his way into the car. Another big man, with a shiny, bald head just like a cue ball, filled the seat behind the driver.

"In the middle," Bulldog said and then got in beside Max.

"Where're we going?"

"You'll know shortly," Bulldog said.

"Whom do you work for?"

"We talk; you listen. Got that, Kenworth?" Bulldog tapped Max on the head with his pistol.

"Bart Madison, right?"

Bulldog struck Max on the head again, harder this time, and then said, "Stuff it! What part of *we talk you listen* don't you understand?"

Cue Ball entered a series of numbers into a cell phone and then placed it to his ear. "We have him. We're on our way," he said and then ended the call and returned the phone to his shirt pocket.

***

9:46 a.m.
Lake Mead, Nevada

"You son of a bitch! I told you to be back here by eight thirty," Bart, red faced, said through clenched teeth as he watched al-Muhaymin and the sniper enter the tent.

"We are back now. Everything is fine," al-Muhaymin said and shifted his stance. A smirk spread across his face, displaying his stained teeth. "We made the delivery and picked up the weapons. There were no problems."

"No, it's not fine. I told you no women. That prostitute is going to land you and the rest of us behind bars. Give me your cell phone."

"Bart, I—"

"I know you took her with you. There's no telling what you bragged about to her. Hell, she's probably working for Kenworth. I've collected the others' phones. We execute tonight." Bart looked at the sniper who had accompanied al-Muhaymin to Barstow. "The weapons checkout?"

"They are sufficient," he said with a nod.

Bart looked back at al-Muhaymin and said, "Here's a list of things for you to do while I'm gone." Bart handed him a slip of paper. "Double-check everything, and make damned sure we're ready to go. No one leaves or gets boozed, and no women. You can have your victory party tomorrow. Everyone is to be a model citizen, even you. Got it?"

"Got it," al-Muhaymin said, the smirk turning to a glower.

"I've gotta go back over to the rental house." Bart's tone was harsh. "The men al-Aqrab hired nabbed Kenworth, and they're taking him over there. I'll have 'em hold him there. I haven't decided what to do with him yet. I've several other things to do as well. It may be dark by the time I get back."

"I will have everything ready. You can count on me," al-Muhaymin said and then displayed a grin. He hoped to get back in Bart's good graces.

"Yeah, right."

***

10:51 a.m.
Rental House
Boulder City, Nevada

David was concealed in shrubbery a short distance from where he was supposed to rendezvous with Max and punched in the number to Gail's phone. He placed it to his ear and heard Gail's greeting that she was unavailable.

"Gail *dahling,* call me as soon as you can. I can't find Max." David ended the call and then entered the number for Ludwig. He heard Ludwig's recorded greeting. "Ludwig, call me; I can't find Max." David ended that call and then tapped at the keypad once again in an attempt to reach Danya. He got her voice message instead.

"Geez, is anyone working? Did I miss something?" he said under his breath and then entered Margaret's number at CTC. When she answered, he said, "Oh, thank heavens you're working; I can't get a hold of anyone. I don't know what to do. I—"

"David, hold on!" came Margaret's reply. "What're you talking about? What's happened?" Her voice was attentive and full of concern.

"They sent me out here to this house to relieve Max, and I can't find him."

"Are you sure you're at the right address? You are at the address the FBI geolocated, correct?"

"Yes, I put it in my GPS. I can't get hold of anyone."

"Have you looked everywhere, very carefully, for Max or his car?"

"Yes."

"Is anything happening at the house?" Margaret's tone was calm.

"No. There're a dark Mercedes and a tan car parked in the drive. I haven't seen anything."

"OK, keep watching the house. I'll keep trying to get in touch with Max and the others to find out what's going on.

I'll also touch base with Chugs. Max may have talked to him. I'll let you know what I find out and call you back. Stay alert, and let me know if anything happens."

David calmed down after hearing Margaret's reassuring voice. His inexperience in field operations was showing. As his anxiety began subsiding, David said to himself, "I remember reading about the feelings of vulnerability and helplessness that are common when alone on surveillance or sentry positions. Ludwig told me it can feel very lonely, especially for an inexperienced person. I understand now what he meant."

David knew that he was no exception. With Margaret's lifeline, he was able to concentrate on the mission he had been given. Just knowing he could call her made it seem like David was no longer alone. His attention returned to the front of the house.

He shifted his position to get more comfortable and checked his watch. As boredom replaced David's anxiety, he picked at the leaves of a bush in front of him. Just as he finished shredding the fourth leaf, he looked up to see an SUV pull into the driveway. Devoting his full attention to the vehicle, he watched as a man got out, walked to the door, and went inside.

"It's him," he said under his breath. "Bart Madison. Oh my goodness. Now what?" David punched in Margaret's number.

"Yes, David," came Margaret's voice. She glanced at the clock and recorded the time.

"It's Madison."

"Are you sure it's him?"

"Yes. I have the copy of the photograph Max gave me. The man looks just like the photo. But his hair is just a little bit longer, and he looks a little bit older. He's wearing a tan ball cap. It's him. What do I do? Gail didn't give me a gun."

"Just stay put, and keep watching the house. Gail and the others will be there in a little while."

Inside the house, Max sat in a chair with his hands still bound behind him. His captors had placed him in the center of a room on the main floor. Bulldog and Pug stood guard over him. Cue Ball, smoking a cigar, stood on the patio and talked to the driver of the Mercedes. As soon as Bart entered the house, the two men stepped inside.

"It's been a long time, Kenworth," Bart said as he glared at Max and pitched his ball cap onto a coffee table on the side of the room. "Too bad you didn't wait one more day. You're the one in the hot seat this time."

Bart was unable to control his anger. He blamed Max for his being forced out of the army, never acknowledging that his downfall was his own doing. Max had just followed orders and regulations. Bart had carried a chip on his shoulder after Max had reprimanded him, and his career had deteriorated.

"Madison." Max's sarcasm was thick. "What pound did these two come from? Your two ladies here think they're really tough." He nodded with his head to the two men. "I think that pair of legs you had in the SUV could take either one of them without messing up her nails—especially the one over there who looks like a bulldog." Max nodded again. "Cue Ball there is too dense—"

"Knock it off, Kenworth."

"I can't figure you," Max continued. "Why bring me back here and not just shoot me? We both know how a hostage situation ends."

Bart drew his fist back and hit Max in the face, knocking him out of the chair. Cue Ball's eyes darted to Bulldog and Pug, and then he nodded toward Max. The two men grasped Max by the arms and set him back in the chair. "Don't tempt me!"

"You want to make a deal?" Max asked through numb lips. Hoping to learn more about his plan, Max wanted Bart to talk. So far Max was still alive, although it didn't appear that the odds were in his favor.

"You're not in a good position to make deals. I want information. Who's in charge of the bunch looking for me?"

"You know better than to ask." Max stared into Bart's eyes.

"I do. Sooner or later you'll tell me what I want to know. Everyone does."

"I want that nuke back," Max said, his tone cold. "We've got the other three." Max saw Bart's eyes squint slightly. *He didn't know we got the other one in Barstow.*

"You can *want* all fucking day. You'll get this one up your ass. Who's leading the effort? FBI, DEA, ATF, or Homeland? Where are they?"

"You've screwed up bad this time."

Bart drew his fist back once more and knocked Max out of the chair again. The guards put him back.

"So I've screwed up," Bart said, "but you're in the chair getting your face bashed in. You got lucky on the highway. I'm glad those two idiots didn't kill you. Tell me, who's running the show?" Sweat streaked down Bart's red face. "Who the fuck is it—FBI, Homeland, or ATF? What are the resources the army is providing?"

"You're slipping, Madison. You know this won't work. Where's the other nuke? We can make a deal." Max saw the rage building in Bart's eyes.

Bart slugged him in the midsection. "I should just kill you now. I want information. You want to die now or later?"

Max moaned and then said, "Feel better? You know they're already looking for me. Unless you deal with me, you won't see the morning sun." Max focused on Bart's eyes. *He reminds me of a rabid dog*, Max thought.

"Where are they, and who are they? Tell me now!" Bart's fist slammed into Max's midsection before Max could answer. Then Bart looked at Bulldog and said, "I'll call you later with instructions. Keep your eyes on him, and don't relax for a minute. I got a few things to do."

Bulldog nodded and then shot a glance at Pug and saw his nod.

Bart retrieved his ball cap, placed it on his head, and walked out.

David's attention had drifted from the house yet again. No matter what he did, no position was comfortable behind the bush. For a while, he toyed with a spider until that got boring. Then suddenly David heard the door of the house across the street from him slam, and his attention snapped back. Bart walked out, got into the SUV, and drove off. David picked up his phone and then tapped in the number for Margaret.

"Yes, David," she said, her voice calm.

"Madison just left the house. No one has shown up here to help me. What do I do now?"

"Keep watching the house. Has anyone else been there or come out?"

"No, no one. Do you want me to go over and look around?"

"No, stay there. I finally got in touch with Gail. She's had a little trouble getting the judge to sign the court order. Danya is with Gail. They didn't think it was going to take this long. Seems like the judge was fishing. Ludwig knows your situation, and when I talked to him, he was about to head in your direction. Chugs was expecting a call from Max, but he never called."

"This is not sounding good," David replied, his voice full of anxiety.

***

Where's Ludwig? David thought as he checked his watch again. *It's been almost thirty minutes since Margaret said he was leaving.* A movement caught his attention. He turned his head and saw the welcome form of Ludwig.

The mercenary crouched and maneuvered to reach the bushes that concealed David. "What's the situation?" he asked in a low voice.

"Madison was here a while ago and then left. I haven't seen anyone else enter or leave the house. Those two cars were here when I arrived."

"Sandwich for you." Ludwig handed David a wrinkled sack. "You like McDonald's and *pommes frittes, ja*? I thought you would be hungry."

"Hamburger and french fries. I'm starved. Wait, you mean we're going to sit here and have a picnic when Max has disappeared and that house may have a nuclear bomb in it?"

"*Ja*." Ludwig shrugged and shifted his position to get comfortable. "We will wait and watch."

David's mouth opened, and he started to speak. But he didn't. He hesitated, opened the bag, and withdrew his lunch.

"Are you armed?" Ludwig asked as he picked up a couple of fries.

"No. Gail said I was just supposed to watch."

"Here." Ludwig handed a forty-five-caliber automatic to David.

"Wha…what am I supposed to do with this?" David asked as he warily took the pistol grip.

"Use it."

David shook his head. "Gail won't like this."

"She won't like you getting shot, either, *ja*. It's Max's." Ludwig's tone was blasé.

"Where—how did you get it?" David asked.

"I spotted Max's rental car in a church parking lot on my way over here. Someone hit the rear end. The pistol was inside the car. I believe Max is in that house over there."

"They have him as a hostage?" David's eyes opened wide.

"Perhaps, *ja*. We will have a look. You do know how to use that, don't you?" Ludwig pointed at the pistol.

"Well, yes. I've been to the range a few times." David's voice was full of reservations. He had never faced what Ludwig had just proposed—a possible shootout.

"Then you know this is the business end, *ja*?" Ludwig pointed to the muzzle. "When we go in, if I start shooting, you point that end at the bad guys and squeeze the trigger."

"OK, then what?" David was struggling; his voice revealed a bit of faintheartedness.

"We kill the bad guys, assess the situation, and go from there." Ludwig's callous response was full of confidence.

"I've never shot anyone before," David said. He had never contemplated such an act. The image of Senator Bradbourne's corpse lying on the ground in Rock Creek Park flashed into David's mind, and his stomach tightened.

"I know. You just make noise, and I will do the rest, *ja*." Ludwig scanned the neighborhood.

"Ludwig," David said as he sat up. "Look." He lifted his hand and pointed to the house.

Two men, one bald and the other slender with short-cropped, brown hair, emerged, got into the Mercedes, and drove off. Neither of them was Max.

"This is why we wait and watch," Ludwig said, maintaining his attention on the house. "One car left. Two fewer guns to worry about. We will go take a look now, *ja*?"

Chapter 20

2:11 p.m.
November 8, 2013
CTC
Tysons Corner, Virginia

"Gail," Margaret said into the phone, "Ludwig believes Max is being held inside the house. Madison entered the house, and then a little while later, he left."

"I'm on my way there now."

"We've got another problem; the president has relieved the SOCOM commander."

"What?" Gail's voice was full of shock. "What did you say?"

"The president has relieved the SOCOM commander. Dawn has everybody convinced that the other weapon is in New York and that they're going to attack one of the dams there. The president won't hear of anything else. I've talked to Chugs about five times already today. He's livid."

"Doesn't Dawn know we recovered one of them in Barstow?" Gail's tone was full of frustration.

"She believes New York will be the main attack," Margaret continued. "The Internet chatter is up, and ISIS is back recruiting former US service members. We've already identified a number of ISIS-trained individuals mixed in with the refugees flooding the borders in the United States and Europe. It's a disaster."

"We're basically screwed," Gail said, astounded.

"You've got about twenty-four hours to get Max and recover that other weapon. I hope to hell he's all right. Chugs said that SOCOM has been set back on its heels and is being micromanaged from the White House. He's sending assets to

New York to please the president. Chugs wants Max to put in an appearance in New York. You may be getting a call from your director."

"I have already," Gail replied. "He's letting me stay here. He agrees with us, but he's feeling the heat as well. Max thinks we may be too late and may not have twenty-four hours."

"The latest Global Hawk imagery still doesn't show anything unusual, just a few people out fishing on the lake, a few people swimming, and a number of campers. That's about it. Do you need anything else?"

"Just Max. I'll keep you posted."

***

Rental House
Boulder City, Nevada

Ludwig made another examination of the surrounding area and then focused on the windows of the house. With a critical eye, he methodically scrutinized each one and then the perimeter. Satisfied that no one was lurking outside or observing from the windows, he looked back to David and said, "Remember what I told you. If I start shooting, you shoot. But don't shoot me or Max, *ja*?" Ludwig saw David's hand trembling.

"OK." David forced the words out. "I think I'm going to be sick." His voice broke.

"No time for that now. Time to move out. Let's go." Ludwig knew he had to get David going, as the longer David thought about what was about to happen, the more likely it was that David's fear would overtake him. In a low voice, Ludwig said, "We will go around to the back of the property; it's too open here, *ja*. They could spot us right away." He tugged on David's arm, began backing out of the shrubbery, and led David back to his car.

Reaching the rental, Ludwig had the key in the ignition by the time David closed the door. Just as he was about to pull out, Gail, with Danya, eased her car to a stop behind his.

"Wait here," Ludwig said as he glanced at David and then got out of the car and walked back to talk to the two women.

"Margaret filled me in. She said Madison was here. Anything else happened?" Gail said as she looked up at Ludwig.

"*Nein.* We were just going to have a look around the back of the house. I don't know how many are inside."

Gail nodded. "I have the search warrant. Let's go check it out."

"Wait," Ludwig said and motioned with his hand. "We need to know what the situation is and where they are holding Max, if he's in there."

"Why don't I pose as a neighbor looking for a cat?" Danya asked. "Maybe I can see enough to tell what the situation is."

"*Ja*, it is good. You come from one side posing as a neighbor. Gail, you come from the other. David and I'll go around to the back. When we get into position, I'll send you a text. If I can locate Max, I'll go in from the rear. Then you and Gail come in. Wait for my text."

"Understood," Danya said and then reached for her purse.

"Ludwig," Gail said, "David is not—"

"He is fine. I have instructed him."

Gail nodded but didn't quite understand his meaning. Ludwig, finished with the conversation, stepped back to his car, got in, and drove off. Gail gave a slight shake of her head and then refreshed her face.

Danya bent down the rearview mirror to see her reflection and then hurriedly applied a fresh coat of makeup, a little heavier than normal. Once the blush accentuating her cheeks was complete, she fluffed up her wavy brown hair. Then Danya applied red lipstick. With a tissue, she blotted at the corners of her mouth to ensure that her lips were perfect. A touch of her perfume behind her ears and at the top of her cleavage rounded out the presentation.

Pleased with the results, Danya slid out of the car and shoved her breasts up to highlight them even more. Next she began tucking in her blouse. She worked the garment to fit snug against her flat stomach, emphasizing her thirty-four double-Ds. She slipped the top buttons of her blouse free to expose an ample amount of cleavage and a hint of her lace bra. As a final touch, Danya massaged her nipples to make them erect, and then leaning forward and looking into the car, she said, "How do I look?"

"Honey, you look hot," Gail said. "Turning on the headlights is a nice touch. I'll pull the car down the street and walk back to the house."

Danya nodded as she stuffed her pistol into the back of her waistband and then closed the car door.

After receiving the text that Ludwig was in position, Danya strolled to the house and pretended she was looking for something in the event someone saw her. She made another check of her headlights to ensure that they were still visible and then rang the doorbell. She stood facing the peephole, as she expected that someone would check before opening the door. Assuming it would be male occupants, Danya ensured that whoever peeked out would get an eyeful of her cleavage. The stage was set.

The sound of the doorbell alerted the men inside. Pug motioned to Bulldog, and they raised their defenses. "Sit there, and be quiet," Pug said as he shot a glance at Max. Both men grasped their pistols and looked to the front door. Bulldog, with his pistol behind his back, approached the door, stooped, and looked through the peephole. A smile emerged on his face. He turned to look at Pug and nodded toward the door. "Check out this chick."

Pug stood and walked closer to the door. He stopped near Bulldog to get a look at what his partner wanted him to see but was careful to stay where he could see Max, if he turned his head.

Bulldog opened the door and eyed Danya and then looked over her shoulder to see if anyone else was near. His eyes landed back on her chest. "Yes?"

Danya, knowing she was correct in believing that he had more testosterone than brains, hesitated momentarily to allow him to look. She gave him the impression she was interested in him by slowly looking him over with her sparkling brown eyes and then said, "Well, hello."

Danya was very sexy and alluring. She placed her right hand on the wall where Gail could see her fingers. Danya's eyes focused beyond the two men as she looked for others deeper inside the house. Her focus returned to the man in front of her, and she said, "I'm sorry to bother you. But my cat got out, and I can't find her." Danya lifted two fingers of her hand, indicating to Gail that she identified two men. "By chance, have you seen a Siamese cat anywhere, possibly in your backyard?"

"No, I haven't seen any cat," Bulldog said, his eyes never venturing above Danya's neck. He then turned to Pug and said, "Have you seen a cat around here?"

Pug shook his head, but his attention remained locked on Danya.

"Perhaps you and your friend would like to come over later for some wine," Danya said as she looked past the two men again to see Ludwig waiting poised by the patio door. She gave Gail the signal that Ludwig was in position and ready to enter. "I just live two doors down." Danya pointed to her left.

"Oh, this is my roommate," she continued as Gail walked up beside her.

Gail smiled as she stopped beside Danya. "Gentlemen," Gail said, her voice enticing. She grasped her identification and continued, "FBI!" Her voice rang out as she thrust her identification out where they could see it. "I have a warrant to search this house."

Gail barged in.

Danya had her pistol leveled at the two men. She saw a look of rage in Bulldog's eyes. "Don't try anything," Danya said. "I'll take the guns."

"Do as she says," Ludwig commanded, his SIG Sauer P220 pistol pointing at them.

The voice behind them told them everything. Bulldog and Pug had been outsmarted and were outgunned; they surrendered their weapons.

"Who's upstairs?" Danya asked, her voice now commanding.

"No one," Bulldog replied.

"In there." Danya motioned toward the inside where Max sat. "On the floor, facedown," she said.

Ludwig cut the zip-tie handcuffs from Max's wrists as Gail started up the stairs and then stopped. "Where's David?"

"Here," he said as he entered the back door, brushing at his pants legs.

"Are you all right?" Gail saw David's skinned forearm and palms.

"Yes. Ludwig had me crawling in the bushes, and there were spiders. I don't do spiders!"

David turned and darted back outside.

Ludwig looked up at Gail and said, "Too much sandwich and *pommes frites*." His tone was prosaic.

Gail rolled her eyes. She continued up the stairs, withdrawing her cell on the way, and called to have the two men picked up and held.

Guarding the two men, Danya couldn't suppress the grin when she heard David. "You all right, Max?" Danya asked, glancing at him.

"I'm fine. We've got work to do." Max rubbed his wrists.

For the next several minutes, they made a thorough inspection of the house, looking for any information or clues left behind. Unfortunately the house was clean. When Gail and Max completed their scrutiny of the rooms, they began questioning the two men.

After about thirty-five minutes, Bulldog said, "We were hired to get Kenworth and bring him here. That was it. Madison didn't tell us anything else. Madison said he'd call later with more instructions. That's all we know."

"All right, get these guys outta here," Gail said to the two men who had arrived to pick them up.

Max watched as the two were escorted out. "He's going to execute his plan tonight," Max said as he looked at Gail. "Madison said, 'Too bad you didn't wait one more day.' That means tonight." He paused and then continued, "Ludwig, you, Gail, and David go meet with Chief Taite at the dam. Tell her Madison has set his plan in motion and will strike tonight. Get her to alert her people."

"Max, it'll be dark soon, and she's probably gone home," David said.

"Right. Have the duty officer call her in. Better yet, Gail, call over there. You'll probably have to use some influence to get them to call her."

"Ludwig," Max continued, "tell her the army will be in charge of the operation. Nothing else. Be sure and get their radio frequencies and send 'em to me. The delta commander'll need them in order to coordinate with the police. I'm going to meet with the commander. I'll take Danya with me, and we'll meet you at the dam."

Max called the delta-team commander. "I'm heading your way. Send your Blackhawk on a reconnaissance of the lake. Just one pass, and circle wide when finished so as not to be seen when landing."

"Yes, sir. I'd like to get the radio frequencies for the Boulder Dam police. It'll be dark by the time they get on station, but the visibility is supposed to be good. Weather isn't a problem."

"I'll have the frequencies for you by the time I get there. I've gotta call Chugs, and I'll have him call you."

"Good, that was my next request." The conversation ended.

Max called Chugs and briefed him on the situation. "I'm OK, General." Max said into the phone.

"Good. Margaret has kept me up to speed all day," Chugs replied.

"The house was clean; we've got two gunmen. Unfortunately they don't know anything. I am convinced Madison will launch tonight. He made one slip. He said it was too bad I didn't wait one more day."

"I agree," came the reply. "I'll get you whatever you need, but it will take a little time to get it to you."

"I know. I just don't know what I need right now, other than a nuclear-explosive ordnance-disposal team," Max replied. If he found the SADM in time, that was one scenario, but if he wasn't in time, the resources would be different. The NAIRA team would be in charge of the situation then—Max, his team, the delta team, many of the Boulder Dam police, and a number of civilians would be dead.

"I'll kick the team out the door and get 'em to your area as soon as possible. I'm calling the delta commander now," said Chugs.

***

The delta commander looked over Max's shoulder as Max examined the Global Hawk images on his smartphone. Danya was on Max's other side. Max quickly roamed over the image chip, focusing from the water's edge to about two hundred meters on land and from the dam north to where the Colorado River narrowed at Flamingo Cove. Numerous campsites and coves dotted the area of interest.

He was studying the same images the analysts at SOCOM had examined without noting any anomalies. Reaching the same conclusion as the analyst, Max loaded all image chips and blended them, each one slightly more transparent than the one below it. Again Max roamed over the area of interest.

"Max, we're drawing a blank," the commander said as he wiped his brow. "I talked to the Blackhawk pilot just before you arrived. He made a pass over this entire area." The commander motioned to the smartphone screen. "And he didn't see anything. I hesitate to start flying all over this area, as we'll tip 'em off."

"I know. Madison is here, and we're just not seeing him." Max began roaming over the water on the image, looking for any change, starting at the dam and going up the canyon. "Hold on a minute. That boat was there three nights ago, for two nights, and then last night it wasn't."

"So?" the commander asked. "Fishermen change all the time depending on where the fish are."

Max zoomed out on the image to reveal a wider area. "The boat is just inside the canyon, almost a straight shot into the dam." Max looked at Danya and said, "I need a pointer of some kind."

She turned and picked up a twig and handed it to Max.

Taking it from her, Max traced a line with the twig from the boat to the dam. "Last night al-Muhaymin delivered one weapon to Barstow, and he couldn't make a rehearsal. If that boat is there tonight, that's them." Max positioned the curser over the craft on the image and revealed the grid coordinates. He copied them down and handed the paper to the commander. "I'll call and get someone focused on that area."

The Blackhawk landed, kicking up sand and dust. As soon as it touched down, three commandos slid out of the helicopter. The turbine engines whined as the rotors slowed to a stop. The smell of the exhaust filled the air. One of the commandos approached the commander. "Hold on just a minute, Max," he said and then stepped toward the approaching soldier.

As soon as the commander returned, Max said, "We need the people in the boat alive to locate the nuke, if they've already emplaced it."

"Got it."

"Here are the radio frequencies." Max turned his smartphone so that the commander could see the frequencies.

"Thanks."

Max called Ludwig and told him about the boat he suspected. "Have someone check it out, and let me know. If the police go, no flashing lights. Don't do anything to tip 'em off. Better to observe from a distance."

"Roger, out," Ludwig replied, and the connection went dead.

Max turned back to the commander and said, "We'll know shortly about the boat."

I hope we have time to wait, Max thought.

***

Lake Mead, Nevada

Bart gathered his men inside the tent on the lake in preparation for the evening. Before he started, he turned up the radio in front of the tent to prevent eavesdropping. The volume matched that of several other campsites. The two sniper teams had departed earlier to get into their positions, as they needed the most time.

"We go tonight," Bart said; his tone was cold. He looked at each man. "We've rehearsed this several times, and you know what to do. We'll kick off in about half an hour. It'll be dark enough by then. The authorities are getting close, so do exactly as I have instructed you—obey all the laws, don't get in any hurry, be polite—do exactly as we have practiced.

Remember, they don't know who you are, so don't give yourself away. Got it?" He looked at each of them. "Remember, you are on a fishing trip."

Each man nodded that he understood.

"Is everything gassed up?" Bart looked at al-Muhaymin.

He nodded.

Bart looked next to the Syrian. "The diving gear ready? Refilled with the carbon-dioxide-scrubbing chemical?"

The Syrian nodded.

"Timing is critical. After you complete your part of the task, be very orderly in your evacuation. If either one of us—" Bart motioned to the Syrian and then himself and continued, "is not on time getting back to the boat, the boat leaves. No search."

He then looked at the Syrian and said, "Don't miss a way point or get lost."

The Syrian nodded.

Bart continued, checking over every detail, each man's duties, and the equipment they were responsible for. He left nothing to chance, and his attention to detail was paying off. Every man was prepared and recited what he was to do exactly. "Take one last look around and at the items you are leaving behind; make sure nothing is left that can identify any of us," Bart said. "Get ready to go."

Bart pulled the Syrian aside. "You have your slate?"

He withdrew the slate and handed it to Bart.

Bart looked it over, first the front and then the back. "Good."

He handed it back and then casually stepped out of the tent. Bart's eyes swept the other campsites nearby and then the area farther out and back toward the dam. He continued strolling around the camp to scan the horizon and parts of the lake he could see from different vantage points.

Nothing unusual, he thought. *Show time.*

He signaled to al-Muhaymin to commence.

***

Max and Danya arrived at the lake just after Scarlet. Gail, Scarlet, and her deputy were already engaged in a discussion. "None of my officers have reported anything out of the ordinary," Scarlet said as Max walked up.

"They probably won't," Max said. "Your officers'll need to look for little things or inconsistencies. Madison probably has them trained to look and act like everyone else here at the lake."

"How valid is this threat?" Scarlet considered her career if the situation should prove to be a hoax. "I still haven't seen anything or any alerts that concern us from Homeland Security. Why haven't I seen something? There are several references to dams and facilities in New York. Are you sure about this? I checked for any alerts just before I left this afternoon."

"Very." Max's tone was curt as he became impatient with the bureaucrat. "I spent a good portion of the day with some of their representatives."

Scarlet looked at his bruises but hesitated.

"Hell, I can't tell you why you haven't been alerted by Homeland," Max continued, his patience slipping away. "I don't make those decisions. It doesn't surprise me, though. Homeland is as worthless as tits on a boar hog. Scarlet, we need to get our asses in gear. Every second counts."

"I need to call my boss. I talked to him on the way over here, and I'm supposed to get back to him as soon as I've talked to you. He doesn't know of any specific threat to the dam either."

"Make it damned quick, Scarlet," Gail said, her tone harsh and impatient. "There's a fucking madman with a nuclear bomb about to blow up the dam. Hell, we may all vaporize while we're standing around working through the bureaucratic bullshit."

Scarlet's eyes shot at Gail. The redhead's look was not pleasant.

"Scarlet," Max said. "Tell your boss that we are ninety-five percent certain there will be an attempt on the dam tonight."

"Are you suggesting I close the recreation facility?"

"Unfortunately it's too late for that. Closing this place down'll cause panic and make it more difficult to prevent the attack. I want you to place your police under my control."

Unsure about what to do, Scarlet shot Max a fleeting look and then nodded.

"I want Ludwig to start briefing and organizing your force while you make your call," Max pushed. He turned to Gail and said, "You and Danya, make sure the officers can identify us and instruct the police not to use their warning lights unless it is an absolute emergency."

They both nodded.

***

Bart made one last observation of the area and then shoved the Bayliner powerboat off the beach and climbed in. Drew Wyman, the ISIS-recruited US Army veteran, slid the throttle lever forward and steered toward the small cove near the entrance to Black Canyon. No one spoke. As soon as the boat was away from the shore, Bart and the Syrian began preparing their diving gear. Once it was ready, they took their seats and joined al-Muhaymin in watching for trouble or for anything that appeared different from their previous rehearsals. The black sky with bright stars was only partly cloudy; visibility was good. So far nothing appeared unusual, and no one was interested in their activities. To any observer, they were just another boat out fishing.

Once the small craft was in the cove, Wyman slipped the throttle into neutral, allowing the boat to glide to a near stop. Bart lifted a pair of night-vision binoculars to his eyes and inspected the entire area around them to ensure that no one was in the vicinity. The only sound, other than the purr of their MerCruiser engine, was the infrequent, distant drone of other boats on the dark water.

On previous occasions, they hadn't been armed and certainly hadn't had a nuclear bomb with them. This night appeared the same as the other nights they had been on the lake. Bart breathed a sigh of relief and paused to look around once again. *So far so good,* he thought. *Still, anything can happen in the next few hours. I'll be glad to be rid of al-Muhaymin.*

Bart and the Syrian donned their equipment and quietly slipped into the water. When the two men were ready, Bart nodded. Wyman eased the lever forward and engaged the transmission; the boat slowly made its approach into the canyon—the divers clinging to the tow harnesses on the side of the boat—to the designated position.

Within a few minutes, Wyman brought the Bayliner to a stop at the drop point. As soon as the divers were ready, Bart nodded, and the two descended to forty feet.

Chapter 21

Secluded Desert Landing Zone
Vicinity of Lake Mead

The Night Stalkers were living up to their name and making their final preparations for the night operation. Not knowing what to expect or how much resistance they would encounter, the elite helicopter crew of the US Army's 160th Special Operations Aviation Regiment prepared for the worst; all weapons were loaded and checked. The MH-6 Little Bird's rotors began to spin as the turbine whined. Four mission-loaded delta-force commandos, two on either side on outboard benches, strapped in. The pilot and copilot of the ominous, armed MH-60 Blackhawk ran through the preflight checklist and started the twin engines. In a few moments, the two birds would launch into their mission, carrying the commandos to recover the SADM.

"Max, we're ready and are waiting your authorization to launch," the commander said into his radio.

"Roger, stand by," the radio cracked with Max's voice.

Tension and activity in the command center spiked as everyone anticipated the upcoming events. Max looked at Scarlet before he gave the final authorization and saw her wring her hands and bite her lip.

The security command center of the police station—a state-of-the-art facility complete with closed-circuit televisions to monitor the area, sensors, and security enhancements to thwart a terrorist attack—became Max's operations center at the dam. It looked and sounded like chaos to the casual observer, but Max was in control, never missing a beat in responding to communications and actions taking place.

On any given night, the police were busy assisting visitors, performing traffic control, patrolling the twenty-three-mile security zone, engaging in public relations, and ensuring safety. This night was no exception. One woman was delivering a baby, there were two minor traffic accidents, a beer party got out of hand, someone got a snakebite, and two people tried to sneak into the recreation facility. Those problems were enough to keep the small police force busy, but Ludwig had directed that additional patrols—foot and mounted—be added, which stretched the force very thin.

Reports streamed in as Ludwig had instructed; all security personnel were reporting everything. Max was in constant communication with Ludwig, the delta commander, Gail, Chugs, and Scarlet. Ludwig directed a team of officers to discreetly evacuate anyone near the boat they suspected and the entrance to Black Canyon. Two police boats were working the coves under the auspices of safety checks on the lake. Danya sifted through bits and pieces of information and looked for pertinent intelligence. She had talked to Margaret twice, giving her a status report and two pieces of information Danya thought were worth running by her. Max was like the conductor directing Mozart's opera, *Don Giovanni.*

"Max, hold up!" Scarlet said as she stepped closer, her voice full of apprehension. She had spent the last several minutes on the phone with her boss. "Homeland Security has just put New York on high alert. They say one of the dams in New York is the target. Still nothing on Boulder Dam. Something isn't right here."

"Scarlet, the bomb—" Gail said, her face as red as Scarlet's hair.

Max held up his hand and said, "Scarlet, that nuke is here and could go off any moment." His voice was cold. "You've got to make a decision right now. I have two aircraft ready to go and waiting my order." Max pointed to the canyon. "That boat down there is the key."

Unable to hold her tongue, Gail said, "You're going to get a lot of people killed, including us. This is no time to be a bureaucrat. Earn your damned salary for once."

Terrified of making a mistake, Scarlet bit her lip, looked at the boat, and then forced a nod.

Max cued the radio, and as soon as he heard the commander's voice, Max said, "Execute. Let me know when you clear the last ridge before the lake."

"Roger, out," came the snappy reply.

***

Wyman and al-Muhaymin relaxed under the star-filled sky as the Bayliner gently bobbed on the water. They had their fishing poles up and the bait down—they looked like the other anglers on the lake. Al-Muhaymin withdrew a cigar from his pocket, looked at Wyman, and asked, "Want one?"

"I've got somethin' better." Wyman turned and rummaged through a tackle box. When he turned back, he held a small tin box. "Want one?" He smiled.

A grin spread across al-Muhaymin's face as he returned the cigar to his shirt pocket. He started to reach for the joint and then stopped. "No, Bart said no drugs or alcohol until tomorrow. Better do as he said. You know how mad he gets."

"Screw Bart!" said Wyman. "He's not here and won't return for quite a while. We've been out here several times, and no one pays any attention to us. Tonight'll be just like the other nights…boring. We're not even catchin' any fish." Wyman pushed the bill of his cap up and then picked out a joint and put it between his lips.

"OK, I will have one. Just one." The grin returned to al-Muhaymin's face as he selected a reefer and inserted it between his puckered lips and then leaned toward Wyman to get a light. The two men leaned back and breathed the smoke deep into their lungs.

Wyman opened his eyes and stared into the star-filled sky. The peaceful night, gentle rocking of the boat, and water slapping against the sides made for a very relaxing evening. The marijuana certainly didn't hurt any. It became more difficult to keep up the facade of fishing as the two men fought off the boredom and the weed-packed roll-ups dwindled.

"I think I'm going to get a girl and go to the beach for a few days. Wanna join me?" Wyman said, his head resting on the back of the seat as he gazed at the stars.

"That's what we can do. Have a party to celebrate. I can have Candy get you a girl. We could go to one of the other lakes around here."

"Duh! If Bart is right, there won't be any lakes around here. Besides, the military and police will be all over this place for a while. I was thinking California."

"I'm not very familiar with California. Do they have good beaches?"

"Beautiful ones. Have her get me a girl with nice, big boobs and a narrow waist." Wyman gestured with his hands.

"We can get a boat like this and drink and screw all night." Al-Muhaymin grinned.

"I'd like to have her straddled across me right now." Wyman wrinkled his face, reached out with his arms as if he were holding a woman, and then thrust his pelvis forward a couple of times.

Al-Muhaymin laughed at Wyman's antics and then sucked on his beer. "I'll call Candy in the morning and set it up." He took another hit on his reefer.

Wyman had smoked half of his second joint. While al-Muhaymin was thinking of Candy, Wyman rose, stepped to the storage compartment, and dug out two more cans of beer. Without speaking, he handed one to al-Muhaymin and then slid back into his seat.

"We must be very careful," al-Muhaymin said as he took the can. "We only have a few hours to go." He inhaled on his reefer and then opened the beer and took a swig.

"This has been easy money, except for putting up with Bart."

Al-Muhaymin nodded. His thoughts were with Candy. "I like you, Wyman. What are you going to do when we finish? You should come to work for us full-time. I will tell them you are a good soldier."

"I don't know. I'll think about it." Wyman sipped his beer.

***

As soon as the commander of the delta team received word from Max to launch their mission, he signaled to the pilots, and in a swirl of dust and sand, the Night Stalkers took off. The Little Bird flew nap of the earth along a planned course from the northwest. In this technique, the aircraft flies just above the ground, using the geographical features as cover to avoid detection. The low-flying helicopter followed the lowest features of the terrain, just about treetop height, to mask them from the skyline and to keep from being heard.

There were few trees in the area, which meant they were flying along and following the terrain features at a hundred knots, twenty feet off the ground, with assistance from the onboard terrain-avoidance radar. It was not a ride for the faint of heart. Approaching the ridge, the pilot maintained the same height above ground to the top of the ridge and then followed it back down on the other side and across Boulder Basin. Hemenway Wall, the ridge that formed the northwest wall of Black Canyon, masked their approach.

The Blackhawk's route, at a higher altitude, was from the south of Hoover Dam to the canyon. North of Kingman Wash Access Road, the helicopter would take an overwatch position that would make it possible for the sensors to scan the terrain on both sides of the canyon looking for threats and provide support to the Little Bird.

Back in the command center, the tension was unabated, and everyone intently listened for the next report from the delta commander. Although Max believed Madison would attack the dam from the water, he could not afford to ignore the possibility of an attack from the land by vehicle or individual. Madison was smart and cunning; Max knew that he was capable of anything. He did consider that the boat in the canyon could be a ruse and that the strike would be elsewhere.

Gail coordinated the building searches as Ludwig focused on the terrain. All the metal halide lights were on and operational; the intrusion-detection system and vehicle barriers were thoroughly checked. The police were methodically inspecting every structure and possible hiding place in the security zone, starting first with the dam. It appeared that the dam was secure and that no one could enter without passing through the sensors and checkpoints. All this bothered Max. He knew that Madison was no slouch, and bypassing dam security was the type of challenge Madison was good at exploiting. One slip or overconfidence of any of the security personnel would play right into Madison's hands.

Max was confident the delta team could slip up on the boat before the occupants would be able to react or get away. What he wasn't confident about was how much they would resist. He wasn't even sure who was in the boat. If they were Madison's men, he needed them alive. Those questions would be answered in the next several minutes, but the most important one—would they recover the SADM in time?—was the gut-wrenching question.

"We just cleared the last ridge; starting across the basin." The radio cracked with the delta commander's voice.

"Roger, out," Max replied and then turned and signaled to Ludwig. He radioed the police boat working the coves to start the approach toward the boat in Black Canyon. The police boat was to converge on the Bayliner as soon as the Little Bird was ready to round Hemenway Wall. Just prior to the Little Bird entering the canyon, the Blackhawk would rise over the rugged ridge to its designated overwatch position.

***

Wyman looked over at al-Muhaymin, who was asleep in the seat of the Bayliner, and then looked around the canyon. *Gotta piss*, he thought. *I'm ready to go to town.* He tugged his ball cap down and then pushed himself out of the seat and stepped to the boat's rear. He unzipped his pants and relieved himself over the side. When finished, he zipped his pants and then grabbed another beer from the storage compartment. *Hell, just as well get him one,* Wyman thought. He took another one, stepped back to his seat, and flopped onto it. With the beer in his hand, he nudged al-Muhaymin. "Wake up. Here."

Al-Muhaymin opened his eyes and then lifted his head. He rubbed his face and saw the can in Wyman's hand. "Ah, good," he said as he took the beer, opened it, and took a swig. "Listen!" Al-Muhaymin paused and then said, "I thought I heard a helicopter."

"I don't hear anything," Wyman replied. "I just hear a boat." He looked over the canyon and then shrugged. "You're imagining things. Relax. Drink your beer."

"I'm hungry," al-Muhaymin said. "Hand me that bag of pretzels." He pointed to the bag in the cubbyhole beside his partner.

Without speaking, Wyman grabbed the bag, withdrew a handful of pretzels, and then pitched the bag to him.

***

The radio's speaker fractured the din of the command center.

"Sniper! Request permission to fire," the delta commander on board the Blackhawk said, his voice cold and confident. "He's on the last finger of Hemenway Wall, about halfway up, near the target boat."

Max looked at Gail; his eyes signaled the question. He then spoke into the mic. "Have shots been fired?"

"Negative," came the reply.

"Take them alive, if possible," Gail said and then stepped to a large map of the lake area that hung on the wall and located the position where the team had spotted the sniper. She looked at Scarlet, who stepped next to her. "That's pretty rugged. Can your officers get up there?"

Scarlet looked at Gail and then at Max and said, "We've got a couple of dirt bikes that'll get them pretty close."

Max said into the mic, "Two police on dirt bikes are heading to the location. Drop off a couple of men to assist the police. Try to keep track of the sniper, and keep the Little Bird behind the ridgeline."

"Roger, out," the commander replied.

"Keep your boat back," Ludwig said to the police radio operator.

The operator relayed the message to the boat as instructed.

"Ludwig," Max said, "it's going to take some time to get up to the sniper."

"*Ja*, too much time."

"That sniper is covering Madison's operation," Max continued. "That boat dropped him off and is waiting to pick him up. If we could get on it, we could grab Madison when he returns."

"That might work," Ludwig said. "But how are you going to get on it? The sniper is covering them. It will be very risky to approach from the air or another boat. Madison may return to the boat before we can take the sniper."

"I know. Let me think just a minute."

***

Wyman sat upright, adjusted his ball cap again, and nudged al-Muhaymin. "That was a Blackhawk."

"I didn't see anything," al-Muhaymin replied and then sipped his beer.

"Down there, on the left-hand side of the dam. It rose above the ridge and then dropped back down. It *was* a helicopter you heard a while ago."

Without speaking, al-Muhaymin stood and dug out the Kalashnikov AK-103 assault rifle he had stowed beneath his seat.

"Hey, that's the fucking army. We won't have a chance against them." Wyman's voice was full of panic.

"You just saw one helicopter. Have you seen any others? We can shoot it down."

"We need to get outta here."

"No! We will fight." Al-Muhaymin's training kicked in. "Get ready."

***

Max looked at Ludwig and then at the police communications officer. "Have a boat pick us up at Lake Mead Marina just around the ridge."

The officer nodded and said, "Yes, sir." He turned and directed a police boat to pick them up.

"Gail, take over here. I'll be monitoring in the boat."

She nodded. "What do you have in mind?"

"If we can spook the boat so that they will try to make a run for it, we can nab them. Hopefully they will run back around the ridgeline, since that's the only way out for them. That'll be out of the line of sight of the sniper."

"What if they decide to start firing?"

"We'll deal with them. The sniper first."

"Do you really think this will work?" Gail's forehead wrinkled, and one eyebrow rose.

"I'm open for suggestions if you've got one," Max replied, his tone serious. "Every second counts, and we've got to break the standoff. I don't want to lose any troops or an aircraft."

Gail shook her head. "I don't have one."

"Scarlet, get us to the marina as quick as you can," Max said, his tone authoritative. He started for the door without waiting for a reply.

Scarlet nodded and picked up two police walkie-talkies as she passed by the communications desk.

Several people had gathered on the marina and the nearby shore, looking at the Little Bird maneuvering about the lake. Their curiosity had been aroused when the small armed helicopter had first appeared over the ridge and flown low over the basin. More people approached the water's edge as they became aware of activity near the ridge. All along the shoreline and on the marina, the conversation was the same. *What happened? What's going on? What's the army doing? Was there an accident?* But no one could provide answers. Two police boats were patrolling the basin and keeping everyone away from the entrance to Black Canyon.

Scarlet, driving a police cruiser with the red and blue lights flashing, sped along the route to the marina. Max grasped the mic to the police radio and provided details of his plan and instructions to the delta commander, the police, and to Gail.

"I want the Little Bird to surprise the boat with a pass and avoid the sniper," he said. "Scarlet has authorized the Little Bird to use small-arms fire in response—if the sniper fires on them. Hopefully the occupants in the boat will try to escape out of the canyon."

"That's pretty risky," the commander said. "I prefer not to get these guys shot up."

"Come in low and fast. Have two men ready to return fire as necessary. If the sniper fires, take him out."

"Roger," the commander replied.

"The police boat will intercept the Bayliner," Max continued. "Then Ludwig and I'll replace the occupants and take the boat back to the former position to wait for the divers. I'll brief the boat skipper on the way."

Their route would take several minutes, as they needed to travel from the dam around the ridge forming the canyon wall. Scarlet proved her driving ability on the curve-filled road leading back to the Great Basin Highway. Once on the highway, she floored the pedal; the car reached 120 miles per hour until she slowed to exit onto Lakeshore Road. The car slid to a stop at the entrance to the marina; Max and Ludwig immediately sprang from the car. Scarlet, not as fast, followed them. A police boat was waiting at the marina by the time they arrived.

Once the two men stepped aboard, Max said, "OK, let's go."

As the police boat reached Cape Horn, a point on the ridge out of sight of the sniper, Max directed the Little Bird to commence its run.

In the Bayliner, al-Muhaymin and Wyman heard the Little Bird behind them as it shot past, just over their heads. The two men ducked low, and then Wyman started the engine.

"Death to the infidels!" al-Muhaymin screamed. He raised the Kalashnikov AK-103 assault rifle and squeezed the trigger. "*Allahu Akbar!*" The 7.62-millimeter ammunition sprayed wildly into the night sky. The thirty-round magazine emptied in about three seconds. He paused briefly and then reached for another magazine.

Wyman, not having the same training as al-Muhaymin, realized that any resistance against the army was futile. He had seen the horrors of battle and the capability of special-forces soldiers. He knew they would bring him death. He threw up his arms in surrender.

As soon as the Little Bird passed over the boat, it swerved and zigzagged in the sky to avoid the sniper. The commandos on the outboard seats, watching for the sniper, saw the muzzle flash of his rifle. Immediately both returned fire. The sniper's body slumped onto the rocks, and the commandos returned their attention to the boat in time to see the crazed al-Muhaymin wave his rifle and then fire without aiming. They again returned fire. Al-Muhaymin's body fell onto the deck of the boat as Wyman's hands reached for the sky.

The Blackhawk had resumed its overwatch position, its sensors scouring the rugged terrain once again, just as Max ordered the Little Bird to make the pass over the boat. Two crew chiefs manned the miniguns on both doors, and commandos filled the seats next to them. They saw the sniper fire at the Little Bird and then watched the bodies of the sniper and his spotter fall as the army shooters took them out. The pilot eased the bird toward the canyon to get a sensor reading on the east side of the canyon, which had been blocked by the jagged rocks.

"Sniper at two o'clock, low," the pilot said over the intercom and pointed toward the spot where he saw the sniper. The delta commander tapped the soldier next to him as a signal to neutralize the threat. The pilot swerved as the sniper raised and fired at them. He stabilized the helicopter, and the soldier fired twice and then again. The sniper and his spotter fell silent. The commander sent the coordinates of the bodies' location to the command center.

As the Little Bird approached the Bayliner, the pilot gestured for Wyman to head the boat back toward the entrance of Black Canyon. The police boat with Max and Ludwig met the Bayliner as it rounded the point of the entrance. As the Bayliner came alongside the police boat, Max and Ludwig stepped onto it. Max removed Wyman's ball cap and placed it on his own head as Ludwig checked al-Muhaymin's body. The police took Wyman onto their boat, placed handcuffs on his wrists, and seated him. Ludwig passed the corpse to the police boat and shoved off to separate the boats.

The police boat eased away and circled back to the marina. Max gave a wave to the Little Bird and the Blackhawk, and the Night Stalkers disappeared into the night. Ludwig sat in the seat across from Max as the boat returned to the position it had occupied only a few minutes previously. Another police boat waited around Cape Horn, in case Max and Ludwig needed assistance. The two men sat quietly in the boat and pretended to fish. Their silhouettes closely matched those of the previous occupants. If the divers surfaced at a distance to check out the boat before coming up next to it, the boat would look as they expected—dark, quiet, with two men fishing leisurely.

Max and Ludwig sat silently, waiting and scanning the water as the boat gently rocked. Peace and calm had returned to the canyon. There was no way to know when the divers would return or even if that was their plan. How long to wait was the real question, as they knew that terrorists, with the intent to do horrific damage and cause terror, had emplaced a nuclear bomb. Neither spoke of it, but it was on their minds. Were they waiting for their own deaths?

After a while, a head broke the surface of the water about ten meters from the boat.

"Ludwig, you see him?" Max asked quietly.

"*Ja*," he whispered. "Just one, though. The other should be near." His eyes scanned the water.

"As he grasps the ladder, grab his arms, and we'll pull him aboard before he knows what's going on."

Ludwig nodded.

"He's swimming in. Let's get ready."

Ludwig stood and stepped to the rear of the boat. Max stepped next to him. Both were ready to grasp the diver and pull him aboard.

They watched as the head bobbed along the surface of the water. Finally the diver reached the boat and paused. One dive fin emerged from the water in the diver's hand. Max took it. Then another fin appeared, and Max took that one, pitching both on the deck behind him. The diver's hands rose, searched for a firm hold on the boarding ladder, and then slid up the rail. Max and Ludwig grasped both of the man's arms, as was normal when helping a diver onto a boat, and steadied him as he stepped onto the deck.

Max glanced back to the water but didn't see a second diver. Out of the water, the bulky rebreather and weights made the man awkward and unstable. Max and Ludwig had control over him. Max held him as Ludwig began removing the man's gear, beginning with his mask, to reveal his startled and wide-open eyes. Ludwig continued stripping the diver of his equipment.

Chapter 22

12:37 a.m.
November 9, 2013
Lake Mead, Nevada

Ludwig reached down to the diver's calf and removed his titanium knife. "I have used a knife just like this once on a man. Do not make any sudden moves, or you will become fish bait, *ja*?" Ludwig's tone was cold. He held the sharp blade next to the man's neck.

The diver nodded.

Max slipped the dripping rebreather off the man's shoulders as Ludwig unzipped the wet-suit top; a diving slate fell to the deck. In a sudden burst, the man kicked at the slate in an attempt to knock it into the water. Max popped the man, knocking him back, as Ludwig scrambled and grasped the slate.

"Where's Madison?" Max asked through clenched teeth.

"I do not know Madison." The man forced the words through his bleeding lips.

Max hit him again in the face, and he went down. "Don't waste my time. Where's Madison?" Max asked the diver as he towered over the groaning man. Max kicked him in the side.

"I want lawyer," the man groaned as he held his side. "You must get me lawyer."

"We're not the police and don't need to get you shit! I want to know where Madison is."

The man spat at Max.

Max kicked him, and the man drew up in pain.

"Max, look here. The slate, it shows the location of the SADM." Ludwig pointed to the slate with the tip of the knife.

Max took it from Ludwig and shone a light onto the slate. He traced along the line that was drawn to each one of the points and read each notation, and Max followed the line to the end, where a tick mark was placed. "That's it," Max said. "I'll call Scarlet. Scan the water and the shoreline again for Madison. He coulda spotted us and could be swimming to shore."

"Or that was his plan all along, not return to the boat," Ludwig said as he locked eyes with Max.

"Could be. These guys take the fall, and while we're dealing with them, he gets away. That'd be the smart thing to do. Let's not waste any more time with this guy; the nuke is the priority."

Max alerted the police boat waiting behind Cape Horn. "We're heading your way," Max said into the walkie-talkie. "We captured one and will drop him off to you."

"Roger, we'll stand by."

Next Max called Scarlet. "We're on our way back to the marina now. I think we've located it. Do you have two sets of scuba gear?"

"Yes, we use it often," Scarlet replied. "I'll have two divers waiting for you at the dam."

Max immediately called the delta commander. "We're missing Madison, the leader. He didn't surface with the other diver. Have your birds start a search along the canyon out to the basin. He could've gone to either side." Max slid a map of the area closer to him. "Looking at the map, it appears to be less populated on the Arizona side."

"We're on the ground now, and it'll take about twenty to thirty minutes for us to be on station. It's pretty rugged on that side," the commander replied. "It'll be slow going for him, if he went that way. There's one ravine on the Arizona side that could provide him a good escape route. It's close to where the boat was. Vicinity—hill four, eight, niner. The wadi leads to Kingman Wash Access Road."

"Roger, I see it," Max said. "If he makes it to that road, we may lose him. I'll get the police to cover that area. Maybe we can head him off. Out."

Max immediately punched in the numbers for Scarlet and directed her to send the police to the area the delta commander described.

"I know the area you're talking about," she replied.

"Remind them that Madison is probably armed and very dangerous."

Max guided the Bayliner alongside the police boat and allowed it to coast to a stop. Ludwig seized the other craft and held it as Max and one of the police officers lashed the boats' cleats together. Another officer stepped onto the Bayliner. Ludwig turned and grabbed the Syrian, guiding him to his feet. The policeman placed handcuffs around his wrists and then assisted him onto the police boat.

"He's all yours, and he's been schooled, already demanding a lawyer," Max said as he bent over to release the line from the cleat.

The officer nodded. "Figures. We'll process him in."

"He'll be out in twenty-four to forty-eight hours." Max looked at the officer and then at Ludwig.

The officer wrinkled up the corner of his mouth and gave a nod as he said, "Unfortunately."

As Ludwig looked at Max, his expression was one of astonishment. "Why, Max? That doesn't make sense; he just—"

"I know, Ludwig. Don't get me started. Let's go."

As soon as the ropes were free from the cleats, Max shoved the throttle forward, and the two boats parted.

Just as Max and Ludwig stepped onto the dock, they were met by Scarlet. "My two divers are on the way and will meet us here in about forty-five minutes. They advised me that since the water level is so low, they'll need to leave from here. There's no place to get in and out of the water close to the dam. A police boat will take you back around to the dam."

"Shit!" Max exclaimed. "We don't have that kinda time."

Max looked beyond Scarlet and saw a number of people approaching and crowding onto the dock. He looked toward Lakeshore Road. Several vehicles, their lights bouncing off the road, obviously were already making their escape from the area.

The marina was filling with people of all ages—disheveled and dressed haphazardly—trying to find out about the activity of the army helicopters and the gunfire. The shoreline of the basin came to life with onlookers. Lights popped on at every campsite. Lanterns and flashlights dotted the landscape. The tranquility turned into a din of anxious questions, speculation, and rumors.

No one knew what was happening, and like an infectious disease, fear began to take hold spreading through the crowd. *What's happening? Is it terrorists? Is there a bomb? It must be bad if the army is here.* Max recognized their tension and suspected that the slightest incident would trigger a panic. His eyes darted back to the water, and he saw the police boat working to keep boaters at a safe distance from the entrance to the canyon.

Max grabbed Scarlet's arm and led her to the end of the rocking dock. He nodded to Ludwig to keep the people back. In a low voice, Max said, "You're gonna have a panic if you don't make some kind of statement. Ya gotta show 'em you're in charge and need to instill confidence. Get several of your officers focused back on the traffic and clear the dock of people. Check all the cars for Madison. This could be his way out. Only essential personnel at the dam."

"Right. OK, what'll I tell them?" Scarlet wrung her hands as bewilderment covered her face.

"Don't you have some prepared press release in case of an emergency?" Max asked. He could tell that Scarlet was allowing her own fear to overtake her. Even though emergency-training exercises were conducted at the dam, those were scripted, and Scarlet always knew the outcome. This time it was real, and there was no script. She didn't know how this situation would end. She'd never faced a real crisis before, and it showed.

"Oh yeah! I'll get it," Scarlet said.

"Go back to the dam, and get with Gail. She'll help you. Get a statement out, and notify all the officers as soon as you can. The news media will be here soon, so get ready. Keep them back from the marina and the dam. This is going to turn into chaos real quick if you don't head it off."

"How do you know the news will be here soon?"

"Scarlet, look at the damned road." Max pointed toward several cars speeding along the road leading to the marina and Lakeshore Road. "That's people panicking. They'll alert the media, if they haven't already."

"Oh, right."

"This is going to make finding Madison very difficult. Get going."

Scarlet turned and started to walk away.

"Scarlet, wait." Max clutched her arm and gently pulled her back around. "Show me where your dive locker is; we can't wait for your divers. Ludwig and I'll locate the device."

"OK, come on." She turned and walked through the crowd without speaking.

Max took a step and then stopped.

"Listen up, everyone," Max said over the clamor of the frustrated mass of people. "That was Chief Taite of Hoover Dam Police, and she'll be making a statement in a few minutes. There's nothing to worry about. Please, return to your camps or boats. No questions right now. As soon as Chief Taite makes her statement, she'll answer questions. There's nothing for you to worry about; the police will notify you about her statement. There will be a press conference later. Just give them a few minutes."

Max, followed by Ludwig, stepped through the murmuring crowd and caught up with Scarlet.

Scarlet turned her head toward Max and said, "Thank you, Max. I wasn't sure what to say back there."

"I know," Max said. "As soon as we get the diving gear, you go back to the dam and brief Gail. Ludwig and I'll head back to the canyon and start searching."

Scarlet nodded.

Max slipped his cell phone from his pocket and called Gail. He told her, "We can't wait for the police divers. Ludwig and I are goin' to try to locate it."

Max stepped away from the others and then continued, "Listen, Scarlet is letting her fear get the best of her. Coach her along. She should have a prepared statement in her emergency-operations procedures. Go over it with her, and keep her straight. Panic is about to set in down here. Take charge, but put the chief out front."

"Got it." Gail's voice was crisp. "The phone lines are flooded with people asking what is going on with the gunshots and helicopters. It's going to turn into a circus pretty soon. Several news organizations have already called in to check out a number of rumors."

"I was afraid of that," replied Max. "Don't waste any time in getting the statement out, and make sure that Scarlet looks like she's in charge."

"Will do. Be careful, Max." Gail hung up.

Max stepped onto the police boat and briefed the skipper. He handed him the slate and pointed to where he thought the SADM was located.

The skipper said, "I know that area well. I think I can get you right on top of it."

"Good." Max nodded. "We're just about ready to go."

As soon as the diving gear was loaded and stored on board, the police boat sped away from the dock. So as not to waste any time, the two men began assembling and adjusting the equipment to fit properly and then pulled on the wet suits. They smoothed the neoprene suits to fit comfortably on their muscular frames. Satisfied with the fit, they sat and waited.

Max picked up the dive slate they had retrieved from the Syrian and then slid closer to Ludwig. They studied the drawings and annotations on the slate again as the craft bounced along the course into Black Canyon. Within a few minutes, the police skipper slowed to a near stop to negotiate the net barrier. Once they were clear of the net, the skipper guided the boat to the canyon wall close to the position marked on the slate.

"This should be it," the skipper said.

Max and Ludwig donned the rest of the equipment, and then, with the help of the skipper, they stepped to the side of the boat and entered the water, one after the other. Max grasped the dive computer and checked to ensure that it was working. He noted the chilly water's temperature at sixty-three degrees and a slight current flowing toward the dam. One-thousand-watt metal halide lights provided illumination of the area and the surface of the water.

As soon as he saw Ludwig's nod indicating he was ready, Max submerged. They switched on their dive lights, as they knew that the overhead lights would soon fade and the expanse beneath any rock ledges would be dark. Max withdrew the slate and oriented it to the rock wall in front of them, and they slowly started an S-pattern search, sweeping the area.

***

Security Command Center
Hoover Dam

Lights indicating incoming calls blinked on the control panel at the communications desk. A police officer went from call to call and repeatedly told each caller that the chief of police would be making a statement in the next few minutes and that a press conference would follow later. Gail also answered phone calls in rapid succession, first from her boss at the

FBI, then Homeland Security, and then from two of the local television stations. David was in constant contact with Margaret at CTC. Danya reviewed and prioritized the reports as they streamed in. Scarlet entered the center and headed straight to her office.

Catching a glimpse of Scarlet as she darted in, Gail ended the call and followed her into the office. "You don't have much time," Gail said as she closed the door behind her. "First thing is, going over your statement. I've already taken calls from two news stations."

"Yeah, I know," Scarlet said, her voice labored. "I talked to my boss on the way over here. He got calls from some reporter and a congressman as well." Scarlet, her face pale, sat at the desk and glared at the door. "I…I'm not—"

"Scarlet," Gail said, harshly and abruptly. "Your statement. We'll practice it a few times; then you give it. Don't answer any questions."

"I don't think I can. I think I'm going to be sick."

"You don't have time to be sick. You're going to give your statement and act as if you're in charge. Just five short minutes. I'll be right next to you. Where's your emergency-procedures book?"

"There, on the second shelf. The black binder." Scarlet forced the words as she pointed to the shelf on the opposite wall.

Gail looked to the shelf and then pulled the bulging binder from its hiding place. She flipped open the cover, scanned down the index to the emergency section, flipped to the page, and began skimming over the information.

A police officer opened the door, stepped in, and looked at Scarlet. "There's a news crew that wants to set up and do an interview. What do you want me to tell them?"

Without hesitation, Gail said, "Tell them to set up at the public bathrooms—back up the hill. There's plenty of parking, and it's away from the dam. Make sure there're a couple of police officers there as well. Block off Hoover Dam Access Road below the restrooms, and don't let any traffic in without checking with the chief first. I don't want that road jammed with traffic. Got that?"

"Yes, ma'am." The officer closed the door as he withdrew.

"OK, Scarlet," Gail said. "Let's go over your statement. Do it just like you have done on those exercises."

"OK." Scarlet's hand trembled as she took the page.

After coaching Scarlet through several iterations of her presentation, Gail said, "OK, that's about as good as it's going to get. Let's go."

Without hesitation, she marched Scarlet to the car.

One of the security guards at the public-restroom parking area directed Gail to stop in the designated VIP section. As the two women emerged from the car and walked to the podium beneath a canopy and bright lights, a news helicopter flew overhead. Gail leaned toward Scarlet and said in a low voice, "The circus has started."

Several news crews were set up, and a number of uneasy onlookers, presumably curious visitors to the recreation area center who had taken notice of the occurrence, anticipated answers from the police chief. The cameramen switched on their bright lights as Scarlet approached. Scarlet, with Gail at her side, was poised as she stood there, and a pleasant smile emerged on her face. The small but growing crowd fell silent in anticipation of her statement. Gail nudged Scarlet's hip slightly as a signal to start her briefing.

"Thank you all for coming," Scarlet began. "I will hold a press conference later, after I have received a detailed report from my officers and all the facts are known. Final checks are being conducted now. I want to assure you, first of all, that the dam and security zone are safe. Earlier this evening we received a report that two individuals were in a suicide pact. As most of you know, that does happen on occasion. When the officers responded, shots were fired, and the officers took appropriate precautions to protect themselves. I don't have the details yet but will have them for you at the press conference.

"Those helicopters you may have seen belong to the national guard. They've been here participating in a national-preparedness exercise we conduct routinely. The helicopters are used in the event of an emergency and had our officers on board. Anytime there is a threat, we take the safety of the visitors and the dam very seriously. I will not take any questions at this time. Thank you."

Scarlet turned, and the two women headed back to the car.

A barrage of questions ensued from the pushy reporters hoping for a scoop on a story.

"Why were shots fired?"

"There was a report of automatic weapons firing. Who was that?"

"How many were killed?"

"Was there a bomb?"

Gail sensed that Scarlet was slowing her stride, so she leaned in close to Scarlet and said, "Just keep walking, and don't answer any questions. Just get into the car."

Scarlet nodded and continued her pace.

Once in the car, Gail eased the car out of the parking lot and headed back to the dam.

"Well," Scarlet said, "do you think they bought the story?"

"No. You just gained a little relief. The press conference will be much different, and your ass will be puckering."

"It is now."

"You're going to think the entire world has descended on you. We've got a lot of work to do. I just hope Max locates that nuke and disarms it in time."

"If he doesn't, then what?"

"Sister, then it won't matter," Gail said, her voice cold. "There won't be a press conference, and everyone around here will be dead—including you and me."

***

Dive Location
Lake Mead

The chilly water turned dark as the two divers descended to where the slate indicated the SADM was located. The only sound was their breathing and the air bubbles against their cheeks that made their way to the surface as they exhaled. Their bright light beams disappeared a few feet in front of them along the jagged wall. Numerous places provided possibilities for the small nuclear device; however, none of them harbored the weapon.

Max and Ludwig were lucky in that they had the slate showing the location of the nuke, but they could be within a few feet and never see it. The SADM, encased in an olive-green canvas cover, would be difficult to spot on land or in rubble; it would be even more difficult to find in the underwater achromatic world of the lake.

Arm's length apart, the two divers methodically searched the area, their light beams leading the way. *Could the location on the slate be another one of Madison's tricks?* Max thought as he probed along. *Would he have intentionally marked a different location and set up his accomplice to take the fall? We did find the slate very easily.*

Suddenly Ludwig signaled for Max to stop. Something had attracted his attention and required a closer inspection.

Ludwig turned and faced the wall and directed his light into a recess that had once held a small boulder. As he moved his light farther, the movement of the water stirred up silt that had accumulated, only to reveal a vacant hole. He looked back toward Max and shook his head. The two resumed their search, and the next few moments provided several more false positives. At about ten meters from where they had started, Max turned and descended, with Ludwig beside him. He checked the dive computer again and saw forty-three feet displayed as they headed back to the starting point.

Max signaled for Ludwig to stop. His eyes had landed on something of interest. Max guided his light closer to the object. In an opening, about three feet in diameter in the rock wall, several rocks were stacked in a mound. *That's not natural,* Max thought.

He gently removed one of the rocks and then another as the silt swirled in the nippy water. The canvas cover began to emerge. Max pointed to his discovery so that Ludwig could see it. The two men carefully removed the remainder of the rocks. Max then opened the cover to reveal the mechanical timer—thirty-one minutes remained. Reflexively both men pushed back.

Why didn't we upgrade those mechanical timers to something a little more accurate? At best we've got twenty-three minutes, Max thought. *Will this be the one that functions eight minutes early or thirteen minutes late?*

They were mere inches from an armed nuclear device that was slowly ticking down to zero. Both divers looked at each other with alarm. There was no way they could escape the blast if the bomb detonated. They would simply cease to exist. Their only option was to try to disarm the weapon.

Unfortunately they could not disarm or neutralize the device under water, and any sane ordnance-disposal technician, if there were such a thing, would want a well-lit, stable platform to work on the armed device. Max painstakingly began inspecting the dark interior of the recess in the wall, looking for any other booby traps or surprises Madison might have left behind. Satisfied that there was none, Max motioned to Ludwig his intent to take the nuke to the boat.

Ludwig nodded and withdrew a small coil of nylon cord and then passed the end to Max, who, in turn, fastened the cord to one of the rings on the harness of the canvas cover. Accidently dropping the weapon was not an option. The lake was too deep at that location to make any recovery possible without special diving gear. Acquiring such equipment and finding the nuke again would take time, which they didn't have.

Max gently cradled the nuke as Ludwig took the slack out of the line. Once it was clear of the rocks, Max signaled, and the two divers, clutching the harness around the weapon, slowly ascended toward the waiting boat. At the surface Max checked to ensure that the tether was still secure as Ludwig clung onto the ladder. Then Max handed the skipper his fins and climbed the ladder.

"Help Ludwig," Max said as he released the buckles and slid the buoyancy-control device, with tank, from his shoulders. He placed it on the opposite side of the ladder near the corner of the deck. Max stepped back to assist the skipper who was hoisting the nuke onboard, and they set the device against the buoyancy-control device as Ludwig climbed the ladder.

"Head back toward the marina as fast as you can," Max said, his voice commanding, and then Max looked at Ludwig. "Are you ready? Hold on."

"*Ja.* Go! Go!" Ludwig said, motioning with his hand. He began removing his gear as the boat headed toward the net, the only thing slowing them down.

Max retrieved his phone and then punched in the number to Gail. "We have it," he said as soon as he heard her voice.

"Thank God!"

"Not yet. We've got it, but it's not disarmed. Start clearing everyone away from the marina, including campers nearby."

"Will do. The disposal guys just arrived."

"Good. Have them meet us at the marina. Start looking for some place where they can work on this thing."

"Don't go to the marina; go to the boat-launch area north of Las Vegas Boat Harbor, on Hemenway Cove Road."

Max looked to the skipper and shouted over the rumbling engine. "Go to the boat launch on Hemenway Cove Road."

The police skipper nodded that he understood.

"We've got less than twenty-five minutes," Max said into his phone. "Be waiting for us."

Max ended the call and then punched in Danya's number. "I want you to get out of the area now," Max said when Danya answered. "I don't think we're going to make it."

"Max, no!" she said. "Max, I—"

"Danya, no. Go now, and don't look back. *Ani ohev otach.*"

Max had ended the call with *I love you.*

Chapter 23

Bedlam had replaced the usual serenity at the recreation area. Rumors spread wildly about the developing situation. The appearance of army helicopters, sound of gunshots, and flashing of police lights fueled the anxiety. Scarlet's statement did little to satisfy the angst of the visitors.

After receiving Max's transmission that he had the nuke on the police boat, Scarlet ordered the area evacuated. Her order did not mention anything about the SADM. Max, monitoring the communications, followed up as soon as Scarlet ended her message.

Max said, "Shut down all operations at the dam, and turn all electronics off. Leave the police communication on until we reach the ramp. Prepare for an electromagnetic pulse."

"Max, I—" Scarlet began.

"Will do!" Gail replied, cutting in, obviously taking over for Scarlet.

Hysterical rumors seemed to spread faster than the police transmissions. Order and discipline were replaced with people's basic instinct—survival. However, most people misplaced their priorities and chose personal possessions above their personal safety. Fights erupted at the boat launches, campgrounds, and marinas. Fender benders, some worse than others, could be seen everywhere. Terrified people scrambled to leave, only to be met with traffic jams as everyone competed for the exit. It was more than the police at the dam could handle; they only dealt with the more serious issues. The boat ramp at Hemenway Cove Road, where Max was directed to go, was no exception. There were frightened people trying to get their boats out of the water, car accidents, a sunken boat, and an abandoned pickup with trailer clogged the ramp.

As the police boat sped across the basin, Max leaned to the side to see around the skipper and check their progress. The area surrounding the marina was full of lights in all directions—amid them were the demanding flashes from police vehicles. Another police boat, its lights pulsing, was on the far side of the marina, about fifty yards from the ramp.

Max looked at Ludwig and said, "It's lit up like Dulles Airport at night."

"*Ja*, and we are going right into that mess. We have no time for traffic jams."

The police skipper turned toward the two men and said, "We have very few alternatives and none nearby. The lake is so low that we've had to close a number of ramps that are no longer in the water."

"I know," Max said as he picked up the walkie-talkie. "Gail, clear the ramp; we're getting close."

"We see you," her crisp voice blared out. "The police are trying to clear the people out."

At that moment a man's voice could be heard over a loudspeaker, directing all boats to clear the ramp. He announced his instructions again, more specifically this time. He followed with, "An extreme emergency exists. Evacuate the area immediately!"

The skipper guided the boat, its lights throbbing, to the ramp area and met the congestion of boats competing for the ramp. The skipper turned on his siren.

"Clear the way!" he shouted over the public address system. "Make way! Clear the ramp!"

People, seemingly flouting the first police boat, stopped and turned to the approaching boat; their faces displayed uncertainty. One by one, the coxswains began to move their boats clear of the ramp. Some just backed out of the way, while others—the smarter ones—retreated to presumably safer locations. Standing at the front of a small crowd congregated on the ramp, Gail and Danya met the arriving police boat. The skipper reversed the transmission of the boat as it approached the shore. The bow dipped, and their vessel gently bumped to a stop.

Max eased out of the boat into about two feet of water and reached back to the side as Ludwig handed the SADM to him. Ludwig followed Max's example, took his position next to Max, and grasped one of the straps of the canvas cover.

Max looked at the skipper and shouted, "Go! Go! Get to the cove as we discussed!"

Acknowledging Max's instruction, the skipper waved his hand and then backed the boat off the ramp and maneuvered to leave.

"This is an extreme emergency," the other police-boat skipper announced. "Leave immediately. This is your last warning!" Both boats sped away. All police communications shut down as instructed.

Carrying the device, Max and Ludwig cautiously waded out of the water to meet Gail. Seeing them, the crowd immediately began to disperse like cockroaches when illuminated by bright lights. Voices could be heard in different directions. *It's a bomb! That's the emergency! Let's get out of here! Look out!* They would never know how correct they were and would never know that they were mere feet from a nuclear bomb that could detonate at any moment.

"What are you doing here?" Max scolded when his eyes landed on Danya.

"Being with you," she said as her eyes found his.

"This way, Max," Gail said, pointing up the ramp. "The disposal guys are waiting for you up the hill."

Max look toward Danya. "Danya, please—"

"Shut up. I'm staying."

Master Sergeant Blake "Buck" Ormond and Sergeant Glen Seaver took the nuke from Max and Ludwig and then placed it on a sturdy platform. They gently slid sandbags snug around the device to hold it securely in position. Captain Tracy "Stormy" Warden, explosive ordnance officer in charge, looked at the timer on the weapon.

Then he looked at Max and said, "This'll be dicey. This thing could go off any second; we're inside the plus or minus critical range on the timer."

"I know," Max said. "You don't have to do this." Max didn't have to tell him that it was suicide.

"Kinda late now. I couldn't get far enough away from here to be safe anyway. I told the chief when I met with her earlier to keep everyone back as far as they can but not to tell 'em this is a nuclear weapon. They'll do more damage trying to get out of here than if it goes off," Stormy said through a crooked smile. His voice was full of sarcasm. "If it does, they'll never know. We've got a communications link back to the dam. We've designated a safe area at Hoover Dam Lodge. That big ridge between here and the lodge will provide protection from the blast. Now clear out, sir. I've got work to do."

"Good luck, Stormy," Max said as he stepped back to Danya.

Stormy nodded.

"Danya, Gail, let's go!" Max barked. "Where's Scarlet?"

"Bringing the vehicle," Danya replied. At that moment Scarlet arrived, the wheels sliding on the crushed rocks.

Scarlet lowered the window and shouted, "Get in!"

The four piled into the SUV. Before the doors closed, Scarlet stomped on the accelerator, and the SUV sped away.

"Hold on!" she shouted. "I'm taking a trail to get us back to the highway. Hemenway Road and Lakeshore Road are jammed with traffic." The vehicle bounced several times before anyone could say anything.

Max directed Scarlet to back the SUV in as close as possible to the base of the ridge on the east side of the Hoover Dam Lodge. He hoped that the ridge would provide protection from the ensuing explosion when the nuke detonated. He was now concerned with their survival—the blast, shock wave, radiation, or fallout could end their lives. Flying debris caused by the shock wave was a major concern. However, Max believed that the ridge would shield them from whatever was picked up by the high winds. At least he hoped it would provide protection.

"Maybe I've got time to get my last fucking drink," Gail said.

"I don't know, Gail," Max replied. "I'm going to sit down and wait right over there." He pointed to a spot next to the base of the ridge.

Ludwig stepped to the same place without speaking.

Danya slid her hand into Max's and said, "I'm with you." She smiled and leaned into him.

"Come on, Scarlet. You're buying," Gail said as she tugged on Scarlet's arm. The two women darted toward the entrance of the lodge.

Max watched the steady stream of cars that apparently had seen the police vehicle tear out over the trail, bypassing the main road. Like sheep, they followed the SUV's flashing lights to the lodge. One man jumped out of his car and headed toward Max and Danya, stopped about ten feet in front of them, and shouted, "What do we do now?"

Realizing that fear had overtaken the man, Max said, "Have a drink." A crooked smile appeared on Max's face as he held up his palms and then pointed to the lodge. Max shot a glance at Ludwig, who shook his head and then rubbed his face.

"They said it was a bomb. How much time do we have?" the newcomer asked.

Max shrugged and said, "Don't know."

The frightened individual turned and headed to the lodge, followed by another man and two women.

Max checked his watch again as he and Danya sat arm in arm. Neither spoke. Max had done everything he possibly could. There were too many ifs to contemplate what was next. The outcome was out of his hands. They simply had to wait. He closed his eyes and felt Danya lean into him. They waited for the flash to light up the night sky.

The past twenty-four hours had taken their toll on Max. He pushed all thoughts of the nuke out of his mind as best as he could and allowed himself to relax. He preferred to be in countless other places; sitting on rocks, waiting for a nuclear explosion was not one of them. Feeling Danya's warmth, Max's thoughts were of her. He closed his eyes. Moments later a car pulled to a stop in front and to the left of them, and its headlights illuminated the trio. The sudden light on his face startled Max awake.

"Don't look at the flash!" Max shouted.

"Max, they're car lights," Danya said as she placed her hand on his cheek. "You're sweating."

Ludwig, snoozing as well, woke to Max's outburst. He knew what was on Max's mind but didn't speak.

"I'm OK," Max said. "I guess I was dreaming." He squeezed Danya's hand and checked his watch again.

A Humvee appeared in the parking lot and circled the cars, apparently looking for a spot. It turned and came to a stop in front of where Max, Danya, and Ludwig sat. The silhouette of a soldier got out of the vehicle and crossed in front of the light.

"There you are; I was looking for you," Captain Warden said with a smile. "All the communications are down in anticipation of the EMP. Buck and Sergeant Seaver are packing everything up."

Max and Danya looked at the soldier in disbelief and slowly stood.

"It's safe." Stormy grinned and then pulled a piece of wire from his breast pocket and handed it to Max. "A souvenir for you."

Max's brow dipped as he looked at the wire and then back at Stormy.

"Bad solder job," Stormy said as he read the quizzical look on Max's face. "The bomb guy must have been in a hurry. Kinda sloppy. The timer did function. But somewhere along the line, the connection broke free, and it wasn't in contact when it fired. You were very lucky, sir. You must be living right."

"Thank God."

"I've notified SOCOM, and a helicopter is on the way," Stormy said as he shoved his ball cap up. "I don't wanna do that again. I think it's time for a drink or several."

Ludwig stood and signaled his agreement. "I will be charging Chugs extra for this job. You tell him, *ja*? I will visit him on my way back home."

"A drink is a good idea. I'll join you in a minute. I need to call Chugs," said Max. He looked at Danya and continued, "Danya, go on with Stormy. I'll be in a minute."

"Nope! I'm staying with you," Danya replied.

***

9:05 a.m.
Monday
November 11, 2013
CTC
Tysons Corner, Virginia

After Gail entered the conference room, David closed the door. Already seated at the table were Margaret and Max. Gail rolled her eyes and said, "I'm sorry I'm late. Captain Hadley, DC Metropolitan Police, always knows when I'm in town or heading to a meeting."

"Gail *dahling*, he likes you." David grinned.

"Can it, David. It's too damned early for your shit, and I'm in no mood," Gail said as she took her place at the table and sipped her coffee.

"Does he have anything we need to know about?" Margaret asked.

"Naw, just clearing with me a public notice he wants to release and asking if I had any more info on Madison."

"What's he going to say?" Max asked.

"He's going to show the photo of Madison and announce that he's a person of interest in the death of Senator Carlton Bradbourne, whose body was found on the morning of October twenty-fourth in Rock Creek Park."

"OK, thanks." Max nodded and took a sip of his coffee. "Ludwig sends his regards. He's on his way to Tampa to visit Chugs."

Margaret passed out folders containing information she had captured since their last meeting. Then Margaret said, "Please take a couple of minutes to review this. Let me know if I've missed something or if you see an error."

They each agreed with her notes. Margret then slid another sheet of paper in front of them. It was a summary report she had received from Mossad titled *Habib Abd al Jabbar*. It outlined the details about the bomb maker and lieutenant to the ISIS bomb scientist, Hamdan Talib Dhul Fiqar. A picture of the contorted, blood-smeared corpse of Abd al Jabbar was inserted near the top. The bomb maker and two of his bodyguards had been killed at a house about three miles from Tocumen International Airport in Panama.

Margaret said, "We don't know yet if Abd al Jabbar sent any pictures or information about the SADM to Dhul Fiqar, but we are assuming he did." She looked at each of them and then continued. "The LA division is working with Mossad in Panama. They are searching his laptop and cell phone."

"What's the status of the diver we captured?" Max asked.

"He's Fathi Mustafa," Gail said. "He's currently in federal custody, booked on terrorism charges. Unfortunately the DOJ thinks the case against him is weak. *Circumstantial* is what they called it." Gail summarized Mustafa's story. "He claims he was night diving for catfish. When he speared one, it jerked the spear gun out of his hands, and he lost it. He surfaced, and that's when he was arrested. He had his story ready to go, and he's sticking to it."

"Hold on a minute," Margaret said as she grabbed the remote and turned up the volume on the TV. The news broadcast flashed *Breaking News Alert*. The four people fell silent and turned their attention to the screen. The governor of New York, the attorney general of New York, and Dawn Blakey of Homeland Security were giving a press conference. The governor elaborated about a plot to blow up one of the dams in New York by terrorists.

"We had creditable information and had the people involved under twenty-four-hour surveillance," the governor said. "One was killed, and two were taken into custody and booked on terrorism charges. I assure you that the dam and the people of New York are safe and were never in any danger. I wish to thank Dawn Blakey and her team from Homeland Security for their excellent work. I—"

"Please turn that shit off! I'm going to be sick!" Gail blurted out, her face red and expression exaggerated.

"Right scenario, wrong dam," Max said, more to himself than to the others. He wrinkled up the corner of his mouth and shook his head.

The meeting continued for another twenty minutes as they reviewed the details of the last several days. They formulated a report with recommendation that would make its way to the director and then to the National Security Council and president.

"That just leaves Bart Madison," Margaret said and then dropped her glasses onto the table. "Max, can you share any information on him?"

"Nothin' yet," Max said, his expression serious and tone cold.

***

1:16 p.m.
Wednesday
November 13, 2013
SOCOM Headquarters
Tampa, Florida

Back at his office in Florida, Max was finishing his report on the theft of the SADMs before he started his vacation. Just as he placed the *Top Secret* cover on his report, the phone on his desk rang. "Kenworth," he said.

"This is Prestin Woosley at Livermore Labs."

"Hello, Prestin," Max replied. "What do you have for me?"

"I've finished with my inspection of the SADMs. I couldn't find any evidence that the first two were tampered with. However, the last two are a different story. It appears that they went all over the damned things. I've got quite a bit of work to do on 'em to get 'em back in service. If that solder connection would've held, we wouldn't be having this conversation."

"I thought so. The timers—"

"Yeah, the timers. Crappy things aren't too reliable. That one appears to function about six minutes early. I think we should look into upgrading them. What do you think?"

"I vote for that."

"By the way, I got a call from the CIA. They want a copy of my findings. They're not too happy about ISIS examining one of our classified weapons. Have you talked to them? They said they were going to contact you."

"Thanks for the info," said Max. "I haven't heard from 'em and may not for a few weeks. I'm going on leave and will be out of the office for the next ten days."

"Have fun. I'll talk to you when you get back."

Max ended the call and picked up the report prepared by Captain Greg Garnett, the officer in charge of the team that had secured the Balboa site after the attack. He had just finished the first page when Chugs entered his office.

"Yes, sir," Max said, placing the papers on his desk as he stood.

Chugs closed the door, sat in one of the side chairs, and said, "Captain Garnett did a good job on that report." He pointed to the papers on the desk. "I had a chance to make a trip down there to look at the site. They're about finished repairing the damage."

"Good. I'll make a trip to visit the site when I get back," said Max. "I'd like to do a complete review of the contractor providing the guards."

"That's a good idea." Chugs nodded.

Max said, "I still think we need to have soldiers guarding the facility."

"We can discuss it when you get back. The CIA boys in Panama are going to take care of the Madison problem. I'll let you know when it goes down."

"I understand." There was nothing else Max could say.

The terrifying ordeal was over. Max and his team had been able to avoid a catastrophe. All four nuclear weapons were back in the custody of SOCOM. A number of flaws in the national-preparedness plans had been identified and noted. The flaws may have been documented, but the same administration was still in power. And ISIS still wanted to destroy the United States. A disaster had been averted, mainly by a faulty solder connection. The same people, most of them rewarded, were still occupying their positions. Only a handful of people would know what had really happened and how close ISIS had come to creating a cataclysmic event of unequalled scale in the heartland of the country.

Max sat back in the chair and briefly reflected on what had happened over the past few weeks and how close ISIS had come to succeeding.

Max picked up the receiver, placed it to his ear, and punched in a series of numbers.

"This is Danya," the soft voice replied.

"I'm leaving now. I'll be there soon."

***

10:11 a.m.
Friday
November 15, 2013
Somewhere in the Caribbean

The morning sky was blue, and a soft, warm breeze danced about. It was a beautiful day to be at the beach. The rhythmic sounds of the waves lapping the white sand were relaxing. The world was far away, until the ringing cell phone broke Max's trance.

"Hello," Max said, his attention reentering the real world. It was Chugs's number on the screen.

"It's done." The call went dead.

Max looked at Danya and nodded with a slight smile.

She nodded in reply. No words were spoken, but she knew.

Also by Patrick Parker

War Merchant

A suspense-filled novel that crosses the globe in a world of corrupt politics, a ruthless greedy opportunist, terrorists, and a pawn with deadly skills.

Dydre Rowyn wants out, but to leave her working relationship with Clayborne Zsigmond, a ruthless black market arms broker, could be a bullet.

Dydre uses the next assignment Zsigmond gives her—the deliverance of new technology to terrorists—to escape his merciless grip. The risk she takes puts her on the firing line when her plan goes deadly wrong. Not only is her life in jeopardy but also her son's as she finds herself pitted against Zsigmond, his mercenaries, a double-crossing businessman, terrorists, the FBI, and a man from the Defense Department.

Get your copy here: http://amzn.to/2eCfavS

Treasures of the Fourth Reich

A Titian, a Bruegel, and a panel from the Amber Room—vanished during WWII—come to life again.

A string of deaths drags Dix Connor and his art expert wife into a suspense-filled game of cat & mouse with a clandestine organization dating back to WWII.

It was one of the greatest crimes of the century.... Grand museums and families lost countless valuables and works of art to Nazi lootings in what has been called "the rape of Europa." Parker's story begins just outside the Bavarian salt mines as the American and Russian armies are closing in. Amid the chaos, SS officers scramble to hide ill-gotten treasures that will finance the "Fourth Reich." Only a precious journal detailing an inventory of treasure caches around the Tirol holds a clue.

Forty plus years later, the hunt for Europe's lost art falls to a husband and wife team who become entangled in this web of stolen treasures. Dix and Maria Connor face down a secret and deadly network trafficking in Titians, Bruegels and remnants of Peter the Great's magnificent Amber Room. From northeast Italy to Brussels, these amateur detectives risk everything to right the wrongs of history. Crisscross Europe's past and present in this thinking man's action novel.

The lust for loot crosses paths with history's ghosts in this high-octane thriller.

Acknowledgments

I want to thank my wife and best friend, Carole, for her confidence and support. You have been my best critic and provided invaluable input.

New Braunfels Writers Guild—Betty Cook, Deborah Ellison, Don Burquest, Donna Heath, Irene Keller, Lewis Sarkozi, and Liz Lautner. You are a great group and helped me to bring my story to life. Through the many writings, critiques, edits and rewrites, thank you. I appreciate your candor, support and confidence.

Bob Sabasteanski, a big thank you for your critique, suggestions and attention to detail. My go to guy for a reality check and a weapons expert. Thank you.

To the Createspace editors, superb editors, who are terrific! You very quickly understood what the story was about and took it to the next level. Your attention to detail kept me straight.

Elizabeth Mackey, you took the story to a graphic form with a fantastic cover. It has been a real pleasure to work with you on this project.

Thank you.

About The Author

Patrick Parker received his bachelor's degree in management and his master's degree in international relations. He joined the US Army and spent five years in Italy. After retiring from the military, Parker spent an additional fifteen years in the defense industry. Now retired again, Parker enjoys writing, scuba diving, astronomy, and going to the beach. He lives in Texas.

Parker is also the author of *Treasures of the Fourth Reich* and *War Merchant*. Both are available through Amazon.com.

For questions and comments click:

Amazon Author page: http://amzn.to/1izsnBH

Facebook page: http://on.fb.me/1pnfAoM

Twitter: https://twitter.com/pparkerntx

Goodreads Profile page: http://bit.ly/1pnLth0

Blog: http://bit.ly/1tTUjjv

Webpage: http://bit.ly/1ZEoYGu

Did you like *Six Minutes Early*?

Please take few minutes to let everyone know by posting a review. This link will take you to the reviews page: http://amzn.to/2kYNuQW. People get to know what you are reading and I will be forever grateful to you.

Best Regards,

Patrick Parker

Made in the USA
Columbia, SC
04 December 2022

72676572R00190